THE SOLAR QUEEN

ALSO BY ANDRE NORTON FROM TOR BOOKS

THE SOLAR QUEEN
  (with Sherwood Smith)
Derelict for Trade
A Mind for Trade

The Crystal Gryphon
Dare to Go A-Hunting
Flight in Yiktor
Forerunner
Forerunner: The Second Venture
Here Abide Monsters
Moon Called
Moon Mirror
The Prince Commands
Ralestone Luck
Stand and Deliver
Wheel of Stars
Wizards' Worlds
Wraiths of Time

Grandmasters' Choice (Editor)
The Jekyll Legacy (with Robert Bloch)
Gryphon's Eyrie (with A. C. Crispin)
Songsmith (with A. C. Crispin)
Caroline (with Enid Cushing)
Firehand (with P. M. Griffin)
Redline the Stars (with P. M. Griffin)
Sneeze on Sunday (with Grace Allen
  Hogarth)

House of Shadows (with Phyllis
  Miller)
Empire of the Eagle (with Susan
  Shwartz)
Imperial Lady (with Susan Shwartz)

CAROLUS REX
  (with Rosemary Edghill)
The Shadow of Albion
Leopard in Exile

BEAST MASTER
  (with Lyn McConchie)
Beast Master's Ark
Beast Master's Circus

THE GATES TO WITCH WORLD
  (omnibus comprising *Witch World,*
  Web of the Witch World, and *Year of*
  the Unicorn)

THE WITCH WORLD (Editor)
Four from the Witch World
Tales from the Witch World 1
Tales from the Witch World 2
Tales from the Witch World 3

WITCH WORLD: THE TURNING
I *Storms of Victory* (with P. M.
  Griffin)
II *Flight of Vengeance* (with P. M.
  Griffin & Mary Schaub)
III *On Wings of Magic* (with Patricia
  Mathews & Sasha Miller)

MAGIC IN ITHKAR
  (Editor, with Robert Adams)
Magic in Ithkar 1
Magic in Ithkar 2
Magic in Ithkar 3
Magic in Ithkar 4

THE TIME TRADERS
  (with Sherwood Smith)
Echoes in Time
Atlantis Endgame

THE OAK, YEW, ASH, AND ROWAN
To the King a Daughter
Knight or Knave
A Crown Disowned

THE HALFBLOOD CHRONICLES
  (with Mercedes Lackey)
The Elvenbane
Elvenblood
Elvenborn

THE SOLAR QUEEN

QUEEN

ANDRE NORTON

A TOM DOHERTY ASSOCIATES BOOK
NEW YORK

TOR®

THE SOLAR QUEEN

The Solar Queen (as omnibus), copyright © 2003 by Andre Norton
Sargasso of Space, copyright © 1955, renewed 1983, by Andre Norton
Plague Ship, copyright © 1956, renewed 1984, by Andre Norton

Book design by Milenda Nan Ok Lee

Omnibus edited by James Frenkel

Tor® is a registered trademark of Tom Doherty Associates, LLC.

ISBN 0-765-30054-0

Printed in the United States of America

CONTENTS

PUBLISHER'S NOTE

Andre Norton published the first *Solar Queen* novel, *Sargasso of Space,* under the name "Andrew North" in 1955, following it with *Plague Ship*, also by "Andrew North," in 1956. Miss Norton wrote a number of science fiction adventures under that male pseudonym, in a time when women supposedly didn't write science fiction. Andre Norton's marvelous works, both under a pseudonym and under her own name, have rightly inspired many women to write science fiction.

These novels were the start of a series that Miss Norton continued with two additional novels, *Postmarked the Stars* and *Voodoo Planet,* which will comprise a second *Solar Queen* omnibus.

The four *Solar Queen* novels are classic science fiction adventure, full of the excitement and daring that have made Andre Norton one of the most popular science fiction adventure writers of all time. They also were written in a time when technology was very little like what is available today, so there are some bits of jargon and technology which may seem archaic. None of this has been changed, however. These are tales that stand the test of time, even if the jargon is a bit different from that found in more recent books.

New *Solar Queen* novels have been written more recently by Miss Norton in collaboration, *Redline the Stars* (with P. M. Griffin), and *Derelict for Trade* and *A Mind for Trade* (with Sherwood Smith).

The *Solar Queen* omnibus you hold in your hands is the original, the two novels that started it all. Enjoy!

SARGASSO
OF SPACE

THE SOLAR QUEEN

1
   The lanky, very young man in the ill-fitting Trader's tunic tried to stretch the cramp out of his long legs. You'd think, Dane Thorson considered the point with a certain amount of irritation, the men who designed these under-surface transcontinental cars would take into mind that there would be tall passengers—not just midgets—using them. Not for the first time he wished that he could have used air transport. But he had only to finger the money belt, too flat about his middle, to remember who and what he was—a recruit new to the Service, without a ship or backer.

   There was his muster pay from Training Pool, and a thin pad of crumpled credit slips which remained from the sale of all those belongings which could not follow him into space. And he had his minimum kit—that was the total sum of his possessions—except for that slender wafer of metal, notched and incised with a code beyond his reading, which would be his passport to what he determined was going to be a brighter future.

   Not that he should question the luck he had had so far, Dane told himself firmly. After all it wasn't every boy from a Federation Home who could get an appointment to the Pool and emerge ten years later an apprentice-cargo-master ready for ship assignment off-world. Even recalling the stiff examinations of the past few weeks could set him to squirming now. Basic mechanics, astrogation grounding, and then the more severe testing in his own specialization—cargo handling, stowage, trade procedure, Galactic markets, Extraterrestrial psychology, and all the other items he had had to try and cram into his skull until he sometimes thought that he had nothing but bits and patches which he would never be able to sort into common sense. Not only had the course been tough, but he had been bucking the new trend in selection, too. Most of his classmates were from Service families—they had grown up in Trade.

Dane frowned at the back of the seat before him. Wasn't Trade becoming more and more a closed clan? Sons followed fathers or brothers into the Service—it was increasingly difficult for a man without connections to get an appointment to the Pool. His luck had been good there—

Look at Sands, he had two older brothers, an uncle and a cousin all with Inter-Solar. And he never let anyone forget it either. Just let an apprentice get assigned into one of the big Companies and he was set for the rest of his life. The Companies had regular runs from one system to another. Their employees were always sure of a steady berth, you could buy Company stock. There were pensions and administrative jobs when you had to quit space—if you'd shown any promise. They had the cream of Trade—Inter-Solar, The Combine, Deneb-Galactic, Falworth-Ignesti—

Dane blinked at the tele-screen at eye level at the far end of the bullet-shaped car—not really seeing the commercial which at that moment was singing the praises of a Falworth-Ignesti import. It all depended on the Psycho. He patted his money belt again to be sure of the safety of his ID wafer, sealed into its most secret pocket.

The commercial faded into the red bar announcing a station. Dane waited for the faint jar which signalized the end of his two-hour trip.

He was glad to be free of the projectile, able to drag his kit bag out of the mound of luggage from the van.

Most of his fellow travelers were Trade men. But few of them sported Company badges. The majority were drifters or Free Traders, men who either from faults of temperament or other reasons could not find a niche in the large parental organizations, but shipped out on one independent spacer or another, the bottom layer of the Trade world.

Dane shouldered his bag into the lift which swept him up to ground level and out into the sunshine of a baking southwestern summer day. He lingered on the concrete apron which rimmed this side of the take-off Field, looking out over its pitted and blasted surface at the rows of cradles which held those ships now readying for flight. He had scant attention for the stubby interplanetary traders, the Martian and Asteroid lines, the dull dark ships which plowed out to Saturn's and Jupiter's moons. What he wanted lay beyond—the star ships—their sleek sides newly sprayed against dust friction, the soil of strange worlds perhaps still clinging to their standing fins.

"Well, if it isn't the Viking! Hunting for your long boat, Dane?"

Only someone who knew Dane very well could have read the real meaning in that twitch of his lower lip. When he turned to face the speaker his expression was under its usual tight control.

Artur Sands had assumed the swagger of a hundred voyage man, which contrasted oddly, Dane was pleased to note, with his too shiny boots and unworn tunic. But as ever the other's poise aroused his own secret resentment. And Artur was heading his usual chorus of followers too, Ricki Warren and Hanlaf Bauta.

"Just come in, Viking? Haven't tried your luck yet, I take it? Neither have we. So let's go together to learn the worst."

Dane hesitated. The last thing in the world he wanted to do was to face the Psycho in Artur Sands' company. To him the other's supreme self-confidence was somewhat unnerving. Sands expected the best, and judging from various incidents at the Pool, what Artur expected he usually got.

On the other hand Dane had often good reason to worry about the future. And if he were going to have hard luck now he would rather learn it without witnesses. But there was no getting rid of Artur he realized. So philosophically he checked his kit while the others waited impatiently.

They had come by air—the best was none too good for Artur and his crowd. Why hadn't they been to the cargo department assignment Psycho before this? Why had they waited the extra hour—or had they spent their last truly free time sightseeing? Surely—Dane knew a little lift of heart at the thought—it couldn't be that *they* were dubious about the machine's answer too?

But that hope was quenched as he joined them in time to hear Artur expound his favorite theme.

"The machine is impartial! That's just the comet dust they feed you back at the Pool. Sure, we know the story they set up—that a man has to be fitted by temperament and background to his job, that each ship had to carry a well integrated crew—but that's all moon gas! When Inter-Solar wants a man, they get him—and no Psycho fits him into their ships if they don't want him! That's for the guys who don't know how to fire the right jets—or haven't brains enough to look around for good berths. I'm not worrying about being stuck on some starving Free Trader on the fringe—"

Ricki and Hanlaf were swallowing every word of that. Dane didn't want to. His belief in the incorruptibility of the Psycho was the one thing he had clung to during the past few weeks when Artur and those like him had strutted about the Pool confident about their speedy transition to the higher levels of Trade.

He had preferred to believe that the official statements were correct, that a machine, a collection of impulses and relays which could be in no way influenced, decided the fate of all who applied for assignment to off-world ships. He wanted to believe that when he fed his ID plate into the Psycho at the star port here it would make no difference that he was an orphan without kin in the Service, that the flatness of his money belt could not turn or twist a decision which would be based only on his knowledge, his past record at the Pool, his temperament and potentialities.

But doubt had been planted and it was that lack of faith which worked on him now, slowing his pace as they approached the assignment room. On the other hand Dane had no intention of allowing Artur or either of his satellites to guess he was bothered.

So a stubborn pride pushed him forward to be the first of the four to fit his ID into the waiting slot. His fingers twitched to snatch it back again before it disappeared, but he controlled that impulse and stood aside for Artur.

The Psycho was nothing but a box, a square of solid metal—or so it looked to the waiting apprentices. And that wait might have been easier, Dane speculated, had they been able to watch the complicated processes inside the bulk, could have seen how those lines and notches incised on their plates were assessed, matched, paired, until a ship now in port and seeking apprentices was found for them.

Long voyaging for small crews sealed into star spacers, with little chance for recreation or amusement, had created many horrible personnel problems in the past. Some tragic cases were now required reading in the "History of Trade" courses at the Pool. Then came the Psycho and through its impersonal selection the right men were sent to the right ships, fitted into the type of work, the type of crew where they could function best with the least friction. No one at the Pool had told them how the Psycho worked—or how it could actually read an ID strip. But when the machine decided, its decision was final and the verdict was recorded—there was no appeal.

That was what they had been taught, what Dane had always accepted as fact, and how could it be wrong?

His thoughts were interrupted by a gong note from the machine, one ID strip had been returned, with a new line on its surface. Artur pounced. A moment later his triumph was open.

"Inter-Solar's *Star Runner*! Knew you wouldn't let the old man down, boy!" He patted the flat top of the Psycho patronizingly. "Didn't I tell you how it would work for me?"

Ricki nodded his head eagerly and Hanlaf went so far as to slap Artur on the back. Sands was the magician who had successfully pulled off a trick.

The next two sounds of the gong came almost together, as the strips clicked in the holder on top of one another. Ricki and Hanlaf scooped them up. There was disappointment on Ricki's face.

"Martian-Terran Incorporated—the *Venturer*," he read aloud. And Dane noted that the hand with which he tucked his ID into his belt was shaking. Not for Ricki the far stars and big adventures, but a small berth in a crowded planetary service where there was little chance for fame or fortune.

"The Combine's *Deneb Warrior*!" Hanlaf was openly exultant, paying no attention to Ricki's announcement.

"Shake, enemy!" Artur held out his hand with a grin. He, too, ignored Ricki as if his late close companion had been removed bodily from their midst by the decision of the Psycho.

"Put her there, rival!" Hanlaf had been completely shaken out of his usual subservience by this amazing good fortune.

The Combine was big, big enough to offer a challenge to Inter-Solar these past two years. They had copped a Federation mail contract from under I-S's nose and pounded through, at least one monopolistic concession on an inner system's route. Artur and his former follower might never meet in open friendship again. But at the present their mutual luck in getting posts in the Companies was all that mattered.

Dane continued to wait for the Psycho to answer him. Was it possible for an ID to jam somewhere in the interior of that box? Should he hunt for someone in authority and ask a question or two? His strip had been the first to go in—but it was not coming out. And Artur was waking up to that fact—

"Well, well, no ship for the Viking? Maybe they haven't got one to fit your particular scrambled talents, big boy—"

Could that be true, Dane hazarded? Maybe no ship now in the Port cradles needed the type of service his strip said he had to offer.

Did that mean that he would have to stay right here until such a ship came in?

It was as if Artur could read his thoughts. Sands' grin changed from one of triumph to a malicious half-sneer.

"What did I tell you?" he demanded. "Viking doesn't know the right people. Going to bring in your kit and camp out until Psycho breaks down and gives you an answer?"

Hanlaf was impatient. His self-confidence had been given a vast jolt toward independence, so that now he dared to question Artur.

"I'm starved," he announced. "Let's mess—and then look up our ships—"

Artur shook his head. "Give it a minute or two. I want to see if the Viking gets his long boat—if it's in dock now—"

Dane could only do what he had done many times before, pretend that this did not matter, that Artur and his followers meant nothing. But was the machine functioning, or had his ID been lost somewhere within its mysterious interior? Had Artur not been there, watching him with that irritating amusement, Dane would have gone to find help.

Hanlaf started to walk away and Ricki was already at the door, as if *his* assignment had removed him forever from the ranks of those who mattered—when the gong sounded for the fourth time. With a speed the average observer would not have credited to him, Dane moved. His hands dashed under Artur's fingers and caught the ID before the smaller youth could grab it.

There was no bright line of a Company insignia on it—Dane's first glance told him that. Was—was he going to be confined to the system—follow in Ricki's uninspired wake?

But, no, there was a star on it right enough—the star which granted him the Galaxy—and by that emblem the name of a ship—not a Company but a ship—the *Solar Queen*. It took a long instant for that to make sense, though he had never considered himself a slow thinker.

A ship's name only—a Free Trader! One of the roving, exploring spacers which plied lanes too dangerous, too new, too lacking in quick profits to attract the Companies. Part of the Trade Service right enough, and the uninitiated thought of them as romantic. But Dane knew a pinched sinking in his middle. Free Trade was almost a dead end for the ambitious. Even the instructors at the Pool had skimmed over that angle in the lectures, as carefully as the students were briefed. Free Trade was too often a gamble with death, with plague, with hostile alien races. You could lose not only your profit and your ship, but your life. And the Free Traders rated close to the bottom of the scale in the Service. Why, even Ricki's appointment would be hailed by any apprentice as better than this!

He should have been prepared for Artur's hand over his shoulder to snatch the ID, for the other's quick appraisement of his shame.

"Free Trader!"

It seemed to Dane that Sands' voice rang out as loudly as the telecast.

Ricki paused in his retreat and stared. Hanlaf allowed himself a snicker and Artur laughed.

"So that's how *your* pattern reads, big boy? You're to be a viking of space—a Columbus of the star lanes—a far rover! How's your blaster aim, man? And hadn't you better go back for a refresher in X-Tee contacts? Free Traders don't see much of civilization, you know. Come on, boys," he turned to the other two, "we've got to treat the Viking to a super-spread meal, he'll be on con-rations for the rest of his life no doubt." His grip tightened on Dane's arm. And, though his captive might easily have twisted free, the prisoner knew that he could better save face and dignity by going along with the plan and bottling down all signs of anger.

Sure—maybe the Free Traders did not rate so high in the Service, maybe few of them swanked around the big ports as did the Company men. But there had been plenty of fortunes made in the outer reaches and no one could deny that a Free Trader got around. Artur's attitude set Dane's inborn stubbornness to finding the good in the future. His spirit had hit bottom during the second when he had read his assignment, now it was rising again.

There were no strict caste lines in Trade, the divisions were not by rank but by employer. The large dining room at the Port was open to every man wearing the tunic of active service. Most of the Companies maintained their own sections there, their employees paying with vouchers. But transients and newly assigned men who had not yet joined their ships drifted together among the tables by the door.

Dane got to an empty one first and triggered the check button. He might be a Free Trader but this party was his, he was not going to eat any meal provided by Artur—even if this gesture swept away most of his credits.

They had some minutes to look around them after dialing for meals. A short distance away a man wearing the lightning flash badge of a com-tech was arising from the table. He left two companions still methodically chewing as he went off, his wide chest—that of a second or third generation Martian colonist—unmistakable, though his features were those of a Terran Oriental.

The two he left behind were both apprentices. One bore on his tunic the chart insignia of an astrogator-to-be and the other an engineer's cogwheel. It was the latter who caught and held Dane's gaze.

The cargo-apprentice thought that never before had he seen such a handsome, daredevil face. The crisp black hair which framed the finely cut, space tanned features, was cropped short, but not short enough to hide a wave. The heavy lidded eyes were dark, and a little amused smile held more than a hint of cynicism as it quirked the corners of his too-perfectly cut lips. He was a Video idea of the heroic space man and Dane disliked him on sight.

But the perfect one's companion was as rough hewn as he was faceted. His naturally brown skin could have taken no deeper tan for he was a Negro. And he was talking animatedly about something which sparked languid answers from the budding engineer.

Dane's attention was brought back to his own table by a waspish sting from Artur.

"*Solar Queen.*" He spoke the name much too loudly to suit Dane. "A Free Trader. Well, you'll get to see life, Viking, that you will. At any rate we can continue to speak to you—since you aren't on any rival listing—"

Dane achieved something close to a smile. "That's big-minded of you, Sands. How dare I complain if an Inter-Solar man is willing to acknowledge my existence?"

Ricki broke in. "That's dangerous—the Free Trade, I mean—"

But Artur frowned. To a dangerous Trade some glamor might still cling, and he refused to allow that. "Oh, not all the Free Traders are explorers or fringe system men, Ricki. Some have regular runs among the poorer planets where it doesn't pay the Companies to operate. Dane'll probably find himself on a back and forth job between a couple of dome-citied worlds where he can't even take a breath outside his helmet—"

Which is just what you would like, isn't it? Dane concluded inside. The picture isn't black enough to suit you yet, is it, Sands? And for a second or two he wondered why Sands got pleasure out of riding him.

"Yes—" Ricki subsided fast. But Dane was aware that his eyes continued to watch the new Free Trader wistfully.

"Here's to Trade any way you have it!" Artur raised his mug with a theatrical gesture. "Best of luck to the *Solar Queen*. You'll probably need it, Viking."

Dane was stung anew. "I don't know about that, Sands. Free Traders have made big strikes. And the gamble—"

"That's just it, old man, the gamble! And the chips can fall down as well as up. For one Free Trader who has made a stroke, there're a hundred or so who can't pay their Field fees. Too bad you didn't have some pull with the powers that be."

Dane had had enough. He pushed back from the table and looked at Artur straightly. "I'm going where the Psycho assigned me," he said steadily. "All this talk about Free Trading being so tough may be just meteor light. Give us both a year in space, Sands, and then you can talk—"

Artur laughed. "Sure—give me a year with Inter-Solar and you a year in that broken-down bucket. I'll buy the dinner next time, Viking, you won't have credits enough to settle the bill—I'll wager an extra ten on that. Now," he glanced at his watch, "I'm going to have a look at the *Star Runner*. Any of you care to join me?"

It seemed that Ricki and Hanlaf would, at least they arose with dispatch to join him. But Dane remained where he was, finishing the last of a very good dinner, certain that it would be a long time before he tasted its like again. He had, he hoped, put up a good front and he was heartily tired of Sands.

But he was not left to his own company. Someone slipped into Ricki's chair across the table and spoke:

"You for the *Solar Queen,* man?"

Dane's head snapped up. Was this to be more of Artur's pleasantries? But now he was looking at the open face of the astrogator-apprentice from the neighboring table. He lost part of his bristling antagonism.

"Just been assigned to her." He passed his ID across to the other.

"Dane Thorson," the other read aloud. "I am Rip Shannon—Ripley Shannon if you wish to be formal. And," he beckoned to the Video hero, "this is Ali Kamil. We are both of the *Queen*. You are a cargo-apprentice," he ended with a statement rather than a question.

Dane nodded and then greeted Kamil, hoping that the stiffness he felt was not apparent in his voice or manner. He thought that the other looked him over too appraisingly, and that in some mysterious way he had been found wanting after the instant of swift measurement.

"We are going to the *Queen* now, come with us?" Rip's simple friendliness was warming and Dane agreed.

As they boarded the scooter which trundled down the length of the Field toward the distant cradles of the star ships, Rip kept up a flow of conversation and Dane warmed more and more to the big young man. Shannon was older, he must be in his last year of apprenticeship, and the newcomer was grateful for the scraps of information about the *Queen* and her present crew which were being passed along to him.

Compared to the big super ships of the Companies the *Solar Queen* was a negligible midget. She carried a crew of twelve, and each man was necessarily responsible for more than one set of duties—there were no airtight compartments of specialization aboard a Free Trader spacer.

"Got us a routine cargo haul to Naxos," Rip's soft voice continued. "From there," he shrugged, "it may be anywhere—"

"Except back to Terra," Kamil's crisper tone cut in. "Better say good-bye to home for a long while, Thorson. We won't be hitting this lane for some time. Only came in on this voyage because we had a special run and that doesn't happen once in ten years or more." Dane thought that the other was getting some obscure pleasure in voicing that piece of daunting information.

The scooter rounded the first of the towering cradles. Here were the Company ships in their private docks, their needle points lifted to the sky, cargoes being loaded, activity webbing them. Dane stared in spite of himself, but he did not turn his head to keep them in sight as the scooter steered to the left and made for the other line of berths, not so well filled, where the half dozen smaller Free Trade ships stood awaiting blastoff. And somehow he was not surprised when they drew up at the foot of the ramp leading to the most battered one.

But there was affection and honest pride in Rip's voice as he announced:

"There she is, man, the best trading spacer along the lanes. She's a real lady, is the *Queen*!"

WORLDS FOR SALE

2

Dane stepped inside the cargo-master's office cabin. The man who sat there, surrounded by files of microtape and all the other apparatus of an experienced Trader, was not at all what he expected. Those masters who had given lectures at the Pool had been sleek, well groomed men, their outward shells differing little from the successful earthbound executive. It had been difficult to associate some of them with space at all.

But more than J. Van Rycke's uniform proclaimed him of the Service. His thinning hair was white-blond, his broad face reddened rather than tanned. And he was a big man—though not in fatty tissue, but solid bulk. He occupied every inch of his cushioned seat, eyeing Dane with a sleepy indifference, an attitude shared by a large tiger-striped tom cat who sprawled across a third of the limited desk space.

Dane saluted. "Apprentice-Cargo-Master Thorson come aboard, sir," he rapped out with the snap approved by Pool officers, laying his ID on the desk when his new commander made no attempt to reach for it.

"Thorson—" The bass voice seemingly rumbled not from the broad chest but from deep in the barrel body facing him. "First voyage?"

"Yes, sir."

The cat blinked and yawned, but Van Rycke's measuring stare did not change. Then—

"Better report to the Captain and sign on." There was no other greeting.

A little at a loss Dane climbed on to the control section. He flattened against the wall of the narrow corridor as another officer swung along behind him at a hurried pace. It was the com-tech who had been eating with Rip and Kamil.

"New?" The single word came from him with some of the same snap as the impulses in his communicators.

"Yes, sir. I'm to sign on—"

"Captain's office—next level," and he was gone.

Dane followed him at a more modest pace. It was true that the *Queen* was no giant of the spaceways, and she doubtless lacked a great many refinements and luxurious fittings which the Company ships boasted. But Dane, green as he was, appreciated the smartly kept interior of the ship. Her sides might be battered and she had a rakish, too worn appearance without—inside she was a smooth running, tight held vessel. He reached the next level and knocked at a half open panel. At an impatient order he entered.

For one dazed moment he felt as if he had stepped into the Terra-port X-Tee Zoo. The walls of the confined space were a montage of pictures—but such pictures! Off-world animals he had seen, had heard described, overlapped others which were strictly culled from more gruesome nightmares. In a small swinging cage sat a blue creature which could only be an utterly impossible combination of toad—if toads had six legs, two of them ending in claws—and parrot. It leaned forward, gripped the cage bars with its claws, and calmly spat at him.

Fascinated, Dane stood rooted until a rasping bark aroused him.

"Well—what is it?"

Dane hastily averted his eyes from the blue horror and looked at the man who sat beneath its cage. Grizzled hair showed an inch or so beneath the Captain's winged cap. His harsh features had not been improved by a scar across one cheek, a seam which could only have been a blaster-blister. And his eyes were as cold and imperious as the pop ones of his blue captive.

Dane found his tongue. "Apprentice-Cargo-Master Thorson come aboard, sir." Again he tendered the ID.

Captain Jellico caught it up impatiently. "First voyage?"

Once more Dane was forced to answer in the affirmative. It would have been, he thought bleakly, so much better had he been able to say "tenth."

At that moment the blue thing sirened an ear-piercing shriek and the Captain swung back in his chair to strike the door of the cage a resounding slap which bounced its occupant into silence, if not better manners. Then he dropped the ID into the ship's recorder and punched the button. Dane dared to relax, it was official now, he was signed on as a crew member, he would not be booted off the *Queen*.

"Blastoff at eighteen hours," the Captain told him. "Find your quarters."

"Yes, sir." He rightly took that for dismissal and saluted, glad to be out of Captain Jellico's zoo—even if only one inhabitant was living.

As he dropped down again to the cargo section, Dane wondered from what strange world the blue thing had come and why the Captain was so enamored of it that he carried it about in the *Queen*. As far as Dane could see it had no endearing qualities at all.

Whatever cargo the *Queen* had shipped for Naxos was already aboard. He saw the hatch seals in place as he passed the hold. So his department's duties were done for this port. He was free to explore the small cabin Rip Shannon had indicated was his and pack away in its lockers his few personal belongings.

At the Pool he had lived in a hammock and locker, to him the new quarters were a comfortable expansion. When the signal came to strap down for blastoff, he was fast gaining the contentment Artur Sands had threatened to destroy.

They were space borne before Dane met the other members of the crew. In addition to Captain Jellico, the control station was manned by Steen Wilcox, a lean Scot in his early thirties who had served a hitch in the Galactic Survey before going into Trade, and now held a full rating as Astrogator. Then there was the Martian com-tech— Tang Ya—and Rip, the apprentice.

The engine-room section was an equal number, consisting of the Chief, Johan Stotz, a silent young man who appeared to have little interest save his engines (Dane gathered from Rip's scraps of information that Stotz was in his way a mechanical genius who could have had much better berths than the aging *Queen,* but chose to stay with the challenge she offered), and his apprentice—the immaculate, almost foppish Kamil. But, Dane soon knew, the *Queen* carried no dead weight and Kamil must—in spite of his airs and graces—be able to meet the exacting standards such a chief as Stotz could set. The engine-room staff was rounded out by a giant-dwarf combination, startling to see.

Karl Kosti was a lumbering bear of a man, almost bovine, but as alert to his duties with the jets as a piece of perfectly working machinery. While around him buzzed his opposite number, a fly about a bull, the small Jasper Weeks, his thin face pallid with that bleach produced on Venus, a pallor not even the rays of space could color to a natural brown.

Dane's own fellows housed on the cargo level were a varied lot. There was Van Rycke himself, a superior so competent when it came to the matters of his own section that he might have been a computer. He kept Dane in a permanent state of awe, there appeared to be nothing concerning the fine points of Free Trade Van Rycke had ever missed hearing or learning, and, having once added any fact to his prodigious store of memories, it was embedded forever. But he had his soft spot, his enduring pride that as a Van Rycke he was one of a line stretching far back into the dim past when ships only plied the waters of a single planet, coming of a family which had been in Trade from the days of sails to the days of stars.

Two others who were partly of the cargo world shared this section. The medic, Craig Tau, and the cook-steward Frank Mura. Tau Dane met in the course of working hours now and then, but Mura kept so closely to his own quarters and labors that they seldom saw much of him.

In the meantime the new apprentice was kept busy, laboring in an infinitesimal space afforded him in the cargo office to check the rolls, being informally but mercilessly quizzed by Van Rycke and learning to his dismay what large gaps unfortunately existed in his training. Dane was speedily reduced to a humble wonder that Captain Jellico had ever shipped him at all—in spite of the assignment of the Psycho. It was too evident that in his present state of overwhelming ignorance he was more of a liability than an asset.

But Van Rycke was not just a machine of facts and figures, he was also a superb raconteur, a collector of legends who could keep the whole mess spellbound as he spun one of his tales. No one but he could pay such perfect tribute to the small details of the eerie story of the *New Hope,* that ship which had blasted off with refugees from the Martian rebellion, never to be sighted until a century later—the *New Hope* wandering forever in free fall, its dead lights glowing evilly red at its nose, its escape ports ominously sealed—the *New Hope* never boarded, never salvaged because it was only sighted by ships which were themselves in dire trouble, so that "to sight the *New Hope*" had become a synonym for the worst of luck.

Then there were the "Whisperers," whose siren voices were heard by those men who had been too long in space, and about whom a whole mythology had developed. Van Rycke could list the human demi-gods of the star lanes, too. Sanford Jones, the first man who had dared Galactic flight, whose lost ship had suddenly lashed out of Hyperspace, over a Sirius world three centuries after it had lifted from Terra, the mummified body of the pilot still at the frozen controls, Sanford Jones who now welcomed on board that misty "Comet" all spacemen who died with their magnetic boots on. Yes, in his way, Van Rycke made his new assistant free of more than one kind of space knowledge.

The voyage to Naxos was routine. And the frontier world where they set down at its end was enough like Terra to be unexciting too. Not that Dane got any planet-side leave. Van Rycke put him in charge of the hustlers at the unloading. And the days he had spent poring over the hold charts suddenly paid off as he discovered that he could locate everything with surprising ease.

Van Rycke went off with the Captain. Upon their bargaining ability, their collective nose for trade, depended the next flight of the *Queen*. And no ship lingered in port longer than it took her to discharge one cargo and locate another.

Mid-afternoon of the second day found Dane unemployed. He was lounging a little dispiritedly by the crew hatch with Kosti. None of the *Queen*'s men had gone into the sprawling frontier town half encircled by the bulbous trees with the red-yellow foliage, there was too much chance that they might be needed for cargo hustling, since the Field men were celebrating a local holiday and were not at their posts. Thus both Dane and the jetman witnessed the return of the hired scooter which tore down the field toward them at top speed.

It slewed around, raising more dust, and came to a skidding stop at the foot of the ramp. Captain Jellico leaped for that, almost reaching the hatch before Van Rycke had pried himself from behind the controls. And the Captain threw a single order at Kosti:

"Order assembly in the mess cabin!"

Dane stared back over the field, half expecting to see at least a squad of police in pursuit. The officers' return had smacked of the need for a quick getaway. But all he saw was his own superior ascending the ramp at his usual dignified pace. Only Van Rycke was whistling, a sign Dane had come to know meant that all was very well with the Dutchman's world. Whatever the Captain's news, the cargo-master considered it good.

As the latest and most junior member of the crew, Dane squeezed into the last small portion of room just inside the mess cabin door a few minutes later. From Tau to the usually absent Mura, the entire complement of the ship was present, their attention for Captain Jellico who sat at the head of the small table, moving his fingertips back and forth across the old blaster scar on his cheek.

"And what pot of gold has fallen into our hands this time, Captain?" That was Steen Wilcox asking the question which was in all their minds.

"Survey auction!" the words burst out of Jellico as if he simply could not restrain them any longer.

Somebody whistled, and someone else gasped. Dane blinked, he was too new to the game to understand at once. But when the full purport of the announcement burst upon him he knew a surge of red hot excitement. A Survey auction—a Free Trader got a chance at one of those maybe once in a lifetime. And that was how fortunes were made.

"Who's in town?" Engineer Stotz's eyes were narrowed, he was looking at the Captain almost accusingly.

Jellico shrugged. "All the usual. But it's been a long trip, and there are four Class Ds listed as up for bids—"

Dane calculated rapidly. The Companies would automatically scoop up the A and B listings—there would be tussles over the Cs. And four Ds—four newly discovered planets whose trading rights auctioned off under Federation law would come within range of the price Free Traders could raise. Would the *Queen* be able to enter the contest for one of them? A complete five- or ten-year monopoly on the rights of Trade with a just chartered world could make them all wealthy—if luck rode their jets!

"How much in the strong box?" Tau asked Van Rycke.

"When we pick up the voucher for this last load and pay our Field fees there'll be— But what about supplies, Frank?"

The thin little steward was visibly doing sums in his head. "Say a thousand for restocking—that gives us a good margin—unless we're in for a rim haul—"

"All right, Van, cutting out that thousand—what can we raise?" It was Jellico's turn to ask.

There was no need for the cargo-master to consult his books, the figures were part of the amazing catalogue within his mind. "Twenty-five thousand—maybe six hundred more—"

There was a deflated silence. No Survey auctioneer would accept that amount. It was Wilcox who broke the quiet.

"Why are they having an auction here, anyway? Naxos is no Federation district planet."

It was queer, come to think of it, Dane agreed. He had never before heard of a trading auction being held on any world which was not at least a sector capitol.

"The Survey ship *Rimwold* has been reported too long overdue," Jellico's voice came flatly. "All available ships have been ordered to conclude business and get into space to quarter for her. This ship here—the *Griswold*—came in to the nearest planet to hold auction. It's some kind of legal rocket wash—"

Van Rycke's broad fingertips drummed on the tabletop. "There are Company agents here. On the other hand there are only two other independent Traders in port. Unless another planets before sixteen hours today, we have four worlds to share between the three of us. The Companies don't want Ds—their agents have definite orders not to bid for them."

"Look here, sir," that was Rip. "In that twenty-five thousand—did you include the pay-roll?"

When Van Rycke shook his head Dane guessed what Rip was about to suggest. And for a moment he knew resentment. To be asked to throw one's voyage earnings into a wild gamble—and that was what would happen he was sure—was pretty tough. He wouldn't have the courage to vote no against it either—

"With the pay-roll in?" Tau's soft, unaccented voice questioned.

"About thirty-eight thousand—"

"Pretty lean for a Survey auction," Wilcox was openly dubious.

"Miracles have happened," Tang Ya pointed out. "I say—try it. If we lose we're not any the worse—"

It was agreed by a hand vote, no one dissenting, that the crew of the *Queen* would add their pay to the reserve—sharing in proportion to the sum they had surrendered in any profits to come. Van Rycke by common consent was appointed the bidder. But none of them would have willingly stayed away from the scene of action and Captain Jellico agreed to hire a Field guard as they left the ship in a body to try their luck.

The dusk of Naxos was early, the air away from the fuel vapors of the Field, scented with growing things, almost too much so to suit their Terran nostrils. It was a typical frontier town, alive with the flashing signs of noisy cafés. But the men from the *Queen* went straight to the open market which was to be the auction place.

A pile of boxes made a none-too-stable platform on which stood several men, two in the blue-green uniforms of the Survey, one in rough leather and fabric of the town, and one in the black and silver of the Patrol. All the legalities would be strictly observed even if Naxos was sparsely settled frontier.

Nor were the men gathering there all wearing brown Trade tunics. Some were from the town, come to see the fun. Dane tried to check the badges of rivals by the limited light of the portable flares. Yes, there was an Inter-Solar man, and slightly to his left, the triple circle of the Combine.

The As and Bs would be put up first—planets newly contacted by Galactic Survey but with a high degree of civilization—perhaps carrying on interplanetary trade within their own systems, planets which the Companies would find worth dealing with. The Cs— worlds with backward cultures—were more of a gamble and would not be so feverishly sought. And the Ds, those with only the most primitive of intelligent life, or perhaps no intelligent life at all—were the chances within the reach of the *Queen*.

"Cofort is here—" He heard Wilcox tell the Captain and caught Jellico's bitter answering exclamation.

Dane looked more closely at the milling crowd. Which one of the men without Company insignia was the legendary prince of Free Traders; the man who had made so many strikes that his luck was fabulous along the star lanes? But he could not guess.

One of the Survey officers came to the edge of the platform and the noise of the crowd died. His cohort held up a box—the box containing the sealed packets of micro-film—each with the coordinates and the description of a newly discovered planet.

The As went. There were only three and the Combine man snaffled two of them from the Inter-Solar bidder. But Inter-Solar did much better with the Bs, scooping up both of them. And another Company who specialized in opening up backward worlds plunged on the four Cs. The Ds—

The men of the *Queen* pressed forward, until with a handful of their independent fellows they were right below the platform.

Rip's thumb caught Dane in the lower ribs and his lips shaped the name, "Cofort!"

The famous Free Trader was surprisingly young. He looked more like a tough Patrol Officer than a Trader, and Dane noted that he wore a blaster which fitted so exactly to the curve of his hip that he must never be without it. Otherwise, though rumor credited him with several fortunes, he was little different in outward appearance from the other Free Traders. He made no display of wrist bands, rings, or the single earring the more spectacular of the well-to-do Traders flaunted, and his tunic was as plain and worn as Jellico's.

"Four planets—D class—" the voice of the Survey officer brought Dane's attention back to the business at hand. "Number One—Federation minimum bid—Twenty thousand credits—"

There was a concentrated sigh from the *Queen*'s crew. No use trying for that. With such a high minimum they would be edged out almost before they had begun. To Dane's surprise Cofort did not bid either and it went to a Trader from the rim for fifty thousand.

But at the presentation of planet number two, Cofort came to life and briskly walked away from the rest of the field with a bid of close to a hundred thousand. No one was supposed to know what information was inside each of those packets, but now they began to wonder if Cofort did have an advance tip.

"Planet Three—D class—Federation minimum bid—Fifteen thousand—"

That was more like it! Dane was certain Van Rycke would rise to that. And he did, until Cofort over-topped him with a jump from thirty to fifty thousand in a single offer. Only one chance left. The men from the *Queen* drew together, forming a knot behind Van Rycke as if they were backing the cargo-master in a do or die effort.

"Planet Four—D Class—Federation minimum bid fourteen thousand—"

"Sixteen—" Van Rycke's boom tripped over the Survey announcement.

"Twenty—" That was not Cofort, but a dark man they did not know.

"Twenty-five—" Van Rycke was pushing it.

"Thirty—" The other man matching him in haste.

"Thirty-five!" Van Rycke sounded confident as if he had Cofort's resources to draw upon.

"Thirty-six—" The dark trader turned cautious.

"Thirty-eight!" Van Rycke made his last offer.

There was no answer. Dane glancing saw that Cofort was passing over a voucher and collecting his two packets. The dark man shook his head when the Survey man turned to him. They had it!

For an instant the *Queen*'s men could hardly believe in their good luck. Then Kamil let out a whoop and the staid Wilcox could be seen pounding Jellico on the back as Van Rycke stepped up to claim their purchase. They spilled out into the street, piling in and on the scooter with but one thought in mind—to get back to the *Queen* and find out what they had bought.

CHARTERED GAMBLE

3 They were all in the mess cabin again, the only space in the *Queen* large enough for the crew to assemble. Tang Ya set a reader on the table while Captain Jellico slit the packet and brought out the tiny roll of film it contained. Dane believed afterward that few of them drew a really deep breath until it was fitted into place and the machine focused on the wall in lieu of the regular screen.

"Planet—Limbo—only habitable one of three in a yellow star system—" the impersonal voice of some bored Survey clerk droned through the cabin.

On the wall of the *Queen* appeared a flat representation of a three world system with the sun in the center. Yellow sun—perhaps the planet had the same climate as Terra! Dane's spirits soared. Maybe they were in luck—real luck.

"Limbo—" that was Rip wedged beside him. "Man, oh, man, that's no lucky name—that sure isn't!"

But Dane could not identify the title. Half the planets on the trade lanes had outlandish names didn't they—any a Survey man slapped on them.

"Coordinates—" the voice rippled out lines of formalae which Wilcox took down in quick notes. It would be his job to set the course to Limbo.

"Climate—resembling colder section of Terra. Atmosphere—" more code numbers which were Tau's concern. But Dane gathered that it was one in which human beings could live and work.

The image in the screen changed. Now they might be hanging above Limbo, looking at it through their own view ports. And that vision was greeted with at least one exclamation of shocked horror.

For there was no mistaking the cause of those brown-gray patches disfiguring the land masses. It was the leprosy of war—a war so vast and terrible that no Terran could be able to visualize its details.

"A burnt off!" that was Tau, but above his voice rose that of the Captain's.

"It's a filthy trick!"

"Hold it!" Van Rycke's rumble drowned out both outbursts, his big hand shot out to the reader's control button. "Let's have a close-up. North a bit, along those burn scars—"

The globe on the screen shot toward them, enlarging so that its limits vanished and they might have been going in for a landing. The awful waste of the long-ago war was plain, earth burned and tortured into slag, maybe still even poisonous with radioactive wastes. But the cargo-master had not been mistaken, along the horrible scars to the north was a band of strangely tinted green which could only be vegetation. Van Rycke gave a sigh of satisfaction.

"She isn't a total loss—" he pointed out.

"No," retorted Jellico bitterly, "probably shows just enough life so we can't claim fraud and get back our money."

"Forerunner ruins?" The suggestion came from Rip, timidly as if he felt he might be laughed down.

Jellico shrugged. "We aren't museum men," he snapped. "And where would we have to go to make a deal with them—off Naxos anyway. And how are we going to lift from here now without cash for the cargo bond?"

He had hammered home every bad point of their present situation. They owned ten-year trading rights to a planet which obviously had no trade—they had paid for those rights with the cash they needed to assemble a cargo. They might not be able to lift from Naxos. They had taken a Free Trader's gamble and had lost.

Only the cargo-master showed no dejection. He was still studying the picture of Limbo.

"Let's don't go off with only half our jets spitting," he said mildly. "Survey doesn't sell worlds which can't be exploited—"

"Not to the Companies, no," Wilcox commented, "but who's going to listen to a kick from a Free Trader—unless he's Cofort!"

"I still say," Van Rycke continued in the same even tone, "that we ought to explore a little farther—"

"Yes?" Jellico's eyes held a spark of smoldering anger. "You want us to go there and be stranded? She's burnt off—so she's got to be written off our books. You know there's never any life left on a Forerunner planet that was assaulted—"

"Most of them are just bare rock now," Van Rycke said reasonably. "It looks to me as if Limbo didn't get the full treatment. After all—what do we know about the Forerunners—precious little! They were gone centuries, maybe even thousands of years, before we broke into space. They were a great race, ruling whole systems of planets and they went out in a war which left dead worlds and even dead suns swinging in its wake. All right.

"But maybe Limbo was struck in the last years of that war, when their power was on the wane. I've seen the other blasted worlds— Hades and Hel, Sodom, and Satan, and they're nothing but cinders. This Limbo still has vegetation. And because it isn't as badly hit as those others I think we might just have something—"

He is winning his point, Dane told himself—noticing the change of expression on the faces around the table. Maybe it's because we don't want to believe that we've been taken so badly, because we want to hope that we can win even yet. Only Captain Jellico looked stubbornly unconvinced.

"We can't take the chance," he repeated, his lips in an obstinate line. "We can fuel this ship for one trip—*one* trip. If we make it to Limbo and there's no return cargo—well," he slapped his hand on the table, "you know what that will mean—dirt-side for us!"

Steen Wilcox cleared his throat with a sharp rasp which drew their attention. "Any chance of a deal with Survey?" he wanted to know.

Kamil laughed, scorn more than amusement in the sound. "Do the Feds ever give up any cash once they get their fingers on it?" he inquired.

No one answered him until Captain Jellico got to his feet, moving heavily as if some of the resilience had oozed out of his tough body.

"We'll see them in the morning. You willing to try it, Van?"

The cargo-master shrugged. "All right, I'll tag along. Not that it'll do us any good."

"Blasted—right off course—"

Dane stood again at the open hatch looking out into a night made almost too bright by Naxos' twin moons. Kamil's words were not directed to him, he was sure. And a moment later that was confirmed by an answer from Rip.

"I don't call luck bad, man, 'til it up and slaps me in the face. Van had an idea—that planet wasn't blasted black. You've seen pictures of Hel and Sodom, haven't you? They're cinders, as Van said. This Limbo, now—it shows green. Did you ever think, Ali, what might happen if we walked onto a world where some of the Forerunners' stuff was lying around?"

"Hm—" The idea Rip presented struck home. "But would trading rights give us ownership of such a find?"

"Van would know—that's part of his job. Why—" for the first time Rip must have sighted Dane at the hatch, "here's Thorson. How about it, Dane? If we found Forerunner material could we claim it legally?"

Dane was forced to admit that he didn't know. But he determined to hunt up the answer in the cargo-master's tape library of rules and regulations.

"I don't think that the question has ever come up," he said dubiously. "Have they ever found usable Forerunner remains—anything except empty ruins? The planets on which their big installations must have been are the burnt-off ones—"

"I wonder," Kamil leaned back against the hatch door and looked at the winking lights of the town, "what they were like. All of the strictly human races we have encountered are descended from Terran colonies. And the five non-human ones we know are all as ignorant of the Forerunners as we are. If they left any descendants we haven't contacted them yet. And—" he paused for a long moment before he added, "did you ever think it is just as well we haven't found any of their installations? It's been exactly ten years since the Crater War—"

His words trailed off into a thick silence which had a faint menacing quality Dane could not identify, though he understood what Kamil must be aiming at. Terrans fought, viciously, devastatingly. The Crater War on Mars had been only the tail end of a long struggle between home planet and colonist across the void. The Federation kept an uneasy peace, the men of Trade worked frantically to make that permanent before another and more deadly conflict might wreck the whole Service and perhaps end their own precarious civilization.

What *would* happen if weapons, such as the Forerunners had wielded in their last struggle, or even the knowledge of such weapons, fell into the wrong Terran hands? Would Sol become a dead star circled by burnt-off cinder worlds?

"Sure, it might cause trouble if we found weapons," Rip had followed the same argument. "But they had other things besides arms. And maybe on Limbo—"

Kamil straightened. "Maybe on Limbo they left a treasure house stored with bags of Thork gems and Lamgrim silk—or their equivalent, sure. But I don't think the Captain is in the mood to hunt for it. We're twelve men and one ship—how long do you think it would take us to comb a whole planet? And our scout flitters eat fuel too, remember? How'd you like to be stranded dirt-side on some planet like this Naxos—have to turn farmer to get food? You wouldn't care for it."

Dane had to admit inwardly that *he* certainly wouldn't care for that. And if the *Queen* did set down so—locked in some port for the lack of funds to get her off-world again, he wouldn't even have his back pay as a meager stake to tide him over until he could get another ship. The others must be thinking of that also.

Sometime later Dane lay awake on his narrow bunk amazed at how quickly all their hopes had crashed. If Limbo had only proved to be what they first thought—or even if they only had a big enough reserve to go and inspect their purchase— But—suddenly Dane sat up—there had been that other Trader who had bid against Van Rycke at the auction. Could he be persuaded to take Limbo off their hands at a big discount?

But with a burnt off, he wouldn't want it even at half what they had paid Survey. The risk was too great—no one would make a dry-run on such short odds. Only a man with Cofort's backing could take a chance—and Cofort had shown no interest in this particular "bargain."

In the morning it was a glum crew who trailed in and out of the mess cabin. All of them carefully avoided the end of the table where a grim Captain Jellico sat sipping at a cup of Mura's own secret brew which was usually served only at moments of rejoicing. This was no celebration—it must be that the steward believed they needed heartening.

Van Rycke came in, his tunic sealed trimly from his belt to his broad chin, his winged officer's cap perched on his head, ready for a town visit. Jellico grunted and pushed away his cup as he arose to join him. And so daunting was the Captain's scowl that not one of the others dared to wish them good luck on their mission.

Dane climbed down into the cargo hold, studying its empty space and making a few measurements of his own. If they were fortunate enough to get a pay load he wanted to be ready for its stowing. The hold was in two sections—a wide chamber which took in almost a third of the ship and a small cabin-sized space above it in which choice or unusual items could be stored.

In addition, on the same level, was the tiny room where was shelved and boxed their "trade goods," small items used to attract the attention of savages or backward civilizations—gadgets, mechanical toys, trinkets of glass, wire, enameled metal. Dane, trying out his memorization of the store catalogue, made the rounds of the cases. He had been taken on two tours of inspection by Van Rycke, but he had not yet lost his sense of wonder at the kinds and quality of the goods, and the display of knowledge and imagination of the cargo-master who had assembled this collection. Here were the presents for chieftains and petty kings, the exciters which would bring the people of primitive villages flocking to view such off-world wonders. Of course the supply was strictly limited, but it had been chosen with such care, such insight into humanoid and X-Tee psychology that it must go a long way to win customers for the *Queen*.

Only on Limbo such preparations would be useless. It was not possible that any intelligent life had survived the burn off. If there had been any natives the Survey team would certainly have reported them and that might have raised the value of the planet—even kept it out of the Trade auction until government men had more time to study it.

Dane tried to forget the fiasco of Limbo by applying himself to the study of the "contact" goods. Van Rycke had been patient with him on their rounds of this storehouse, using incidents from his own past to point up the use of each object in the cases or on the protected shelves. Some of the material, Dane gathered, was the handiwork of the crew.

Long drives through space, with the ship locked on its automatic controls, with few duties for her crew, tended to become monotonous. Boredom led to space mania and those who followed the Galactic lanes had early learned that skills of brain and hand were the answer. These could vary widely.

On board the *Queen*, Captain Jellico was a xenobiologist, far past amateur standing. While he could not bring back his specimens alive—save for such "pets" as the blue Hoobat now caged in his cabin—the tri-dee shots he had taken of animal life on unknown worlds had earned him fame among naturalists. Steen Wilcox, whose days were spent wrestling with obtuse mathematics, was laboring to transpose such formulae into musical patterns. And the oddest employ Dane had so far uncovered among his new companions was that of Medic Tau who collected magic, consorting with witch doctors and medicine men of alien primitives, seeking to discover the core of truth lying beneath the mumbo-jumbo.

Dane picked up a piece of Mura's handiwork, a plasta-crystal ball in which floated, to all examination alive, a rainbow winged insect totally unfamiliar to him. But a shadow gliding in the panel to his left brought him out of his absorption. Sinbad, the *Queen*'s cat, leaped gracefully to the top of a case and sat there, regarding the apprentice. Of all the native Terran animals the one which had most easily followed man into space was the feline.

Cats took to acceleration, to free fall, to all the other discomforts of star flight, with such ease that there were some odd legends growing up about their tribe. One was that *Domestica felinus* was not really native to Terra, but had descended from the survivors of an early and forgotten invasion and in the star ships he was only returning to his former golden age.

But Sinbad and those of his species served a definite purpose onboard ship and earned their pay. Pests, not only the rats and mice of Terra, but other and odder creatures from alien worlds, came aboard with cargo, sometimes not to be ordinarily detected for weeks, even months after they had set up housekeeping in the hidden corners of the ship. These were Sinbad's concern. When and where he caught them the crew might never learn, but he presented the bodies of the slain to Van Rycke. And, from all accounts, on past voyages some of the bodies had been very weird indeed!

Dane held out his hand and Sinbad sniffed lazily at his fingers and then blinked. He accepted this new human. It was right and proper for Dane to be here. Sinbad stretched and then leaped lightly down from the box to go about the room on regular patrol. He lingered near one bale with such profound sniffing that Dane wondered if he shouldn't open it for the cat's closer inspection. But a distant gong startled them both and Sinbad, one who never overlooked the summons to a meal, flashed out of the room, leaving Dane to follow at a more dignified pace.

Neither the Captain nor the cargo-master had returned, and the atmosphere at mess continued to be sober. With two other Free Traders in port any cargoes, too small to attempt Company ships, would be at a premium. But they were all startled when the communication light from the outer hatch clicked on overhead.

Steen Wilcox jumped for the corridor and Dane was only seconds behind him. With Jellico and Van Rycke off ship, Wilcox was the nominal commander of the *Queen,* and Dane the representative of *his* section—on duty until the cargo-master returned.

A scooter was drawn up at the foot of the ramp, its driver sitting behind the controls. But a tall man, thin and burnt brown, was climbing confidently up to the entrance hatch.

He wore a scuffed, hard-duty leather tunic and frabcord breeches, with thigh-high boots of corval skin, the dress of a field man on a pioneer world. On the other hand he did not affect the wide brimmed hat of the men Dane had seen in town. Instead his head was covered with a helmet of Metaplast which had the detachable visor and the bubble ear pockets of a built-in short wave receiver—the usual head gear of a Survey man.

"Captain Jellico?" his voice was crisp, authoritative, the voice of a man who was used to giving orders and having them unquestioningly obeyed.

The astrogator shook his head. "Captain's planet-side, sir."

The stranger halted, drumming his fingers on his wide, pocketwalled belt. It was plain he was annoyed at not finding the commander of the *Queen* on board.

"When will he be back?"

"Don't know." Wilcox was not cordial. Apparently he had not taken a fancy to the caller.

"You are open to charter?" was the other's surprising inquiry.

"You'll have to see the Captain—" Wilcox's coolness grew.

The tattoo of fingers on the belt became faster. "All right, I'll see your captain! Where is he—can you tell me that?"

A second scooter was approaching the *Queen* and there was no mistaking the bulk of its driver. Van Rycke was returning to the ship. Wilcox had sighted him too.

"You'll know in a minute. Here's our cargo-master—"

"So—" the man swung around on the ramp, his lithe body moving with trained speed.

Dane grew intent. This stranger was an intriguing mixture. His dress was that of a pioneer-explorer, his movements those of a trained fighting man. Dane's memory presented him with a picture—the exercise ground at the Pool on a hot summer afternoon. That under swing of the arm—the betraying hunch of the shoulder— This fellow was a force-blade man—and a practiced one! But force-blades—illegal—no civilian was supposed to be familiar with their use.

Van Rycke circled the waiting scooter which had delivered the stranger and came at his usual ponderous pace up the ramp.

"Looking for someone?"

"Is your ship up for charter?" the stranger asked for the second time.

Van Rycke's bushy brows twitched. "Any Trader is always open to a good deal," he answered calmly. "Thorson—" his attention swept past the other's impatience to Dane, "go into the Green Whirly Bird and ask Captain Jellico to return—"

Dane ran down the ramp and got into Van Rycke's scooter. He glanced back as he put the small vehicle in gear and saw that the stranger was now following the cargo-master into the *Queen*.

The Green Whirly Bird was half café, half restaurant and Captain Jellico was seated at a table near the door, talking to the dark man who had bid for Limbo at the auction. But as Dane came into the murky room the other Trader shook his head firmly and got to his feet. The Captain made no move to detain him, only shoved the tankard before him an inch or so to the right, concentrating upon that action as if it were some intricate process he must master.

"Sir—" Dane dared to put a hand on the table to attract attention.

The Captain looked up, and his eyes were bleak and cold. "Yes?"

"There's a man at the *Queen,* sir. He's asking about a charter. Mr. Van Rycke sent me for you—"

"Charter!" The tankard went over on its side, to bump to the floor. Captain Jellico flung a piece of the local metal money on the table and was already on his way to the door, Dane hurrying after.

Jellico took control of the scooter, starting off at a wild pace. But before they had gone the length of the street the Captain slowed and when they drew up before the *Queen* no one could have guessed they were in a hurry.

It was two hours later that the crew assembled once more to hear the news. And the stranger sat with Jellico as the Captain told the crew of their luck.

"This is Dr. Salzar Rich," he made a brief introduction. "He is one of the Federation experts on Forerunner remains. It seems that Limbo isn't such a flame-out after all, men. The Doctor informs me that Survey located some quite sizable ruins on the northern hemisphere. He's chartered the *Queen* to transport his expedition there—"

"And," Van Rycke smiled benignly, "this in no way interferes with our own trading rights. We shall have a chance to explore too."

"When do we lift?" Johan Stotz wanted to know.

"When can you be ready, Dr. Rich?" Jellico turned to the archaeologist.

"As soon as you can stow my equipment and men, Captain. I can bring my supplies up right away."

Van Rycke got to his feet. "Thorson." He brought Dane to him with that call. "We'll make ready to load. Send in your material as soon as you wish, Doctor."

LIMBO LANDING

4

During the next few hours Dane learned more in practice about the stowage of cargo than he had ever been taught in theory at the Pool. And, cramped as the crew of the *Queen* were, they also discovered that they must find space for not only Rich but for three assistants as well.

The supplies went into the large cargo hold, most of the work being volunteer labor on the part of Rich's men, since the Doctor hammered home the fact that delicate instruments and perishable goods were included and he had no intention of allowing any of the boxes to be tossed about by the hustlers hired by the Field.

But inside the ship the final stowage of material was, as Van Rycke speedily let him know, solely the problem of the crew. And they could do it without any amateur advice. So Dane and Kosti sweated, swore and tugged, with the cargo-master himself not above lending a hand, until all the supplies were in place according to the mechanics of weight for takeoff. Then they sealed the hatch for the duration of the flight.

On their way up they discovered Mura in the smaller cargo compartment rigging space hammocks for Rich's assistants. The accommodations were crude but the archaeologist had been warned of that before he had thumb-printed the charter contract—the *Queen* had no extra passenger cabins. And none of the newcomers were grumbling.

Like their leader they were a type new to Dane, giving an impression of tough endurance—a quality which, he supposed, was very necessary in any field man sent out to prospect on strange worlds for the relics of vanished races. One of them wasn't even human—the green-tinted skin and hairless head stamped him a Rigellian. But his faintly scaled body, in spite of its odd sinuosity, was clad just like the others. Dane was trying not to stare at him when Mura came up and touched his arm.

"Dr. Rich is in your cabin. You've been moved into the store cubby—along here—"

A little irked by being so high-handedly assigned to new quarters, Dane followed Mura down to the domain, which was the steward's own. There was the galley, the food storage freezers, and, beyond, the hydro garden which was half Mura's concern, half Tau's, as air officer.

"Dr. Rich," Mura explained as they went, "asked to be near his men. He made quite a point of it—"

Dane looked down at the small man. Just why had Mura added that last?

More than any of the crew Mura presented an enigma to Dane. The steward was of Japanese descent—and the apprentice had been familiar from his early training days with the terrifying story of what had happened to those islands which had once existed across the sea from his own native country. Volcanic action, followed by tidal waves, had overwhelmed a whole nation in two days and a night—so that Japan had utterly ceased to be—washed from the maps of Terra.

"Here," Mura reached the end of the corridor and waved Dane through a half-open panel.

The steward had made no effort to decorate the walls of his private quarters, and the extreme neatness of the cabin tended to have a bleak effect. But on a pull-down table rested a globe of plasta-crystal and what it contained drew Dane's attention.

A Terran butterfly, its jeweled wings spread wide, hung by some magic in the very center of the orb, sealed so for all time, and yet giving every appearance of vibrant life.

Mura, noting Dane's absorption, leaned forward and tapped the top of the globe lightly. In answer to that touch the wings seemed to quiver, the imprisoned beauty moved a fraction.

Dane drew a deep breath. He had seen the globe in the storeroom, he knew that Mura collected the insect life of a hundred worlds to fashion the balls—there were two others on board the *Queen*. One a tiny world, an aquatic one with fronds of weed curling to provide shelter for a school of gemmed insect-fish which were stalked by a weird creature two-legged, two-armed, but equipped with wing-like fins and a wicked pronged spear. That was in a place of honor in Van Rycke's cabin. Then there was the other—a vista of elfin towers of silver among which flitted nearly transparent things of pearly luster. That was the com-tech's particular treasure.

"One may create such, yes," Mura shrugged. "It is a way of passing time—like many others."

He picked up the globe, rolled it in protecting fiber and stowed it away in a partitioned drawer, cushioned against the takeoff of the *Queen*. Then he pulled aside a second panel to show Dane his new quarters.

It was a secondary storeroom which Mura had stripped and refurnished with a hammock and a foot locker. It was not as comfortable as his old cabin, but on the other hand it was no worse than the quarters he had had on both the Martian and Lunar training ships during his Pool cruises.

They blasted off for Limbo before dawn and were space borne before Dane aroused from an exhausted sleep. He had made his way to the mess hall when the warning sounded again and he clutched the table, swallowing painfully as he endured the vertigo which signaled their snap into Hyperspace. Up in the control compartment Wilcox, the Captain, and Rip would be at their stations, not able to relax until the break-through was assured.

He wouldn't, Dane decided not for the first time since he had entered training for space, be an astrogator for any reward the Federation could dream up. One fractional mistake in calculations—even with two computers taking most of the burden of the formula run-off—would warp your ship into a totally unknown lane, might bring you *inside* a planet instead of the necessary distance off its surface. He had had the theory of the break-through pounded into him, he could go through the motions of setting up a course, but he privately doubted if he would ever have the courage to actually take a ship into Hyperspace and out again.

Frowning at the unoffending wall he was once more listing his own shortcomings when Rip called.

"Man—" the astrogator-apprentice dropped down on a seat with a deep sigh, "well, we're in once more and nothing cracked!"

Dane was honestly surprised. He was no astrogator, it was all right for him to feel some doubts. But that Rip should display relief at having his own particular share of duty behind him for a while was something else.

"What's the matter?" Dane wondered if something *had* threatened to go wrong.

"Nothing, nothing," the other waved a hand. "But we all feel easier after the jump." Rip laughed now. "Man, you think *we* don't sweat it out? We maybe hate it more than you do. What have you got to worry about until we planet again? Nothing—"

Dane bristled. "No? We've only cargo control, supplies, hydro—" he began to enumerate the duties of his section. "What good does a successful break-through do when your air goes bad—"

Rip nodded. "All right, none of us are dead weight. Though this trip—" he stopped suddenly and glanced over his shoulder in a way which surprised Dane.

"Did you ever meet an archaeologist before, Dane?"

The cargo-apprentice shook his head. "This is my first trip out, remember? And we don't get much briefing in history at the Pool— except where it influences Trade—"

Rip lounged back on the bench, but kept his voice trained low, until it was hardly above a murmur.

"I've always been interested in the Forerunners," he began. "Got the tapes of Haverson's 'Voyages' and Kagle's 'Survey' in my gear now. Those are the two most complete studies that have been made so far. I messed with Dr. Rich this morning. And I'll swear he never heard of the Twin Towers!"

Since Dane had never heard of them either, he couldn't quite see what Rip was trying to prove. But, before he could ask any questions, the blankness of his look must have betrayed his ignorance for the other made a quick explanation.

"Up to now the Twin Towers are about the most important Forerunner find Federation Survey has ever made. They're on Corvo— standing right in the center of a silicon desert—two hundred feet high, looking like two big fingers pointing into the sky. And as far as the experts have been able to discover, they're solid clear through— made of some substance which is neither stone nor metal, but which certainly has lasting properties. Rich was able to cover his slip pretty well, but I'm sure he'd not heard of them."

"But if they're so important," began Dane and then he grasped what the Doctor's ignorance could mean.

"Yes, why doesn't the Doctor know all about the most important find in his field? That presents a problem doesn't it? I wonder if the Captain checked up on him before he took the charter—"

But Dane could answer that. "His ID was correct, we flashed it through to Patrol Headquarters. They gave *us* clearance on the expedition or we couldn't have lifted from Naxos—"

Rip conceded that point. Field regulations on any planet in the Federation were strict enough to make at least ninety percent sure that the men who passed them were carrying proper IDs and clearance. And on the frontier worlds, which might attract poachers or criminals, the Patrol would be twice as vigilant about flight permission.

"Only he didn't know about the Twin Towers," the astrogator-apprentice repeated stubbornly.

And Dane was impressed by the argument. It was impossible to spend a voyage on any star ship with another man and not come to know him with an intimacy which was unknown by civilization outside the small dedicated band of those who manned the Galactic fleets. If Rip said that Dr. Rich was not what he seemed, then Rip was speaking the truth as far as he knew it and Dane was willing to back him.

"What about the law regarding Forerunner remains?" Shannon asked a moment later.

"Not much about it in the records. There've never been any big finds made by a Trader and claimed under Trading rights—"

"So there's nothing we could quote as a precedent if we did find something worthwhile?"

"That can work both ways," Dane pointed out. "Survey released Limbo for Trade auction. If they did that, it seems to me, they've forfeited any Federation claims on the planet. It would make a nice legal tangle—"

"A beautifully complicated case—" Van Rycke rumbled over their heads. "One which half the law sharks of the systems would be eager to see come to trial. It's the sort of thing which would drag on for years, until all parties concerned were either heartily sick of it or safely dead. Which is just why we are traveling with a Federation Free Claim in our strong box."

Dane grinned. He might have known that such an old hand in Trade as his superior officer would not be caught without every angle covered as far as it was humanly possible. A Free Claim to any finds on Limbo!

"For how long?" Rip was still ridden by doubts.

"The usual—a year and a day. I don't think Survey is as impressed by the possibility of unusual finds as our passengers seem to be."

"Do *you* think we'll discover anything there, sir?" Dane struck in.

"I never advance any guesses on what we'll find on any new planet," Van Rycke answered tranquilly. "There are entirely too many booby-traps in our business. If a man gets away with a whole skin, a space-worthy ship, and a reasonable percentage of profit, the Lords of High Space have been good to him. We can't ask for more."

During the days which followed Rich's men kept very much to themselves, using their own supplies and seldom venturing out of their very constrained quarters, nor did they in turn invite visitors. Mura reported that they seemed to spend more of their time either in sleep or engrossed in some complicated gambling game the Rigellian had introduced.

While Dr. Rich messed with the crew of the *Queen,* he dropped in for his meals at hours when there were few in the cabin. And, either by choice or a too well regulated coincidence, those few were generally members of the engineering staff. On the plea of studying the scene of his future operations he had tried to borrow the Survey tape of Limbo, but the times he had been allowed to use it were under the eye of the cargo-master. An eye which, Dane was certain, missed nothing, no matter how abstracted Van Rycke might appear to be.

The *Queen* made transition into normal space on schedule within Limbo's system. Two of the other planets who shared this sun were so far away from that core of light and heat that they were frozen, lifeless worlds. But Limbo swung around on its appointed orbit at about the same range as Mars held in their native system. As they approached to come in on a "breaking orbit," allowing the friction of the planet's atmosphere to slow the ship to landing speed, the com-tech switched on the vision screens throughout the ship. Strapped down on their pads, those not on duty watched the loom of the new world fill the screen.

The ugly brown-gray scars of the burn off faced them first, but as the ship bored in, always at an angle which would coast it along the layers of air gradually, the watchers sighted the fingers of green, and traces of small seas or large lakes which proved that Limbo was not wholly dead, blasted though she had been.

Day became night as they passed on, and then day again. If they had been following the strict regulations for landing on a normal "primitive" world they would have tried for a set-down in a desert country, planning to explore by flitter, learning something in secret of the inhabitants before they made open contact. But Limbo would have no intelligent inhabitants—they could use the best possible landing.

Wilcox had brought them through Hyperspace by his reckoning, but it was Jellico who would set them down after choosing his site. And he was maneuvering to place them on the very edge of the burned area with the healthy ground within easy reach.

It was a tricky landing, not the easy one any tyro could make on a cleared Field with a beam to ride in. But the *Queen* had made such landings before and Jellico nursed her down, riding her tail flames until she settled with a jar which was mild under the circumstances.

"Grounded—" the pilot's voice echoed thinly over the com.

Stotz replied from the engine room with the proper answer: "Secure."

"Planet routine—" Jellico's voice gathered volume.

Dane unstrapped and headed for Van Rycke's office to get his orders. But he had hardly reached the door when he bumped into Dr. Rich.

"How soon can you get the supplies moving out?" the archaeologist demanded.

Van Rycke was still unfastening his shock belts. He looked up in surprise.

"You want to unload at once?"

"Certainly. As soon as you unseal hatches—"

The cargo-master settled his uniform cap on his light hair. "We don't move quite that fast, Doctor. Not on an unknown world."

"There are no savages here. And Survey has certified it fit for human exploration." The Doctor's impatience was fast becoming open irritation. It was as if during their time in space he had so built up his desire to get to work on Limbo that now he begrudged a single wasted moment.

"Brake your jets, Doctor," the cargo-master returned tranquilly. "We move at the Captain's orders. And it doesn't pay to take chances—whether Survey has given us an open sky or not." He touched the ship-com board on the wall by his elbow.

"Control here!" Tang's voice came through.

"Cargo-Master to Control—report all clear?"

"Report not ready," was the return. "Sampler still working—"

Dr. Rich slammed his fist against the door panel. "Sampler!" he exploded. "With a Survey report you want to play around with a sampler!"

"We're still alive," was Van Rycke's comment. "In this business there are risks you take and those you don't. We take the proper ones." He lowered himself into his desk chair and Dane leaned against the wall. The indications were that they were not going to be in a rush unloading.

Dr. Rich, reminding Dane of the Captain's caged Hoobat—though, of course, the archaeologist had not reached the point of spitting at them—snarled and went on toward the cabin where his men were waiting.

"Well," Van Rycke leaned back in his seat and flipped a finger at the visa-screen, "we can't call that a pleasant vista—"

In the distance were mountains, a saw-toothed chain of gray-brown rock crowned in some instances with snow. And their foothills were a ragged fringe cut by narrow, crooked valleys, in the mouths of which a pallid, unhealthy vegetation grew. Even in the sunlight the place looked dreary—a background for a nightmare.

"Sampler reports livable conditions—" the disembodied voice from control suddenly proclaimed.

Van Rycke touched the com-call again. "Cargo-Master to Captain, do you wish exploring parties prepared?"

But he had no answer for that as Dr. Rich burst in upon them again. And this time he pushed past Van Rycke to shout into the com-mike:

"Captain Jellico—this is Salzar Rich. I demand that you release my supplies at once, sir, at once!"

His first answer was complete silence. And Dane, awed, questioned within himself whether the Captain was simply so angry that he couldn't reply coherently. One didn't demand that a star ship captain do this or that—even the Patrol had to "request."

"For what reason, Dr. Rich?" To Dane's surprise the voice was quiet, unruffled.

"Reason!" sputtered the man leaning across Van Rycke's desk, "why, so that we may establish our camp before nightfall—"

"Ruins to the west—" Tang's calm announcement cut through Rich's raised voice.

All three of them looked at the visa-screen where the mountains to the north had disappeared, to be replaced by the western vista as the com-tech swung the detector from one compass point to the next.

Now they were gazing out over the burnt ground, where the unknown weapons of the Forerunners had scored down to rock and then scarred the rock itself with deep grooves filled with a glassy slag which caught and reflected the sun's rays in bright flashes. But beyond this desolation was something else, a tumble of edifices which reached on into the undevastated circle of vegetation.

The ruins were a blotch of bright color in the general somberness, spilling in violent reds and yellows, strident greens and blues. They were, perhaps, some twenty miles from the *Queen*, and they were spectacular enough to amaze the three in the cargo-master's office. Perhaps because Dr. Rich was now treading on familiar ground he was the first to regain speech.

"There—" he jabbed an impatient finger at the screen, "that's where we'll camp!" He whirled back to the mike and spoke into it:

"Captain Jellico—I wish to establish my camp by those ruins. As soon as your cargo-master will release our supplies—"

His vehemence appeared to win, for a short time later Van Rycke broke the seals on the cargo hatch, the Doctor impatient beside him, the three other members of his expedition lined up in the corridor behind.

"We will take over now, Van Rycke—"

But the cargo-master's arm was up, barring the Doctor's advance.

"No, thank you, Doctor. No load goes out of the *Queen* unless my department oversees the job."

And with that Rich had to be content, though he was fuming as Dane operated the crane swinging out and down the ship's radar controlled crawler. And it was the apprentice who supervised the unloading. The Rigellian climbed up on the crawler, using its manual controls to guide it to the ruins. Once unloaded there it could return by itself, guided by the ship's beam, for a second cargo.

Rich and two of the others rode away on the second trip and Dane was left with the silent fourth member of the expedition to wait for the crawler. The last load was a small, miscellaneous one, mostly the personal baggage of the men.

Over the manifest disapproval of the expedition man the cargo-apprentice piled the bags up ready for a quick packing. But it was the other who dropped a battered kit bag. It fell heavily, its handle catching on a spur of rock ripping it open.

With a muffled exclamation the man sprang to stuff back the contents, but he was not quick enough to hide the book which had been wrapped in an undershirt.

That book! Dane's eyes narrowed aganst the sun. But he had no time for a second glance at it—the man was already strapping shut the bag. Only Dane was sure he had seen its twin—sitting on Wilcox's flight desk. Why should an archaeologist be carrying an astrogator's computer text?

FIRST SCOUT

5 Dusk on Limbo had an odd, thick quality as if the shadows were of a tangible dimension. Dane saw to the closing of the outer cargo hatch, leaving the crawler, which had returned empty from its last trip across the barrens, parked on the scorched earth under the fins of the *Queen*. They had taken all the other precautions of a ship on an unknown planet. The ramp had been warped in, the air locks closed. To Limbo at large the *Queen* presented sleek smooth sides which nothing outside of some very modern and highly technical weapons could breach. No star Trader ever took to space except in a ship which could serve as a fort if the need arose.

Intent on his own problem Dane climbed from level to level until he reached Rip's confined quarters on the fringe of control territory. The astrogator-apprentice was huddled on a snap-down seat, a T-camera in his hands.

"I got a whole strip of the ruins," he told Dane excitedly as the other paused in the doorway. "But that Rich— He's a free-rider if I ever saw one. Wonder Sinbad didn't hunt him out with the rest of the cargo gnawers and turn him in as legitimate prey—"

"What's he done now?"

"With the biggest thing yet in Forerunner finds out there," stabbing a finger toward the wall, "he's sitting on it as if it is his own personal property. Told Captain Jellico that he didn't want any of us going over to see things—that 'the encroachment of untrained sightseers too often ruined unusual finds'! Untrained sightseers!" Rip repeated the words deep in his throat, and, for the first time since Dane had known him, he registered real resentment.

"Well," Dane pointed out reasonably, "even with four to help him he can't cover the whole planet. We're going to send out a scouting team after the regular system, aren't we? What's to prevent your running down some class-A ruins of your own? I don't think Rich's found the only remains on the whole planet. And there's nothing in the rules which says we can't explore the ones *we* find."

Rip brightened. "You're blasting with all jets now, man!" He put the T-camera down.

"At least," Kamil's carefully enunciated words cut in from the corridor, "one can never accuse the dear Doctor of neglect of duty. The way he rushed off to the scene of his labors you'd think he expected to find someone there cutting large slices out of the best exhibits. The dear Doctor *is* a bit of a puzzle all around, isn't he?"

Rip voiced his old suspicion. "He didn't know about Twin Towers—"

"And that red-headed assistant of his carries an astrogator's computer text in his kit bag." Dane was very glad to have information of his own to add to the discussion, especially since Kamil was there to hear it. The quiet with which his statement was received was flattering. But as usual Ali provided the first prick.

"How did that amazing fact come to your attention?"

Dane decided to ignore the faint but unpleasant accent on "your."

"He dropped his kit bag, the book rolled out, and he was in a big hurry to get it out of sight again."

Rip reached out to pull open a cupboard. From within he produced a thick book with a water-and-use-proof cover. "You saw one like this?"

Dane shook his head. "His had a red band—like the one on Wilcox's control cabin desk."

Kamil whistled softly and Rip's dark eyes went wide. "But that's a master book!" he protested. "No one but a signed-on astrogator has one of those, and when he signs out of any ship *that* goes into the Captain's safe until his replacement comes on board. There's just one on every ship by Federation law. When a ship is decommissioned the master book for it is destroyed—"

Ali laughed. "Don't be so naïve, my friend. How do you suppose poachers and smugglers operate? Do they comb their computations out of the air? It wouldn't surprise me if there was a brisk black market trade in computer texts, long since supposed to be burnt."

But Rip still shook his head. "They wouldn't have the new data— that's added on each planet as we check in. Why do you suppose Wilcox goes to the Field control office with our volume every time we set down on another world? That book is sent straight to the local Survey office and is processed to add the latest dope. And you couldn't present anything but a legit text—they'd spot it in a minute!"

"Listen, my innocent child," drawled Kamil, "for every law the Federation produces in their idealist vacuum there is some bright boy—or boys—working day and night to break it. I'm not telling you how they work it, but I'm willing to wager all my cut of this particular venture, that it's being done. If Thorson saw a red badge text book in that fellow's possession, then it's being done right here and now—on Limbo."

Rip got to his feet. "We should tell Steen—"

"Tell him what? That Thorson saw a book which looked like a text fall out of that digger's personal baggage? You didn't pick it up, did you, Thorson, or examine it closely?"

Dane was forced to admit that he had not. And his deflation began. What proof had he that the man from the expedition possessed a forbidden master text? And Steen Wilcox, of all people, was the last man on the ship to approach with a story founded on anything but concrete evidence. Unless Dane had the volume in question in his hand and ready to show, he would have little chance of being believed.

"So you see," Kamil turned back to Rip, "we'll have to have much better proof in our hot little hands before we go bursting in on our elders in the guise of intrepid Fed Agents or Boy Patrolmen."

Rip sat down again, as convinced of the reasonableness of that argument as Dane was. "But," he pounced upon the bit of encouragment in that crushing speech, "you say 'we'll have to have'— Then you *do* believe that there's something wrong with the Doctor!"

Kamil shrugged. "To my mind he's as crooked as a Red Desert dust dancer, but that's just my own private and confidential opinion, and I'm keeping it behind my nice white teeth until I can really impress the powers that be. In the meantime, we're going to be busy on our own. We're drawing for flitter assignments within the hour."

The small flitters carried by the *Queen* for exploration work held with comfort a two-man crew—with crowding, three. Both of the planes had been carefully checked by the engineering section that afternoon while Dane had been busied with unloading the expedition supplies. And there was no doubt that the next morning would see the first of the scouting parties out on duty.

There were no lights to break the somber dark of Limbo's night. And then men of the *Queen* lost interest in the uniformly black visascreens which kept them in touch with the outside. It was after the evening meal that they drew for membership on the flitter teams. As usual the threefold organization of the ship determined the drawing; one man of the engineers, one of the control deck, and one of Van Rycke's elastic department being grouped together.

Dane wanted to be teamed with Rip if he had open choice. He thought rather bitterly afterward that maybe it was because of that strong desire that he was served just the opposite. For, when he drew his slip, he discovered that his running mates were Kamil and Tang.

A rearrangement by the Captain left him in the end with the Medic Tau in place of the com-tech who—for some purpose of his own—Jellico decreed must remain with the *Queen*.

More than a little disgusted at such luck he moved back into his old cabin. Curiosity led him to a minute search of the limited storage space, in a faint hope that perhaps he could find some forgotten possession of the enigmatic doctor. Now if this were a Tel-Video melodrama he, as the intrepid young hero, would discover the secret plans of— But that thought led him to remember Kamil's common sense appraisal of their position with regard to unsubstantial suspicions.

And then he was thinking of Kamil, trying to analyze why he so much disliked the engineer-apprentice. Ali's spectacular good looks and poise were part of it. Dane was not yet past the time when he felt awkward and ill at ease on social occasions—he still bumped into objects—just as on the parade ground at the Pool the instructors had used him as an example of how not to execute any maneuver. And when he looked in the small mirror above him on the cabin wall, his eyes did not observe any outward charm. No, physically Kamil was all Dane was not.

In addition the Cargo-apprentice suspected that the other had a quickness of wit which also left him at the post. He, himself, was more of the bulldog type, slow and sure, while Kamil leaped ahead with grasshopper bounds. The right sort of bounds, too. That was the worst of it, Dane had argued himself into a rueful amusement. You wouldn't dislike the engineer so much if he were wrong just once in a while. But so far Ali Kamil had proved to be disgustingly right.

Well, even though the Psycho fitted you to a ship and its crew—you couldn't be expected to like everyone on board. Machines had their limitations. He could rub along with most people, that was one good and useful thing he had learned at the Pool.

Deciding there was no profit in seeking trouble before it sneaked up to use a blaster on one, Dane went to sleep. And in the early dawn of the next day he was eager for the adventure of a scout.

Captain Jellico respected the wishes of Dr. Rich to the extent of not setting any course toward the ruins. But on the other hand he made his instructions plain to the crews of both small ships. Any signs of new Forerunner finds were to be reported directly to him—and not on the broadcast beam of the flitters—a broadcast which could be picked up by those in Rich's camp.

Dane strapped on his helmet with its short wave installation, fastened about his waist an explorer's belt with its coil of tough, though slender rope, its beam light, and compact envelope of tools. Though they did not expect to be long from the *Queen,* into the underseat storage place on the flitter went concentrated supplies, a small medical kit, and their full canteens, as well as a packet of trade "contact" goods. Not that they would have any use for that in Dane's estimation.

Ali took the controls of the tiny ship while Dane and Tau shared a cramped seat behind him. The engineer-apprentice pushed a button on the board and the curved windbreak slid up and over, enclosing them. They lifted smoothly from the side of the *Queen,* to level off at the height of her nose, swinging north for the route Jellico and Van Rycke had charted them.

The sun was up now, striking fire from the slag rivers on the burnt land, bringing to life the sickly green of the distant vegetation which formed tattered edging on the foothill valleys. Dane triggered the recording camera as they winged straight for the northern range of mountains.

As they crossed into the sparse clusters of brush, Ali automatically lost altitude and slowed pace, giving them a chance for a searching examination of what lay below. But Dane could see no signs of life, insect or animal, and no winged things shared the morning air with them.

They followed the first narrow valley to its end, combing it for anything of interest. Then Ali turned to the right, zooming up over a saw-edged ridge of naked black rock, to seek the next cut of fertile soil. Again only scant brush and scattered clumps of grass were to be seen.

But the third valley they explored was more promising. Down its center coursed a small stream and the vegetation was not only thicker but a darker, more normal shade of green. Dane and Tau sighted the first find almost together and their voices formed a duet:

"Down!"

"There!"

Ali had swept over the spot, but now he cut speed and circled back while the other two plastered themselves against the transparent windbreak, trying to sight that strange break in the natural spread below.

There it was! And Dane's excitement grew as he knew that he had been right at his first guess. That pocket-sized, regularly fenced space was a field under cultivation. But what a field! The enclosure, with its wall of pebbles and brush, couldn't have been more than four feet square.

Growing in straight rows was a small plant with yellow, fern-like leaves, a plant which trembled and shook as if beaten by a breeze—when none of the neighboring bushes moved at all.

Ali circled the spot twice and then coasted down the valley toward the devastated plain. They passed three more separate fields and then a larger space where the valley widened out and accommodated three or four together. All of them were fenced and bore evidence of careful tending. But there were no pathways, no buildings, no traces of who or what had planted and would harvest those crops.

"Of course," Tau broke the perplexed silence first, "we may have here a flora civilization instead of a fauna—"

"If you mean those carrot-topped things down there built the walls and then planted themselves in rows—" began Ali, but Dane could think of an answer for that. As a cargo man he had been too firmly indoctrinated with the need for keeping an open mind when dealing with X-Tee races to refuse any suggestion without investigation.

"This could be the nursery—the adults could have planted seeds—"

Ali's answer to that was a snort of derision. But Dane did not allow himself to show irritation. "Can we set down? We ought to have a closer look at this—

"Well away from the fields," he added that caution a moment later.

"Listen, you bead merchant," Ali snapped, "I'm not green and rocket shaken—"

He'd deserved that, Dane decided honestly. This was *his* first field trip—Ali was his superior in experience. No more backseat flitter control from now on. He shut his mouth tight as Ali spiraled them down toward a space of bare rock well away from both the stream and the fields it watered.

Tau made contact with the *Queen,* reporting their discovery, and orders came that they were to explore the valley discreetly, seeking any other signs of intelligent life.

The medic studied the cliffs near which they had landed. "Caves—" he suggested.

But, though they walked for some distance beside those towering reaches of bare black rock, there were no hollows nor crevices deep enough to shelter a creature even the size of Sinbad.

"They may have hidden from the flitter," remarked Ali. "And they could be watching us from cover right now."

Dane turned in a full circle, scanning with wary eyes not only the cliff walls, but the clumps of brush and the taller stands of coarse grass.

"They must be small," he muttered half to himself. "Those fields are so limited in area."

"Plants," Tau returned to his own pet theory. But Dane was not yet ready to agree.

"Traders have contacted eight X-Tee races so far," he said slowly. "The Sliths are reptilian, the Arvas remotely feline, the Fifftocs brachiopod. Of the rest, three are chemically different from us, and two—the Kanddoyds and the Mimsis—are insects. But a vegetable intelligence—"

"Is perfectly possible," Tau finished for him.

They made a careful inspection of the nearest field. The quivering plants stood about two feet high, their lacy foliage in constant flickering motion. They had been carefully spaced apart by the planters and between them the ground was bare of any weed or encroaching spear of grass. The Terrans could see no fruit or seeds on the slender stems, though, as they stooped for a closer look they became aware of a strong spicy scent.

Ali sniffed: "Clove—cinnamon? Somebody's herb garden?"

"Why herbs and nothing else?" Dane squatted on his heels. What was the most puzzling to him was the absence of paths. These miniature gardens were carefully tended, yet there were no roads connecting them, no indication that the invisible farmers approached them on foot. On foot—! Was that a clue, a winged race? He mentioned that.

"Sure," Ali used his usual deflating tactics, "a bunch of bats and they only come out at night. That's why there's no greeting committee on hand—"

Nocturnal? It was entirely possible, Dane thought. That meant that the Terrans must establish a contact station and man it through the dark hours. But if the farmers went about their work in utter darkness they were going to be difficult to watch. All the men from the *Queen* could do was to set up the station and look after it for the rest of the day, hoping it was only that their strange presence was what had terrified the inhabitants of the valley into hiding.

But, though Tau and Dane concealed themselves thoroughly in the shadow of tall rocks while Ali lifted the flitter to the top of the cliff well out of sight, the hours crawled on and there was nothing to be seen but the shivering spicy plants and their wild cousins along the stream.

Whatever life did exist on Limbo must be limited both in numbers and varieties. Along with samples of water and vegetation, Tau captured an earth-colored insect bearing a close resemblance to a Terran beetle, imprisoning it in a small tube for transportation to the *Queen,* and future study. And another insect with pale, wide wings dipped toward the water an hour later. But animals, birds, reptiles, all were missing.

"Anything which survived the burn-off," Tau half whispered, "must have been far down the scale—"

"But the fields," protested Dane. He had been trying to figure out a possible lure for the mysterious Limbians, if and when they appeared. Having no idea as to their nature, he was faced with a real problem in contact. What if their eyesight differed—the brightly colored trifles designed to attract the usual primitive races would then be worthless. And if their auditory sense was not within human range the music boxes which had been used to such excellent advantage in establishing friendly relations with the Kanddoyds could not be brought out. He was inclined to dwell on the scent of the field plants. Their spiciness, which was so strong that it was thick to notoriously dull human nostrils, was the only distinctive attribute he had to follow. A contact baited with scent—spicy scent—might just work. He asked Tau a question:

"Those plants are aromatic. Do you have anything like that scent in your medical stores? I've some perfumed soap from Garatole in my trade kit, but that's pretty strong—"

Tau smiled. "The problem of bait, eh? Yes, scent might just bring them in. But, look here, I'd try Mura's stores instead of the medical ones. Get some pinches of his spices—"

Dane leaned back against the rock. Now why hadn't he thought of that! Flavors used in cooking—sure, Mura might have some substance in the galley which would attract a people who raised the lacy leaved herbs. But he'd have to go back to the *Queen* to see—

"I'd say," the medic continued, "that we're not going to make contact today. It's my guess they're nocturnal and we should rig a contact point on that theory. Let's go—"

As the senior officer of the scouting party, Tau had the right to make such a decision. And Dane, eager to start his own preparations for contact, was ready to agree. They waved the flitter down and reported back to the *Queen,* getting orders to return.

They were received in the Captain's office and the cargo-master and Jellico heard them out, allowing Dane to state his suggestion concerning the use of spice to draw the Limbians from hiding. When he had spilled it out in eager enthusiasm, the Captain turned to Van Rycke.

"What about it, Van? Ever use spices in a contact?"

The cargo-master shrugged. "You can make contact with anything which will attract an X-Tee, Captain. I'd say this is worth a try—along with the rest of the usual stuff."

Jellico picked up his com-mike. "Frank," he said into the phone, "come up here and bring samples of all your spices—anything with a strong, pleasant odor."

Two hours later Dane studied his handiwork with what he hoped was the necessary critical appraisal. He had selected a broad rock mid-way between two of the small fields. On the stone he had arranged materials from a basic trade kit. There was a selection of jewelry, small toys, metallic objects, which would easily catch the eye, then a music box arranged to be triggered into tune if handled. And last of all three plastic bowls, each covered with a fine gauze through which came the aroma of mixed spices.

Behind a bush was concealed the contact visa-view which would record any approach to that rock for the benefit of those in the flitter on the cliffs above—where he, Tau, and Kamil would spend the night on watch.

He was still a trifle amazed that he had been allowed to take over this presentation—but he had discovered that the creed of the *Queen* was just—the idea was his, he was to carry it out—the success or failure would depend on him. And he was uncertain within as he climbed into the flitter for the rise to the cliff tops.

SINISTER VALLEY

6 Again Dane was conscious of the thick quality of the Limbian night. Since the planet possessed no satellite, there was nothing to break the dark but those cold pin points which marked the stars. Even the visa-screen they had set up below could hardly pierce the gloom, though it was equipped with a tri-strength delve-ray.

Tau stretched and shifted in his seat, inadvertently nudging Dane. Although they were wearing double-lined winter outer tunics and the temperature of the closed flitter was supposedly akin to the interior of the *Queen,* an insidious chill caught at them. They had divided the night into watches, the two off duty at the tiny receiving screen trying to nap. But Dane found rest beyond him. He stared out at the dark which folded about them like a smothering curtain.

He did not know what time it was that he saw the first flash—a red sword of light striking up into the sky in the west. At his exclamation Ali on duty at the screen glanced up and Tau stirred into wakefulness.

"Over there!" They might not be able to follow his pointing finger but by now they needed no such guide. The flashes of light were multiplied—then they were gone—leaving the night darker than ever.

It was Ali who spoke first: "Blaster fire!" His fingers were already busy on the keys, flashing a message to the *Queen*.

For an instant Dane felt a prick of panic and then he realized that the disturbance was far westward of the *Queen*. The ship had *not* been attacked in their absence.

Ali reported the evidences of distant battle. From the ship the flares had not been sighted and the men there knew nothing of any trouble. Nor had they seen, across the barrens, any disturbance at the ruins where Rich was encamped.

"Do we stick here?" Ali asked a last question. And the reply came promptly that they should—unless forced to withdraw. It was more than ever necessary to discover the nature of any native Limbian life.

But the screen which connected them with the valley below remained obstinately dark. There was the rock, the trade goods, and nothing else.

They kept two watches now, one for the screen and the other westward. But no more flares split the night. If a battle had been in progress it was now over.

By Dane's reckoning it was close to dawn and it was his trick at the screen when the first hint of change came. The movement on the plate before him was so slight that at first he thought he had been mistaken. But a bush to the right of the rock below provided a dark background for something so weird he could not believe he was seeing aright. Luck alone, and reflex action, pressed his finger down on the button of the recorder at the right moment.

For the thing was not only insubstantial, it was also fast, moving at a speed which blurred its already wispy outline. Dane had seen something, he was sure of that. But what it had been, even its general form, he could not have sworn to.

With both Ali and Tau breathing down the back of his neck, Dane hung over the screen, alert to the slightest movement on its surface.

But, though dawn was upon them, and the light was growing better all the time, they could see nothing now but leaves fluttered by the wind. Whatever had passed that way had had no interest in the trade display. They would have to depend upon the film from the recorder to discover what it was.

Limbo's sun began the upward climb. The rime of nightborn frost which had gathered on the stones of the heights was lapped away. But the valley remained deserted, Dane's visitor did not return.

The other flitter arrived with a fresh crew to take over the post. Rip walked over to speak to the yawning crew of the first.

"Any luck?" he wanted to know.

"Got something with the recorder—I hope," Dane replied, but he was feeling more apologetic than triumphant. That faint shadowy thing might not be the owner of the fields—just some passing animal.

"Captain says for you to take a look-see down west before you check in," Rip added to Tau. "Use your own judgment, but don't run into anything serious if you can help it."

The medic nodded. Ali was at the controls and they took to the air, leaving the relieving crew of the other flitter to take over their watch. Below them spread the now familiar pattern of small, narrow valleys, two or three showing squares of fields. But though Ali buzzed at a low altitude over these, there was no life but vegetation below. The Terran flitter was perhaps five miles on to the west before it came down over a scene of horror.

Smoke still curled sluggishly from smoldering brush and the black burns of high voltage blaster fire crossed and re-crossed the ground, cutting noisome paths through greenery and searing soil and rock.

But it was not that which attracted their attention. It was the *things,* three of them, huddled together in a rock pocket as if they had tried to make a last stand there against a weapon they did not understand. The contorted, badly burned bodies had been little recognizable form now, but the three in the flitter knew that they had once been living creatures.

Ali went for a short run above the valley floor. There was no sign of any life. He maneuvered for a landing close to that pocket. But it wasn't until they had left the flitter and started to cross a rocky out-crop that they came upon the fourth victim.

He—or it—had been singed by the flame, but not killed at once. Enough will to live had remained to send the pitiful wreckage crawl-ing into a narrow crevice where it must have clung until death loos-ened its hold and allowed it to tumble slackly into sight again.

Tau went down on one knee beside the twisted body. But Dane, his nostrils filled with a sickening stench which was not all born of the smoldering green stuff, took only one quick look before he closed his eyes and fought a masterly engagement with his churning stomach.

That hadn't been a man! It resembled nothing he had ever seen or heard described. It—it wasn't real—it couldn't be! He gained a minor victory, opened his eyes, and forced himself to look again.

Even allowing for the injuries which had killed it, the creature was bizarre to the point of nightmare. Its body consisted of two globes, one half as large as the other. There was no discernible head at all. From the larger globe protruded two pair of very thin, four-jointed limbs which must have been highly flexible. From the small globe, another pair which separated at the second joint into limber tentacles, each of which ended in a cluster of hair-fine appendages. The globes were joined by a wasp's slenderness of waist. As far as Dane could see, and he couldn't bring himself to the close examina-tion which absorbed Tau, there were no features at all—no eyes, ears, or mouth.

But the oddest sight of all were the globes which formed the body. They were a grayish-white, but semi-transparent. And through the surface one could sight reddish structural supports which must have served the creature as bones, as well as organs Dane had no wish to explore.

"Great space!" Ali exploded. "You can look right through them!"

He was exaggerating—but not so much. The Limbians—if this was a Limbian—were far more tenuous than any creature the Ter-rans had found before. And Dane was sure that the record film would show that it was a thing such as this which had passed the contact point in the other valley.

Ali stepped around the body to examine the scars left by the blast which had driven the creature into the crevice. He touched a finger gingerly to a blackened smear on the rock and then held it close to his nose.

"Blaster right enough."

"Do you think Rich—?"

Ali gazed down the valley. Like all the others they had yet sighted it ran from the towering mountains to the blasted plain, and they could not be too far from the ruins where the archaeologists had gone to earth.

"But—why?" Dane asked a second question before his first had been answered.

Had the globe things attacked Rich and his men? Somehow Dane could not accept that. To his mind the limp body Tau was working over was pitifully defenseless. It held not the slightest hint of menace.

"That's the big question." Ali tramped on, past the hollow where lay those other dreadfully contorted bodies, down to the edge of the stream, which this valley, as did all the cultivated ones, cradled in its center, the fields strung out along it.

Plain to read here was the mark of the invader. No feet had left that pair of wide ruts crushed deep into the soft ground of the fields. Dane stopped short.

"Crawler! But our crawlers—"

"Are just where they should be, parked under the *Queen* or in their storage compartments," Ali finished for him. "And since Rich couldn't have brought one here in a kit bag, we must believe that Limbo is not as barren of life as Survey certified it to be." He stood at the edge of the stream and then squatted to study a patch of drying mud. "Track's odd though—"

Although his opinion had not been asked, Dane joined the engineer-apprentice. The tread marks had left a pattern, clear as print, for about four inches. He was familiar with the operation of crawlers as they pertained to his own duties. He could even, if the need arose, make minor repairs on one. But he couldn't have identified any difference in vehicles from their tread patterns. There he was willing to accept Ali's superior learning.

Kamil's next move was a complete mystery to Dane. Still on his knees he began measuring the distance between the two furrows, using a small rule from his belt tool kit for a gauge. At last Dane dared to ask a question:

"What's wrong?"

For a moment he thought that Ali wasn't going to answer. Then the other sat back on his heels, wiped dust from the rule, and looked up.

"A standard crawler's a four-two-eight," he stated didactically. "A scooter is a three-seven-eight. A flamer's carriage runs five-seven-twelve."

The actual figures meant very little to Dane, but he knew their significance. Within the Federation machinery was now completely standardized. It had to be so that repairs from one world to the next would be simplified. Ali had recited the measurements of the three types of ground vehicles in common use on the majority of Federation planets. Though, by rights, a flamer was a war machine, used only by the military or Patrol forces, except on pioneer worlds where its wide heat beam could be turned against rank forest or jungle growth.

"And this isn't any of those," Dane guessed.

"Right. It's three-two-four—but it's heavy, too. Or else it was transporting close to an overload. You don't get ruts like these from a scooter or crawler traveling light." He was an engineer, he should know, Dane conceded.

"Then what was it?"

Ali shrugged. "Something not standard—low, narrow, or it couldn't snake through here, and able to carry a good load. But nothing on our books is like it."

It was Dane's turn to study the cliffs about them. "Only one way it could go—up—or down—"

Ali got to his feet. "I'll go down," he glanced over at the busy Tau engrossed in his grisly task, "nobody's going to drag him away from there until he learns all he can." He shuddered, perhaps in exaggeration, perhaps in earnest. "I have a feeling that it isn't wise to stay here too long. Any scout will have to be a quick one—"

Dane turned upstream. "I'll go up," he said firmly, it was not Ali's place to give orders, they were equal in rank. He started off, walking between the tracks without looking back.

He was concentrating so on his determination to prove that he could think properly for himself that he made a fatal slip, inexcusable in any Trade-explorer. Though he continued to wear his helmet, along with all the other field equipment, he totally forgot to set his personal com-unit on alert, and so went blindly off into the unknown with no contact with either of the others.

But at the moment he was far more intent on those tracks which lured him on, up a gradually narrowing valley toward the mountain walls. The climbing sun struck across his path, out there were pools of purple shadow where the cliffs walled off its rays.

The trail left by the crawler ran as straight as the general contour of the ground allowed. Two of the lacy winged flying things they had glimpsed in the other valley skimmed close to the surface of the stream and then took off high into the chill air.

Now the greenery was sparser. He had not passed a field for some time. And underfoot the surface of the valley was inclining up in a gentle slope. The walls curved, so that Dane walked more warily, having no desire to round a projection and meet a blaster user face-to-face.

He was certain in his own mind that Dr. Rich had something to do with this. But where did this crawler come from? Had the Doctor been on Limbo before? Or had he broken into some cache of Survey supplies? But there was Ali's certainty that the vehicle was not orthodox.

The trail ended abruptly and in such a manner as to stop Dane short, staring in unbelief. For those ruts led straight to a solid, blank wall of rock, vanishing beneath it as if the machine which had made them had been driven straight through!

There is always, Dane hastily reminded himself, some logical explanation for the impossible. And not Video ones about "force walls" and such either. If those tracks went into the rock, it was an illusion—or an opening—and it was up to him to discover which.

His boots crunched on sand and gravel until he was in touching distance of the barrier. It was then that he became aware of something else, a vibration. It was very silent there in the cramped pocket which was the end of the valley, no wind blew, no leaves rustled. And yet there was something unquiet in the air, a stirring just at the far edge of his sensitiveness to sound and movement.

On impulse he set the palms of his hands against the stone of the cliff. And he felt it instantly, running up his arms into his body until his flesh and bones were only a recorder for that monstrous beat-beat-beat—relayed to him through the stuff of Limbo itself. Yet, when he passed his fingers searchingly over the rough stone, studied each inch of it intently, he could see no break in its surface, no sign of a door, no reason for that heavy thump, thump which shook his nerves. The vibration was unpleasant, almost menacing. He snatched his hands away, suddenly afraid of being trapped in that dull rhythm. But now he was sure that Limbo was not what it seemed—a lifeless, dead world.

For the first time he remembered that he should have maintained contact with the others, and hurriedly turned the key on his com-unit. Instantly Tau's voice rang thinly in his ears.

"Calling Ali—Calling Thorson—come in—come in!" There was an urgency in the medic's voice which brought Dane away from the wall, set him on the back trail even as he replied:

"Thorson here. Am at end of valley. Wish to report—"

But the other cut into that impatiently. "Return to flitter! Ali, Thorson, return to flitter!"

"Thorson returning." Dane started at the best pace he could

muster down the valley. But as he trotted, slipping and sliding on the loose stones and gravel, Tau's voice continued to call Ali. And from the engineer-apprentice there came no answer at all.

Breathing hard, Dane reached the place where they had left the medic. As he came into sight Tau waved him to the side of the flitter.

"Where's Ali?" "Where's Kamil?" Their demands came together and they stared at each other.

Dane answered first. "He said he was going downstream—to follow the crawler tracks we found. I went upstream—"

"Then it must have been he who—" Tau was frowning. He turned on his heel and studied the valley leading to the plains. The presence of water had encouraged a thicker growth of brush there and it presented a wall except for where the stream cut a passage.

"But what happened?" Dane wanted to know.

"I got a call on com—it was cut off almost immediately—"

"Not mine, I was off circuit," returned Dane before he thought. It was only then that he realized what he had done. No one on field duty goes off circuit out on scout, that was a rule even a First Circler in the Pool had by heart. And he had done it the first time he was on duty! He could feel the heat spreading up into his cheeks. But he offered no explanations nor excuses. The fault was his and he would have to stand up to the consequences.

"Ali must be in trouble." Tau made no other comment as he climbed in behind the controls of the flitter, a very quiet Dane followed him.

They arose jerkily, with none of the smooth perfection Ali's piloting had supplied. But once in the air Tau pointed the nose of the flitter down valley, cutting speed to just enough to keep them airborne. They watched the ground below. But there was nothing to see but the marks of blaster fire and beyond undisturbed green broken by bare patches of gravel and jutting rock.

They could also sight the crawler tracks and Dane related the information he had. Tau's countenance was sober.

"If we don't find Ali, we must report to the *Queen*—"

That was only common sense, Dane knew, but he dreaded having to admit his own negligence. And perhaps his act was worse than just carelessness in not using the com-unit, perhaps he should have insisted on their sticking together, deserted though the valley appeared to be.

"We're up against something nasty here," Tau continued. "Whoever used those blasters was outside the law—"

The Federation law dealing with X-Tees was severe, as Dane well knew. Parts of the code, stripped of the legal verbiage, had to be memorized at the Pool. You could defend yourself against the attack of aliens, but on no provocation, except in defense of his life, could a Trader use a blaster or other weapon against an X-Tee. Even sleep rays were frowned upon, though most Traders packed them when going into unknown territory among primitive tribes.

The men of the *Queen* had landed unarmed on Limbo, and they would continue unarmed until such a time as the situation was so grave that either their lives or the ship was in danger. But in this valley a blaster had been used in the wanton indulgence of someone's sadistic hatred for the globe creatures.

"They weren't attacking—those globe things, I mean?"

Tau's brown face was grim as he shook his head. "They had no weapons at all. I'd say from the evidence that they were attacked without warning, just mown down. Maybe for the fun of it!"

And that projected such a picture of horror that Tau, conditioned by life under the Trade Creed, stopped short.

Below them the valley began to widen out, cutting in a fan shape into the plain. There was no sign of Ali anywhere on that fan. He had vanished as if he had stepped through the cliff wall. The cliff! Dane remembering the end of the crawler trail, pressed against the windshield to inspect those walls. But there were no tracks ending before them.

The flitter lost altitude as Tau concentrated on landing. "We must report to the *Queen*," he said as he set them down. Not leaving his seat he reached for the long-range beam mike.

SHIP OUT OF SPACE

7 Tau's fingers clicked the call key of the far-range caster when that sound was drowned out by a wail, both weirdly familiar and strangely menacing. Here on the edge of the burnt-off land there was no soughing of the wind, nothing to break the eternal silence of the blasted country. But this tearing overhead brought both of the Terrans to their feet. Tau, out of his greater experience, identified it first.

"A ship!"

Dane was no hundred-flight man, but something in that shrieking crescendo splitting the sky above them argued that if a ship were coming in, all was not well with it. He caught at Tau's arm.

"What's the matter?"

The medic's face paled beneath the dark space tan. He bit hard on his lower lip. And the eyes still fastened on the arch of sky were haunted. When he answered he had to scream to be heard over the rumble.

"She's coming in too fast—not on a braking orbit!"

And now they could see as well as hear—a dark shape in the morning sky, a shape which tore across that same sky to be gone in an instant to a landing somewhere among those jagged peaks which were the mountains of Limbo's northern continent.

The sound was gone. It was broodingly quiet. Tau shook his head slowly.

"She must have crashed. She couldn't have come out of that one in time."

"What was she?" puzzled Dane. The passage of that shadow had been so quick that he had not been conscious of any identifying outline.

"Too small for a liner, thank the Lord of Far Space. Or at least—I hope it was no liner—"

For a passenger ship to crash would be utter horror. Dane could understand that.

"A freighter maybe," Tau sat down and his hand went out to the click keys. "She must have been out of control when she entered atmosphere." He began to relay this last information on to the *Queen*.

They did not have to wait long for an answer. They were to remain where they were until the second flitter joined them carrying Tau's full medical kit. This flyer would then head out into the mountains in an attempt to locate the scene of the crash, so if there were any survivors the men from the *Queen* could render aid. While a smaller party would stay and try to trace Kamil.

It was only a matter of minutes before the other flitter did appear. Kosti and Mura dropped from it almost before it hit dirt and Tau hurried across to change places. The flyer whirled up into the sun of mid-morning and cut a straight course toward the rock teeth of the range, following the line of flight Dane and Tau had seen that shadow travel.

"Did you see her from the *Queen*?" Dane demanded of the other two.

Mura shook his head. "See her, no, hear her, yes. She was out of control!"

Kosti's broad face wrinkled in concern. "She must have hit hard. A bad smash—no one living, perhaps. I once saw a smack landing like that on Juno—very bad—all dead. That ship—she must have been out of control before they started down. She was not even fighting the fall—she came in like a thing already dead."

Mura whistled softly. "Plague ship, maybe—"

Dane shivered. Plague ships were the terrifying ghosts of the space lanes. Wandering derelicts, free roving tombs holding the bodies of the crews who on some uncharted world had contracted some new and virulent disease, dying alone in the reaches of the heavens—perhaps by stern choice—before they could bring their infection to inhabited worlds. The solar system guards had the unenviable task of rounding up such drifting threats of death and sending them into cleansing suns or giving them some other final end. But here, beyond the frontiers of civilization, a derelict could drift for years, even centuries, before some freak of chance brought it into the gravitational pull of a planet and so crash it on an unwary world.

But the men of the *Queen* knew the score, there would be no rash exploration of the ship if they did locate it. And its smash-up might have been a thousand miles away, well out of the range of the flitter. Tau was there—and of all men a medic was the last to take any chances with a plague.

"Ali—he has disappeared?" Kosti brought them back to the business at hand.

Dane, not overlooking his own carelessness, reported in detail what had happened in the valley. To his relief neither of the newcomers made any comment on his part in the affair, but centered their attention on the task at hand. Mura was the first to suggest a plan of action.

"Let Kosti take up the flitter and cruise above us. Then you and I shall search the ground. There may be some trace left which you could not easily sight from the air."

So it was arranged. The flitter, cut to its lowest cruising speed, circled slowly around, never venturing too far ahead. While Dane and Mura on foot, having to swing bush knives in places against the thick mat of vegetation, made their way into the sinister valley. They found the place where the track of the crawler came from the rock of the burnt-off land to bite into the soft soil of the healthy area.

Mura turned there and stared back, over the plain. They could not sight from this point the blotch of brightly colored ruins. But they were certain that the crawler had come out of the blasted area, to be driven with intelligent purpose toward the mountains—until it vanished into the solid rock of a cliff wall!

"Dr. Rich's party—?" Dane aired his suspicions.

"Perhaps—perhaps not," was Mura's ambiguous reply. "Did you not say that Ali thought this machine was not of the usual type?"

"But—" Dane gaped, "you can't mean that the Forerunners survived—here!"

Mura laughed. "They say that all things are possible in space, do they not? But no, I do not think that those ancient rulers of the lanes have here left their sons to greet us. Only they may have left other things—which are now being put to use. I would like to know more about those ruins—a great deal more."

Perhaps the guess Rip had made days earlier—that on some planet might lie, waiting to be discovered, possessions of the legendary Forerunners—was close to the truth. Had such a cache been discovered by parties unknown here on Limbo? But with that marched the grim warning voiced by Ali that Forerunner material in Terran hands might be a threat to all of them.

Slowly they combed the mouth of the valley, reassured by the flitter cruising above. Dane broke open his field rations, chewing as he went, on a cube of rubbery, tasteless stuff which was supposed to provide his lank young body with all it needed in the way of balanced nourishment—and yet which was so savorless and far removed from real food.

He hacked at a mass of prickly shrubs and stumbled through the clutch of longer branches to come into a pocket-sized clearing entirely ringed with thorn-studded greenery. Under foot was a thick mat of decaying leaves through which not even the spears of grass could grow.

Dane stopped short. The brown muck of the mat had been disturbed. He was conscious of an unwholesome reek of decay which came from scuffed patches where a green slime had been recently uncovered.

He went down on his hands and knees, circling that plowed up patch. He was no tracker, but even to his inexperienced eyes this had been the site of a scuffle. And since the slime was still uncrusted, that event had taken place not too long ago. Dane surveyed the brush which walled in the tiny area. It was just the place for an ambush. If Kamil had come through—over there—

Taking care not to disturb the churned muck, Dane made his way to the opposite side of the clearing. He was right! The cut of a bush knife showed where a branch had been lopped away. Someone, armed with regulation Terran field equipment, had come through here.

Come through here—to find someone, or something, waiting for him!

The globe creatures? Or those who had used the strange crawler and burnt the globes in the valley?

But Dane was certain that he had discovered where Ali had been surprised—not only surprised but overpowered by a superior force. Overpowered—to be taken where? He subjected the walling shrubs to a careful scrutiny. But in no other place did he see any suggestion of disturbance or break. It was almost as if the hunter, having made certain of his prey, had vanished into thin air, transporting the prisoner with him.

Dane was startled by a crashing in the brush. His sleep ray-rod was out as he spun around. But it was Mura's pleasant brown face which was framed in a circle of torn leaves. At Dane's wave he came into the clearing. It was not necessary to point out the signs of battle—he had already noted them.

"They jumped him here," Dane was convinced.

"But who or what are 'they'?" was Mura's counter. And seconds later he added the unanswerable question, "And how did they leave?"

"The tracks of the crawler went right through the wall of the cliff—"

Mura edged out on the carpet of muck. "No indications of any trap door here," he observed, gravely as if he *had* expected to find something of the sort. "There remains—" He jerked a thumb into the air where the purr of the flitter grew louder as Kosti circled back toward them.

"But we would have heard—have seen—" protested Dane, all the time wondering if they would have. He had been at the other end of the valley when Tau had caught that interrupted cry for help. And from this point the place where the Medic had been at that moment was hidden by at least two miles of broken ground.

"Something smaller than one of our flitters." Mura was thinking aloud. "It could be done. One thing we may be sure of—they have collected Kamil and we must find out who they are and where they are before we can get him back!"

He plowed away through the brush and Dane followed him out on a bare strip of ground from which they could signal to the flitter.

"Found him?" Kosti called as he brought the machine down.

"Found where someone scooped him up." Mura went to the keyboard of the caster.

Dane turned for a last look up that sinister valley. But all at once his attention was drawn from the valley and its cliffs to a new phenomenon in evidence on a higher level. He had not noticed that the sun had disappeared while they had been making their search of the brush. But now clouds were gathering—and not only clouds.

The naked, snow-touched peaks of the range, which had been so sharp set against the pallid sky of Limbo when the ship out of space had swept over them, were gone! It was as if that milky, faded sky had fallen as a curtain to blot them out. Where the peaks had been swirled fog—fog so thick that it erased half the horizon as a painter might draw a blotting brush across an unsuccessful landscape. Dane had never seen anything like it. And it was moving so fast, visibly cutting off miles of territory in the few moments he had watched it. To be lost in that—!

"Look!" he ran to the flitter and jogged Mura's arm pointing to the fast disappearing mountains. "Look at that!"

Kosti spit out an oath in the slurred speech of Venus. Mura simply obeyed orders and looked. Another huge section to the north was swallowed up as he did so. And now they noted another thing. From the tops of the valley cliffs curls of grayish, yellow vapor were rising, to cling and render misty the outlines of the rocks. Whether this was all part of the same they did not know, but the three Terrans insensibly drew closer together, chilled as much by what they saw, as the cold apparent with the going of the sun.

They were shaken out of their absorption by the click of the caster summoning them back to the ship. The change on the mountains had been noted on the *Queen* and both the flitter searching for the wreck and their own were ordered to report in at once.

There was further change in the atmosphere, a speeding up of the mists— The swirls above the valley walls combined, formed banks and began to drop, cutting visibility.

Kosti watched them anxiously. "We'll have to swing out—away from the valleys. That stuff is moving too fast. We *can* ride the beam in, but I'd rather not unless I have to—"

But, by the time they were airborne, the mist was down to the level of the valley floor and was puffing out in threatening tendrils onto the rough terrain of the burnt-off land. The mountains had vanished and the foothills were being fast swallowed up. It was uncanny, terrifying in a way, this wiping away of solid earth, the substitution of a dirty, rolling mist which swirled and spun within its mass until one suspicioned movement there, alien, menacing movement.

Kosti set the controls to full speed, but they had covered little more than a mile of the return journey before he was forced to throttle down. For the mist was not only spilling out of the valleys, it was also curling up from the land under them, each thread of haze spinning to join and thicken with others.

It was true that they were in no danger of being lost. The thin reed of sound humming in their ears provided a guide to bring the flitter back to the parent ship. But they were none the easier knowing that as they coasted above a curdling sea of mist.

The stuff rose about them forming viscid bubbles on the wind-break. Only the constant hum of the radar beam linked them with reality.

"Hope our boys made it down from the mountains before the worst of this hit," Kosti broke the strained silence.

"If they didn't," Mura replied, "they will have to land until it clears."

Kosti throttled down once more as the radar hum sharpened. "No use crashing into the old lady—"

Within the blanket of mist all sense of direction, of distance was lost. They might have been up ten thousand feet, or skimming but one above the broken surface of the rock plain. Kosti hunched over the controls, his usually good-humored face pinched, his eyes moving from the mist to the dials before him and back again.

They sighted the ship—a dark shadow looming through the veil. With masterly precision Kosti brought the flitter down until it jarred against the ground. But he was in no hurry to climb out. Instead he wiped his face with the back of his hand. Mura leaned forward and patted the big man's shoulder.

"That was a good job!"

Kosti grinned. "It had to be!"

They crawled out of the flitter and, on impulse, linked hands as they started for the dim pillar which was the *Queen*. The contact of palm against palm was not only insurance and reassurance, but it was also security of a type Dane felt he needed—and guessed that his companions wanted also. The menacing, alien mist pressed in upon them. Its damp congealed greasily on their helmets, dripped from them as they moved.

But ten paces took them to the welcome arch of the ramp and they went up, to stand a moment later in the pleasant light and warmth of the entrance hatch. Jasper Weeks teetered back and forth there, his pallid little face expressing worry.

"Oh—you—" was his unflattering greeting.

Kosti laughed. "Who did you expect, little man—a Sensor dragon breathing fire? Sure, it's us, and we're glad to be back—"

"Something wrong?" Mura interrupted.

Weeks stepped to the outer opening of the hatch once more. "The other flitter—we haven't heard from them for an hour. Captain ordered them back as soon as he saw the fog closing in. Survey tape says these fogs sometimes last a couple of days—but they aren't usual this time of the year."

Kosti whistled and Mura leaned back against the wall, unbuckling his helmet.

"Several days." Dane thought of that. To be lost out in that soup for days! You'd just have to stay grounded and hope for the best. But an emergency landing in the mountains under such conditions—! Now he could understand why Weeks fidgeted at the hatch. Their own journey over the unobstructed plain was, under the circumstances, a stroll in a Terran park, compared to the difficulties those on the other flitter might be forced to face.

They went up to make their report to the Captain. But all through it he sat with at least half of his attention given to the com where Tang Ya sat before the master visa-screen, his hand ready for the key of the caster or to tend the rider beam which might guide the missing flyer in. Somewhere out in the mystery which was now Limbo was not only Ali, but Rip, Tau and Steen Wilcox—a good section of their crew.

"There it is again!" Tang's forehead creased, his hands pulled the phones from close contact with his ears. As he did so the rest heard the clamor which had jolted him. Not unlike the drone of the rider beam—it scaled up to a screech which was real pain.

It continued steadily for a space and as Dane listened to it he became conscious of something else—a muffled rhythm deep within that drone—a rhythm he had known before—when he laid his hands upon the wall of the sinister valley. This disturbance was akin to the vibration in the distant rock!

Then, as suddenly as it had begun, the sound was gone. Tang put on his earphones once more and listened for a signal—either from the missing flitter or from Ali's personal com-unit.

"What is that?" Mura asked.

Captain Jellico shrugged. "Your guess is as good as ours. It may be a signal of some sort—been cutting in at regular intervals all day."

"So we must admit—" that was Van Rycke looming in the door of the control cabin, "that we are not alone on Limbo. In fact there is much more to Limbo than meets the casual eye."

Dane voiced his own suspicion. "Those archaeologists—" he began, but the Captain favored him with a sharp pointed stare that stopped him almost in mid-word.

"We have no idea what is at the root of this," Jellico said coldly. "You men get some food and rest—"

Dane, smarting from his abrupt dismissal, trailed Mura and Kosti down to the mess cabin. As they passed the Captain's private quarters they could hear the wild shrieks of the Hoobat. That thing sounded, Dane thought, just the way he felt. And even warm food, bearing no resemblance to the iron rations he had eaten earlier, did little to raise the general curtain of gloom.

But the meal had an excellent effect on Kosti's spirits. "That Rip," he announced to the table at large, "he's got a lot of sense. And Mr. Wilcox, he knows what he's doing. They're all snug somewhere and'll stay holed up until this stuff clears. Nobody'll come out in this—"

Was Kosti right there, Dane wondered. Suppose there were those on Limbo who knew the tricks of the climate, who were familiar enough with such fogs to be able to navigate through them—use them as a cover—? That signal they had heard blatting out of the com—could it be a beam to guide some expedition creeping through the mist? An expedition heading toward the unsuspecting *Queen*!

FOG BOUND

8 Those of the *Queen*'s men, who had no definite duties engaging them elsewhere, drifted to the hatch which gave upon the gray wool of the new Limbian landscape. They would have liked to hole up close to the control section and Tang's com, but the presence of the Captain there was a dampener. It was better to hunker down at the top of the ramp, look out into the mist, and strain one's ears for the motor purr of a flitter which did not arrive.

"They're smart," observed Kosti for the twentieth time. "They won't risk their necks plowing through this muck. But Ali—that's different. He was snatched before this started."

"You think it is poachers?" ventured Weeks.

His big partner considered the point. "Poachers? Yeah—but on this Limbo what have they got to poach—tell me that? We aren't pulling in a cargo of sveek furs, nor arlun crystals—leastways I haven't seen any of those lying around waiting to be picked up. What about those dead things back in the valley, Thorson," he turned to Dane, "did they look as if they had anything worth poaching?"

"They weren't armed—or even clothed—as far as we could tell,"

Dane replied a bit absently. "And their fields grew spicy stuff I never saw before—"

"Drugs—could it be drugs now?" inquired Weeks.

"A new kind then—Tau didn't recognize the leaves." Dane's head was up as he faced out into the mist. He was almost sure—there— there it was again! "Listen," he caught at Kosti, dragged the big man out on the ramp.

"Hear anything now?" he demanded a moment later.

There was sound in the fog, a fog which was now three parts night, through which the signal light on the nose of the *Queen* could not cut. The regular beat of a true running motor was magnified by some trick of the mist until it seemed that a whole fleet of small flyers was bearing down upon the space ship from all points of the compass.

Dane whirled and brought his hand down on the lever which controlled the lights along the ramp. Even swirled in the fog as they were, some faint gleam might break through to offer a landing mark for the flitter. Weeks had disappeared. Dane could hear the clatter of his space boots on the ladder within as he sped with the news. But before the wiper could have reached control a new marker blazed into view, the full powered searchlight from the nose, a beacon which could not be blanketed out, no matter how its rays were diffused.

And in that same instant a dark object swept by, so close that Dane leaped back, certain it was going to graze the ramp. The beat of the motor was loud, then it thinned, to grow into a roar once more as the shadow appeared for a second time, circling closer to the ground.

It landed with an audible smacking grind which suggested that the fog spoiled distance judgment. And to the foot of the ramp came three figures which continued to be muffled shapes until they were nearly at the hatch.

"Man—oh, man!" Rip's rich voice came to the ears of the watchers as he halted to pat the side of the ship. "It's good to see the old girl again—Lordy, it's good!"

"How did you make it back through this?" Dane asked.

"We had to," the astrogator-apprentice told him simply. "There was no place back in the ranges to set down. Those mountains are straight up and down—or they look that way. We got on the beam— except when— Say, what's the cause of the interference? We were thrown off twice by it. Couldn't cut it out—"

Steen Wilcox and Tau followed him at a slower pace. The medic moved wearily, his emergency kit in his hand. And Wilcox had only a grunt for the reception party, pushing past them to climb to control. But Rip ingered to ask another question.

"Ali—?"

Dane retold the story of what they had discovered in the valley clearing.

"But how—?" was Rip's second puzzled question.

"We don't know. Unless they went straight up. And it wasn't space enough to hold a flitter. But look how those crawler tracks ran straight into the cliff. Rip, there's something queer about Limbo—"

"How far was that valley from the ruins?" the astrogator-apprentice's voice lost much of its warmth, it was quieter, with a new crispness.

"We were nearer to those than to the *Queen*. But the fog hit us on the way back and we didn't see them—if we did pass over the location."

"And you couldn't raise Ali on the com-unit after that one interrupted signal?"

"Tang's been trying. And we kept open all the time we were out."

"They might have stripped that off him at once," Rip conceded. "It would be a wise move for them. He could give us a fix otherwise—"

"But could we get a fix on a com-unit? On one which no one was using—" Dane began to see a thin chance. "That is if its power was still working?"

"I don't know. But the range would be pretty limited. We could ask Tang—" Rip was already on his way up the ladder to where the com-tech was on duty.

Dane glanced at his watch, making a swift calculation squaring ship time with hours measured on Limbo. It was night. Suppose

Tang was able to pick up a call from Ali's com-unit—they could not trace it now.

They did not find the com-tech alone. All the officers of the *Queen* were there and again Tang was holding the earphones well away from his head so that they could hear the discordance which beat out from some hidden point in the fog-bound world.

Wilcox spoke as the two younger men came in. "That's it! Cut right across the rider beam. I got two fixes on it. But," he shrugged, "with the atmospherics what they are and this soup covering everything, how accurate those are is a big question. It comes from the mountains—"

"Not just some form of static?" Captain Jellico appealed to Tang.

"Decidedly not! I don't think it's a signal—though it may be a rider beam. More like a big installation—"

"What kind of installation would produce a broadcast such as that?" Van Rycke wanted to know.

Tang put the earphones down on the snap desk at his elbow. "A good sized one—about as big as the HG computer on Terra!"

There was a moment of startled silence. An installation with the same force as HG on this deserted world! They had to have time to assimilate that. But, Dane noted, not one of them questioned Tang's statement.

"What is it doing here?" Van Rycke's voice held a note of real wonder. "What *could* it be used for—?"

"It might be well," Tang warned, "to know who is running it. Remember, Kamil has been picked up. They probably know a lot about us while we're still in the dark—"

"Poachers—" That was Jellico but he advanced the suggestion as if he didn't really believe in it himself.

"With something as big as an HG com under their control? Maybe—" But Van Rycke was plainly dubious. "Anyway we can't get out and look around until the fog clears—"

The ramp was drawn in, the ship put under regular routine once more. But Dane wondered how many of the crew were able to sleep. He hadn't expected to, until the fatigue produced from the adventures of the past twenty-four hours of duty pushed him under and he spun from one dream to another, always pursuing Ali through crooked valleys and finally between the towering banks of the HG computer, unable to catch the speeding engineer-apprentice.

His watch registered nine the next morning when he approached the hatch open once more on Limbo. But it might have been the depths of night—save the gray of the mist was three or four shades lighter than it had been when he had seen it last. To his eyes however it was as thick as in the hour when they had returned to the ship.

Rip stood halfway down the ramp, wiping his hand on his thigh as he lifted it from the dripping guide rope where the moisture condensed in large oily drops. He raised a worried face to Dane as the other edged along the slippery surface to join him.

"It doesn't seem to be clearing any," Dane stated the obvious.

"Tang thinks he got a fix—a fix on Ali's unit!" Shannon burst out. He reached once more for the guide rope and faced west, staring out into those cottony swirls hungrily as if by will alone he could force the stuff away from his line of vision.

"From where—north?"

"No, west!"

From the west where the ruins lay—where Rich's party were encamped! Then they were right, Rich had something to do with Limbo's mystery.

"That interference was cut out sometime early this morning," Rip continued. "Conditions must have been better for about ten minutes. Tang won't swear to it, but he's sure himself that he caught the buzz of a live helmet com."

"Pretty far—the ruins," Dane made the one objection. But he was as certain as Rip that if the com-tech mentioned it at all, it was because he had been nine-tenths sure he was right. Tang was not given to wild guesses.

"What are we going to do about it?" the cargo-apprentice added.

Rip twisted his big hands about the rope. "What can we do?" he wanted to know helplessly. "We can't just go off and hope to come up against the ruins. If they had a caster on it would be different—"

"What about that? Aren't they supposed to keep in touch with the ship? Couldn't a flitter get to them riding in on their caster beam?" Dane asked.

"It could—if there were a beam," Rip returned. "They went off the air when the fog came in. Tang has been calling them at ten minute intervals all night—had the emergency frequency in use so they'd be sure and answer. Only they haven't!"

And, without any caster beam to guide it, no flitter could pierce this murk and be sure of landing at the ruins. Yet a com-unit had registered there—perhaps Ali's—and that only a short time ago.

"I've been out there," Rip pointed to the ground they could not see from the ramp. "If I hadn't had a line fastened I'd been lost before I got four feet away—"

Dane could believe that. But he knew the restlessness which must be needling Rip now. To be kept prisoner here just when they had their first clue as to where Kamil might be—! It was maddening in a way. He edged down the slippery ramp, found the cord Rip had left looped there, and took an end firmly in hand, venturing out into the gray cloud.

The mist condensed in droplets on his tunic, trickled down his face, left an odd metallic taint on his lips. He walked on, taking one cautious step at a time, using the rope to keep him oriented.

A dark object loomed out of the gray and he neared it warily, only to recognize it with an embarrassed laugh as one of the crawlers—the one which had made the journey back and forth to deliver Rich's material to his chosen camp site.

Back and forth—

Dane's hand closed on the tread. What if—? They couldn't be sure—they could only hope—

He used the cord to haul himself back to the ramp, the need for haste making him stumble. If what he hoped was true—then they had the answer to their problem. They could find the camp, make a surprise descent upon the archaeologist, a descent which the other might not be prepared to meet.

There was the ramp and Rip waiting. The astrogator-apprentice must have guessed from Dane's expression that he had discovered something, but he asked no questions, only fell in behind as the other hurried into the ship.

"Where's Van Rycke—Captain Jellico?"

"Captain's asleep—Tau made him take a rest," Rip answered. "Van Rycke is in his cabin, I think."

So Dane made his way to his own superior's office. If only what he hoped *was* true! It would be a stroke of luck—the best luck they had had since that auction had brought them this headache which was Limbo.

The cargo-master was stretched out on his bunk, his hands behind his head. Dane hesitated in the doorway but Van Rycke's blue eyes were not closed and they did roll in his direction. He asked a question first:

"Have you used the crawler in the past two days, sir?"

"To my knowledge no one has—why?"

"Then it was only used for one purpose here," Dane's excitement grew, "and that was to carry Dr. Rich's supplies to his camp—"

Van Rycke sat up. Not only sat up, but reached for his boots and pulled them on his feet.

"And you think that the fix has been left on that camp. It might just be, son, it might just be." He was tugging on his tunic now.

Rip caught on. "A guide all ready to go!" he exulted.

"We hope," Van Rycke applied a cautious warning.

It was the cargo-master who led the way out of the *Queen* once more, back to the parked crawler. The low-slung cargo shifter was standing just as Dane had left it in the shelter of the *Queen*'s fins, its blunt nose pointing forward, out of the enclosure of the fins, to make a quarter turn to the west! The auto-fix was still on the camp. Dane took a running jump for the slow moving vehicle and brought it to a stop. But it was on a line which would take it, fog or no fog, straight to the camp where it had carried supplies two days before. And it would provide an unerring guide for men roped to it. They had a chance now to locate Ali.

The cargo-master made no comment but started toward the *Queen*, the others following. Dane glanced over his shoulder at the crawler.

"If we had one of those portable flamers—" he muttered and Rip caught him up on that.

"A sonic screamer would be more to the point!"

Dane was startled. A flamer could be used as a threat or a tool with which to force one's way into a fortification. It need not be a weapon. But a sonic screamer—there was no protection against the unseen waves which could literally tear a man apart. If Rip wanted a screamer he must fear real trouble. Since the *Queen* was a law abiding ship and carried neither fitting the point must remain purely academic.

Van Rycke climbed to control. And as he rapped at the Captain's private cabin they could hear the screaming of the Hoobat. Jellico opened the panel, his face wearing a weary frown. Before he greeted the cargo-master he slapped the cage of the blue creature, setting it to oscillating crazily, but the shaking up did nothing to discourage the throat-splitting squalls.

The cargo-master watched the frenzied Hoobat. "How long has Queex been acting that way, Captain?"

Jellico gave the caged captive a baneful glare and then stepped into the corridor away from the din.

"Most of the night. The thing's gone mad, I think." He shut the panel and the shrieks were muffled. "I can't see what sets it off like that."

"Its hearing range goes into the super-sonic, doesn't it?" Van Rycke persisted.

"Four points. But what—" The Captain bit off that "what" and his eyes narrowed. "That blasted interference! Do you suppose that's sonic?"

"Could be. Does Queex howl when it cuts out?"

"We can see—" Jellico made as if to return to his cabin but Van Rycke caught his arm.

"Something more important on the launching cradle now, Captain."

"Such as what?"

"We've found a guide to take us to Rich's camp." Van Rycke explained about the crawler. Jellico leaned against the wall of the corridor, his face impassive. Van Rycke might have been reciting the table of cargo stowing.

"Could just work," was his only comment when the cargo-master concluded. But he did not appear in any hurry to put it to the proof.

Once more the crew assembled by order in the mess room—without Tang who stayed by the com. When Jellico came in he was holding a small silver rod, fastened to a chain locked on his belt.

"We've discovered," he began without preliminaries, "that the supply crawler is still on auto-beam to Rich's camp. It can act as a guide—"

He was answered by a murmur which separated into individual demands to know when they could start. But these died as Jellico hammered the rod on the tabletop for their attention.

"Lots—" he said.

Mura had them ready, slips of white straw he dropped into a bowl and stirred about with his finger.

"Tang has to stay with the com," Jellico reminded them. "That leaves ten of us—the five with short straws go—"

The steward passed around, holding the bowl above eye level of the seated men. Each, Dane noticed, palmed his choice, not even looking at it. When all had one they opened their hands together displaying their luck.

Short straw! Dane felt a thrill—was it of pleasure or apprehension— He looked around to see who would be his companions on the trip. Rip—Rip's straw was also short! And so was the one between

Kosti's grimed fingers. Steen Wilcox showed the next, and the last was Mura's.

Wilcox would be in command—that was good. Dane had every confidence in the taciturn astrogator. And it was odd how luck had ruled. In a way, those whom fate had chosen were the most expendable of the crew. Should disaster strike, the *Queen* could safely lift from Limbo. Dane tried not to think of that.

Jellico grunted when he found himself ruled out of the expedition. He got to his feet and crossed to the wall on the right. There he applied the rod, unsealing some concealed panel. There was a grating sound as if some catch had not been activated for a long time.

Then a rack was revealed—a rack of hand blasters! And below them holster belts swung on pegs, full refills, glinting evilly in the light. The arsenal of the *Queen,* which could only be opened when the Captain deemed the situation highly serious.

One by one Jellico lifted out blasters, passing each in turn to Stotz who inspected it closely, flipping the charge slot open and shut before putting it down on the table. Five blasters, five belts complete with recharges. It appeared that Jellico expected war.

The Captain closed the panel and locked it with that master control rod which by Federation law could not leave his person day or night. Now he returned to the table, facing the five who had been chosen. He gestured to the arms. By training they knew how to use blasters, but a Trader might not have to carry one more than once in a lifetime among the stars.

"They're all yours, boys," he said. And he needed to add nothing to impress upon them just how bad he considered their task to be.

BLIND HUNT

9 Once more Dane put on his field equipment, making a fervid promise to himself as he adjusted his helmet that this time his com would be on—all the time. No one had said anything to him about his slip-up in the valley. He had thought that his carelessness would condemn him to the sidelines. Yet here he was being given a second chance, merely because he had been lucky in the drawing. And no one had challenged his right to go out. So it was up to him to prove that their confidence was not misplaced.

Since the fog was as heavy as ever there was no day or night outside. They ate a hot and nourishing meal before they tramped into a gloom which their watches told them was mid-afternoon.

With the weight of the blaster resting unfamiliarly against his thigh, Dane followed Rip as Shannon tagged Wilcox's heels down the ramp. Kosti and Mura were already busy at the crawler.

There was room for one man, two if they crowded, on the flat surface of the small vehicle. But, since the platform had no sides and there was nothing to cling to in order to keep from sliding from its fog-slick surface on the rough terrain, the party was content to be infantry, attaching themselves to the guide by lengths of rope.

Kosti triggered the starter and the crawler ground forward, its treads crushing gravel and bits of porous stone. The pace was that of a walk and none of them had any difficulty keeping up.

Dane looked back. Aleady the *Queen* had vanished. Only a radiance high in the mist marked the searchlight which under ordinary conditions could be seen for miles. It was then that he realized what it would mean to lose touch with the crawler, and his hand tugged the rope which tied them together, testing its safety.

Luckily the ground was fairly even and only once did they have to slip and scramble over one of the rivers of slag. The man who had piloted the crawler across the waste on its first trip to the ruins had chosen the best path he could find.

But they became aware now of another peculiarity of the fog—the noises. Whether those were the sounds they made, flung back and magnified, or some other natural change, they could not tell. But several times they paused, Kosti snapping off the crawler, and listened, sure that they were surrounded by another party moving confidently through the murk, that they were about to be the focus of an attack. But when they so halted the sounds ceased, and it was only when they plodded on once more that the sensation of being dogged by unseen travelers grew strong again. After those two stops, by mutual and unspoken consent, they ignored the noises and pushed on, seeing each other as shadows, the ground under their boots visible only for inches.

The moisture which trickled down their helmets and clothing was an added discomfort. It had, at least to Dane's sensitive senses, an unpleasant smell and it left the skin feeling slimy and unclean. He tried wiping his face vigorously, only to discover that such motion apparently smeared it deeper.

Nothing interfered with the steady advance of the crawler. Though the men who followed it could no longer see the ship, nor sight the ruins for which they were bound, the machine's electronic memory guided them unerringly. They were about three quarters of the way across the waste when they heard a new noise—not raised as an echo of their own passing.

Someone or something running!

And yet that thudding was not the pound of space boots, the rhythm was oddly different—as if the creature who passed had more than two feet, Dane thought.

He faced into the gloom, trying to gauge the quarter from which that sound came. But in the mist the compass points were lost. It could have been speeding toward them or away. Then his guide rope tautened and pulled him on.

"What was that?" the voice was muffled, but it was unmistakably Rip's.

"Your guess is as good as mine." Dane could no longer hear that pattering. Had it been one of the globe things?

A dark object rose out of the fog and then Dane was startled by a shout. His boots rasped from gravel and sand to smoother flooring. He was standing on a square of pavement and that shadow to the left was a jagged wall of ancient ruin. They had crossed the waste!

"Thorson! Dane—!"

Rip's summons was imperative and Dane hurried to answer it. Kosti must have stopped the crawler for his rope did not tug him forward. Then he came upon the astrogator-apprentice bending over a sprawled form.

It was Rip's own chief, Wilcox, who had taken that misstep and now lay partly in the crevice which had clamped knee-high on his leg.

In the end it took all four of them to pry the astrogator loose. And it was at least a half hour before he sat on the crawler, nursing his leg where the tough material of the age-old building had punched a jagged hole through the calf of his high boot and drawn blood. They applied first aid, but from now on Wilcox would have to ride.

They closed in a tight escort about the crawler as it moved on. Wilcox sat with a drawn blaster balanced on his good knee. The scraps of ruin became whole walls, sections of oddly shaped structures. And yet they saw nothing which had any signs of a Terran camp.

Here among the relics of an older and alien life Dane felt again that sensation of being spied upon, that just beyond vision limited by the fog lurked something else, something to which these drifting mists were no sight barrier. The treads of the crawler no longer crackled on rock and an eerie silence wrapped them about. The smooth walls ran with dank water, it gathered in puddles here and there. But the liquid was tainted, noisome, with an evil metallic smell clinging about it.

They came into a region where the buildings appeared to be untouched, with roofs and walls still guarding pitch dark interiors. The last thing Dane wanted to do was to explore any of those fetid openings.

But the crawler was not pausing anywhere along the street, instead crunching on over buckled strips of pavement. Perhaps the walls banked off some of the fog, for Dane now found it possible to see not only the forms but the faces of his companions. And all of them, he saw, had a tendency to look over their shoulders, and to stare into the interior of every structure they passed.

It was Rip who made the first find. He had taken out his hand torch and was using it at pavement level. Now he centered that ring of light on a dark splotch which marked a wall a little above ground surface. He tugged a signal to halt and went down on one knee beside his find as Dane joined him.

The cargo-apprentice found the other smelling that splotch, sniffing as if he were some hound on a muddled trail. But to Dane it was only a dark blotch.

"What is it?"

Rip's light swept from the stain on the wall to move over the pavement as if in search. Then it centered on a brownish wad. But though Rip inspected that with care he avoided touching it.

"Crax seed—"

Dane had been stooping. Now, in instant reaction to those words, he straightened. "Sure?"

"Smell it."

But Dane made no move to follow that suggestion. The less one meddled with crax seed the safer one was.

Rip got to his feet and hurried on to the crawler. "There's a cud of crax seed been spit out here. Fairly fresh—maybe this morning—"

"Told you—poachers!" Kosti broke in.

"So——" Wilcox gripped his blaster more firmly. Crax seed was one of the Galaxy-wide outlawed drugs. Those unwise enough to chew it had—for a period of time—an abnormal reaction speed, a heightened intellect, a superman control. What occurred to them later was not pretty at all. But to come up against a crax chewer was to face an opponent who at his peak was twice as wily, twice as fast, twice as strong as yourself. And it was not an assignment to be lightly undertaken.

Save for that betraying wad of crax seed, in spite of the search they now made in the vicinity, they could find no other indication that any life but themselves had walked this way since the forgotten war had blasted the city. If Dr. Rich had begun any archaeological excavations, the site of the investigation was still to be found.

Wilcox set the crawler on the lowest speed and started on. Nor was he the only one to travel with his blaster ready. All four of the rest took the same precaution.

"I wonder—" Dane had been surveying the broken line of roofs. "The fog," he added to Rip, "doesn't it appear to be thinner ahead?"

"It's been thinning out ever since we made that last halt. Good thing, too. Just look at that, man!"

What in a deeper murk, might have been a death trap gaped before them, a vast crevice slicing the pavement, opening a pit large enough to swallow both the crawler and the men escorting it. But the machine was prepared for that. Ponderously it altered course eastward, pulling up over a mound of rubble while Wilcox had to reholster his blaster and cling with both hands to keep his seat. The machine reached the top of the mound and began to crawl down the opposite side, a crawl which became a slide as the earth gave way beneath its weight.

Surely that rumble was enough to rouse any of Rich's men. But though those from the *Queen* took cover and waited out long minutes, there was nothing to indicate they had been heard.

"They can't be here," Kosti said as he crept out of cover at Wilcox's signal.

"Probably haven't been here for some time," Rip observed. "I knew he wasn't a real archaeologist!"

"What about Ali's com?" cut in Dane. Tang *had* got that faint fix from this general direction—though it was true that the ruins had not been pinpointed as the source of the faint cast-beam.

Wilcox made a long survey of their surroundings. Before them the gap in the ground had been filled in with wreckage until a bridge of uncertain stability faced the crawler. Its "memory" had brought them there so it must have crossed here during the trips to carry Rich's supplies. They would have to take the chance and go on if they wanted to know what had become of the archaeologists.

The astrogator started the motor and then clung with iron fingers as the machine under him bucked and heaved over the loose bridge stuff. Once the treads hit a pocket and the crawler canted to the left. A foot more and it would have spilled its passenger down into the black depths of the gulf.

Kosti went next, both hands on the rope which still tied him to the machine. He took tiny steps in the middle of the bridge, and beneath his helmet drops of sweat washed the fog slick from his cheeks. The others picked their way slowly, testing each step. The fact that they could not see the bottom of the crevice on either side did not make the trip any easier.

Beyond, the crawler picked up speed again and made a quick turn back to its original course. The lifting of the mist was even more apparent—though it did not vanish entirely. But their range of vision, from a foot or two about their persons, had increased to half a block.

"They did have bubble tents," Dane said suddenly. "And regulation camping gear."

"So—where's the camp?" Rip sounded almost peevish. Since he had found the crax cud his buoyant good humor had vanished.

"They wouldn't camp in the city." Dane was convinced of that. There was about these ruins an alien, brooding atmosphere which dragged at one's spirits. He had never regarded himself as a particularly sensitive person, but he felt this strongly. And he believed that the others did also. Little Mura had hardly spoken since they had sighted the ruins, he had dragged back on his guide rope, his eyes darting from one side of the street to the other as if at any moment he expected some formless horror to dash at him out of the murk. Who would dare to set up a tent here, sleep, eat, and carry on the business of daily living fenced in with the age-old effluvium which clung to the blasted and broken dwellings—dwellings which perhaps had never harbored human creatures at all?

The crawler drew them on through the maze until the structures which still had a semblance of completeness were behind them once again and only broken walls and shattered mounds of blocks and earth made obstructions around which their machine led them in the pattern it must follow.

It was halfway around one towering mound when Wilcox brought it to a quick stop by smashing his hand down on the control button. That gesture and the frantic haste in which he made it were not lost on the others. They dived into hiding and then began working forward to edge in behind the crawler.

From a cleared space arose—though its lines were still blurred by the fog—a bubble tent, its puffed surface slick with the moisture. They had reached Rich's camp at last.

But Wilcox gave no order to advance. Though they had nothing but suspicion against the archaeologist, the attitude of the astrogator suggested that he was about to reconnoiter a position held by open enemies.

He tightened his helmet strap after adjusting his throat mike. But his orders did not come audibly—instead he gestured them out to encircle the sealed bubble. Dane crept to the right with Rip, automatically keeping cover between them and the tent.

They had gone a quarter of the circle when Rip's hand came down on Dane's arm and the astrogator-apprentice motioned that Thorson was to remain where he was while Rip crawled on to another vantage point in the circle they were drawing about Rich's headquarters.

Dane studied the lay of the ground between his station and the bubble. Here the rubble had been leveled off, packed down, as if the men who camped here needed room to accommodate either crawlers or flitters. But as far as Dane could see, and he was frankly ignorant of the archaeologist's trade, there was no indication of work on uncovering the ruins. Vague memories of items he had seen on news tapes, and Rip's briefings, were his only guides. But surely they should have come across excavations, things waiting for study, maybe even crates ready to pack with transportable finds. But this place had rather the stripped look of a field headquarters for some action team of pioneers or Survey. Could it be left by Survey and not Rich's camp at all?

Then he saw the crawler come into sight, Wilcox on it, his lame leg drawn up so that the fact that he was inactive would not be apparent to anyone watching from the bubble. The crawler crunched on toward the tent without rousing any sign of life within.

But to the astonishment of Dane and the surprise of Wilcox—judging by his expression—the machine did not come to a stop at the level space before the tent. Instead it changed course to evade the bubble and kept steadily on until Wilcox halted it. The astrogator stared at the tent and then his voice whispered in Dane's earphones:

"Come on in—but take it slow!"

They converged on the bubble, slipping from cover and racing across the clearing to new protections. But the tent might be deserted for all the attention their actions aroused. Mura reached the structure first, his sensitive fingers searching for the sealing catch. When the flap peeled down, all of them stared in.

The bubble was only an empty shell. None of its interior partitions had been put into place, even the tilo-floor was missing, so that bare rubble of the field showed. And there was not a box or bag of all the supplies which had been brought from the *Queen* present in that wide space.

"A fake!" Kosti sputtered. "This was set up just to make us think—"

"That they were still here," Wilcox finished for him. "Looks that way, doesn't it?"

"Passing over here in a flitter," Rip murmured, "we'd believe everything was just as it should be. But where *are* they?"

Mura resealed the bubble's flap. "Not here," he announced as if that were a new discovery. "But, Mr. Wilcox, did not the crawler attempt to proceed past this area? Perhaps it knows far more than we have given it credit for—"

Wilcox fingered the throat strap of his helmet. About them the fog was fading—though far more slowly than it had descended. His eyes went from the bubble to the mist beyond. Perhaps if Ali had not been involved he would have ordered a return to the *Queen*. But now, after a pause, he switched on the crawler's motor once more.

The machine circled around the bubble and kept on. There were clumps of vegetation appearing now—the tough grass, the stunted bushes. And knots of rock slanting up signaled their approach to the foothills.

Here the fog which was thinning on the plains curdled again, shutting down until they bunched about the crawler in a tight cluster, each man within arms-distance of his fellows.

That feeling of being spied upon, of being dogged by something they could not see grew strong once more. Underfoot the ground became rougher. But Kosti pointed out other tracks, rutted in the soft patches of soil, indications that they were on a road the crawler had used before.

As the mist thickened they strained ears and eyes—but they saw nothing but each other and their machine guide. And what they heard they could not believe.

"Look out!" Rip grabbed at Dane, jerking him back just in time to avoid a painful meeting with a rock wall which loomed out of the fog. From the echo of their boots on the ground they gained the impression that they were entering a narrow defile. Linking hands they spread out—to discover that the four of them marching at arms-length could span the road they now followed.

Once more Wilcox slowed to a halt. He was uneasy. Marching blind this way, they could walk into a trap. On the other hand those they hunted must believe that the crew of the *Queen* would not attempt to travel through the fog. The astrogator had to weigh the possibility of a surprise descent upon the unseen enemy against the chance that he was going into an ambush.

And being imbued with that extra amount of caution which made him an excellent astrogator, Wilcox was not given to snap decisions. Those with him knew that no argument could move him once his mind had been made up. Therefore they sighed with relief when he started the crawler once more.

But the strange solution to their chase came so shortly that it was a shock. For, within feet, they were fronted by towering rock, rock against which the crawler stubbed its flat nose, as its treads continued to bite into the ground as if to force it into the solid, unmoving stone.

THE WRECK

10

"She's trying to dig into *that*!" Kosti marveled.

Wilcox snapped out of his surprise and turned off the motor so that the crawler stopped heaving, nuzzling the rock wall through which its "memory" urged it.

"They must have put a false set of coordinates on purpose," suggested Rip.

But Dane, remembering that earlier trail which had ended in the same fashion, stepped around Shannon and pressed his palms against the slimy, wet surface of the rock. He was right!

Fainter than it had been in that other valley, the vibration crept up his arms into his body. Not only that, but it was building up, growing in strength even as he stood there. He could feel it now in the ground, striking through the soles of his boots. And the others caught it too.

"What in the—!" exploded Wilcox who hitched forward on the crawler to copy the experiment. "This stuff must be hollow—that installation Tang talked about—"

That was it, of course, the installation which the com-tech was sure must rival Terra's largest computer, was broadcasting—not only in the sound waves picked up on the *Queen,* but through the stuff of Limbo itself! But what was that vast power being used for and why? And what was the trick which could send a crawler through solid rock? For Dane did not agree with Rip that the radar guide had been tampered with. If that had been done it would have been more sensible to set it on a point far out in the barrens, leading any would-be trackers into the midst of nowhere.

"There's a trick in this—" Wilcox muttered as he moved his hand with patting motions across the stone.

But Dane was sure that the astrogator was not going to spring any hidden latch that way. His own examination of that other wall in the bright light of day had taught him the futility of such a hunt.

Kosti leaned against one of the caterpillar treads of the crawler. "If it went through there once, it isn't going to do it now. We don't know how to open the right door. A stick of thorlite might just get us in."

"Now that's a course I *can* compute, man." Rip hunkered down, running his hands along the ground line of that exasperating cliff. "How big a stick would do it, do you think?"

But Wilcox shook his head. "You don't lift a ship without co-ordinates. Here," he swung to Kosti, "link com-units with me and let's see if with double power we can raise the *Queen.*"

The jetman unhooked the energy core of his helmet com and joined it to Wilcox's in an emergency linkage.

"The installation is picking up voltage," Dane warned, judging by the vibration singing through his fingertips. "Do you think you can break through the interference, sir?"

"That's a thought." Wilcox pulled at his mike. "But they've never been on steady. We can wait for a break in their broadcast."

Rip and Mura came back to the wall. The vibration was a steady beat. Dane walked along to the right. He found a corner where the narrow valley went on—masked by the fog. And he was sure that as he shuffled along, his hand against the stone as a guide, that beat grew stronger. Could one by the sense of touch trace the installation? That was something to think about. What if they unfastened the ropes which had linked them to the crawler and made one long cord of them—an anchorage for a man to explore northeast? He retraced his path and reported to Wilcox, adding his suggestion.

"We'll see what the Captain says," was the astrogator's answer.

The chill which was a part of the fog struck into them now that they were halted. Dane wondered how long Wilcox proposed to linger there. But through their touch on the wall they became aware that the beat of that distant discharge or energy was lessening, that one of the silent intervals was at hand. Wilcox, his fingers on the wall, adjusted the mike with his other hand, determined to make contact the first instant that he could.

And when all but the faintest rumble was gone from the rock, he spoke swiftly in the verbal shorthand of the Traders. Their discoveries among the ruins were reported, as was the present impasse.

There followed an anxious wait. They might be out of range of the *Queen,* even using the stepped-up com. But at last, through the crackle of static, their orders reached them—to make a short exploration along the valley if they wished. But to start back to the ship within the hour.

Wilcox was helped from the crawler before they manhandled the unwieldy vehicle around and reset its dial for the return journey. Then they tied the ropes into two longer lines for the explorers' use.

Dane did not wait for orders—after all, this was his project. He knotted one of those lines about his middle, leaving his hands free. Just as matter-of-factly Kosti took up the other, almost out of Rip's hands, nor did the jetman pay any attention to Shannon's protests.

"It's starting up again," Mura reported from beside the cliff.

Dane put his left hand on the wall and started off, with Kosti falling into step. They rounded the bend Dane had discovered into the continuation of the valley which was still packed with the cotton wool of the fog.

It was plain that no crawler had ever advanced this far. The narrow way was choked with piles of loose debris over which they helped each other to keep their footing. And the vibration in the wall grew stronger as they went.

Kosti thumped his fist against the stone as they paused for a breather.

"Those drums—they sure keep it up."

The distant beat did carry with it some of the roll of a heavy drum.

"Kinda like the Storm Dancers on Gorbe—just a little. And that's devilish stuff, gets into your blood 'til you want to get out and prance along with them. This—well, it's nasty down deep—plain nasty. And you get to believing something's waiting out there—" the jetman's hand indicated the fog, "just waiting to pounce!"

They kept on, climbing now as each ridge of rubble they surmounted was a little higher than the preceding one. They must have been well above the surface of the valley where they had left the crawler when they came upon the strangest find of all.

Dane, clinging to an outcrop in the wall to retain his balance, teetered on the top of a mound. His boot slipped and he tumbled forward before Kosti could snatch him back, rolling down until he brought up with a bruising bump against a dark object. Under his clawing hands he felt, not the rough gravel and earth of the valley, but something else—a smooth sleekness— Had he come upon another ruined building this far from the city?

"Are you hurt?" Kosti called from above. "Look out, I'm coming down."

Dane backed away from his find as Kosti came down feet first in a slide, his boots ringing against that buried thing with the unmistakable clang of metal.

"What the—!" The jetman was on his knees, feeling over that exposed surface. And he was able to identify it. "A ship!"

"What?" Dane crowded in. But now he was able to see the curve of the plates, various other familiar details. They *had* come upon the wreckage of a crash—a bad crash. The ship had jammed its way into the narrow neck of the valley as if it were a cork pounded into a bottle. If they were to go any farther they would have to climb over it. Dane took up his helmet mike and reported the find to the three at the crawler.

"The wreck of that ship you heard coming in?" Wilcox wanted to know. But Dane had seen enough to know that it was not.

"No, sir. This has been here a long time—almost buried and there's rust eaten in. Years since this one lifted, I think—"

"Stay where you are—we're coming up!"

"You can't bring the crawler, sir. Footing is bad."

In the end they did come, supporting Wilcox over the worst bits, keeping contact with the crawler by rope only. In the meantime Kosti prowled around and over the wreck, trying to find a hatch.

"It's a rim prospector of a sort," he reported as soon as Wilcox was settled on a rock to view the find. "But there's something odd about it. I can't name the type. And it's been rooted here a good time. That hatch ought to be about here." He kicked at a pile of loose gravel which banked in one side of the metal hulk. "I think we could dig in."

Rip and Dane returned to the crawler and got the pioneer tools, always kept lashed to the under-carriage of that vehicle. With the shovel and lever they came back to work, taking turns at clearing the debris of years.

"What did I tell you!" Kosti was exultant as a black arc which must mark the top of an open hatch was uncovered.

But it was necessary to shift a lot more of the native soil of Limbo before any one of them could crawl into that hole. Rim prospectors were notoriously sturdy ships, if not swift travelers. They had to be designed to withstand conditions which would shatter liners or disturb even the crack freight- and mail-ships of the Companies.

And the condition of this one proved that its unknown builder had wrought even better than he had hoped. For the smash of its landing had not broken it into bits. Its carcass still hung together, although parts were telescoped.

Kosti leaned on the shovel after he threw out the last scoop of earth. "I can't place it—" He shook his head as if his inability to identify the type of ship worried him.

"How could anyone?" demanded Rip impatiently. "She's nothing but a scrap heap."

"I've seen 'em smashed worse than this." Kosti sounded annoyed. "But the structure—it's wrong—"

Mura smiled. "Rather I would say, Karl, that it is right. I know of no modern ship which could so well survive the landing this one made."

" 'No modern ship'?" Wilcox seized upon that. "You have seen one like this before then?"

Mura's smile grew broader. "If I had seen one such as this plying its trade—then I would be five hundred, perhaps eight hundred years old. This resembles the Class Three, Asteroid Belt ships. There is one, I believe, on display in the Trade Museum at Terraport East. But how it came here—" He shrugged.

Dane's historical cramming had not covered the fine points of ship design, but Kosti and Rip both understood the significance of that, and so did Wilcox.

"But," the astrogator was the first to protest, "they didn't have hyper-drive five hundred years ago. We were still confined to our own solar system—"

"Except for a few crazy experimenters," Mura corrected.

"There are Terran colonies in other systems which are over a thousand years old, you know that. And the details of their flights are sagas in themselves. There were those who went out to cross the gap in frozen sleep, and those who lived for four, six, and eight generations in ships before their far-off descendants trod the worlds their ancestors had set course for. And there were earlier variations of the hyper-drive, some of which may have worked, though their inventors never returned to Terra to report success. How an Asteroid prospector came to Limbo I can not tell you. But it has been here a very long time, that I will swear to."

Kosti flashed his torch into the hole they had uncovered. "We can get in—at least for a way—"

Before the smash the prospector had been a small ship with painfully confined quarters. Compared to her the *Queen* was closer to a liner. And Kosti had to turn back at the inner hatch, unable to squeeze his bulk through the jammed door space. In the end Mura and Dane alone were able to force a path to what had been a combined storage and living quarters.

But under the beam of their torches a fact was immediately clear. A great gap through which soil shifted faced them. This section had been ripped open on the other side, the hole later buried by a slide. But the smash had not done that, the marks of a flamer were plain on the metal. Sometime after its crack-up the prospector had been burnt open, the reason plain. For the portion where they now stood had been stripped—although the traces of cargo containers were on the floor and along the crumpled walls.

"Looted!" Dane exclaimed as the light swept from floor to wall.

To his right was the telescoped section which must have contained the control cabin. There, too, were signs of the flamer but the unknown looters had had little luck beyond. For the holes revealed a mixture of rock and twisted metal which could never be salvaged. Everything forward of the one cargo section they stood in was a total loss.

Mura fingered that slit in the wall. "This was done some time ago—maybe even years. But I think that it was done a long, long time after the ship crashed."

"Why did they want to get in here?"

"Curiosity—a desire to see what she was carrying. A prospector on a long course is apt to make surprising discoveries. And this ship must have had something worth the taking. It was looted. Then, so lightened, the wreckage may have turned over, perhaps earthquakes resettled it and buried it more completely. But it was looted—"

"You don't think that the survivors of its crew may have returned? They could have taken off in an escape flitter before the crash—"

"No, there was too long a time between the crash and the looting.

This ship was discovered by someone else and stripped. I do not think that they—" Mura pointed to the fore-compartment, "escaped."

Did Limbo have intelligent inhabitants, natives who could use a flamer to cut through ship alloy? But the globe things—Dane refused to believe that those queer creatures had looted the prospector.

Before they climbed out of the ship Mura pushed as far as he could into the fore-section. And when he inched out again he was repeating a number.

"Xc—4 over 9532600," he said. "Her registry, by some chance it is still visible. Remember that: Xc—4 over 9532600."

But Dane was interested in another point. "That's Terran registry!"

"I suspected that it would be. She is Asteroid class—perhaps an experimental ship with one of the very early hyper-drives. She might have been a private ship, the work of one or two men, an attempt to pioneer in a new direction. Could that tangle ever be uncoiled our engineers ought to discover some interesting alternate of the usual engine. It could be worth the effort to break through just for that—"

"Ahoy!" the voice from the outer air summoned. "What are you doing in there?"

Dane spoke into his mike, outlining what they had found. Then they squeezed out through the hatch.

"Stripped bare!" Kosti was openly disappointed. "Opened up and stripped bare. She must have been carrying something really worth-while for all the trouble they took to do it."

"I'd rather know who stripped her. Even if it was done years ago," was Rip's comment and it was evident that Wilcox agreed with him.

The astrogator pulled himself to his feet, leaning against a rock. "We'd better get back to the *Queen*."

Dane glanced around. He was sure that the fog was thinning here as it had back around the ruins. If it would just clear—then they could take up a flitter and really comb this district! They had discovered no trace of Ali anywhere, and each step they took seemed to plunge them only deeper into mystery.

Rich and his party had vanished—into a stone wall if the crawler was to be relied upon. Now here was a ship which had been looted long after it had crashed. And somewhere deep in the heart of Limbo beat an unknown installation which might offer the worst threat of all!

They went back to the crawler and by the time Wilcox was once more established on it, the fog was retreating, more swiftly now. As it lifted they read on the scraped walls, in the rutted soil that this was or had been a thoroughfare in good use. Those who had come and gone this path had made it a lane of travel before the arrival of the *Queen,* some of those marks were far more than a few days old.

Survey's tapes had said nothing of all this—the ruins, the installation, the wrecked ships. Why not? Had Survey's report been edited? But Limbo had been put up to legal auction just as usual. Did it mean that Survey's scout teams had not explored this continent to any extent—that seeing the evidences of a burn-off their investigation had been only superficial?

It was raining now, a drizzle which worked into the high collars of their tunics and soaked the upper linings of their boots. Unconsciously their pace quickened as the crawler took the homeward trundle. Dane wished that there was some way they could cut cross country and shorten the march which lay between them and the *Queen.* But at least they no longer had to rope themselves to the carrier.

They came into the ruins again, maintaining a careful watch for any signs of life there. The brilliant hues of the buildings were subdued by the lack of sunlight, but they still warred with one another and jolted Terran senses in a subtle fashion. Either the people who had built this city had a different type of vision, or a chemical reaction from the burn-off had altered the color schemes for the worse. As it was, none of the Traders felt exactly comfortable if they looked too long at those walls.

"It isn't altogether the color—" Rip spoke aloud. "It's their shape, too. Those angles are wrong—just enough wrong to be disturbing—"

"The burn-off blast may have shaken them up," offered Dane. But Mura was not ready to accept that.

"No, Rip has it right. The colors, they are wrong for us, also the shapes. See that tower—over there? Only three floors remain, but once it was taller. Let your eyes rise along the lines of those floors into space—where once must have been other walls. It is all wrong—those lines—"

Dane saw what he meant. With imagination one could add more floors to the tower—but when one did! For a moment he was dizzy as he tried that feat. It was very easy, after studying all this, to believe that the Forerunners had been alien, alien beyond any race that the Terrans, newly come to the Galactic lanes, had encountered.

He hurriedly averted his eyes from that tower, winced as his gaze swept across an impossibly scarlet foundation and fastened with relief on the comfortable monotone of the crawler and Wilcox's square back in the drab brown Service tunic.

But the astrogator had not joined his companions in their speculations concerning their surroundings. He was hunched over, both hands clutching the mike of the stepped-up com Kosti had not yet altered. And there was something in his posture which altered the others as they watched him.

SARGASSO WORLD

11 Dane strained to hear a hint of sound in his helmet phones. There was a far-off click which faded quickly. But it was evident that Wilcox with his double-powered com received more than that.

The astrogator took one hand from the mike and gestured the others to come to the stalled crawler. Luckily no drone from the interference blanketed the air waves. And by some freak the word "stay" boomed suddenly in Dane's ears.

Wilcox looked up at them. "We're not to go back now—"

"What's wrong?" Mura's voice lost none of its mild tone.

"The *Queen*'s surrounded—"

"Surrounded!" "By whom?" "What happened?" the questions came together in a confused gabble.

"They were fired upon when they tried to leave the ship. And there's some reason why they can't lift. We're to keep clear until they can find out what's behind it all—"

Mura glanced over his shoulder at the valleys now unveiled as the mist drifted away in tattered streamers.

"If we cut across the open," he said slowly, "we can be seen with ease now that the fog is gone. But suppose we go back—along the valley mouths, paralleling the burnt-off country. We should reach a point opposite the *Queen,* and then we can climb the heights until we are able to see what is going on about her—"

Wilcox nodded. "We're not to try contact by com. They're afraid we might be picked up."

Though the fog had lifted visibility was not good. It must be well into evening and the astrogator surveyed their present surroundings with disfavor. It was plain that they could not move through the rough foothill country in the dark. Their travels must wait until morning. But he did not order them to find shelter in the city buildings. Mura broke the short silence first.

"There is the bubble—we could camp there for the night. I do not think it has been used since it was erected as a blind."

They seized upon that thankfully and the crawler made the return trip to the abandoned camp of the archaeologists. They unsealed the full door flap, allowing their carrier space to enter. And when the portal was closed again Dane had a feeling of relief. The walls enclosing them were Terran made, he had slept in such shelters before. And that familiarity was in a measure security against the alien quality of the city without.

The bubble cut off the night winds and they were not too uncomfortable in spite of the lack of heat. Kosti who had been wandering about the hollow shell kicked at an inoffensive bit of rock.

"They could have left the heating unit. That's supposed to be part of one of these—"

Rip laughed. "But they didn't know we were coming."

Kosti stared at him, inclined to be affronted, and then he chuckled.

"No, they did not know. We can't complain—" his deep roar of laughter was directed at himself.

Mura busied himself with duties which were part of his usual job, collecting their emergency rations and parceling out to each one of the tasteless cubes and so many sips from their canteens. Dane wondered at the steward's careful measurements. It was as if Mura did not believe they were going to return to the *Queen* in the near future and thought that these limited supplies might have to last for a long time.

Once they had eaten, they drew together for warmth, stretching out on the bare floor. Outside the bubble they could hear the moan of the night winds, rising to a crescendo of weird cries as it wailed through fissures of the ruins.

Dane's thoughts were restless. What was wrong with the *Queen*? If the ship was besieged why hadn't she simply lifted from the landing and set down elsewhere, giving them directions where to join her, or sending out the flitter to pick them up? What kept the freighter planet bound?

Perhaps the others shared his worries, but there were no speculations voiced in the dark, no questions asked. Having their orders they had determined upon a course of action for themselves and now they were getting what rest they could.

Shortly after dawn the haggard Wilcox sat up and then limped to the crawler. In the pinched gray light he looked years older and there was a tight set to his lips as he bent over the machine, making the adjustments which would leave it on manual control during the hours to come.

None of them could have been asleep for Wilcox's action acted as a signal and they were all on their feet, stretching the cramp out of arms and legs. Greetings were grunts as they ate what Mura allowed them. Then they were out in the crispness of the morning. Streaks of color heralded the sun they had not seen for so long and the last of the fog was gone. In the north the mountains were stark and bare against the sky.

Wilcox pointed the crawler north where the foothill valleys pushed out in a ragged fringe. There was plenty of cover there and they could slip east undetected. Of them all the astrogator had the most difficult job. Here was no smooth path for the crawler. And within a half mile he had to throttle down to a slow walking pace or be bounced from his seat.

In the end they separated into two parties. Two of them at a time scouted ahead, while the two remaining stayed with Wilcox and the crawler at the slower pace. From all signs they might have been alone in a dead world. No tracks broke the soil, there were no sounds, and they did not even sight one of the rare insects which must keep to the more hospitable inner portions of the valleys.

Dane was on advance patrol with Mura when the steward gave a grunt and raised his hands as if to shade his eyes. Above them the sun had struck fire from some gleaming surface, struck it strong enough to flash a burning beam down at the Terrans.

"Metal!" Dane cried. Could this be another clue to the installation?

He started toward that spot, first clambering with difficulty over the debris left by a recent slide of small rocks. Then he pulled himself up on a ledge the slide had uncovered and made his way to the source of that flash. What he expected he did not really know. But what he found was wreckage—wreckage of another space ship— although the outlines were strange, even allowing for alterations made by the force of its landing. It was smaller than the prospector they had discovered the day before, and in a greater state of disintegration, the parts which had been exposed before the slide brought it all to the surface were only rust-eaten scraps.

Mura joined him and looked down at the crumpled thing which had once navigated space.

"This is old—very, very old." He tried to pick up a rod-shaped bit. Between his fingers it became red dust. "Old—I do not think a Terran ever flew this one."

"A Forerunner ship?" Dane was startled. If that were true—this *was* a find—a find which might bring Survey and its kindred services back to Limbo with all jets blazing.

"Not that old—or it would not exist. But the Rigellians and that vanished race of Angol Two were in Galactic space before we were. This may be an ancient vessel of their building. It is so very old—"

"What brought it here?" Dane wondered. "That was a smash landing, and the prospector ended the same way. Then there was that ship we heard come in before the fog closed down. Yet the *Queen* didn't have any trouble making a good landing. I don't get it. One crack up—but three—?"

"It makes one think," Mura agreed. "Perhaps we should look about a bit more. The solution to this puzzle may lie within sight and sound and yet we are not clever enough to learn it."

They waited on the ledge until they could signal to the slowly advancing party with the crawler. The astrogator took careful bearings on the site. If and when they had time, they might later send a party to explore this discovery—since its age and alien origin might make it of value.

"This reminds me somehow," Kosti said, "of how those Sissiti catch the purple lizards they make boots of. They set up a thing that waggles back and forth—just a thin wire attached to a motor. But the lizard sees it and—pow—he's sunk. Sits there watching that stupid thing wiggle-waggle until a Sissit comes along and pops him into a bag. Maybe someone's set up a wiggle-waggle here to draw in ships—that would be something!"

Wilcox stared at him. "Could be you have something at that," he replied, as he fingered his mike. It was apparent he longed to report this second find to the *Queen*. And he had a suggestion for the scouting parties. "Take a look up these valleys if you can without wasting too much time. I'd like to know if there are any more wrecks strewn about in this general area."

So from then on, though they continued to work their way east to flank the *Queen,* they also made side trips into the valleys for short distances. And it was Kosti and Rip who found the third ship.

Where the two other shattered discoveries had been of an earlier day, this was not only of their own time but a type of craft they were able to recognize at once. Through some freak its disastrous ending had not been as bad as those which had telescoped the prospector and smashed the alien. While the new find lay on its side showing buckled and broken plates, it was not crushed.

"Survey." Rip yelled almost before they were within hearing distance.

There was no reason to mistake the insignia on the battered nose—the crossed, tailed comets were as well known along the star trails as the jagged lightning swords of the Patrol.

Wilcox limped forward with the rest as they trailed along its length.

"The hatch is open—" Rip called down from the pinnacle he had climbed for a better look.

It was what dangled from that open hatch which centered their attention. A rope hanging like that could mean only one thing—that there had been survivors! Was this the explanation for all the puzzling happenings on Limbo? Dane tried to remember how many men comprised the crew of a Survey ship—they usually had a group of specialists—perhaps as many as rode in the *Queen*—perhaps more—

Though there was no reason why anyone would have remained in the wrecked ship, the men from the *Queen* prepared to explore. Rip dropped from the pinnacle and balanced across to that hatch. Only Wilcox had to remain where he was as the others climbed the rope.

It was a strange experience to lower oneself down a well which was once a corridor, Dane found. Ahead, torches picked out fugitive gleams from smooth surfaces as the explorers poked into the cabins.

"She's been stripped!" Rip's words rang in the helmet coms back along the line. "I'm for control—"

Dane knew very little of the geography of a Survey ship. He could only follow the others, halting at the first open panel to peer inside with the aid of his own torch. This must have been the storage for space suits and exploring gear as it was on the *Queen*. But it was empty now—cupboards gaping as if their contents had been hurriedly ripped loose. Had the crew left the boat in space before the crash? No, that did not explain the rope.

"Lord above us!" The shock in that cry stopped Dane where he was. Rip's voice in the com was so strained, horrified— What *had* the other discovered in the control section?

"What's the matter?" that was Wilcox, impatient at being left out.

"Coming—" Kosti's growl came next.

And a few moments later the jetman's voice was loud with a crackle of expletives as shocked as Rip's exclamation had been.

"What *is* it?" fumed Wilcox.

Dane left the storage space and made his way quickly to the passageway tying together all sections of the ship, which should lead him directly to what the others had found. Mura was ahead of him there and he soon caught up with the steward.

"We've found them," Rip's voice was bleak and old as he answered the astrogator.

"Found who?" Wilcox wanted to know.

"The crew!"

The passage ahead of Dane was blocked. He could see past Mura, but Kosti's bulk and Rip's shut out what lay beyond. Then Rip spoke again and Dane hardly knew it for his voice.

"Got—to—get—out—of—here—"

"Yes!" that was Kosti.

Both of them turned and Mura and Dane had to retrace their way to the hatch, hurried on by the impatience of the two behind them. They climbed out on the curving side of the ship, giving way to the others. Rip crawled down toward the fins. He held fast to the braces of one and proceeded to be thoroughly sick.

Kosti's face was greenish, but he maintained control with a visible effort. None of the other three quite dared at that moment to ask what either man had seen. It wasn't until Rip, shivering, crept back and slid down the rope to the ground that Wilcox lost patience.

"Well, what happened to them?"

"Murder!" Rip's voice rang too loudly, echoed by some freak of the stone abutments about them until "murrrderrr" was shouted in their ears.

Dane glanced around in time to see Mura descend again into the ship. In the shadow of his helmet the small man's face was composed and he gave no reason for his return.

Nor did Wilcox ask any more questions. After a minute or two Mura's voice sounded in their coms.

"This ship has also been stripped by looters—"

First the prospector hulk and then this—which must have been far more rewarding. Survivors of earlier crashes could have been searching for supplies, for material to make life more endurable but— Rip had an answer to that line of thought and he gave it in a single outburst:

"The Survey men were blaster burned!"

Blaster burned! Just as the globe things had been killed in that valley. Ruthless cruelty of a sort unknown to the civilized space lanes was in power on Limbo. Then another announcement from Mura electrified them all.

"This, I believe, is the missing *Rimbold*!"

The Survey ship whose disappearance had indirectly led to the auction on Naxos, and so their own arrival on Limbo! But how had it reached here and what had brought it crashing down on this world? Survey ships, because of the nature of their duty, were as nearly foolproof as any ships could be. In a hundred years perhaps two had been lost. Yet the *Rimbold,* for all of its safety devices and the drilled know-how of its experienced crew, had been as luckless as the earlier ships they had discovered.

Dane slid down on the rope, Kosti following him. The sun had gone under a cloud and there was a spatter of rain on the rocks about. It was thickening into a drizzle as the steward joined them. Whatever he had seen within the *Rimbold,* it had not upset him as completely as it had Rip and Kosti. Instead he had a thoughtful, almost puzzled look.

"Does not Van tell a story like this?" he asked suddenly. "It is one from the old days when ships rode the sea waves, not the star lanes. Then there was said to be a place in a western ocean of our own earth where no winds blew and a weed grew thick, trapping within it the ships of those days so that they were matted together into a kind of floating land of decay and death—"

Rip's attention was caught, Dane saw him nod. "The Sago—no—the Sargasso Sea!"

"That is so. Here, too, we have something like—a Sargasso of space which in some way traps ships, bringing them in to smash against its rocks and be held forever captive. And whatever it is must have great power. This Survey ship is no experimental prospector of the early days when calculations were faulty and engines could easily fail."

"But," Wilcox protested, "the *Queen* made a routine landing without any trouble at all!"

"Did it occur to you," Mura said, "that she might have been permitted to make such a landing—for a reason—"

That would explain a great many things, but the idea was chilling. It suggested that the *Solar Queen* was a pawn in someone's game—Rich's? And that she no longer had any control over her destiny.

"Let's get along!" Wilcox shifted his weight and started limping back to where they had left the crawler.

And from then on they made no more side expeditions hunting wrecks. There were probably more of them to be found, Dane suspected. Mura's idea had taken hold of his imagination—a Sargasso of space, drawing into its clutch wanderers of the lanes which came into the area of its baleful influence—whatever that influence could be. Why had the *Queen* been able to make a normal landing on a world where other ships crashed? Was it because they had had Rich and his men on board? Who and what was Rich?

They splashed through a stream which had been fed by the rain. It was there that Wilcox pulled up the crawler and spoke: "We must be getting close to a point opposite the *Queen*. If we don't want to miss her we should get aloft—" He pointed to the cliff.

In the end it was decided to make temporary camp with the crawler for their base, leaving Wilcox and two others there, while two more in turn climbed the heights and scouted ahead. It was now past noon and with the coming of night they would be able to move freely. So they must discover their vantage point before dark.

Rip and Mura made the first scout, but when Shannon came back to report—since they dared no longer trust to the com-calls which others might catch—it was to say that the *Queen* was in sight but farther ahead.

With caution Wilcox started up the crawler, taking it out of the valley they had just selected, through the rough edge of the plains, until he had gained a mile beyond their first proposed base. Concealed there behind a tall outcrop, he waited for a second report—and this time Mura made it.

"From there," he indicated a pinnacle of rock, "one can see well. The *Queen* is sealed—and there are others around her. As yet we have not had a chance to count them or see their arms—"

Kosti, his fear of the heights still operating to keep him from climbing, had prowled along on the plain. Now he returned with news as much to the point as Mura's.

"There is a place, right up there behind the lookout, where you can park the crawler and it can't be seen from any angle—"

Wilcox headed the machine for that point and the jetman took the astrogator's place to maneuver the crawler into the confined quarters. While Kosti and Wilcox stayed there, Dane climbed with Mura up to the spy post where Rip was already stationed, his back supported by a rock, far-distance glasses to his eyes as he faced south, looking out over the burnt-off land.

There was the sky-pointing needle of the *Queen*. It was true she was sealed, the ramp was in, the hatch closed, she might have made ready for a blastoff. Dane unhooked his own glasses and adjusted the range until the rocky terrain about the ship's fins leaped up at him.

SHIP BESIEGED

12

Even after he had the glasses focused he could not be sure that he saw more than just one strangely shaped vehicle and the two men by it. To Dane's angle of sight the party appeared to be fully exposed to those in the *Queen*. And he wondered why the Traders had not attacked—if this was the enemy.

"Right out in the open—" he said aloud. But Rip was not so sure.

"I don't think so. There's a ridge there. Visibility's poor now, but it would show in sunlight. With a stun rifle—"

Yes, with a stun rifle, and this elevation to aid him, a man might pick off those foreshortened figures—even with the range as great as it was. Unfortunately their full armament now consisted of only short range weapons—the close-to-innocuous sleep ray rods, and the blasters—potent enough, but only for in-fighting.

"Might as well wish for a bopper while you're about it," Dane commented.

Both flitters had disappeared from the landing place near the ship. He supposed they had been warped in for safety. Now he swept the ground slowly, trying to pick out any shapes which did not seem natural. And within five minutes he was sure he had pinpointed at least as many posts of two or three watchers staked out in an irregular circle about the ship. Four of the groups had transportation—machines which resembled their own crawlers to some degree but were narrower and longer, as if they had been designed to negotiate the valleys of this planet.

"Speaking of boppers," Rip's voice startled Dane because of its tenseness, "what's that? Over there—"

Dane's glasses obediently turned west. "Where?"

"See that rock that looks a little like a hoobat's head—to the left of that."

Dane searched for a rock suggesting Captain Jellico's pet monstrosity. He finally found it. To the left—now. Yes! A straight barrel. Was that—could that be the barrel of a portable bopper, wheeled into a position which commanded the ship, from which it could drop its deadly little eggs right under her fins?

A bopper couldn't begin to make any impression on a sealed ship, that was true. But it could and would bring sudden death to those venturing out into the gas which burst from its easily shattered ammunition. One had to take a bopper seriously.

"Space!" he spit out. "We must have strayed into a darcon's nest—"

"With the clawed one breathing down our necks into the bargain," agreed Rip. "Why doesn't the *Queen* lift? They could set down anywhere and pick us up later. Why stay boxed in here?"

"Do you not think," asked Mura, "that perhaps the odd behavior of our ship may have something to do with the wrecks? That maybe if the *Queen* takes to the air she might become as they are?"

"I'm no engineer," Dane said, "but I don't see how they could bring her down. They haven't any big stuff lined up out there. It'd take a maul to push her off course—"

"Did you see any signs of an attack by a maul on the *Rimbold*? There were none. She crashed as if she were drawn to this planet by some force she could not resist. Those who wait down there may have

the secret of such a force. It could be that they rule not only the surface of Limbo, but some portion of the heavens above—"

"You think that the installation is a part of it?" Rip inquired.

"Who knows?" the steward's quiet voice continued. "It might well
be." He was watching the plain through his own glasses. "I would
like to slip down there after nightfall and prowl about. If we could
have a quiet and informative talk with one of those sentries—"

Mura's tone did not change, he was his usual placid, unexcited
self. But Dane knew that the last person he would care to change
places with at that particular moment was one of the sentries Mura
wished to "talk."

"Hmmm—" Rip was studying the terrain. "It might be done at
that. Or a man could get to the *Queen* and find out what this was all
about—"

"You don't think we could reach them by com?" suggested Dane.
"We're close enough for a clear reception."

"Notice those helmets on the sentries' heads?" Rip pointed out.
"I'll bet you earth-side pay that they're linked up on our frequency
now. If we talk they'll listen—not only listen but get a fix on us. And
they know this ground better than we do. Would you like to play hide
and seek across this country in the dark?"

Dane decidedly would not. But it was difficult to relinquish using
the coms. So easy to just call and find out what might take hours and
hours of spying and risk to discover by themselves. Only, as the Masters had dinned into them for years back in the Pool, there were few
easy shortcuts in Trade. It was a matter of using your wits from first
to last, of being able to improvise on the spur of the moment such
dodges as would save your profit, your ship or your skin. And the last
two precious articles appeared to be at stake on this occasion.

"At least," Rip was continuing, "we are sure now that more than
Rich and his hand-picked boys are involved."

"Yes," Mura nodded, "it would seem that the forces ranged against
us are numerically stronger." His glasses coursed from one group of
hidden men to the next, until he had made the complete circle con-

cealed from those aboard the *Queen*. "There are perhaps fifteen out there."

"To say nothing of reinforcements they may have back in the mountains. But who in the Black Reaches of Outer Space are they?" Rip asked of the air about them.

"Something is about to happen." Mura stiffened, his attention settling on one spot.

Dane followed the steward's lead. The other was right. One of the besiegers had walked boldly out of cover and now approached the ship, waving vigorously over his head the age-old sign for parley—a strip of white cloth.

For a moment or two it appeared as if the *Queen* was not going to answer that. And then the hatch opened far above the surface of the ground. No ramp was lowered. Instead a figure paused in the opening and Dane recognized Captain Jellico.

The bearer of the white flag hesitated some distance away. Though the watchers could not see too clearly in the growing dusk, they could hear, for a voice crackled in their helmet phones, thus proving Rip right—the coms of the raiders were on the same band as their own.

"Thought it over, Captain? Ready to be sensible?"

"Is that all you want to know?" Jellico's rasp could not be mistaken. "I gave you my decision last night."

"You can sit here until you starve, Captain. Just try to get off-world—"

"If we can't get off—neither can you get in!"

"And there he speaks the truth," Mura observed. "Nothing they have down there is capable of forcing an entrance to the *Queen*. And if they are able to smash her—she will be of no use to them."

"You think that that is what they are after—the *Queen*?" hazarded Dane.

Rip snorted. "That's obvious. They don't want her to lift—they have a use for her. I'll bet that Rich brought us here just to get the *Queen*."

"There is the matter of supplies, Captain," the besieger's voice purred in their earphones. "We can afford to sit here half a year if it is necessary—you can not! Come, do not be so childish. We have offered you a fair deal all around. And you have been caught in a pinch, have you not? Your ready funds went at the auction when you bought trading rights here. Well, we are offering you better than trading rights. And we have the patience to sit it out."

But, if the speaker had the patience he vaunted, one of his fellows did not. Through the air came the crack of a stun rifle. Jellico either ducked or fell back into the ship and the hatch was clapped to. The three Traders on the cliff sat very still. It appeared that the man with the flag had not expected that move on the part of his own side. He stayed where he was for a moment before he dropped the treacherous strip of white and dived for the cover of an outcrop, from which point he squirmed back to his original post.

"That was not planned," remarked Mura. "Someone was a fraction impatient. He will suffer for his zeal—since he has just put an end to the chance of future negotiation."

"Do you think the Captain was hurt?" Dane asked.

"The old man knows all the tricks." Rip did not seem worried. "I'd say he got out in a hurry. But now they'll have to starve him into surrender. That shot is not going to get our men to come out with their hands up—"

"Meanwhile," Mura dropped his glasses to his knee, "there is the little matter of our own action. We might be able to slip through those lines in the dark, but with the ship sealed, how can we get in? They are not going to lower a line at the first hail out of the night. Not now."

Dane gazed across the rough ground which lay between the heights on which he perched and the distant ship. Yes, it might be simple to avoid the sentry post of the besiegers, they would be more intent on the ship than on the territory behind their own lines. Maybe they did not even know that some of the *Queen*'s crew had escaped their trap. But, having reached the ship, how could one get on board?

"A problem, a problem," Mura murmured.

"Aren't we on a level with the control section here?" Rip asked suddenly. "Maybe we could rig up some kind of a signal to let them know we were sending someone in—"

Dane was willing to try. He squinted along the line from where he sat to the nose of the ship.

"It will have to be done very soon," Mura warned. "Night is coming fast."

Rip looked up at the sky. The sun of the morning had long since vanished. Leaden clouds hung over them. And it was clearly twilight.

"Suppose we make a shelter—maybe out of our tunics—and light a torch in it. The range of the light would be limited at the sides—it could not be seen from below. But those on the *Queen* might catch it—"

The steward's answer was to unbuckle his equipment belt and pull at the seal latch of his tunic. Dane hurriedly followed his example. Then they crouched shivering in the cold, holding their tunics as side screens, while Rip squatted between, flashing his torch on and off in the distress signal of the Trading code. It was such a slim chance, someone would have to be in the control cabin watching at just the right angle to catch that click, click of light—a mere pinprick of radiance.

Then the night beacon of the *Queen* flashed on, striking up into the gray sky as it had fought the fog a day earlier. Only now it lit the surrounding clouds. And as the three on the cliff watched, hoping to read in this some reply to their improvised com, the yellowish beam took on a ruddier tinge.

Mura sighed with relief. "They have read us—"

"How do you know?" Dane could see nothing to lead the steward to believe that.

"They had switched on the storm ray. See, now it fades once more. But they read us!" He was smiling as he donned his tunic. "I would suggest that we compose a proper message among us and also inform Wilcox of this development. If we can communicate with the *Queen*, even if she cannot with us, something may be done to our advantage after all."

So they went down to the crawler. It did not take long to relay the news.

"But they cannot answer us." Wilcox put his finger on the weakness of the whole setup. "They wouldn't have used the storm ray if they had had any other means of letting us know they read you—"

"We'll have to send someone in. Now we can signal that he is coming and they will be waiting to take him aboard," Rip said eagerly.

Wilcox's manner suggested that he did not wholly agree with that plan. But, though they discussed it point by point, there did not seem to be any other solution.

Mura got to his feet. "The dark is coming fast. We must decide upon a plan at once, for the climb to our signal post is not one to be taken when it cannot be seen. Who is to go and when? That much we can send in code—"

"Shannon," Wilcox singled out the astrogator-apprentice, "this is the time those cat's eyes of yours will come in handy. You can see as much in the dark as Sinbad—or you seemed to that time on Baldur. Want to try to make it at, say," he consulted his watch, "twenty-one hours? That will give our playmates on the sentry posts time to settle down."

Rip's beaming face was answer enough. And he was humming as the three once more ascended the rock and took over the task of beaming the message.

"You will add," Mura remarked, "that your safe arrival is to be signaled back to us with the storm ray. We would like to rejoice in your success."

"Sure, man. But I'm not worrying." Rip's natural buoyance was returning for the first time since he had made that horrible discovery in the wrecked *Rimbold*. "This is a stroll compared to that job we had on Baldur."

Mura looked grave. "Never underestimate what may stand against you. You are experienced enough in Trade to remember that, Rip. This is no time to take unnecessary chances—"

"Not me, man! I'll be as silent and slippery as a snake out there. They will never know I passed by."

Once again the steward and Dane shed their tunics and shivered in the damp cold as Rip flashed the news of his mission across to the silent, sealed ship. There was no answer but they were certain that after their first assay at communication there had been a watcher stationed to wait for a second message.

It was arranged that Mura and Dane were to bed down on the heights while Rip went back to the crawler and waited to set out from there. When the astrogator-apprentice disappeared below, Dane moved rocks to provide them with a windbreak.

They had no source of warmth but their nearness to each other, so they crouched together in the pocket Dane had devised, with nothing to do but wait out the hours until the signal came that Rip had reached his goal.

"Lighting up," Mura murmured.

The beam from the *Queen* still beaconed in the night. But what Mura referred to were the sparks of fire which marked the fixed posts of the unknown sentries.

"Make it easier for Rip—he'll be able to avoid them," ventured Dane but his companion disagreed.

"They will be alert for trouble. Probably they have beats linking each of those with the rest and are doing sentry-go along them."

"You mean—they guess that we are here—that they are only waiting for Rip to come along—"

"That may or may not be true. But they are, of course, alert for a move from the men in the *Queen*. Tell me, Thorson, are you not now aware of something more? Can you not feel it through this rock?"

Of course he could. That beat of the installation, less heavy than it had been near the ruins, but faithful in its pattern. And now there was no fluctuation in its power as the long minutes dragged wearily by. It was running steadily at full strength.

"That," Mura continued, "is what ties the *Queen* to this earth—"

The jigsaw bits of what they had learned during the past two days were beginning to fit into a picture. Suppose these strangers who had enmeshed the *Queen* for some purpose of their own, did control a means of crashing her if she tried to lift from Limbo? It would be necessary to keep that installation, energy broadcaster, beam, or whatever it was, working all the time or the ship would make a sneak escape. Those in her must be fitting the pieces together, too—even if they did not yet know the Sargasso properties of Limbo.

"Then the only way to get out of here," said Dane slowly, "is to find the source of power and—"

"Smash it? Yes. If Rip makes contact—then we must move to that end."

"You say 'if Rip makes contact.' Don't you think he's going to?"

"You are very young in the Service, Thorson. After some voyages a man becomes very humble. He begins to realize that the quality we name on Terra 'luck' has much to do with success or failure. We can never honestly say that this or that plan of action will come to fruition in the manner we hope, there are too many governing factors over which we have no control. We do not count on any fact until it is an established reality. Shannon has many of the odds on his side. He has unusually keen night sight, a fact we discovered on a similar situation not long ago, he is used to field work, he is not easily confused. And from here he has had a chance to study the territory and the positions of the enemy. The odds are perhaps eighty percent in his favor. But there remains that twenty percent. He must be ready and we must be ready to prepare for other moves—until we see the beacon signal that he has made it."

Mura's emotionless voice unsettled Dane. It had the old illusion-pricking touch of Kamil, refined, made even more pointed and cutting. Kamil! Where was Ali? Being held by some of those now ranged about the *Queen*? Or had he been taken on to the mysterious source of power?

"What do you suppose they did with Kamil?" Dane asked aloud.

"He represents to them a source of information about us and our concerns. As such they would see that he reaches the guiding brain behind all this. And he will be safe—just as long as they have a use for him—"

But there was something vaguely sinister in that answer—a hint twisting Dane's memory to a scene he did not like to recall.

"Those men on the *Rimbold*— Was Rip right? Had they been blasted?"

"He was right." The three words were unaccented by any emotion, and the very gentleness of the reply made it the more forceful.

They talked very little after that, and only moved about when the warning stiffness of arm or leg made it necessary. On the plain the beacon continued to point starward from ship without change.

In spite of the cold and the cramp, the beat of the vibration was lulling. Dane had to fight to keep awake, using an old trick of recalling in detail one tape after another in the "Rules of Stores" he had made his study during the voyage out. If he were only back in Van Rycke's cubby now, safely engrossed in his studies, with nothing more exciting than a sharp piece of bargaining to look forward to in the morning!

A whistle, low, yet penetrating, reached their ears from the depths. That was Rip, about to set out on his risky venture. Dane held his glasses to his eyes. Though he knew very well that he could not follow the other's progress through the dark.

The rest of the hours seemed days long. Dane watched the beacon with a single-minded intensity which made his eyes ache. But there was no change. He felt Mura shift beside him, fumbling in the dark and a faint glow told him that beneath the shelter of tunic hem the other was consulting his watch.

"How long?"

"He has been out four hours—"

Four hours! It wouldn't take a man four hours to reach the *Queen* from here. Even if he had to detour and hide out at intervals to escape the sentries. It looked very much as if that twenty percent which Mura had mentioned as standing against the success of Rip's mission was indeed the part to be dealt with now.

ATTACK AND STALEMATE

13 Dawn was hinted at with a light in the east, and still the *Queen*'s beacon had not changed its hue. The watchers did not expect it to now. Something had gone wrong—Rip had never reached the ship.

Unable to stand inaction longer, Dane crept from the improvised shelter and started along the cliff on which they had set up their lookout. It formed a wall between the entrances to two of the tongue-shaped valleys—the one in which Wilcox and Kosti were encamped, the other unknown territory.

Dane sighted a trickle of stream in the second. The presence of water heralded, or had heralded, other life in his experience of Limbo. And here and now that pattern held. For he counted ten of the small checkerboard spice fields.

But this time the fields were not deserted. Two of the globe creatures worked among the plants. They stirred the ground about the roots of the spice ferns with their thread-like tentacles, their round backs bobbing up and down as they moved.

Then both of them stood upright. Since they lacked any discernible heads or features, it was difficult for Dane to guess what they were doing. But their general attitude suggested that they were either listening or watching.

Three more of the globes came noiselessly into sight. Between two of them swung a pole on which was tied the limp body of an animal about the size of a cat. No audible greeting passed between the hunters and the farmers. But they gathered in a group, dropping the pole. Through the glasses Dane saw that their finger tentacles interlocked from globe to globe until they formed a circle.

"Sooo—" The word hissed out of the early morning murk and Dane, who had been absorbed in the scene below, gave a start, as Mura's hand closed on his shoulder.

"There is a crawler coming this way—" the steward whispered.

Once more the group of globes had an aura of expectancy. They scattered, moving with a speed which surprised the Terrans. In seconds they had taken cover, leaving the fields, the stream bank deserted.

The crunch of treads on loose stone and gravel was clear to hear as a vehicle crept into the vision range of the two on the cliff. Just as Kamil had been the first to discover, the crawler was not the usual type favored by Federation men. It was longer, more narrow, and had a curious flexibility when it moved, as if its body was jointed.

One man sat behind its controls. An explorer's helmet shielded his face, but he wore the same mixture of outer garments as Rich and his men had affected.

Mura's hand on Dane's shoulder applied pressure. But Dane, too, was aware of the trap about to be sprung. Masked by a line of brush, there was stealthy movement. A globe thing came into the Traders' sight, clasping close to its upper ball body a large stone. One of its fellows joined it, similarly armed.

"—trouble." Mura's voice was a thin whisper.

The crawler advanced at a steady pace, crunching over the ground, splashing through the edge of the water. It had reached the first field now, and the driver made no effort to avoid the enclosure. Instead he drove on, the wide treads rolling flat, first the low wall, and then the carefully tended plants that it guarded.

The globe things, hidden from their enemy, scuttling on a course which paralleled that of the vehicle. Their stones were still tightly grasped and they moved with a lightning speed. By all the signs the man on the crawler was heading into an ambush.

It was when the machine plowed into the third field that the infuriated owners struck. A rain of stones, accurately hurled, fell on both crawler and driver. One crashed on the man's helmet. He gave a choked cry and half arose before he slumped forward limply over the controls. The machine ground on for a moment and then stopped, one tread tilted up against a boulder at an angle which threatened the stability of the whole vehicle.

Dane and Mura climbed down the side of the cliff. The driver might have deserved just what he had received. But he was human and they could not leave him to some alien vengeance. They could see nothing of the globes. But they took the precaution, when they had reached the valley floor, of spraying the bushes around the crawler with their sleep rays. Mura remained on guard, ready to supply a second dose of the harmless radiation while Dane ran forward to pull free the driver.

He lugged him back in a shoulder carry to the edge of the cliff where they could stand off an attack of the globes if necessary.

But either the sleep ray or the appearance on the scene of two more Terrans discouraged a second sortie. And the valley might well have been completely deserted as the two from the *Queen* stood ready, the limp body of the rescued at their feet.

"Shall we try it—" Dane nodded at the wall behind them. Mura contrived to look amused.

"Unless you are a crax seed chewer, I do not see how you are going to climb with our friend draped across your broad shoulders—"

Dane, now that it was called to his attention, could share that doubt. The cliff climbing act was one which required both hands and feet, and one could never do it with a dead weight to support.

The unconscious man groaned and moved feebly. Mura went down on one knee and studied the face framed by the dented helmet. First he unhooked the fellow's blaster belt and added it to his own armament. Then he loosened the chin strap, took off the battered headcovering and proceeded to slap the stubbled face dispassionately.

The crude resuscitation worked. Eyes blinked up at them and then the man tried to lever himself up, an operation Mura assisted with a jerk at his collar.

"It is time to go," the steward said. "This way—"

Together they got the man on his feet, and urged him along the wall, rounding the spur on which they had been perched all night, so coming to the hidden point where the other two of their party were camped.

The driver showed little interest in them, he was apparently concentrating on his uncertain balance. But Mura's grip was about his wrist and Dane guessed that that grasp was but the preliminary of one of the tricks of wrestling in which the steward was so well versed that no other of the *Queen*'s crew could defeat him.

As for Dane, he kept an eye behind, expecting any moment to be the target of a hail of those expertly thrown rocks. In a way this move they had just made would lead the Limbians to believe them one with the outlaws; and might well ruin any hopes they had cherished of establishing Trade relations with the queer creatures. And yet to leave a human at the mercy of the aliens was more than either of the Terrans could do.

Their charge spit a glob of blood and then spoke to Mura: "You one of the Omber crowd? I didn't know they'd been called in—"

Mura's expression did not change. "But this is a mission of importance, is it not? They have called many of us in—"

"Who beamed me back there? Those damned bogies?"

"The natives, yes. They threw stones—"

The man snarled. "We ought to roast 'em all! They hang around and try to crack our skulls every time we have to come through these hills. We'll have to use the blasters again—if we can catch up with 'em. Trouble is they move too fast—"

"Yes, they provide a problem," Mura returned soothingly. "Around here now—" He urged their captive around the point of the cliff into the other valley. But for the first time the man seemed to sense that something was wrong.

"Why go in here?" he asked, his pale eyes moving from one to the other of the Terrans. "This isn't a through valley."

"We have our crawler here. It would be better for you to ride—in your condition, would it not?" Mura continued persuasively.

"Huh? Yes, it might! I've a bad head, that's sure." His hand arose to his head and he winced as it touched a point above his right ear.

Dane let out his breath. Mura was running this perfectly. They were going to be able to get the fellow back where they wanted him without any trouble at all.

Mura had kept his clasp on their charge's arm, and now he steered him around a screen of boulders to face the crawler, Kosti and Wilcox. It was the machine that gave the truth away.

The captive stiffened and halted so suddenly that Dane bumped into him. His eyes shifted from the machine to the men by it. His hands went to his belt, only to tell him that he was unarmed.

"Who are you?" he demanded.

"That works two ways, fella," Kosti fronted him. "Suppose you tell us who *you* are—"

The man made as if to turn and looked over his shoulder down the valley as if hoping to see a rescue party there. Then Mura's grip screwed him back to his former position.

"Yes," the steward's soft voice added, "we greatly wish to know who you are."

The fact that he was fronted by only four must have triggered the prisoner's courage. "You're from the ship—" he announced triumphantly.

"We are from *a* ship," corrected Mura. "There are many ships on this world, many, many ships."

He might have slapped the fellow with his open hand, for the effect that speech had. And Dane was inspired to add:

"There is a Survey ship—"

The prisoner swayed, his bloodstained face pale under space tan, his lower lip pinched between his teeth as if by that painful gesture he could forego speech.

Wilcox had seated himself on the crawler. Now he calmly drew his blaster, balancing the ugly weapon on his knee pointing in the general direction of the prisoner's middle.

"Yes, there are quite a few ships here," he said. They might have been speaking of the weather, but for the set of the astrogator's jaw. "Which one do you think we hail from?"

But their captive was not yet beaten. "You're from the one out there—the *Solar Queen*."

"Why? Because no one survived in the others?" Mura asked quietly. "You had better tell us what you know, my friend."

"That's right." Kosti moved forward a pace until his many inches loomed over the battered driver. "Save us time and you trouble, if you speak up now, flyboy. And the more time it takes, the more impatient we're going to get—understand?"

It was plain that the prisoner did. The threat which underlay Mura's voice was underlined by Kosti's reaching hands.

"Who are you and what are you doing here?" Wilcox began the interrogation for the second time.

The knockout delivered by the bogies had undoubtedly softened up the driver to begin with. But Dane was inclined to believe that it was Mura and Kosti who finished the process.

"I'm Lav Snall," he said sullenly. "And if you're from the *Solar Queen*, you know what I'm doing here. This isn't going to get you anywhere. We've got your ship grounded for just as long as we want."

"This is most interesting," Wilcox drawled. "So that ship out on the plain is grounded for as long as you want, is it? Where's your maul—invisible?"

The prisoner showed his teeth in a grin which was three quarters sneer. "We don't need a maul—not here on Limbo. This whole world's a trap—when we want to use it."

Wilcox spoke to Mura. "Was his head badly injured?"

The steward nodded. "It must have been—to addle his wits so. I can not judge truly, I am no medic."

Snall rose to the bait. "I'm not space-whirly if that's what you mean. You don't know what we found here—a Forerunner machine and it still operates! It can pull ships right out of space—bring 'em in here to crash. When that's running your *Queen* can't lift—not even if she were a Patrol Battlewagon, she couldn't. In fact we can pull in a battlewagon if and when we want to—!"

"Most enlightening," was Wilcox's comment. "So you've got some sort of an installation which can pull ships right out of space. That's a new one for me. Did the Whisperers tell you all about it?"

Snall's cheeks showed a tinge of dark red. "I'm not whirly, I tell you!"

Kosti laid his hands on the prisoner's shoulders and forced him to sit down on a rock. "We know," he repeated in a mock soothing tone. "Sure—there's a great big machine here with a Forerunner running it. It reaches out and grabs—just like this!" He clutched with his own big fist at the empty air an inch or two beyond Snall's nose.

But the prisoner had recovered a little of his poise. "You don't have to believe me," he returned. "Just watch and see what happens if that pigheaded Captain of yours tries to upship here. It won't be pretty. And it won't be long before you're gathered up, either—"

"I suppose you have ways of running us down?" Wilcox's left eyebrow slanted up under his helmet. "Well, you haven't contacted us yet and we've done quite a bit of traveling lately."

Snall looked from one to another. There was a faint puzzlement in his attitude.

"You're wearing Trade dress," he repeated aloud the evidence gathered by his eyes. "You have to be from the *Queen*."

"But you're not quite sure, are you?" Mura prodded. "We may be from some other spacer you trapped with this Forerunner device. Are you certain that there are no other survivors of crashes roaming through these valleys?"

"If there are—they won't be walking about long!" was Snall's quick retort.

"No. You have your own way of dealing with them, don't you? With this?" Wilcox lifted the blaster so that it now centered upon the prisoner's head rather than his middle. "Just as you handled some of those aboard the *Rimbold*."

"I wasn't in on that!" Snall gabbled. In spite of the morning chill there were drops of moisture ringing his hairline.

"It seems to me that you are all outlaws," Wilcox continued, still in a polite, conversational tone. "Are you sure you haven't been Patrol Posted?"

That did it. Snall jumped. He got about a foot away before Kosti dragged him back.

"All right—so I've been Posted!" he snarled at Wilcox as the jet-man smacked him down on the rock once more. "What are you going to do about it? Burn me when I'm unarmed? Go ahead—do it!"

Traders could be ruthless if the time and place demanded ice-cold tactics, but Dane knew now that the last thing Wilcox would do was to burn Snall down in cold blood. Even if the fact that he was Patrol Posted as a murderous criminal, with a price on his head, put him outside the law and absolved his killer from any future legal complications.

"Why should we kill you?" asked Mura calmly. "We are Free Traders. I think that you know very well what that means. A swift death by a blaster is a very easy way into the Greater Space, is it not? But out on the Rim, in the Wild Worlds, we have learned other tricks. So you do not believe that, Lav Snall?"

The steward had made no threatening grimaces, his pleasant face was as blandly cheerful as ever. But Snall's eyes jerked away from that face. He swallowed in a quick gulp.

"You wouldn't—" he began again, but there was no certainty in his protest. He must have realized that the competition he now faced was far more dangerous than he had estimated. There were tales about Free Traders, they were reputed to be as tough as the Patrol, and not nearly so bound by regulation. He believed that Mura meant exactly what he said.

"What do you want to know—"

"The truth," returned Wilcox.

"I've been giving it to you—straight," Snall protested. "We've found a Forerunner installation back in the mountains. It acts on ships—pulls them right out of space to crack up here after they move into the beam, or ray, or whatever it is. I don't know how it works. Nobody's even seen the thing except a few picked men who know something about com stuff—"

"Why didn't it act on the *Solar Queen* when she came in?" Kosti asked. "She landed perfectly."

"'Cause the thing wasn't turned on. You had Salzar on board, didn't you?"

"And who is Salzar?" It was Mura's turn to ask the question.

"Salzar—Gart Salzar. He was the first to see what a sweet thing we found here. He got us all under cover when Survey was snooping around. We lay low and Salzar knew that if this world was auctioned off we'd be in real trouble. He took a cruiser we'd patched up and beat the *Griswold* back to Naxos, and then contacted you. So we get a nice trader all empty and waiting to load our stuff—"

"Your loot? And how did *you* reach here—crash?"

"Salzar did ten—twelve years ago. He didn't make too bad a landing and he and those men of his who were still alive went snooping. They found the Forerunners' machine and studied it until they learned a bit about working it. Now they can switch it off when they want to. It was dead when Survey was prowling around here because Salzar was off planet and we were afraid we'd get him when he came in."

"A pity you didn't," Wilcox remarked. "And where is this machine?"

Snall shook his head. "I don't know." Kosti moved a step closer and Snall added swiftly, "That's the truth! Only Salzar's boys know where it is or how it works."

"How many of them?" Kosti asked.

"Salzar, and three, maybe four others. It's back in the moun-tains—there somewhere—" He stabbed a finger, a shaking finger, in the general direction of the range.

"I think you can do better than that," Kosti was beginning when Dane cut in:

"What was Snall doing driving that crawler in here—if he didn't know where he was going?"

Mura's eyelids dropped as he adjusted the buckle of his helmet. "I think we have been slightly remiss. We should have a sentry aloft. There may be one of Snall's friends along."

Snall studiously studied the toes of his boots. Dane went to the cliff.

"I'll take a look-see," he offered.

To his first sight the situation on the plain had not changed. The *Queen*, all hatches sealed, rested just as she had at twilight the night before. With his glasses he could make out the small encampments of outlaws. But close to his own post he saw something else.

One of the strange crawlers had pulled away from the nearest camp. Seated behind the driver were two others and between them a fourth passenger, his brown Trade tunic not to be mistaken.

"Rip!" Though Dane could not see that prisoner's face he was sure the captive was Shannon. And the crawler was headed toward the valley where the bogies had ambushed the first!

Now was their chance to not only rescue Rip but make a bigger gap in the besiegers' force. Dane crawled to the edge of the cliff and, not daring to call, waved vigorously to attract the attention of those below. Mura and Wilcox nodded and Kosti headed the prisoner into greater seclusion. Then Dane sought a vantage point and waited with rising excitement for the enemy crawler to enter the valley.

TRUMPET OF JERICHO

14

"It is time, I believe," Mura had come up on the lookout point, "to follow the tactics of our fellow fighters, these 'bogies.' How is your throwing arm, Thorson?" He stooped and searched the ground, rising a few moments later grasping a round stone about as big as his fist.

Taking aim he pitched it at an angle into the valley and they saw and heard it strike against a rock there. Dane saw the reason for such an attack upon the crawler. Blaster fire was no respecter of persons. In an exchange of such potent forces Rip might well be killed or maimed. But rocks expertly thrown from above would not only knock out the outlaws, but would suggest an attack by native Limbians and not betray the identity of the attackers.

Kosti circled around the foot of the cliff and took cover below the perch favored by Mura, while Dane skimmed across the valley and climbed above eye level to a narrow ledge on which he might crouch with a pile of hastily collected ammunition.

They were not given long for such preparations, the clinking passage of the crawler echoed ahead as a warning and the three Traders took to cover as the vehicle crept into sight across the uneven terrain. It crashed through bushes until the driver slowed to a halt. His helmet com-unit must have been on, for, while his natural voice could only have been an undistinguishable murmur to those in hiding, his words were loud in their ears.

"There's Snall's wagon—piled up! What's been—?"

One of Rip's guards scrambled off the crawler as if to go forward and investigate. And in that moment Mura's arm signaled Dane to attack.

A stone thudded against the helmet of the would-be investigator, sending him off balance to clutch at the tread of the crawler for support. Dane slammed another in his direction and then aimed for the driver of the machine.

They were yelling now and Rip had come to life. Though his arms were tied behind him, he threw himself at the man to his left, his effort carrying them both to the ground beyond. The driver turned on the power of the crawler so that it ground ahead through the rain of stones the three Traders hurled at it.

One of the outlaws had pulled himself aboard again and now the other wriggled from under Rip's body. He had his blaster in hand and he bent over Shannon with an evil grin. Then his face was smashed into a red pulp. He screamed horribly and reeled back. The one who had managed to climb aboard looked back in time to witness his fall.

"Kraner—those little beasts got Kraner! No, don't wait to collect that Trader! If you do they'll get us!"

The crawler kept on toward the mountains. For some reason the two on board it had not used their blasters to rake the bushes. The very unexpectedness of the attack and the loss of one of their company left them only with the thought of escape.

They rounded the length of the stranded crawler and were out of sight before Kosti crept out of hiding and went down to Rip, where Dane joined him seconds later.

Shannon lay on his side, his arms bound at a painful angle behind him, his face showing a closed eye surrounded with a dark bruise, a cut lip, raw and bloody.

"You *have* been to the wars," Kosti grunted as he knelt to saw at the cords with his bush knife.

Rip's words were mumbled as he tried to move his torn mouth. "They jumped me—I was almost to the *Queen* when they jumped me. They've the ship pinned here—some sort of ray which crashes any ship within a certain distance of the planet—"

Dane slipped an arm under Rip's shoulders and helped him to sit up. The other gave a grunt and a muffled exclamation as he moved, one hand going to his side.

"More damages?" Kosti reached out to unseal Rip's tunic but Shannon parried the investigating hand.

"Nothing we can fix here and now. Think I've cracked a rib—or maybe two. But, listen, they've the *Queen*—"

"We know. Picked up a prisoner," Dane told him. "He was driving that crawler over there. Told us all about what's going on here. Maybe, using him, we can make some sort of a deal. Can you walk—?"

"Yes, it might be well to withdraw." Mura stepped down to where they were. "They had their coms on when we jumped them. It is uncertain how much of the succeeding events have been overheard by their fellows."

Rip could walk, with support. And they got him around to their own crawler and Wilcox.

"Any sign of Kamil?" Kosti wanted to know.

"They have him all right," Rip replied. "But I think that he's with their main party. They have quite a few men. And they can keep the *Queen* here until she rusts away—if they want to."

"So Snall here has already informed us," Wilcox observed bleakly. "He also says that he does not know where this mysterious installation is. I'm inclined to doubt that—"

At that the bound and gagged prisoner wriggled and made muffled sounds, trying to indicate his sincerity.

"Down that valley is one way in, at least in to their major supply depot and barracks," Rip informed them. "And the installation can't be too far from that."

Dane touched the wriggling Snall with the toe of his boot. "D'you suppose we could exchange this one for Ali? Or at least use him to get us into the place?"

Rip answered that. "I doubt it. They're a pretty hard lot. Snall's life or death wouldn't matter much as far as they are concerned."

And the look in those bloodshot eyes above the gag Kosti had planted, bore out that Snall agreed with that. He had little faith in assistance from his own companions unless his rescue was necessary to their preservation.

"Three of us on our feet and able to go, and two crooks," Wilcox mused. "How many men have they back in the mountains, Shannon, any idea of that?"

"Maybe a hundred. It seems to be a well organized outfit," Rip replied dispiritedly.

"We can sit here until we starve," Kosti broke the ensuing silence, "and that won't get us anywhere, will it? I'd say take some chances and hope for luck. It can't all be bad!"

"Snall could show us the way in—at least into the part he knows," Dane said. "And we could scout around—size up the country and the odds."

"If we could only contact the *Queen*!" Wilcox beat his knee with his fist.

"With the sun up—it is now—there is perhaps a way," Mura began.

His way entailed going back to the wrecked crawler in the second valley, and unscrewing a bright metal plate which backed the driver's seat. With Dane's help, the steward got this to the top of the cliff. And they wedged their prize at an angle until they caught the sun on its surface and flashed the light across the mile or so of rugged territory which lay between them and the ship.

Mura smiled. "This may do it. It should be as good as our torches in the night if it works. And unless those outlaws down there have eyes in the back of their skulls, it will not be seen except from control—"

But once their crude com was in place they had other preparations to make. Wilcox, Rip, Kosti and the prisoner moved from the hideout in one valley on into the other. The strange crawler was righted and found to be undamaged and ready to move. And while the other four waited Mura and Dane climbed once more to the heights where they sweated over the plate until they laboriously flashed twice over their message to the *Queen*.

Then there was nothing to do but stay to see if their code had been read. Only if the ship made the proper reply in action could they move.

And that answer came just as Dane had given up hope. Round ports blinked like eyes on the sides of the *Queen*! There was a bark of sound and smoke arose by a hidden pocket of besiegers—the one which lay between the ship and the valley. Their message had been read, those on the ship would keep the enemy bracketed while the party in the valley made their dash for the outlaw headquarters on a desperate attempt at surprise.

They were all able to ride on this carrier, the prisoner sandwiched in between Dane and Mura, Kosti at the controls. It had what their own crawler had lacked, handholds, and they clung to these as the thing rattled along.

Dane watched the bushy slopes they passed. He had not forgotten the bogie attack. It might be true that the creatures were nocturnal. But on the other hand, once aroused, perhaps the globes might still be in hiding there, waiting to cut off any small party.

The valley curved and narrowed. Now under the jolting carrier the surface was mostly stream bed and the water crept up to lap at the edge of the platform. There were signs here, as there had been in the valley near the ruins, that this way had been in use as a road— scratches on the rocks, tracks crushed in the gravel.

Then before them the stream became a small falls, splashing into a pool and the valley ended in a barrier cliff. Kosti jerked the gag from Snall's mouth.

"All right," he said in the tone of one who was not going to be put off, "what do we do to get through here, bright boy?"

Snall licked his puffed lips and glowered back. Bound and gagged as he had been, helpless as he was, he had regained a large measure of his confidence.

"Find out for yourself," he retorted.

Kosti sighed. "I hate to waste time, fella. But if you must be softened up, you're going to be—get me?"

Something else got them all first. A stone missed Kosti's head by a scant inch as he bent over Snall. And a larger one struck the captive's body, bringing a sharp cry of pain out of him.

"Bogies!" Dane fanned his sleep ray up a wall where he could see nothing move, but from which he was sure the stones had been thrown.

Another rock cracked viciously against the crawler as Wilcox hit dirt on the other side, pulling Rip with him to shelter half under the machine. Mura was using his ray, too, standing unconcerned knee deep in the pool and beaming the cliff foot by foot as if he had all the time in the world and intended to make this a thorough job.

It was Snall who ended that strange blind battle. Kosti had dragged him to safety and must have cut his bonds so that he could move with greater speed. But now the outlaw flung himself out of shelter, straight for the controls of the carrier. He brought his fist down upon a button set in the panel and was rewarded by a high pitched tinkle— a tinkle which resounded in the Terrans' heads until Dane had to fight to keep his hands from his ears.

The answer to this assault upon their eardrums was as preposterous as anything Dane had ever witnessed in a Video performance. The supposedly solid rock wall fronting the end of the valley opened, one piece of the stone falling back to provide a dark gap. And, since their captive was prepared for that he was the first through the door, darting from under Kosti's clutching hands.

With an inarticulate roar the jetman followed Snall. And Dane pounded after both of them into the maw of the cliff. From the sunlight of Limbo they were translated to a twilight gray, strung out like beads on a string, with Snall, proving himself a good distance runner, well at the head.

Dane was inside the straight corridor before his common sense took command once more. He shouted to Kosti and his voice echoed in a hollow boom. Though he slowed, the other two kept on into the dusky reaches ahead.

Dane turned back to the entrance, still undecided. To be cut off here—their party divided. What should he do, run after Kosti, or try to bring in the others? He was in time to see Mura come in at a walking pace. And then, to Dane's horror, the outlet to the world closed! There was a clang of metal meeting metal and the sunlight was instantly cut to evening.

"The door!" Dane hurled himself at the masked opening with the same fervor with which he had followed Snall into the corridor. But before he reached that spot Mura's steadying grip closed on his arm, restraining him with a strength he had forgotten the smaller man possessed.

"Do not be alarmed," the steward said. "There is no danger. Wilcox and Shannon are in safety. They are armed with the sleep rays, in addition they know how to operate the horn to open the gate when necessary. But where is Karl? Has he disappeared?"

Mura's tone had a soothing effect. The little man gave such an impression of unruffled efficiency that Dane lost that panic which had sent him running for the entrance.

"The last I saw he was still after Snall."

"Let us hope that he has caught up with him. I would be better pleased if we walked these ways with Snall under our control—not with him somewhere ahead to warn his companions."

They hurried on and discovered that the corridor made a sharp turn to the left. Dane listened, hoping to hear the sounds of running feet. But when the thump-thump did come it was made by a single pair of boots. And a minute later the jetman barged into view, his face very sober in the wan light radiated from the smooth walls about them.

"Where's Snall?" Dane asked.

Kosti grimaced. "He got through one of those condemned walls back there—"

"Just where?" Mura went in the direction from which the jetman had just come.

"The door snapped shut as I got to it," Kosti protested. "We can't follow him. Unless one of you brought that tootler off the crawler."

The passage stretched only a short distance beyond, ending in a wall as blank of any opening as the cliffs without. Though this was not of stone but of the seamless substance which made the buildings in the Forerunner ruins.

"This wall?" Mura thumped the surface as Kosti nodded gloomily.

"Can't see any opening there now—"

The humming vibration, to which they had become so accustomed that they no longer consciously noted it, sang through the walls, through the flooring under their feet. How much that sonic resonance added to their feeling of uneasiness it was hard to tell. But the narrow corridor, the pallid light, fed their sensation of being trapped.

"Looks as if we are stuck," the jetman observed, "unless we go out into the valley again. How about that? Where's Wilcox and Shannon?"

Dane explained. But he, too, hoped that the others would use the horn and open the outer door. With the intention of getting back to the entrance he walked along the hall. That passage had run straight, he remembered, and then there had been a right angle turn around which Kosti had disappeared in pursuit of Snall—

But when Dane came to that corner and made the turn he was fronted not by the hall he remembered, but a pocket of some three or four feet. He stopped, bewildered. There had been only one corridor—with no openings along its sides. Before him now should be a smooth stretch leading to the outer door. But instead here was another wall. He reached out and his nails scraped on its slick surface. It was there all right—no illusion.

A muffled cry brought him about and he was just in time to see another barrier appear out of the side wall to seal off a second segment of the passage, one to cut him away from the others.

Dane threw himself forward, barely getting through the narrowing space. And he might not have made it had Kosti not come to his aid and used his bull's strength to wrestle against the sliding wall. But as Dane won to the other side, it clicked triumphantly into place and they were boxed in a six foot section of corridor.

"Neat," Kosti commented. "Got us shut up until they have time to attend to us."

Mura shrugged. "It cannot now be doubted that Snall got through with his alarm."

But the steward did not appear bothered. Kosti thumped the wall, listening intently as if he hoped to discover the trick of its opening by the sound he so invoked.

"Remote control, of course," Mura continued in his placid tone. "Yes, they will now believe that they have us safe—"

"Only they don't, do they?" Observance of Mura led Dane to that queston.

"That we shall see. The outer door is controlled by sonics. I heard Tang say that the installation interference lies partly in the non-audible range. So it may be we have an answer to this trap."

He unsealed the front of his tunic and groped in the inner breast pocket all Traders used for their most prized possessions. He took out a three inch tube of polished white substance which might have been bone.

Kosti stopped his thumping. "Say—that's your Feedle call—"

"Just so. Now we shall see if it can be used for another purpose than to summon the insects of Karmuli—"

He put the miniature pipe to his lips and blew though no sound issued to be caught by Terran hearing. Kosti's shade of elation vanished.

"No use—"

Mura smiled. "You have no patience, Karl. This has ten ultrasonic notes. I have only used one. Give me a chance to try the others before you are sure we do not possess a key to these doors."

There followed long moments of silence with no visible result.

"Not going to work—" Kosti shook his head.

But Mura paid no attention. At intervals he took the pipe from his lips, rested, and then tried again. Dane was certain that he must have tried more than ten notes, but the steward showed no sign of discouragement.

"That's more than ten notes," accused Kosti.

"The signal that opened the first door employed three. The same number combination may apply here." He raised the pipe once more.

Kosti sat down on the floor, obviously divorcing himself from proceedings he deemed useless. Dane squatted beside him. But Mura's patience was infinite. One hour passed—by Dane's watch, and they were well into the second. Dane wondered about their air supply. Unless it oozed through the walls as did the light, he could see no way in which it was renewed. And yet that about them was fresh.

"That tootling," Kosti sounded fretful, "isn't going to do any good. You'll wear the pipe out before you get through this—" he struck his hand against the side wall.

And under his touch the section of wall moved, showing a dark crack a couple of inches wide extending from the floor to a point six feet up.

PRISONER'S MAZE

15

"You've done it!" Dane cried to Mura as Kosti tore at the opening, forcing it larger—the door resisting as if it had not moved for a long time.

"This isn't the right way," the jetman protested even as he pushed.

"Not the corridor, no," agreed Mura. "But this *is* a way out of our present trap and as such it is not to be despised. Also it is not one in general use, or so I would judge by its stubbornness. Therefore, an even better path for us. I must have hit upon a rarer sonic combination—" He wiped the tiny pipe carefully and put it away.

Though Kosti forced the door open as wide as it would go, the resulting entrance was a narrow one. Mura negotiated it without trouble, but Dane and the jetman had to squeeze. And for one dangerous moment it seemed that the latter might not be able to make it. Only by shedding his bulky equipment belt and his outdoor tunic could he scrape by.

They found themselves in a second corridor, one more narrow than that in which they had been imprisoned. The same gray light glowed from the walls. But as Dane stepped forward his feet were cushioned and he looked down to see that his boots stirred fine dust, dust thick enough to coat the floor an inch or more in depth.

Mura freed his belt torch and sent its beam ahead. Save where they had disturbed it, that dust was smooth, without track. No one had walked this way for a long, long time—perhaps not since the Forerunners had left this mountain citadel.

"Hey!" Kosti's startled cry drew their attention. Where the narrow door had been was now once more smooth wall. Their retreat had been cut off.

"They've trapped us again!" he added hoarsely. But Mura shook his head.

"I think not. There is perhaps some closing mechanism that operates automatically, which we activated merely by passing it. No one uses this passage—or hasn't for years. I am willing to believe that Rich and the others do not even know of its existence. Let us see where it will lead us." He pattered ahead eagerly.

The corridor paralleled for a space that wider hall which had been turned into a trap. Its smooth walls showed no other hint of openings. There might be innumerable doors along it, all attuned to some combination of whistled notes, Dane thought, but they had neither the time nor the energy to explore that possibility.

"Air—"

Dane did not need that exclamation from Mura—he had already scented it. Cutting across the dusty, dead atmosphere of the way was a breath of stronger air—a puff which carried with it the chill of the outer world, and a very faint hint of growing stuff which out in the open might not have been discernible at all.

The three reached the point from which that came, and found an opening in the wall. Beyond, audible above the beat of the installation, was a rushing sound. Dane thrust his hand out into the square of dark and the current of air, blowing as if sucked in by the mountain, pulled gently at his fingers.

"Ventilation system," Kosti's engineering knowledge was intrigued. He put head and shoulders into the opening. "Big enough to travel through," he reported after using his torch up and down the channel beyond.

"Something to keep in mind," Mura agreed. "But first let us get to the end of this particular way."

In twenty minutes they got to the end, another blank wall. Kosti was not disheartened this time.

"Bring out the tootler, Frank," was his solution, "and open her up for us—"

But Mura did not reach for the pipe. Instead he swept his torch carefully over the wall. This was not the smooth material of the Forerunners' work, but the rough native stone of the mountain.

"I do not think that this will respond to any tootling," he remarked. "This is the end of the road and it is truly sealed—"

"But a passage should lead somewhere!" Dane protested.

"Yes. Undoubtedly there are many openings we cannot see. And we do not know the sonic combinations to unlock them. I do not think it wise to waste time trying to find any such. Let us return to that air duct. If it supplies a series of passages it may let us out into another one—"

So they went back to the duct As Kosti had said, it was large, large enough that the jetman and Dane might travel it—if they went on hands and knees. And it lacked the dust which carpeted the side passage.

One after another they swung into it, and into the dark as they moved from the entrance. For here was none of the ghostly radiance which gave limited light to the corridors.

Mura crawled first, his torch beaming on. They were in a tube of generous proportions, and around them passed air which had come from the outside. But the steady beat of the installation crept up their arms and legs from contact with the surface.

The steward switched off his torch. "Light ahead—" his voice was no more than a husky whisper.

When Dane's eyes adjusted to the lack of torchlight he saw it too—a round circle of pale gray. They had found the end of the vent.

But as they came up to that exit they found themselves fronted by a grille of metal, a mesh wide enough to allow passage of their hands through the squares. And beyond it lay a vast open space. Mura looked through and for the first time since he had known him Dane heard the unusually calm steward give a gasp of real surprise. Dane prodded his back suggesting that he and Kosti also wanted to see.

Mura flattened himself against the wall of the tube so that Dane could take his place. The space beyond was huge—as if the whole of a mountain interior had been hollowed out to hold a most curious structure. For, when the cargo-apprentice squirmed forward he looked down upon the strangest building he had ever seen.

It was roofless, its outer walls coming up to within six feet of the ventilation grille. But those walls—they ran crazily at curves and angles, marking off irregular spaces which bore small resemblances to ordinary rooms. Corridors began nowhere and ended in six, or eight-sided chambers without other exit. Or a whole series of rooms were linked—for no purpose since the end ones possessed neither entrance nor exit.

The walls were thick, at least three feet wide. A man could swing down and walk along them, so discovering the purpose of the muddled maze, or winning completely across the cave. And since there was no way back for them, that is what the Terrans must do. Dane inched back to allow Kosti his turn at the grille.

With a grunt of surprise the jetman viewed the weird scene. "What's it for?" he wanted to know. "It doesn't make sense—"

"Maybe not our brand of sense, no," Mura agreed. "But the solidity of the work suggests a very definite purpose. No one builds such erections for a mere whim."

Dane reached over Kosti's shoulder to pull at the grille. "We'll have to get through this—"

"Yes, and then what?" the jetman wanted to know. "Do we grow wings?"

"We can get down to the top of that wall. They're wide enough to walk on. So we can get across on them—"

Kosti was very quiet. Then his big hands went out to the grille, testing the fastenings. "Take a while to get this loose." From his belt he took his small tool kit and busied himself about the frame of the netting.

They ate while they crouched there, rations from their emergency kits. Since the gray light of the cave neither waxed nor waned, there was no measurement of time save as recorded on their watches. It might have been the middle of the night—their timekeepers said it was afternoon.

Kosti gulped his vita-cube and went back to work on the grille. It was well into the second hour before he put away his tools.

"Now!" he pushed gently at the grille and it folded out, leaving the end of the tube open. But he did not swing through as Dane expected. Instead he crawled back and allowed the others to pass him. Mura thrust his head through the opening and then looked back at Dane.

"I shall have to have help to reach the wall. I am too short—"

He held out his hands and Dane clamped a hold about his wrists. Mura backed cautiously out of the vent and for a moment his weight pulled Dane forward. In that same instant the younger man felt Kosti's grip about his hips giving him the anchorage he needed as he lowered the steward to the wall.

"Made it!" Mura trotted several feet to the right on the wall and stood waiting.

Dane turned to lower himself to the same level.

"Good luck!" Kosti said out of the shadows. Instead of crouching ready to follow, the jetman had moved back in the tube.

"What do you mean?" Dane asked, chilled by something in the other's attitude.

"You've got to go this next stretch by yourselves, fella," Kosti returned calmly enough. "I haven't any head for heights. I can't balance along on those walls down there—two steps and I'd be over the edge."

Dane had forgotten the big man's disability. But what were they going to do? The only way out of here lay across the maze of walls, a maze Kosti could not tread. On the other hand, they could not leave the jetman here.

"Listen, boy," Kosti continued. "You two will have to go on. I'll stay right here. If there is a way out and you find it, well, then maybe I can make it. But, until you are sure, there's no use in my going along to foul you up. That's only good sense—"

Maybe it was good sense, but Dane could not accept it. However, a moment later he had no chance to protest. Kosti's hands were iron about his wrists, the jetman pushed him to the edge of the duct and thrust him through, dangling him until his boots scraped the wall. Then Kosti let go.

"Kosti won't come— He says he can't make it!"

Mura nodded. "To walk these—" he indicated the maze of walls, "would be impossible for him now. But if we can find a way out— then we can return and guide him. We will move faster alone, and Karl knows that—"

Still feeling as if he were deserting Kosti, Dane reluctantly followed the steward who picked a cat's surefooted way along the wall out into the scrambled pattern beyond. The walls were about twenty feet high and the rooms and corridors they formed were bare of any furnishings. There were no signs that anyone had been there for centuries. That is, there was not, until Mura gave a sudden exclamation and aimed the beam of his torch down into a narrow room.

Dane crowded up beside him to see it, too, a tangle of white bones, a skull staring hollow-eyed back at them. The maze had had an inhabitant once, one who remained for eternity.

Mura swung the beam in slow circles about the skeleton. There were some dark rags of clothing, and the light glimmered back at them from a buckle of untarnished metal.

"A prisoner," said the steward slowly. "A man shut into this could wander perhaps forever and never find his way out—"

"You mean that he has been here since—since—" Dane could not

name the stretch of time which had elapsed since the destruction of
the city, the burn-off of Limbo.

"I think not. This one, he was human—like us. He has been here a
long time certainly, but not so long as it has been since the builders left
this maze. Others have found it, and a use for so puzzling a structure."

Now as they went from one wall to the next, twisting and turning,
but always aiming at the center of the maze, they kept careful watch
for other remains in the sections below. The whole space filled with
this curious honeycomb erection was much larger, Dane came to realize, than it had appeared from the air duct. There must be several
square miles of plain solid walls crossing, curving, and crisscrossing
to shut in nothing but oddly shaped emptiness.

"For a reason," Mura murmured. "This must have a purpose, been
made for a reason—but why? The geometry is wrong—as were the
lines of the buildings in the city. This is Forerunner work. But why—
why should they contrive such a thing?"

"For a prison?" Dane suggested. "Put someone in here and they
would never get out. Prison and execution chamber in one."

"No," Mura shook his head. "It is too large an undertaking—men
do not go to such lengths to handle their criminals. There are shorter
and less arduous methods for imposing justice."

"But the Forerunners may not have been 'men.'"

"Not our kind of 'men,' perhaps. But what do we mean by the
word 'man'? We use it loosely to mean an intelligent being, able in
part to rule both his environment and his destiny. Surely the Forerunners were 'men' by those tests. But you can not lead me to think
that they meant this merely as a prison and place of execution!"

In spite of the fact that they were both surefooted and had a head
for heights, neither hurried on these high narrow ways. Dane discovered that to stare too much at the passages and the rooms had an odd
effect on his sense of balance and it was necessary to pause now and
then and gaze up into the neutral gray overhead in order to settle an
uneasy stomach. And all the while through the walls there arose the

beat of the mighty machine which must be housed somewhere within the mountain range of which this maze could be a not insignificant part. As Mura had pointed out the geometry of the place was "wrong" in Terran sight, it produced in the Traders a sensation which bordered on fear.

They found the second dead man well beyond the first. And this time their light picked out a tunic with insignia they knew—a Survey man.

"It may not have been built for a prison," Dane commented, "but they must be using it for one now."

"This one has been dead for months," Mura kept his light trained on the huddled body. But Dane refused to look again. "He may have been from the *Rimbold*—or from some other lost ship."

"They could have bagged more than one Survey ship with that infernal machine of theirs. I'll wager there're a good lot of wrecks lying about."

"That is the truth." Mura arose from his knees. "And for this poor one we can do no good. Let us go—"

Only too eager to get away from that mute evidence of an old tragedy, Dane started on, moving from one wall to the corner of an adjoining one.

"Wait—!" The steward raised his hand as well as his voice in that emphatic order.

Obediently Dane halted. The steward's whole stance expressed listening. Then Dane too caught that sound, the ring of boots on stone, space boots with their magnetic sole plates clicking in an irregular rhythm as if the wearer was reeling as he ran. Mura listened, then he took a quick turn to the right and headed back in the general direction from which they had just come.

The sound died away and Mura quested about like a hunting hound, making short assays right and left, shining his torch into one narrow, angled compartment after another.

He was stopping above a section of corridor which ran reasonably straight when the click of those steps began again. But this time they were slower, with intervals between, as if the runner was almost at the end of his strength. Some other poor devil was trapped in here—if they could only find him! Dane pushed on as avidly as Mura.

But in here sound was a tricky guide. The walls echoed, muffled or broadcast it, so that they could not be sure of anything but the general direction. They worked their way along, about two sections apart, flashing the light into each cornered room.

Dane followed his narrow footing halfway around a room which had six walls, each of a different length, and transferred to the top of one which was part of a curving hallway. Then he sighted movement at one of those curves, a figure who lurched forward, one hand on the wall for support.

"Over here!" he called to the steward.

The man below had come to the end of that hall—another wall—and as he half fell against the obstruction and slipped to the floor he groaned. Then he lay motionless, facedown, twenty feet below his would-be rescuer. And Dane, eyeing that perfectly smooth expanse, did not see how they could get down to offer aid.

Mura ran lightly up the narrow footpaths as if he had spent all his life traveling maze walls. His circle of light touched Dane's as they spotlighted the body.

There was no mistaking the ripped tunic of their Service. The captive was a Trader—one of their own. They did not know whether he was aware of their torches, but suddenly he moaned and rolled over on his back, exposing a face cut and bruised, the result of a skillful and brutal beating. Dane might not have been able to recognize him but Mura was certain.

"Ali!"

Perhaps Kamil heard that, or perhaps it was just his steel will which roused him. He moaned again and then uttered some undistinguishable words through torn lips as his puffed and swollen eyes turned up toward them.

"Ali—" Mura called. "We are here. Can you attend—do you understand?"

Kamil's blackened face was up, he forced out coherent words. "Who—? Can't see!"

"Mura, Thorson," the steward identified them crisply. "You are hurt?"

"Can't see. Lost—Hungry—"

"How are we going to get down?" Dane wanted to know. If they only had the ropes which had linked them to the crawler in the fog! But those were behind and here were no substitutes.

Mura unhooked his belt. "Your belt and mine—"

"They aren't long enough, even together!"

"No, not in themselves, but we shall see—"

Dane shed his belt and watched the steward buckle it end to end with his own. Then the smaller man spoke to Thorson.

"You must lower me. Can you do it?"

Dane looked about doubtfully. The wall top was smooth and bare of anything in the way of an anchor. If he couldn't take the weight of the steward he would be jerked over and they would both fall. But there was no other way.

"Do my best—" He lay belly down on the wall, hooking the toes of his boots on either side and thrusting his left arm out and down into the neighboring room. Mura had drawn his blaster and was making careful adjustments to its barrel.

"Here I go—" With the blaster in one hand the steward swung over, his other fist twisted in the rope of linked belts. Dane held on grimly in spite of the tearing wrench in his shoulders.

He blinked and ducked his head at a sudden flash of burning fire. The fumes of blaster fire assaulted his throat and nose and he understood at last what Mura was attempting. The steward was burning out hand and foot holds in the smooth surface of the wall as he descended, cutting a ladder to reach Ali.

THE HEART OF LIMBO

16

All at once Mura's weight was gone, the strain on his shoulders no longer pulled him apart. Dane looked over the edge of the wall. A series of holes, black near him, still glowing red farther down, were clear to see in the gloom. His aching fingers released hold on the belts and they clattered to the floor.

When the red faded from the last of the holes the blaster had cut, Dane pulled on the gloves, clipped to his tunic cuffs against the cold of Limbo, and swung over to test the ladder. Though it ended well above the floor, he dropped the last few feet without difficulty.

Mura had out his aid kit and was working on Ali's beaten face as Dane came up.

"The torch," the steward ordered impatiently, "give me some light here!"

So Dane provided the light needed for the job of temporary patchwork. When the steward was done, Ali was able to see a little and had been supplied with a vita-cube and a limited drink of emergency stimulant. Ht could not twist his battered features with a smile, but some of the old light tone was back in his voice as he spoke:

"How did you get here—by flitter?"

Mura got to his feet and gazed up into the vast dome which arched above the maze.

"No. But one could be of use here, yes—"

"Yes is right!" Torn and swollen lips kept Kamil's words a mumble, but the engineer-apprentice was determined to talk. "I thought I was coasting with dead jets all right until you showed up. When that Rich shut me in here he said there was a way out if I were just clever enough to find it. But I didn't think it meant you had to have wings!"

"What is this anyway?" Dane asked. "Their prison?"

"Partly that, partly something else. You know what's going on here?" Ali's voice was shrill with excitement. "They've found an installation left by the Forerunners—and the thing still runs! It brings down any ship within a certain range—smash 'em up here. Then this gang of Patrol Posteds goes out and loots the wrecks!"

"They've got the *Queen* pinned down," Dane told him. "If she tries to lift she'll crash—"

"So that's it! They have had to run the machine at a more steady pace than usual and there was some talk—before they threw me in here—about how long it will go without a rest. Seems that before it switched on and off mechanically after some impulse pattern they don't understand. Anyway, the key to the whole setup is somewhere here in this blasted puzzle house!"

"The installation is here?" Mura eyed the walls about them as if he were ready to pull the secret out of their very substance.

"Either that, or something important concerning it. There is a way through here—if you know the trail. Twice since I've been wandering around I heard people talking, once just on the other side of a wall. Only I never could get through to the right halls—" Ali sighed. "I had about reached the end of my orbit when you came jetting out of the ether."

Dane buckled his belt around him and now he drew his blaster. With it on the lowest pressure he began to use it, methodically burning a series of holds to meet those Mura had left at a higher level.

"We can go and see," he said as he worked.

"You will go," Mura told him. "And you will do it with secrecy—avoiding as much as possible any trouble. Ali cannot walk the walls, not now. But see if from above you can find this trail he talks of. Then with your guidance we can move—"

That was sensible enough. Dane waited for the pocks to cool, listening to Mura explain all that had happened since Ali had disappeared, hearing in turn Kamil's account of his own adventures.

"There were two of them waiting in ambush and they jumped me," he said with open disgust at his own lack of caution. "They had individual flyers!" There was awe in his tone. "Something else they found here. Great Space, this place is a storehouse of Forerunner material! Rich is using things he doesn't know the meaning of—or why they work—or anything! These mountains are a regular warehouse. Well, with those flyers on they nipped me up and out—knocked me out. And when I came to I was tied up on one of those worm crawlers of theirs. Then I had a little question session with Rich and a couple of his burn-off boys—" Ali's voice sounded grim and he did not go into details, his face gave evidence enough of that period. "Afterwards they made a few bright remarks and shoved me in here and I've probably been going around in circles ever since. But—do you realize—this place, it's what everyone had been hunting for for years! Forerunner material—good as the day it was made. If we can get out of here—"

"Yes, first the getting out," Mura cut in. "Also the matter of the installation—"

Dane glanced at the top of the wall. "How am I going to find you here again?"

"You will take bearings. Also," Mura brought out his torch, set it up on end and snapped the low power button. "When you are aloft, see what kind of guide this makes—"

Once more Dane made use of the holds and scrambled up on the wall. He looked back. Yes, the beam from the torch cut straight up in the gloom. In a very inferior way it was not unlike the beacon on the

Queen. He waved his hand to the two below and started out, heading for the center of the maze where Ali believed the secret of the installation lay.

Walls angled, curved, took him right or left, so he had to retrace time and again. And nowhere did he see any hall below which led through the puzzle without interruption. If there was such a one, its doorways might be controlled by sonics and so hidden to the casual search.

But through his body coursed the heavy beat of the hidden machine. He must be nearing the source. Then he was conscious of a heightened glow in the grayness ahead. It had none of the sharp quality of a torch ray—rather it was as if the spectral radiance of the walls had been stepped to a more concentrated degree in that section. He slowed his pace to a shuffle as he neared that center, afraid that the click of his metallic boot plates might betray him.

What he came to first was a double wall forming an oval area, a space of three feet between the two smooth surfaces. Determined to see what lay within, he made a risky jump from one to the next and then crouched on his hands and knees, creeping up to peer down into a room which was in stark contrast to the territory about it.

There were machines here—huge towering things—each sealed into a box coating. And a good third of the encircling wall was a bank of controls and dials, centered by a wide plate of smooth metal which bore a likeness to the visaplates he knew.

But that screen mirrored no scene from the outer world on its surface. Instead it was uniformly black and across it moved sparks of light.

Watching this were three men. And, by the brighter light, Dane was able to recognize Salzar Rich as well as the Rigellian who had come in on the *Queen*. The third man, in a seat just before the screen, his hands resting on a wide keyboard, was one he had never seen before.

This was it! This was the rotten heart of Limbo which rendered the blasted planet a menace to her particular corner of space! And as long as that heart beat, as it was doing now in waves which he could feel through his whole body, the *Queen* was tied to danger and her crew were helpless—

But were they? Dane felt a tiny thrill of excitement. Rich was making use of machines he did not really understand. And under other hands the whole setup could be rendered harmless. Perhaps by watching now he himself could discover how to control the broadcast which kept the *Queen* a prisoner.

The points of light moved on the screen and the three men watched with a concentration of interest which argued of some anxiety. None of them made any move to touch the levers or buttons on the panel. Dane wriggled on his belly toward a point from which he could overhear any orders Rich might give.

So he was flattened out of sight a few minutes later when the sound of running feet startled him. Someone was coming through the maze. It was one of the outlaws and he wove a path from crooked hall to angled room in a manner which proved that he knew the secret. As he came up against the barrier he threw back his head and shouted, his voice ringing in the vast dome over their heads:

"Salzar!"

Rich whirled and then he flung out his right hand and made some adjustment on the panel. A section of the wall slid back to admit the newcomer.

Rich's voice, chilly with irritation, floated up to the watcher above: "What's the matter?"

The runner was still puffing, his beefy face showing flushed. "Message from Algar, Chief. He's coming in—with the Patrol riding his fins!"

"Patrol!" the man at the keyboard half turned in his chair, his mouth slightly agape.

"Did you warn him that the pull was on?" demanded Rich.

"Sure we did. But he can't evade much longer. He either earths or the Patrol nets him—"

Rich stood very still, his head slightly cocked so that he could see the vision plates. His other assistant, the Rigellian, spoke first:

"Always said we needed a com hook-up down here," he stated, with some of the content of one who is at last proved to be right in a long argument.

The man at the controls had a quick answer for that. "Yes—and how are you going to cut through the interference to hear anything over it?" he began when Rich snapped an order to the messenger:

"Get back up there and tell Jennis to order Algar to go inert at once. In exactly two hours," he was consulting his watch, "we'll off the pull for an hour—an hour, that's all. He's to set down, make the best landing he can under power. It doesn't matter if he smashes the ship—he'll work to save his own skin all right. Then we'll snap on the power and net the Patroller when she comes in for the kill. Get it?"

"Two hours and then off pull—keep it off for one, and he's to make a landing then—then on pull," parroted the messenger. "Got it!"

He turned and pounded out of the room, back into the maze. For a moment Dane longed to be twins so that he might follow that flight and so find the way out of the puzzle. But it was more important now to see how Rich was going to manipulate the installation to neutralize the power for the landing of his subordinate's ship.

"Think he'll make it?" asked the man at the control board.

"Twelve to two he does," snapped the Rigellian. "Algar's a master pilot."

"He'll have to take the pull coming in and be ready to snap on his braking rockets the minute it fades—tricky stuff—" It was plain that the other was dubious.

Rich was still watching the vision plate. Two new lights appeared on its surface. But their fluttering across it was so erratic that Dane, not being briefed on the use of this alien recorder, could make nothing of that weird dance.

Rich's lips were moving, counting off seconds, his eyes going from his watch to the plate and back again. The atmosphere grew more tense. At the control board the man's shoulders were hunched, his attention glued to the row of buttons at his fingertips. While the Rigellian strode with the peculiar gliding walk of his kind to the far end of the wall panel, his scaled, bluish six-fingered hand outstretched to one lever there.

"Wait—!" It was the man at the keyboard. "It's pulsing again—!"

Rich spat a blistering oath. On the screen the dots were moving up and down in a crazy race. And Dane was conscious that the hum of the installation varied, that the beat had developed a tripping accent.

"Get it back!" Rich sped to the keyboard. "Get it back!"

The man showed a face damp with sweat. "How can I?" he demanded. "We don't know why it does this."

"Shorten the beam—that helped once before," that was the Rigellian, of the three he showed the least emotion.

The man pressed two buttons. All three stared at the screen for the results of that move. The wildly flying dots settled down to a pattern not far different from the one they had made when Dane had first come upon the scene.

"How far out does it pull now?" asked Rich.

"Atmosphere level."

"And the ships?"

His underling squinted at the board, consulted some dials. "They won't come into the pull for one—maybe two hours. When we cut like that it takes time to build up the power again. Anyway this doesn't affect that blasted Trader any—*she* can't lift."

Rich took a small box from his pocket, poured some of its contents into the palm of his hand and licked it up. "It is pleasant to know that *something* is going right," he observed with a chill in his voice which made Dane's skin prickle.

"We don't know much about this," the man thumbed the edge of the keyboard. "None of us have been trained to use it right. And it was alien made to begin with—"

"Let me know when and if you can get it back on full power again," was all the answer Rich made.

Two hours before they could turn on the full power, Dane thought. Now if in those two hours he and Mura—and maybe Kosti and Ali—could move—that lever the Rigellian had reached for—it must control something important. And if they could take over this room and the men in it, they would learn even more about its operation. Suppose the Patrol ship could make a safe landing on the tail of the outlaw they were pursuing—! What should be *his* next move?

Rich decided it for him. His jaws moving in a rhythmical chewing, the outlaw leader walked toward the hidden door. "You say two hours," he spoke over his shoulder as he went. "It'll be much better all around if you halve that, understand? I'll be back in an hour—be ready to cut in the full beam then." He nodded curtly to the Rigellian and stepped through the opening in the wall.

And this time Dane was ready to follow. He allowed Rich a good start and trailed the other through the winding ways which the outlaw threaded with the ease of much practice. Before they had drawn level with the small beacon provided by Mura's torch, a beacon Rich could not sight from the floor, Dane had the secret of the maze. Two right turns, then one left, and then three right once more, skip the next passage opening and repeat. Rich had made the same pattern four times and Dane was sure that it would continue to carry him to the outer door of the puzzle. But, having learned that, the Trader waited on the wall for the other to work his way five corridors ahead before he crossed to the room where he had left Mura and Ali.

He found Kamil up and walking about now, restored by the steward's first aid. And as Dane climbed down their crude ladder they closed in on him.

"—That's it," he ended his report. "The Patrol's riding in on this bird's jet stream. As long as they both stay out of the atmosphere they're safe. But once the pull is working full power again—" He snapped his fingers.

"Our move!" Kamil got out the words between his swollen lips. "We've got to cut that power off—totally!"

"Yes," Mura crossed to the holds on the wall. "But first we collect Kosti—"

"How can you get him here? He said he can't walk the walls—"

"A man can do anything if he is forced to it," Mura replied. "You will stay here—I shall bring Kosti. But first show me the route which takes one to this 'heart'—"

Dane climbed the wall behind the steward, led the way across the three intervening spaces to that corridor he had seen Rich traversing. And there he repeated the pattern the outlaw had followed. Mura smiled his placid smile.

"It is very simple, is it not? Now, you wait with Kamil—and do nothing foolish until I return. This is most interesting—"

Dane obediently went back to the room where they had left the engineer-apprentice. Kamil sat on the floor, his back against one of the walls, his battered face turned to the torch light. As Dane's boots hit the pavement he turned his head.

"Welcome aboard," he mouthed. "Now tell me about that installation—" he went on into a series of questions about what Dane had seen, which sometimes left the cargo-apprentice floundering. Of the machines he had seen little because of their casings. And he could not describe the control panel very well, having been at the time more intent on the actions of the men by it. He admitted this with some of his old feeling of inadequacy. A Trader kept his eyes open, a Trader had to use both his eyes and his brain at one and the same time. Here he had had another opportunity which he had apparently muffed. And a little of the old antagonism sparked to life inside him.

"What is their source of power?" Ali demanded of the room about them. "We've nothing like it—nothing at all! There must be things here which will put us years ahead—generations—"

"Providing, of course," Dane broke in a little sourly, "that we get to use them. We aren't the winners yet."

"Neither are we licked," Ali retorted.

It was as if their roles had been reversed. Now it was Kamil who was building castles, Dane who did the undermining.

"If Stotz and I could have a couple of hours in that place! By the Black Hole, we did pick a winner when we bid on Limbo—"

Ali seemed able to ignore the fact that Rich was still very much in command of the situation, that the *Queen* was pegged down, and that the enemy had a force which could render their headquarters impenetrable. The more Kamil enlarged on the future to come, the more flaws Dane could see in their actions in the immediate present. But they were both lifted out of their thoughts by a soft hail from above.

"Mura!" Dane jumped to his feet. The steward had been successful in his mission, a second man stood on the wall above, one hand resting on the steward's shoulder.

"Yes," was hissed down at them. "Now it is for you to climb. Up quickly, both of you, time runs out!"

Ali went first, and once or twice he bit off an exclamation as his exertions wrung his sore body. Dane caught up the beacon torch, snapped it off, and went after.

"Now this is what we shall do." Mura was clearly in command, as he had been all the time since they had entered the mountain. "Kosti and Ali shall go by the regular path to the room of the installation. While you and I, Thorson, will take the route along the wall top. They are expecting Rich to return there. Your entrance in his place should surprise them long enough for us to go into action. We must get at that switch and immobilize it. And do whatever else we can to make this devil thing incapable of action in the future. So—now we move—"

They made their way back to the path Rich had used, Kosti walking slowly with his hand on the steward's shoulder, visible shudders shaking his big body. There once more they used the linked belts and lowered the jetman and Ali to the floor of the maze.

The brighter glow of the installation sector was their guide now and they reached the oval wall easily. Mura gestured at Kosti and the jetman raised his voice in the same call the messenger had given earlier. The other three stood tense, ready to move if it worked.

"Salzar!"

Dane's attention was fixed on the Rigellian. The alien's head went up, his round eyes sought the hidden doorway. It was going to work because that blue hand went to the proper button among the controls. And outside the barrier Kosti stood waiting, his blaster drawn and ready to fire, the unarmed Ali behind him.

THE HEART CEASES TO BEAT

17

As the door slid back into the wall and Kosti leaped through, Mura raised his voice:

"You are covered! Stand where you are!"

The man at the keyboard started, looking over his shoulder at Kosti, his face a mask of wild surprise. But the Rigellian moved with the superhuman speed of his race, his blue hand whipping toward another point on the control board.

It was Dane who fired and struck, not living flesh but that bank of controls. The man at the keyboard screamed, a thin, inhuman cry to echo through the maze. And the Rigellian dropped to the floor. But he was not yet beaten. He threw himself at Kosti, moving with a speed no Terran muscles could equal.

The big man swerved, but not far or fast enough, and went down into a clawing, gouging scramble on the floor. But the other outlaw remained where he was, sounds which bore small likeness to words still bubbling between his lips.

Ali slipped through the door and started around the room, edging with the wall as a support to his weaving legs. He turned his face up to Dane.

"Which is it?" he cried. "That switch—"

"Just ahead—the black one with the device set in the handle," Dane called back. And now the eyes of the man by the keyboard found the two on the top of the wall. Why the sight of them restored his sense they could never know, but his hand went to the weapon at his belt. And at that same instant blaster fire cut so close to him that he must have felt the sear of the beam.

"Your hands—up with your hands—at once!" Mura gave the order with the same snap as Jellico might have used.

The man obeyed, leaning over to plant his outspread fingers on the screen he had watched for so long. But now he was intent upon Ali's tottering advance and on his face there was a growing horror. When Kamil's hand fell on the switch at last he gave another cry.

"Don't!"

But Ali disregarded the warning and pulled the lever down with all his strength. The outlaw at the keyboard screamed for the second time. And there came another answer. The hum which had filled the walls, beat within their bodies for so long, was gone.

The Rigellian wrenched himself free from Kosti's grip and gathered his feet under him to launch himself at the switch. But Ali had flung his whole weight upon the lever, dragging it down until the metal shaft broke off in his hand, determined that it would not be opened again. And at the sight of that the man at the keyboard went mad, flinging himself at Kamil in spite of the menace of Mura's blaster.

Dane had been caught napping, his attention had been on the Rigellian who, he thought, was the more dangerous of the two. But the steward burned the lunatic down as his tearing hands reached for Ali's throat. The man's shriek was choked in mid cry and he writhed to the floor, on his face. Dane was glad he could not see those blackened features.

The Rigellian got to his feet, his unblinking reptilian eyes fastened on Dane and Mura, very much aware of the two blasters now centered upon him. He pulled his clothing into order and ignored Kosti.

"You have just condemned us all, you know—" his voice speaking the Trade Lingo was flat, unaccented, he might have been exchanging the formal compliments used among his kind.

Kosti moved on him. "Suppose you get your hands up, and don't try the trick your partner pulled—"

The Rigellian shrugged. "There's no need for tricks now. We are all caught in the same trap—"

Ali caught at the chair and lowered himself into it. Behind him the screen was blank—dead.

"And this trap?" asked Mura.

"When you threw that switch and wrecked it—you wrecked all the controls," the Rigellian leaned back against the wall at his ease, no emotion to be read on his scaled face. "We'll never get out of here—in the dark!"

For the first time Dane was aware of a change. The gray radiance which had glowed from the walls of the Forerunners' domain was fading, as the glow might fade from the dying embers of a fire.

"We are locked in," the remorseless voice of their prisoner continued. "And since you've smashed the lock, no one can get us out."

A ray of light answered. The Rigellian showed no interest.

"We don't know all the secrets of this place," he told them. "Wait and see how good your lights will be in here shortly."

Dane turned to the steward. "If we start now—before the light is all gone from the walls—"

The other agreed with a nod and called down to the Rigellian: "Can you open the door?"

His answer came in a detached shake of the alien's head. And Kosti promptly went into action. Using his blaster he burnt holds on the wall. Dane fairly danced in his impatience for them to be out and trying for the entrance, he hated to spare the time for those holds to cool.

But at last they were up and over the wall and all in the road to the outside. In the corridor Kosti pulled the hands of the Rigellian behind him and tied them with the man's own belt before ordering him ahead. Their progress was necessarily slow as even with an aiding hand Ali could not keep a fast pace. And now they were in virtual darkness—the light only a ghostly reflection of the former glow.

Mura snapped on his torch. "We'll use these one at a time. Save the charges for when we need them most."

Dane wondered about that. Torch charges were not easily exhausted, they were made to be in use for months. But the ring of light which guided them now was oddly pallid, grayish, instead of yellow-bright as they expected.

"Why not turn it up?" Ali asked after a moment.

There was a snicker out of the gloom from the direction of the Rigellian. Then Mura answered:

"It is up—top strength—"

No one commented, but Dane knew that he was not the only one to watch that faint circle anxiously. And when it faded to a misty light extending hardly a foot beyond, somehow he was not surprised. Kosti, alone, asked a question:

"What's the matter? Wait—!" The beam of his own torch struck out into the thick darkness. For perhaps two minutes it was clear, uncut, and then it, too, began to diminish as if something in the atmosphere sapped it.

"All energy within this space," the Rigellian's voice expounded, "is affected now. There is much of the installation we do not understand. Light goes, and later the air, also—"

Dane drew a long, testing breath. To his mind the chilly atmosphere was the same as it had always been. Perhaps that last embellishment was merely a flight of imagination on the part of their prisoner. But their pace quickened.

The pallid circle of the torch did not fade totally away for some time and they were able to follow the pattern which Rich had betrayed—the one who should guide them out of the labyrinth. There was a vast and brooding silence now that the great machine had stopped and in it the ring of their boots awoke strange echoes. At length Kosti's torch was sucked dry and Dane's pressed into use. They threaded on, from one room to another, down this short corridor to that, trying to make the best possible use of the dying light. But there was no way of gauging how close they were to the outer door.

When the last flicker of Dane's light was in turn swallowed up, Mura gave a new order.

"Now we link ourselves together—"

Dane's right hand clipped into Mura's belt, his left closed about Ali's wrist, providing one link in the chain. And they went on so, a soft murmur of sound telling the cargo-apprentice that the steward in the lead was counting off paces, seeming to have worked out some method of his own for getting them from one unseen point to the next.

But the dark pressed in upon them, thick, tangible, with that odd sensation that darkness on this planet always possessed. It was like pushing through a sluggish fluid and one lost any belief in ground gained, rather there was the feeling of being thrust back for a loss.

Dane followed Mura mechanically, he could only trust that the steward knew what he was doing and that sooner or later he would bring them to the portal of the maze. He himself was panting, as if they had been running, and yet the pace was the unhurried, ground covering stride of the Pool parade ground which they had fallen into insensibly as they advanced in line.

"How many miles do we have to go, anyway?" Kosti's voice arose.

He was answered by another snicker from their prisoner. "What difference does it make, Trader? From this there is no way out—once you smashed that switch."

Did the Rigellian really believe that? If he did why wasn't he more alarmed himself? Or was he one of those fatalistic races to whom life and death wore much the same face?

There was a surprised grunt from Mura and a second later Dane piled up tight against the steward while Ali and the two following him plowed up in a tangle. To Dane there was only one explanation for that barrier before them—somewhere Mura had miscounted and taken a wrong turn in the dark. They were lost!

"Now where are we?" Kosti asked.

"Lost—" the Rigellian's voice crackled dryly with a cold amusement crisping its tone.

But Dane's hand was on the wall which had brought them up short and now he moved his fingers across its surface. This was not fashioned of the smooth material manufactured by the Forerunners, instead it had the grit of stone. They had reached the native rock of the cave! And Mura confirmed that discovery.

"This is rock—the end of the maze."

"But where's the way out?" persisted Kosti.

"Locked—locked when you broke the switch," the Rigellian replied. "All openings are governed by the installation—"

"If that is so," Ali's voice rose for the first time since they had begun that march, "what happened in the past when you shut off the machine? Were you locked in then until it was turned on once more?"

There was no reply. Then Dane heard a rustle of movement, and queer choking noise, and hard on it the jetman's husky tone:

"When we ask questions, snake man, we get answers! Or take steps. What happened when you shut off that switch before?"

More scuffling sounds. And then a hoarse answer: "We stayed in here until it was switched on again. It was only off occasionally."

"It was off for days while Survey was poking about here," Dane corrected.

"We didn't come near here then," returned the Rigellian promptly— a little too promptly.

"Someone must have stayed in here—to turn it on again when you wanted that done," Ali pointed out. "If the doors were locked you couldn't have gotten in or out—"

"I'm not an engineer," the Rigellian had lost some of his detachment, he was sullen.

"No, you're just one of Rich's lieutenants. If there's a way out of here, you'll know it." That was Kosti.

"How about your pipe?" Dane asked Mura whose continued silence puzzled him.

"That I have been trying," the steward answered.

"Only it doesn't work, eh? All right, snake man, spill—!" More sounds of a scuffle and then Ali's voice across them—

"If this is rock, and it is the right place—how about using a blaster?"

To cut through! Dane's hand went to his holster. A blaster could cut rock, cut it with greater dispatch than it had shorn through the tougher material of the maze. The idea struck Kosti too—the muffled noise made by his "persuasion" methods ceased.

"You'll have to pick just the right spot," Ali continued. "Where is the door—"

"That can be found by this old snake here, can't it?" purred the jetman.

There was an inarticulate whimper in answer to that. Kosti must have heard it as an assent for he pushed past Dane, shoving the captive before him.

"Right there eh? Well, it better be, blue boy, it just better be!"

Dane nearly lost his balance as the Rigellian was thrust back upon him. He elbowed the man back against the wall and stood waiting.

"That you, Frank? Get back, man—all of you get back!"

A second body was pushed against Dane and he gave ground, retreating with the Rigellian and the other.

"Look out for a back wash, you fool!" Ali called out. "Give it low power 'til you see how that cuts—"

Kosti laughed. "I was flipping a polishing rag, son, when you were learning how to walk. You let the old man show his stuff now. Up ship and out!" With that wild slogan which had resounded in countless bars when the Traders hit dirt after long voyages, blazing light spewed out, blinding them all.

Dane peered between the fingers of a shielding hand and watched that core of brilliance center on the rock, saw the stone glow red and then white before rippling in molten streams to the floor. Heat, waves of roasting heat blasted back at them, forcing retreat for all except that one big figure who stood his ground, pointing the weapon at the rock, his helmet, its protecting visor snapped into place, nodding a little in time with the force bolts which jerked his arm and body as they burst from the weapon in his hand to crash against the disintegrating wall. How could Kosti stand up to that back wash? He was taking more than was possible for a man to endure.

But the beam held steady on the point and the hole grew as stone flaked away in patches, the inner rot spreading. The stink of the discharge filled their throats, gave them hacking coughs, cut at their eyes until tears wet their cheeks. And still Kosti stood in his place, with the stability of a command robot.

"Karl!" Ali's voice rose to a scream, "Look out— Let up!"

There was a crash as a piece of rock gave way, bashing down into the corridor of the maze. Just in the last instant the jetman had moved, but he did not give more than the few feet necessary to preserve the minimum safety.

With his free hand he beat at a smoldering patch on his breeches. But his grip on the blaster did not waver and the beam of destruction continued to bore in just where he had aimed it.

By the flame Dane saw the Rigellian's face. His wide eyes centered on Kosti and there was a kind of horror mirrored in them. He edged away from the inferno at the portal, but more as if he feared the man who induced it, than if he were afraid of the blaster work.

"That does it!" Kosti's voice was muffled in his helmet.

As yet they dared not approach the glowing door he had cut for them. But since he had holstered his arm it was plain that he thought the job done. Now he came back to join them, pushing up his visor so by the glow of the cooling rock they could see his face wet and shiny. He pounded vigorously with his gloved hands at places on the front of his tunic and breeches and carried with him the taint of singed leather and fabric.

"What's out there?" Dane wanted to know.

Kosti's nose wrinkled. "Another hallway as black as outer space. But at least we can get out of this whirly-round!"

Impatient as they were to be on their way, they must wait until it was safe to cross that cut which radiated heat. Adjusting helmets, improvising a protection for Ali from the Rigellian's tunic, they made ready. But before they went Kosti gave a last attention to their captive.

"We could pull you through," he observed. "But you might fry on the way, and besides you'd be a dead jet breaking our speed if we tangle with any of your friends outside. So we'll just store you in deep freeze—to be called for." He fastened the man's ankles as well as his wrists and rolled him away from the heated portion of the corridor.

Then with Ali in their midst they hurried through the cut and out into the hall. Darkness closed about them once more, and an experiment proved that here, as well as in the maze, the torches could not fight the blackness. But at least the way before them was smooth and straight and there were no openings along it to betray them into wrong turnings.

They slowed their pace to accommodate Ali, and went linked together by touch as they had in the maze.

"Worm's eye view—" Kosti's grumble came through the sable quiet. "Did the Forerunners have eyes?"

Dane slipped his arm about the swaying Ali's shoulders and gave him support. He felt the engineer-apprentice wince as his clumsy grasp awoke some bruise to life and adjusted his hold quickly, though Ali made no sound of protest.

"Here is an opening, we have reached the end of this way," Mura said. "Yes, beyond is another passage, wider, much wider—"

"A wider road might lead to a more important section," Dane ventured.

"Just so it gets us out of here!" was Kosti's contribution. "I'm tired of jetting around in this muck hole. Go on, Frank, take us in."

The procession of four moved on, making a sharp turn to the

right. They were now marching abreast and Dane had an impression of room about them, though the dark was as complete as ever.

Then they were stopped, not by another barrier but by noise—a shout which exploded along the hall with the crack of a stun rifle. In a moment it was followed by just that—the stun of a rifle.

"Down!" Mura snapped. But the others were already moving.

Dane ducked, pulling Ali with him. Then he was lying flat, trying to sort out some meaning from the wild clamor which floated back to them.

"Small war on—" that was Kosti managing to make himself heard between two bursts of firing.

"And it's coming our way," Ali breathed close to Dane's ear.

The cargo-apprentice drew his blaster, though he did not see how he was going to make much use of it now. To fire blindly in the dark was not a wise move.

"Yaaaah—" That was no shout of rage, it was the yammering scream of a man who had taken his death wound. And Ali was very right—the battle was fast approaching where they lay.

"Back against the walls," again Mura gave tongue to a move they were already making.

Dane clutched a portion of Ali's torn tunic and felt it rip more as he pulled the engineer-apprentice after him to the right. They fetched up against the wall and stayed there, huddled together and listening.

A flash of light cracked open the curtain about them. Dazzled, Dane had an impression of black forms. And then a smoldering patch of red on the wall was all that marked the burst of a blaster.

"Lord of High Space," Ali half whispered. "If they beam those straight down here, we'll fry!"

Feet pounded toward them and Dane stiffened, clutching his weapon. Maybe he should fire at the sound, knock out the runners before they came too close. But he could not bring himself to squeeze the trigger. All a Trader's ingrained distrust of open battle made him hesitate.

There was light up there now. Not the gray, ghostly gloom which had once lit these halls, but a thick yellow shaft which was both normal and reassuring to Terran eyes. And against that the four from the *Queen* saw five figures take cover on the floor, ready—no longer fleeing, but turning to show their teeth to their pursuers.

UP SHIP AND OUT

18 "Surrender! in the name of the Federation—" the voice boomed from the walls about them.

"Patrol!" Ali identified the order.

All right—so the Patrol had landed, Dane was willing to accept that. But which of the parties before them represented law and order? Those waiting attack, or those behind the light, waiting to deliver it?

The light steadily advanced—until one of those in wait shot straight into its heart. There was answering fire through the resulting dark and someone screamed.

If they had any sense, Dane thought, they would now rereat to the maze until the fight was over. This was no time to get caught in a mix-up between Rich's forces and the Patrol. But he made no move to pass that bright thought on to Ali. Instead he found himself leveling his blaster, taking aim through the dark at the roof of the hall in which they lay. He pressed the trigger.

The voltage was still set on "low" but the beam struck the roof and bit in. And he had not misjudged the distance too badly—that burst of light revealed the men who had shot out the Patrol light—he was sure that the Patrol were the light party now. Their white faces, mouths agape, stared up at the glowing core of destruction over their heads as if they were hypnotized by it. Only one moved, throwing himself back, passing under that coruscating splotch, toward the men from the *Queen*. But he did not get past them.

Kosti launched his body out of the shadows, barely visible in the fading gleam from the roof. He should have struck the fleeing man head on. Instead the other made an unbelievable swift twist of his body which carried him almost by the contact point. Had the jetman's fingers not caught in the fugitive's belt, he would have made it.

Dane fired again, sending a second bolt of fire up beside the first to give Kosti light for his fight. But the flash revealed a far different scene. A figure as tall as the jetman was getting to hands and knees for a second forward dash, while Kosti lay limp and still.

Ali moved, clumsily, but at all the speed he could muster, rolling out so that the other stumbled over his body and went down once more. And then Dane used the blaster for the third time, aiming at a point behind them, bracketing the would-be escapee with the blaze.

"Stop!" again the voice boomed about them. "Stop firing or we'll bring a flamer in and sweep this whole hall!"

A wild beast's snarl from the shadows answered. And at the edge of the last glowing splotch, the one meant to barricade the passage, a dark shape prowled back and forth, its crouching outline suggesting something not human.

Then the light went on again, catching them all in its glare. Nearest to the source of it three outlaws stood, their empty hands rising above their heads. But the beam reached on, past them, to reveal Kosti. The big jetman lay still, a trickle of blood on his chin. On the radiance swept, pinpointing Mura as he hurried to Kosti, bringing Ali into focus as he hunched over, clutching at his chest, coughing.

Dane, his back to the glare, was alert, his blaster ready for the next move of that other thing. The thing with slavering lips and slack jaw who prowled up and down at the edge of the burning ring which cut it off from the dark safety beyond, that thing who had once been Salzar, lord of this forgotten kingdom—the thing who had retreated into the Hell of the crax user until it was no longer a man at all!

It turned as the light caught it, snarled and spat at the beam, and then whirled and leaped over the burning area, squalling at the lick of fire, heading for the maze.

"Thorson! Mura!"

Dane shivered. He should be after Salzar but he couldn't force himself to cross those flames to hunt down that thing in the dark. It was with real thankfulness that he heard that sharp call. He looked over his shoulder to its source, but the glare of the light dazzled him and he blinked painfully at the figures advancing around it, able at last to make out the black and silver of the Patrol, the drabber tunics of Trade. He holstered his blaster and waited for them to come up.

It was sometime later that he sat at a table in a strange room. A room with furnishings which betrayed the nature of the trap which was Limbo in bald openness, things which had been looted from fifty—a hundred ships—crowded together to provide a tawdry luxury for the private quarters of the man they had known as Salzar Rich.

Dane wolfed down a meal of real food—no concentrates—as he listened half dreamily to Mura deliver a concise report of their activities for the past three days. He fought an aching fatigue which ordered him to put his head down on the table and sleep—just sleep. Instead he sat and chewed on delicacies he had not tasted since he left Terraport.

Black tunics slipped in and out of the room, delivering reports, taking orders from the Squadron Commander who sat with Captain Jellico listening to Mura's often interrupted story. It was rather like the end of a Video serial, decided Dane groggily, all wrapped up in a neat little package. The Patrol had arrived, the situation was now well in hand—

"As nasty a setup as we've ever come across," that was the Patrol officer.

"I take it," Van Rycke observed, "that this is going to clear up a great many disappearances—"

The Patrolman sighed. "We'll have to comb these hills, maybe chop into them, before we have the roll complete. Though we can do a lot just listing the loot they gathered in. Yes, it's going to clear a lot of records at Headquarters. Thanks to you, we have the chance to do it." He arose and favored Jellico with a sketch of salute. "My compliments, Captain, if you will be free to join me in about—" he consulted his watch—"three hours, we can have a conference. There are several points to be considered."

He was gone. Dane drank from a mug engraved with the Survey crest. And at the sight of those crossed comets, he shuddered and pushed the container from him. It reminded him too vividly of an earlier discovery. Yes, there should be a wealth of strange relics found here. Somehow he was glad that he did not have the task of sorting out and listing them.

"That maze now," Van Rycke's calm seemed ruffled. "That's worth looking over."

Jellico gave a snort of humorless laughter. "As if the Patrol is going to let anyone but themselves and the Fed experts in there!"

The mention of the maze triggered Dane's memory and for the first time he spoke:

"Rich ran back into that. Have they caught him yet, sir?"

"Not yet," Jellico replied. He did not appear much interested in the problem of the missing outlaw leader. "Crax chewer, isn't he? Went right over the edge when we caught up with you—"

"Yes, he was insane at the last, sir," Mura agreed. "However, I trust that the Patrol are not discounting him. To hunt a madman through that puzzle without precautions of a most serious kind—that is a task I would not care to assume."

"Well," the Captain got up, "we're not asked to do it. The whole thing's in Patrol hands now, let them worry about it. The sooner we lift ship from this misbegotten place, the better I'll be satisfied. We're Trade, not police."

"Hmm—" Van Rycke still lounged in a chair which had been

ripped from some liner captain's cabin. "Yes, Trade—a matter of Trade. We must keep our minds on business." But none of Jellico's impatience lurked in his limpid blue eyes. He was bland, and, Dane thought, about to go to work. Van Rycke, Patrol or no Patrol, was not yet through with Limbo.

In spite of Jellico's chaffing to be gone, the Captain did not suggest a return to the *Queen*. Instead he paced warily about the room, stopping now and again to inspect some particular fitting Salzar had fancied enough to have installed there. Van Rycke looked over at Dane and Mura.

"I would suggest," he said mildly, "that you make use of Dr. Rich's bedroom. I think you'll find his bunk soft—"

Still wondering why they were not ordered back to the *Queen* where the injured Kosti and Ali had been sent hours before, Dane followed the steward into the second room of Rich's private suite. Van Rycke had been right about the luxury, but it was no bunk which fronted them, only a wide, real Terra-side bed equipped with self-warming foam blankets and feather down puffs.

Dane shed his helmet, bulky belt, and boots to lie back in the fleecy softness. He was dimly aware of Mura's weight settling down on the other edge of the broad expanse and then he was instantly and deeply asleep.

He was in the control cabin of the *Queen,* it was necessary for him to compute their passage into hyper. And yet across from him sat Salzar Rich, his face disciplined, hard as it had been on that day back on Naxos when they had first met. He, Dane, must get them into hyper, yet if his calculations were wrong Salzar would blast him— and he would fall down, down out of the *Queen* into the maze where something else crouched and yammered in the darkness waiting to hunt him!

Dane's eyes opened, he stared up at a grayness above. His body was shaking with chill, his hands icy cold and wet as he groped for some solid reality among the soft billowy things which melted at his touch.

He willed his hands to be still, he dared not even shift his eyes now. There was something here, something which broadcast such a threat of menace that it tore at his nerves.

Dane forced himself to breathe deeply, evenly. Mura was there, but he could not turn his head to make sure— A fraction of an inch at a time he began to shift his position. He had no idea of what he had to face as yet, but fear was there—he could almost taste it, see it as a murky cloud in the air.

He could see the door now, and from beyond he could hear the murmur of voices. Perhaps both the Captain and Van Rycke were still in the outer room. Yes, the door, and now a scrap of the wall by it. His eyes took in a Tri-Dee painting, a vivid landscape from some eerie world, a world dead, sterile to life, and yet in its way beautiful. Now he dared to move his hand, burrowing under those feather-weight covers, striving to arouse Mura, sure that the other would not betray himself, even when waking.

Hand moved, head moved. The picture—and beyond it a strip of woven stuff hanging, glittering with threads which might have been spun of emerald and diamond, a bright, too bright thing which hurt the eyes. And now by that, his shoulders blotting out part of it—

Salzar!

Only an exercise of will such as he had not known he could command kept Dane immovable. Luckily the outlaw was not watching the bed. He was taking a serpent's silent way to the door.

To all outward appearances he was a man again, but there was no sanity in those dark fixed eyes. And in his hands he fondled a weird tube set on an oddly shaped handstock, a thing which must be a weapon. He was gone from in front of the hanging, his head cut the picture. Three feet more and he would be at the door. But the hand Dane had sent to warn Mura was met, enfolded in a warm grasp. He had an ally!

Dane tried to plan the next move. He was on his back, muffled in the thick covers of the bed. It would be impossible to jump Salzar without warning. Yet the outlaw must not be allowed to reach the door and use that weapon.

The hand which Mura had grasped now received a message—it was pushed back toward him forcefully. He hoped that he interpreted that correctly. He tensed and, as a wild cry broke from the throat of his bedmate, Dane rolled over the edge to the floor.

Lightning rent the air, fire burst from the bed. But Dane's hands closed on a strip of Paravian carpet and he gave it a furious tug. Salzar did not lose his balance, but he fell back against the wall. He swung the weapon toward the scrambling cargo-apprentice. Then hands, competent, unhurried, closed about his throat from behind and dragged him to Van Rycke's barrel chest as the cargo-master proceeded to systematically choke him into submission. Dane and Mura got up from the floor, the blazing bed between them.

There was more confusion, an eruption of Patrolmen, the removal of Salzar and some hasty firefighting. Dane settled down on a bench with a confirmed distaste for beds. Just let him get back to his bunk on the *Queen*—that was all he asked. If he could ever bring himself to try and sleep again.

Van Rycke laid the captured weapon down on the table. "Something new," he commented. "Perhaps another Forerunner toy, or maybe just loot. The Feds can puzzle it out. But at least we know that the dear doctor is now under control."

"Thanks to you, sir!" Dane gave credit where it was due.

Van Rycke's brows raised. "I only supplied the end—there might have been another had we not had warning. Your voice, I believe, Frank," he nodded to the steward.

Mura yawned politely behind his hand. His tunic was hanging open, he had a slightly disheveled air, but his emotions were all neatly undercover as always.

"A joint enterprise, sir," he returned. "I would not have been awake to cry out had not Thorson attended to it. He also delivered the motive power with the carpet. It is a wonder to me why Salzar did not burn us first, before he tried to get at you—"

Dane shivered. The smell of the burned bedclothing was strong enough to turn his stomach. He wanted fresh air and lots of it. Also he did *not* want to think of such alternatives as Mura had just spoken about.

"That seals it up," Captain Jellico came back into the room followed by the Patrol Commander. "You've got Rich—what do we do—continue to sit on our fins while you comb the mountains to discover how many ships he smashed up here with that hellish gadget of his?"

"I don't think, Captain, that you will have to stay much longer," began the Commander when Van Rycke interrupted.

"Oh, we're in no great hurry. There is the problem of our rights on Limbo. That hasn't been discussed as yet. We have a Survey Auction claim, duly paid for and registered, reinforced by an 'All Rights' claim good for twelve Terran months. How much these cover salvage and disposal of wrecks found here, and their contents, must be decided—"

"Wrecks as a result of criminal activity," began the Commander once more, only to have the cargo-master cut in smoothly for the second time:

"But there were wrecks here before Salzar found the planet. The machine appears to have run erratically since the Forerunners left. Historically speaking there must be a mine of priceless relics buried in the soil of these mountains. Since *those* smashups can not be considered the result of criminal activity, I do not doubt we can advance a very legal claim to them. Our men discovered—and without much of a search—at least two ships which antedate Salzar's arrival here. Two—there may be hundreds—" he beamed good naturedly at the Commander.

Captain Jellico, listening, lost much of his impatience. He came to sit down beside his cargo-master as if ready to conduct a perfectly normal trade conference.

The Patrolman laughed. "You're not going to pull *me* into any such squabble, Cargo-master. I can relay your claim and protest to

Headquarters—but at the same time I can send you off to quarantine station on Poldar—that's our nearest post—at once—under escort if necessary. I don't think that the Federation is going to turn over any Limbian rights to anyone for some time to come."

"If they move to cancel contracts made in good faith," Van Rycke pointed out, "they are going to pay for it. In addition there will be Video men on Poldar— And we are not Patrol—your rule of silence does not in any way prevent us from answering questions as to our activities of the past few days. This is colorful news, Commander— in a manner of speaking a legend come to life. 'The Sargasso of Space'—a planet filled with a treasury of long lost ships. The romance of it—" Van Rycke's eyes half closed, as if he were slightly overcome by the romantic aspects of his own speech. "You will draw sightseers from all over the Galaxy."

"Yes," Captain Jellico chimed in, "and they'll come equipped with digging apparatus, too. Van," he spoke to the cargo-master, "this is going to be a *big* thing—"

"How true. Luxury hotels—guided tours—claims staked out for digging. A fortune—a veritable fortune."

"No one will land here without official permission!" The Commander struck back.

"Then I do not envy you the patrol you'll have to keep. How the Video boys will love this story," Van Rycke went back into his day-dream. "And," he opened his eyes wide and stared straight at the Commander, "you needn't have any thoughts about putting us in cold storage either. We shall appeal to Trade in hyper code—that you can't jam."

The Patrolman appeared hurt. "Have we given you any indication that we intend to treat you as criminals?"

"Not at all—just some hints here and there. Oh, we'll go off to quarantine like the good, honest, law-abiding Galactic citizens that we are. But as good, honest, law-abiding citizens we shall also tell our story far and wide—unless some adequate arrangements may be made."

The Commander came directly to the point: "And what is your idea of an 'adequate arrangement'?"

"Suitable reparation for our loss of claims here—along with reward money."

"What reward?"

Van Rycke ticked points off on his fingers. "You landed here intact because men from the *Queen* had turned off that installation. The same party from our ship discovered the *Rimbold*, I believe you have been feverishly seeking her for some time now. And we also delivered Salzar to you, neatly done up in a package. I can undoubtedly make other additions to this list—"

Once more the Patrolman laughed. "Who am I to argue with a Trader over his proper profit? I'll post your claim at Headquarters if you promise to hold your collective tongues at quarantine—"

"For a week," Van Rycke answered. "Just seven Terran days. Then Video shall have the story of our lives. So tell your big brass to get moving. We'll lift today—or rather tonight— And we'll go to Poldar. Also we shall notify Trade just where we are and how *long* we shall be there."

"I'll let you fight it out with the big boys." The Commander sounded resigned. "I have your word you'll go directly to Poldar?"

Captain Jellico nodded. "You need not send for an escort. Good hunting, Commander."

Dane and Mura followed their officers out of the room, but the cargo-apprentice was troubled. To be shut up in a Patrol quarantine station was the usual result of a flight to a new and unknown planet. There would be all the poking and prying of doctors and scientists to make sure that neither men nor ship had brought back any deadly disease. But this had overtones of a longer imprisonment. Yet neither the Captain nor Van Rycke appeared in the least cast-down. In fact they were at peace with their world as they had not been since that auction on Naxos.

"Have something in mind, Van?" Jellico's voice could be heard above the rumble of the crawler taking them back to the *Queen*.

"I looked over Salzar's loot pretty carefully. Remember Traxt Cam, Captain?"

"Traxt Cam—he operates out on the Rim—"

"Operated," Van Rycke's voice lost some of its lightness.

"You mean he was one of Salzar's victims?"

"I don't see how else his private record box got in Salzar's general catch. Traxt was on his way in from a very good thing when he smashed here. He'd bid for Sargol. Got it, and was doing all right there—"

"Sargol," repeated the Captain. "Sargol—isn't that planet where they found the Koros—the new jewels?"

"Yes. And Traxt's claim has a year and a half yet to go. We shall point that out to the powers that be. They might well be ready to settle with us even—our Limbo papers turned in without any back chat from us—a full shipment of supplies for the *Queen*—and the rest of Traxt's claim to exploit. How does it sound, Captain?"

"Just like one of your better deals, Van. Yes, the big boys might go for that. It would cost them little and get us out of their hair—put us out on the Rim where we can't talk too much—"

"Might work?" Van Rycke shook his head solemnly. "Captain, give me more credit. Of course it *will* work. Sargol and the Koros—they're waiting for us."

His confidence built a feeling of security. Dane stared out over the bare bones of Limbo without seeing that seared waste, he was trying so hard to picture Sargol. A mining planet with a rich strike and the *Queen*'s Trade claims paramount! Maybe Limbo had brought them luck after all. They'd be able to answer that better in a month or two.

PLAGUE
SHIP

PERFUMED PLANET

1 Dane Thorson, apprentice-cargo-master of the *Solar Queen*, Galactic Free Trader spacer, Terra registry, stood in the middle of the ship's cramped bather while Rip Shannon, assistant astrogator and his senior in the Service of Trade by some four years, applied gobs of highly scented paste to the skin between Dane's rather prominent shoulder blades. The small cabin was thickly redolent with spicy odors and Rip sniffed appreciatively.

"You're sure going to be about the best smelling Terran who ever set boot on Sargol's soil," his soft slur of speech ended in a rich chuckle.

Dane snorted and tried to estimate progress, over one shoulder.

"The things we have to do for Trade!" his comment carried a hint of present embarrassment. "Get it well in—this stuff's supposed to hold for hours. It'd better. According to Van those Salariki can talk your ears right off your head and say nothing worth hearing. And we have to sit and listen until we get a straight answer out of them. Phew!" He shook his head. In such close quarters the scent, pleasing as it was, was also overpowering. "We would have to pick a world such as this—"

Rip's dark fingers halted their circular motion. "Dane," he warned, "don't you go talking against this venture. We got it soft and we're going to be credit-happy—if it works out—"

But, perversely, Dane held to a gloomier view of the immediate future. "*If,*" he repeated. "There's a galaxy of 'ifs' in this Sargol proposition. All very well for you to rest easy on your fins—you don't have to run about smelling like a spice works before you can get the time of day from one of the natives!"

Rip put down the jar of cream. "Different worlds, different customs," he iterated the old tag of the Service. "Be glad this one is so easy to conform to. There are some I can think of— There," he ended his message with a stinging slap, "you're all evenly greased. Good thing you don't have Van's bulk to cover. It takes him a good hour to get his cream on—even with Frank helping to spread. Your clothes ought to be steamed up and ready, too, by now—"

He opened a tight wall cabinet, originally intended to sterilize clothing which might be contaminated by contact with organisms inimical to Terrans. A cloud of steam fragrant with the same spicy scent poured out.

Dane gingerly tugged loose his Trade uniform, its brown silky fabric damp on his skin as he dressed. Luckily Sargol was warm. When he stepped out on its ruby tinted soil this morning no lingering taint of his off-world origin must remain to disgust the sensitive nostrils of the Salariki. He supposed he would get used to this process. After all this was the first time he had undergone the ritual. But he couldn't lose the secret conviction that it was all very silly. Only what Rip had pointed out was the truth—one adjusted to the customs of aliens or one didn't trade and there were other things he might have had to do on other worlds which would have been far more upsetting to that core of private fastidiousness which few would have suspected existed in his tall, lanky frame.

"Whew—out in the open with you—!" Ali Kamil, apprentice engineer, screwed his too regular features into an expression of extreme distaste and waved Dane by him in the corridor.

For the sake of his shipmates' olfactory nerves, Dane hurried on to the port which gave on the ramp now tying the *Queen* to Sargol's crust. But there he lingered, waiting for Van Rycke, the cargo-master of the spacer and his immediate superior. It was early morning and now that he was out of the confinement of the ship the fresh morning winds cut about him, rippling through the blue-green grass forest beyond, to take much of his momentary-irritation with them.

There were no mountains in this section of Sargol—the highest elevations being rounded hills tightly clothed with the same ten-foot grass which covered the plains. From the *Queen's* observation ports, one could watch the constant ripple of the grass so that the planet appeared to be largely clothed in a shimmering, flowing carpet. To the west were the seas—stretches of shallow water so cut up by strings of islands that they more resembled a series of salty lakes. And it was what was to be found in those seas which had lured the *Solar Queen* to Sargol.

Though, by rights, the discovery was that of another Trader—Traxt Cam—who had bid for trading rights to Sargol, hoping to make a comfortable fortune—or at least expenses with a slight profit—in the perfume trade, exporting from the scented planet some of its most fragrant products. But once on Sargol he had discovered the Koros stones—gems of a new type—a handful of which offered across the board in one of the inner planet trading marts had nearly caused a riot among bidding gem merchants. And Cam had been well on the way to becoming one of the princes of Trade when he had been drawn into the vicious net of the Limbian pirates and finished off.

Because they, too, had stumbled into the trap which was Limbo, and had had a very definite part in breaking up that devilish installation, the crew of the *Solar Queen* had claimed as their reward the trading rights of Traxt Cam in default of legal heirs. And so here they were on Sargol with the notes left by Cam as their guide, and as much lore concerning the Salariki as was known crammed into their minds.

Dane sat down on the end of the ramp, his feet on Sargolian soil, thin, red soil with glittering bits of gold flake in it. He did not doubt that he was under observation from hidden eyes, but he tried to show no sign that he guessed it. The adult Salariki maintained at all times an attitude of aloof and complete indifference toward the Traders, but the juvenile population were as curious as their elders were contemptuous. Perhaps there was a method of approach in that. Dane considered the idea.

Van Rycke and Captain Jellico had handled the first negotiations—and the process had taken most of a day—the result totaling exactly nothing. In their contacts with the off-world men the feline ancestered Salariki were ceremonious, wary, and completely detached. But Cam had gotten to them somehow—or he would not have returned from his first trip with that pouch of Koros stones. Only, among his records, salvaged on Limbo, he had left absolutely no clue as to how he had beaten down native sales resistance. It was baffling. But patience had to be the middle name of every Trader and Dane had complete faith in Van. Sooner or later the cargo-master would find a key to unlock the Salariki.

As if the thought of Dane's chief had summoned him, Van Rycke, his scented tunic sealed to his bull's neck in unaccustomed trimness, his cap on his blond head, strode down the ramp, broadcasting waves of fragrance as he moved. He sniffed vigorously as he approached his assistant and then nodded in approval.

"So you're all greased and ready—"

"Is the Captain coming too, sir?"

Van Rycke shook his head. "This is our headache. Patience, my boy, patience—" He led the way through a thin screen of the grass on the other side of the scorched landing field to a well-packed earth road.

Again Dane felt eyes, knew that they were being watched. But no Salariki stepped out of concealment. At least they had nothing to fear in the way of attack. Traders were immune, taboo, and the trading stations were set up under the white diamond shield of peace, a peace guaranteed on blood oath by every clan chieftain in the district. Even in the midst of interclan feuding deadly enemies met in amity under that shield and would not turn claw knife against each other within a two mile radius of its protection.

The grass forests rustled betrayingly, but the Terrans displayed no interest in those who spied upon them. An insect with wings of brilliant green gauze detached itself from the stalk of a grass tree and fluttered ahead of the Traders as if it were an official herald. From the red soil crushed by their boots arose a pungent odor which fought with the scent they carried with them. Dane swallowed three or four times and hoped that his superior officer had not noted that sign of discomfort. Though Van Rycke, in spite of his general air of sleepy benevolence and careless goodwill, noticed everything, no matter how trivial, which might have a bearing on the delicate negotiations of Galactic Trade. He had not climbed to his present status of expert cargo-master by overlooking anything at all. Now he gave an order:

"Take an equalizer—"

Dane reached for his belt pouch, flushing, fiercely determined inside himself, that no matter how smells warred about him that day, he was not going to let it bother him. He swallowed the tiny pellet Medic Tau had prepared for just such trials and tried to occupy his mind with the work to come. If there would be any work—or would another long day be wasted in futile speeches of mutual esteem which gave formal lip service to Trade and its manifest benefits?

"Houuuu—" The cry which was half wail, half arrogant warning, sounded along the road behind them.

Van Rycke's stride did not vary. He did not turn his head, show any sign he had heard that heralding fanfare for a clan chieftain. And he continued to keep to the exact center of the road, Dane the regulation one pace to the rear and left as befitted his lower rank.

"Houuu—" that blast from the throat of a Salarik especially chosen for his lung power was accompanied now by the hollow drum of many feet. The Terrans neither looked around nor withdrew from the center, nor did their pace quicken.

That, too, was in order, Dane knew. To the rank conscious Salariki clansmen you did not yield precedence unless you wanted at once to acknowledge your inferiority—and if you did that by some slip of admission or omission, there was no use in trying to treat face to face with their chieftains again.

"Houuu—!" The blast behind was a scream as the retinue it announced swept around the bend in the road to catch sight of the two Traders oblivious of it. Dane longed to be able to turn his head, just enough to see which one of the local lordlings they blocked.

"Houu—" There was a questioning note in the cry now and the heavy thud-thud of feet was slacking. The clan party had seen them, were hesitant about the wisdom of trying to shove them aside.

Van Rycke marched steadily onward and Dane matched his pace. They might not possess a leather-lunged herald to clear their road, but they gave every indication of having the right to occupy as much of it as they wished. And that unruffled poise had its affect upon those behind. The pound of feet slowed to a walk, a walk which would keep a careful distance behind the two Terrans. It had worked—the Salariki—or these Salariki—were accepting them at their own valuation—a good omen for the day's business. Dane's spirits rose, but he schooled his features into a mask as wooden as his superior's. After all this was a very minor victory and they had ten or twelve hours of polite, and hidden, maneuvering before them.

The *Solar Queen* had set down as closely as possible to the trading center marked on Traxt Cam's private map and the Terrans now had another five minutes march, in the middle of the road, ahead of the chieftain who must be inwardly boiling at their presence, before they came out in the clearing containing the roofless, circular erection which served the Salariki of the district as a market place and a common meeting ground for truce talks and the mending of private clan alliances. Erect on a pole in the middle, towering well above the nodding fronds of the grass trees, was the pole bearing the trade shield which promised not only peace to those under it, but a three-day sanctuary to any feuder or duelist who managed to win to it and lay hands upon its weathered standard.

They were not the first to arrive, which was also a good thing. Gathered in small groups about the walls of the council place were the personal attendants, liege warriors, and younger relatives of at least four or five clan chieftains. But, Dane noted at once, there was not a single curtained litter or riding orgel to be seen. None of the feminine part of the Salariki species had arrived. Nor would they until the final trade treaty was concluded and established by their fathers, husbands, or sons.

With the assurance of one who was master in his own clan, Van Rycke, displaying no interest at all in the shifting mass of lower rank Salariki, marched straight on to the door of the enclosure. Two or three of the younger warriors got to their feet, their brilliant cloaks flicking out like spreading wings. But when Van Rycke did not even lift an eyelid in their direction, they made no move to block his path.

As fighting men, Dane thought, trying to study the specimens before him with a totally impersonal stare, the Salariki were an impressive lot. Their average height was close to six feet, their distant feline ancestry apparent only in small vestiges. A Salarik's nails on both hands and feet were retractile, his skin was gray, his thick hair, close to the texture of plushy fur, extended down his backbone and along the outside of his well muscled arms and legs, and was tawny-yellow, blue-gray or white. To Terran eyes the broad faces, now all turned in their direction, lacked readable expression. The eyes were large and set slightly aslant in the skull, being startlingly orange-red or a brilliant turquoise green-blue. They wore loin clothes of brightly dyed fabrics with wide sashes forming corselets about their slender middles, from which gleamed the gem-set hilts of their claw knives, the possession of which proved their adulthood. Cloaks as flamboyant as their other garments hung in bat wing folds from their shoulders and each and every one moved in an invisible cloud of perfume.

Brilliant as the assemblage of liege men without had been, the gathering of clan leaders and their upper officers within the council place was a riot of color—and odor. The chieftains were installed on the wooden stools, each with a small table before him on which rested a goblet bearing his own clan sign, a folded strip of patterned cloth—his "trade shield"—and a gemmed box containing the scented paste he would use for refreshment during the ordeal of conference.

A breeze fluttered sash ends and tugged at cloaks, otherwise the assembly was motionless and awesomely quiet. Still making no overtures Van Rycke crossed to a stool and table which stood a little apart and seated himself. Dane went into the action required of him. Before his superior he set out a plastic pocket flask, its color as alive in the sunlight as the crudely cut gems which the Salariki sported, a fine silk handkerchief, and, last of all, a bottle of Terran smelling salts provided by Medic Tau as a necessary restorative after some hours combination of Salariki oratory and Salariki perfumes. Having thus done the duty of liege man, Dane was at liberty to seat himself, cross-legged on the ground behind his chief, as the other sons, heirs, and advisors had gathered behind their lords.

The chieftain whose arrival they had in a manner delayed came in after them and Dane saw that it was Fashdor—another piece of luck—since that clan was a small one and the chieftain had little influence. Had they so slowed Halfer or Paft it might be a different matter altogether.

Fashdor was established at his seat, his belongings spread out, and Dane, counting unobtrusively, was certain that the council was now complete. Seven clans Traxt Cam had recorded divided the sea coast territory and there were seven chieftains here—indicative of the importance of this meeting since some of these clans, beyond the radius of the shield peace, must be fighting a vicious blood feud at that very moment. Yes, seven were here. Yet there still remained a single stool, directly across the circle from Van Rycke. An empty stool— who was the latecomer?

That question was answered almost as it flashed into Dane's mind. But no Salariki lordling came through the door. Dane's self-control kept him in his place, even after he caught the meaning of the insignia emblazoned across the newcomer's tunic. Trader—and not only a Trader but a Company man! But why—and how? The Companies only went after big game—this was a planet thrown open to Free Traders, the independents of the star lanes. By law and right no Company man had any place here. Unless—behind a face Dane strove to keep as impassive as Van's his thoughts raced. Traxt Cam as a Free Trader had bid for the right to exploit Sargol when its sole exportable product was deemed to be perfume—a small, unimportant trade as far as the Companies were concerned. And then the Koros stones had been found and the importance of Sargol must have boomed as far as the big boys could see. They probably knew of Traxt Cam's death as soon as the Patrol report on Limbo had been sent to Headquarters. The Companies all maintained their private information and espionage services. And, with Traxt Cam dead without an heir, they had seen their chance and moved in. Only, Dane's teeth set firmly, they didn't have the ghost of a chance now. Legally there was only one Trader on Sargol and that was the *Solar Queen,* Captain Jellico had his records signed by the Patrol to prove that. And all this Inter-Solar man could do now was to bow out and try poaching elsewhere.

But the I-S man appeared to be in no haste to follow that only possible course. He was seating himself with arrogant dignity on that unoccupied stool, and a younger man in I-S uniform was putting before him the same type of equipment Dane had produced for Van Rycke. The cargo-master of the *Solar Queen* showed no surprise, if the Eysies' appearance had been such to him.

One of the younger warriors in Paft's train got to his feet and brought his hands together with a clap which echoed across the silent gathering with the force of an archaic solid projectal shot. A Salarik, wearing the rich dress of the upper ranks, but also the collar forced upon a captive taken in combat, came into the enclosure carrying a jug in both hands. Preceded by Paft's son he made the rounds of the assembly pouring a purple liquid from his jug into the goblet before each chieftain, a goblet which Paft's heirs tasted ceremoniously before it was presented to the visiting clan leader. When they paused before Van Rycke the Salarik nobleman touched the side of the plasta flask in token. It was recognized that off-world men must be cautious over the sampling of local products and that when they joined in the Taking of the First Cup of Peace, they did so symbolically.

Paft raised his cup, his gesture copied by everyone around the circle. In the harsh tongue of his race he repeated a formula so archaic that few of the Salariki could now translate the sing-song words. They drank and the meeting was formally opened.

But it was an elderly Salarik seated to the right of Halfer, a man who wore no claw knife and whose dusky yellow cloak and sash made a subdued note amid the splendor of his fellows, who spoke first, using the click-clack of the Trade Lingo his nation had learned from Cam.

"Under the white," he pointed to the shield aloft, "we assemble to hear many things. But now come two tongues to speak where once there was but one father of a clan. Tell us, outlanders, which of you must we now hark to in truth?" He looked from Van Rycke to the I-S representative.

The cargo-master from the *Queen* did not reply. He stared across the circle at the Company man. Dane waited eagerly. What *was* the I-S going to say to that?

But the fellow did have an answer, ready and waiting. "It is true, fathers of clans, that here are two voices, where by right and custom there should only be one. But this is a matter which can be decided between us. Give us leave to withdraw from your sight and speak privately together. Then he who returns to you will be the true voice and there shall be no more division—"

It was Paft who broke in before Halfer's spokesman could reply.

"It would have been better to have spoken together before you came to us. Go then until the shadow of the shield is not, then return hither and speak truly. We do not wait upon the pleasure of outlanders—"

A murmur approved that tart comment. "Until the shadow of the shield is not." They had until noon. Van Rycke arose and Dane gathered up his chief's possessions. With the same superiority to his surroundings he had shown upon entering, the cargo-master left the enclosure, the Eysies following. But they were away from the clearing, out upon the road back to the *Queen* before the two from the Company caught up with them.

"Captain Grange will see you right away—" the Eysie cargo-master was beginning when Van Rycke met him with a quelling stare.

"If you poachers have anything to say—you say it at the *Queen* and to Captain Jellico," he stated flatly and started on.

Above his tight tunic collar the other's face flushed, his teeth flashed as he caught his lower lip between them as if to forcibly restrain an answer he longed to make. For a second he hesitated and then he vanished down a side path with his assistant. Van Rycke had gone a quarter of the distance back to the ship before he spoke.

"I thought it was too easy," he muttered. "Now we're in for it— maybe right up the rockets! By the Spiked Tail of Exol, this is certainly *not* our lucky day!" He quickened pace until they were close to trotting.

RIVALS

2

"That's far enough, Eysie!"

Although Traders by law and tradition carried no more potent personal weapons—except in times of great crisis—than hand sleep rods, the resultant shot from the latter was just as unpleasant for temporary periods as a more forceful beam—and the threat of it was enough to halt the three men who had come to the foot of the *Queen*'s ramp and who could see the rod held rather negligently by Ali. Ali's eyes were anything but negligent, however, and Free Traders had reputations to be respected by their rivals of the Companies. The very nature of their roving lives taught them savage lessons—which they either learned or died.

Dane, glancing down over the engineer-apprentice's shoulder, saw that Van Rycke's assumption of confidence had indeed paid off. They had left the trade enclosure of the Salariki barely three-quarters of an hour ago. But below now stood the bebadged Captain of the I-S ship and his cargo-master.

"I want to speak to your Captain—" snarled the Eysie officer.

Ali registered faint amusement, an expression which tended to rouse the worst in the spectator, as Dane knew of old when that same mocking appraisal had been turned on him as the rawest of the *Queen*'s crew.

"But does *he* wish to speak to you?" countered Kamil. "Just stay where you are, Eysie, until we are sure about that fact."

That was his cue to act as messenger. Dane retreated into the ship and swung up the ladder to the command section. As he passed Captain Jellico's private cabin he heard the muffled squall of the commander's unpleasant pet—Queex, the Hoobat—a nightmare combination of crab, parrot and toad, wearing a blue feather coating and inclined to scream and spit at all comers. Since Queex would not be howling in that fashion if its master was present, Dane kept on to the control cabin where he blundered in upon an executive level conference of Captain, cargo-master and astrogator.

"Well?" Jellico's blaster-scarred left cheek twitched as he snapped that impatient inquiry at the messenger.

"Eysie Captain below, sir. With his cargo-master. They want to see you—"

Jellico's mouth was a straight line, his eyes very hard. By instinct Dane's hand went to the grip of the sleep rod slung at his belt. When the Old Man put on his fighting face—look out! Here we go again, he told himself, speculating as to just what type of action lay before them now.

"Oh, they do, do they!" Jellico began and then throttled down the temper he could put under iron control when and if it were necessary. "Very well, tell them to stay where they are. Van, we'll go down—"

For a moment the cargo-master hesitated, his heavy-lidded eyes looked sleepy, he seemed almost disinterested in the suggestion. And when he nodded it was with the air of someone about to perform some boring duty.

"Right, sir." He wriggled his heavy body from behind the small table, resealed his tunic, and settled his cap with as much precision as if he were about to represent the *Queen* before the assembled nobility of Sargol.

Dane hurried down the ladders, coming to a halt beside Ali. It was the turn of the man at the foot of the ramp to bark an impatient demand:

"Well?" (Was that the theme word of every Captain's vocabulary?)

"You wait," Dane replied with no inclination to give the Eysie officer any courtesy address. Close to a Terran year aboard the *Solar Queen* had inoculated him with pride in his own section of Service. A Free Trader was answerable to his own officers and to no one else on earth—or among the stars—no matter how much discipline and official etiquette the Companies used to enhance their power.

He half expected the I-S officers to leave after an answer such as that. For a Company Captain to be forced to wait upon the convenience of a Free Trader must be galling in the extreme. And the fact that this one was doing just that was an indication that the *Queen*'s crew did, perhaps, have the edge of advantage in any coming bargain. In the meantime the Eysie contingent fumed below while Ali lounged whistling against the exit port, playing with his sleep rod and Dane studied the grass forest. His boot nudged a packet just inside the port casing and he glanced inquiringly from it to Ali.

"Cat ransom," the other answered his unspoken question.

So that was it—the fee for Sinbad's return. "What is it today?"

"Sugar—about a tablespoon full," the engineer-assistant returned, "and two colored steelos. So far they haven't run up the price on us. I think they're sharing out the spoil evenly, a new cub brings him back every night."

As did all Terran ships, the *Solar Queen* carried a cat as an important member of her regular crew. And the portly Sinbad, before their landing on Sargol, had never presented any problem. He had done his duty of ridding the ship of unusual and usual pests and cargo despoilers with dispatch, neatness and energy. And when in port on alien worlds had never shown any inclination to go a-roving.

But the scents of Sargol had apparently intoxicated him, shearing away his solid dignity and middle-aged dependability. Now Sinbad flashed out of the *Queen* at the opening of her port in the early morning and was brought back, protesting with both voice and claws, at the end of the day by that member of the juvenile population whose turn it was to collect the standing reward for his forceful delivery. Within three days it had become an accepted business transaction which satisfied everyone but Sinbad.

The scrape of metal boot soles on ladder rungs warned of the arrival of their officers. Ali and Dane withdrew down the corridor, leaving the entrance open for Jellico and Van Rycke. Then they drifted back to witness the meeting with the Eysies.

There were no prolonged greetings between the two parties, no offer of hospitality as might have been expected between Terrans on an alien planet a quarter of the Galaxy away from the earth which had given them a common heritage.

Jellico, with Van Rycke at his shoulder, halted before he stepped from the ramp so that the three Inter-Solar men, Captain, cargo-master and escort, whether they wished or no, were put in the disadvantageous position of having to look up to a Captain whom they, as members of one of the powerful Companies, affected to despise. The lean, well muscled, trim figure of the *Queen*'s commander gave the impression of hard bitten force held in check by will control, just as his face under its thick layer of space burn was that of an adventurer accustomed to making split-second decisions—an estimate underlined by that seam of blaster burn across one flat cheek.

Van Rycke, with a slight change of dress, could have been a Company man in the higher ranks—or so the casual observer would have placed him, until such an observer marked the eyes behind those sleepy drooping lids, or caught a certain note in the calm, unhurried drawl of his voice. To look at the two senior officers of the Free Trading spacer were the antithesis of each other—in action they were each half of a powerful, steamroller whole—as a good many men in the Service—scattered over a half dozen or so planets—had discovered to their cost in the past.

Now Jellico brought the heels of his space boots together with an extravagant click and his hand flourished at the fore of his helmet in a gesture which was better suited to the Patrol hero of a slightly out-of-date Video serial.

"Jellico, *Solar Queen,* Free Trader," he identified himself brusquely, and added, "This is Van Rycke, our cargo-master."

Not all the flush had faded from the face of the I-S Captain.

"Grange of the *Dart,*" he did not even sketch a salute. "Inter-Solar. Kallee, cargo-master—" And he did not name the hovering third member of his party.

Jellico stood waiting and after a long moment of silence Grange was forced to state his business.

"We have until noon—"

Jellico, his fingers hooked in his belt, simply waited. And under his level gaze the Eysie Captain began to find the going hard.

"They have given us until noon," he started once more, "to get together—"

Jellico's voice came, coldly remote. "There is no reason for any 'getting together,' Grange. By rights I can have you up before the Trade Board for poaching. The *Solar Queen* has sole trading rights here. If you up-ship within a reasonable amount of time, I'll be inclined to let it pass. After all I've no desire to run all the way to the nearest Patrol post to report you—"

"You can't expect to buck Inter-Solar. We'll make you an offer—" That was Kallee's contribution, made probably because his commanding officer couldn't find words explosive enough.

Jellico, whose forté was more direct action, took an excursion into heavy-handed sarcasm. "You Eysies have certainly been given excellent briefing. I would advise a little closer study of the Code—and not the sections in small symbols at the end of the tape, either! *We're* not bucking anyone. You'll find our registration for Sargol down on tapes at the Center. And I suggest that the sooner you withdraw the better—before we cite you for illegal planeting."

Grange had gained control of his emotions. "We're pretty far from Center here," he remarked. It was a statement of fact, but it carried over-tones which they were able to assess correctly. The *Solar Queen* was a Free Trader, alone on an alien world. But the I-S ship might be cruising in company, ready to summon aid, men and supplies. Dane drew a deep breath, the Eysies *must* be sure of themselves, not only that, but they must want what Sargol had to offer to the point of being willing to step outside the law to get it.

The I-S Captain took a step forward. "I think we understand each other now," he said, his confidence restored.

Van Rycke answered him, his deep voice cutting across the sighing of the wind in the grass forest.

"Your proposition?"

Perhaps this return to their implied threat bolstered their belief in the infallibility of the Company, their conviction that no independent dared stand up against the might and power of Inter-Solar. Kallee replied:

"We'll take up your contract, at a profit to you, and you up-ship before the Salariki are confused over whom they are to deal with—"

"And the amount of profit?" Van Rycke bored in.

"Oh," Kallee shrugged, "say ten percent of Cam's last shipment—"

Jellico laughed. "Generous, aren't you, Eysie? Ten percent of a cargo which can't be assessed—the gang on Limbo kept no records of what they plundered."

"We don't know what he was carrying when he crashed on Limbo," countered Kallee swiftly. "We'll base our offer on what he carried to Axal."

Now Van Rycke chuckled. "I wonder who figured that one out?" he inquired of the scented winds. "He must save the Company a fair amount of credits one way or another. Interesting offer—"

By the bland satisfaction to be read on the three faces below the I-S men were assured of their victory. The *Solar Queen* would be paid off with a pittance, under the vague threat of Company retaliation she would up-ship from Sargol, and they would be left in possession of the rich Koros trade—to be commended and rewarded by their superiors. Had they, Dane speculated, ever had any dealings with Free Traders before—at least with the brand of independent adventurers such as manned the *Solar Queen*?

Van Rycke burrowed in his belt pouch and then held out his hand. On the broad palm lay a flat disc of metal. "Very interesting—" he repeated. "I shall treasure this recording—"

The sight of that disc wiped all satisfaction from the Eysie faces. Grange's purplish flush spread up from his tight tunic collar, Kallee blinked, and the unknown third's hand dropped to his sleep rod. An action which was not overlooked by either Dane or Ali.

"A smooth set down to you," Jellico gave the conventional leave taking of the Service.

"You'd better—" the Eysie Captain began hotly, and then seeing the disc Van Rycke held—that sensitive bit of metal and plastic which was recording this interview for future reference, he shut his mouth tight.

"Yes?" the *Queen*'s cargo-master prompted politely. But Kallee had taken his Captain's arm and was urging Grange away from the spacer.

"You have until noon to lift," was Jellico's parting shot as the three in Company livery started toward the road.

"I don't think that they will," he added to Van Rycke.

The cargo-master nodded. "You wouldn't in their place," he pointed out reasonably. "On the other hand they've had a bit of a blast they weren't expecting. It's been a long time since Grange heard anyone say 'no.'"

"A shock which is going to wear off," Jellico's habitual distrust of the future gathered force.

"This," Van Rycke tucked the disc back into his pouch, "sent them off vector a parsec or two. Grange is not one of the strong arm blaster boys. Suppose Tang Ya does a little listening in—and maybe we can rig another surprise if Grange does try to ask advice of someone off world. In the meantime I don't think they are going to meddle with the Salariki. They don't want to have to answer awkward questions if

we turn up a Patrol ship to ask them. So—" he stretched and beckoned to Dane, "we shall go to work once more."

Again two paces behind Van Rycke Dane tramped to the trade circle of the Salariki clansmen. They might have walked out only five or
six minutes of ship time before, and the natives betrayed no particular
interest in their return. But, Dane noted, there was only one empty
stool, one ceremonial table in evidence. The Salariki had expected
only one Terran Trader to join them.

What followed was a dreary round of ceremony, an exchange of
platitudes and empty good wishes and greetings. No one mentioned
Koros stones—or even perfume bark—that he was willing to offer
the off-world traders. None lifted so much as a corner of his trade
cloth, under which, if he were ready to deal seriously, his hidden
hand would meet that of the buyer, so that by finger pressure alone
they could agree or disagree on price. But such boring sessions were
part of Trade and Dane, keeping a fraction of attention on the
speeches and "drinkings-together," watched those around him with
an eye which tried to assess and classify what he saw.

The keynote of the Salariki character was a wary independence.
The only form of government they would tolerate was a family-clan
organization. Feuds and deadly duels between individuals and clans
were the accepted way of life and every male who reached adulthood
went armed and ready for combat until he became a "Speaker for the
Past"—too old to bear arms in the field. Due to the nature of their
battling lives, relatively few of the Salariki ever reached that retire-
ment. Short-lived alliances between families sometimes occurred,
usually when they were to face a common enemy greater than either.
But a quarrel between chieftains, a fancied insult would rip that open
in an instant. Only under the Trade Shield could seven clans sit this
way without their warriors being at one another's furred throats.

An hour before sunset Paft turned his goblet upside down on his
table, a move followed speedily by every chieftain in the circle. The
conference was at an end for that day. And as far as Dane could see it
had accomplished exactly nothing—except to bring the Eysies into

the open. What *had* Traxt Cam discovered which had given him the trading contact with these suspicious aliens? Unless the men from the *Queen* learned it, they could go on talking until the contract ran out and get no farther than they had today.

From his training Dane knew that ofttimes contact with an alien race did require long and patient handling. But between study and experiencing the situation himself there was a gulf, and he thought somewhat ruefully that he had much to learn before he could meet such a situation with Van Rycke's unfailing patience and aplomb. The cargo-master seemed in nowise tired by his wasted day and Dane knew that Van would probably sit up half the night, going over for the hundredth time Traxt Cam's sketchy recordings in another painstaking attempt to discover why and how the other Free Trader had succeeded where the *Queen*'s men were up against a stone wall.

The harvesting of Koros stones was, as Dane and all those who had been briefed from Cam's records knew, a perilous job. Though the rule of the Salariki was undisputed on the land masses of Sargol, it was another matter in the watery world of the shallow seas. There the Gorp were in command of the territory and one had to be constantly alert for attack from that sly, reptilian intelligence, so alien to the thinking processes of both Salariki and Terran that there was, or seemed to be, no point of possible contact. One went gathering Koros gems after balancing life against gain. And perhaps the Salariki did not see any profit in that operation. Yet Traxt Cam had brought back his bag of gems—somehow he had managed to secure them in trade.

Van Rycke climbed the ramp, hurrying on into the *Queen* as if he could not get back to his records soon enough. But Dane paused and looked back at the grass jungle a little wistfully. To his mind these early evening hours were the best time on Sargol. The light was golden, the night winds had not yet arisen. He disliked exchanging the freedom of the open for the confinement of the spacer.

And, as he hesitated there, two of the juvenile population of Sargol came out of the forest. Between them they carried one of their hunting nets, a net which now enclosed a quiet but baneful eyed captive—Sinbad being delivered for nightly ransom. Dane was reaching for the pay to give the captors when, to his real astonishment, one of them advanced and pointed with an extended forefinger claw to the open port.

"Go in," he formed the Trade Lingo words with care. And Dane's surprise must have been plain to read for the cub followed his speech with a vigorous nod and set one foot on the ramp to underline his desire.

For one of the Salariki, who had continually manifested their belief that Terrans and their ship were an offence to the nostrils of all right living "men," to wish to enter the spacer was an astonishing about-face. But any advantage no matter how small, which might bring about a closer understanding, must be seized at once.

Dane accepted the growling Sinbad and beckoned, knowing better than to touch the boy. "Come—"

Only one of the junior clansmen obeyed that invitation. The other watched, big-eyed, and then scuttled back to the forest when his fellow called out some suggestion. *He* was not going to be trapped.

Dane led the way up the ramp, paying no visible attention to the young Salarik, nor did he urge the other on when he lingered for a long moment or two at the port. In his mind the cargo-master apprentice was feverishly running over the list of general trade goods. What *did* they carry which would make a suitable and intriguing gift for a small alien with such a promising bump of curiosity? If he had only time to get Van Rycke!

The Salarik was inside the corridor now, his nostrils spread, assaying each and every odor in this strange place. Suddenly his head jerked as if tugged by one of his own net ropes. His interest had been riveted by some scent his sensitive senses had detected. His eyes met Dane's in appeal. Swiftly the Terran nodded and then followed with a lengthened stride as the Salarik sped down into the lower reaches of the *Queen,* obviously in quest of something of great importance.

CONTACT AT LAST

3 "What in"—Frank Mura, steward, storekeeper, and cook of the *Queen,* retreated into the nearest cabin doorway as the young Salarik flashed down the ladder into his section.

Dane, with the now resigned Sinbad in the crook of his arm, had tailed his guest and arrived just in time to see the native come to an abrupt halt before one of the most important doors in the spacer—the portal of the hydro garden which renewed the ship's oxygen and supplied them with fresh fruit and vegetables to vary their diet of concentrates.

The Salarik laid one hand on the smooth surface of the sealed compartment and looked back over his shoulder at Dane with an inquiry to which was added something of a plea. Guided by his instinct—that this was important to them all—Dane spoke to Mura:

"Can you let him in there, Frank?"

It was not sensible, it might even be dangerous. But every member of the crew knew the necessity for making some sort of contact with the natives. Mura did not even nod, but squeezed by the Salarik and pressed the lock. There was a sigh of air, and the crisp smell of growing things, lacking the languorous perfumes of the world outside, puffed into their faces.

The cub remained where he was, his head up, his wide nostrils visibly drinking in that smell. Then he moved with the silent, uncanny speed which was the heritage of his race, darting down the narrow aisle toward a mass of greenery at the far end.

Sinbad kicked and growled. This was his private hunting ground—the preserve he kept free of invaders. Dane put the cat down. The Salarik had found what he was seeking. He stood on tiptoe to sniff at a plant, his yellow eyes half closed, his whole stance spelling ecstasy. Dane looked to the steward for enlightenment.

"What's he so interested in, Frank?"

"Catnip."

"Catnip?" Dane repeated. The word meant nothing to him, but Mura had a habit of picking up strange plants and cultivating them for study. "What is it?"

"One of the Terran mints—an herb," Mura gave a short explanation as he moved down the aisle toward the alien. He broke off a leaf and crushed it between his fingers.

Dane, his sense of smell largely deadened by the pungency with which he had been surrounded by most of that day, could distinguish no new odor. But the young Salarik swung around to face the steward, his eyes wide, his nose questing. And Sinbad gave a whining yowl and made a spring to push his head against the steward's now aromatic hand.

So—now they had it—an opening wedge. Dane came up to the three.

"All right to take a leaf or two?" he asked Mura.

"Why not? I grow it for Sinbad. To a cat it is like heemel smoke or a tankard of lackibod."

And by Sinbad's actions Dane guessed that the plant did hold for the cat the same attraction those stimulants produced in human beings. He carefully broke off a small stem supporting three leaves and presented it to the Salarik, who stared at him and then, snatching the twig, raced from the hydro garden as if pursued by feuding clansmen.

Dane heard the pad of his feet on the ladder—apparently the cub was making sure of escape with his precious find. But the cargo-master apprentice was frowning. As far as he could see there were only five of the plants.

"That's all the catnip you have?"

Mura tucked Sinbad under his arm and shooed Dane before him out of the hydro. "There was no need to grow more. A small portion of the herb goes a long way with this one," he put the cat down in the corridor. "The leaves may be preserved by drying. I believe that there is a small box of them in the galley."

A strictly limited supply. Suppose this was the key which would unlock the Koros trade? And yet it was to be summed up in five plants and a few dried leaves! However, Van Rycke must know of this as soon as possible.

But to Dane's growing discomfiture the cargo-master showed no elation as his junior poured out the particulars of his discovery. Instead there were definite signs of displeasure to be read by those who knew Van Rycke well. He heard Dane out and then got to his feet. Tolling the younger man with him by a crooked finger, he went out of his combined office-living quarters to the domain of Medic Craig Tau.

"Problem for you, Craig." Van Rycke seated his bulk on the wall jump seat Tau pulled down for him. Dane was left standing just within the door, very sure now that instead of being commended for his discovery of a few minutes before, he was about to suffer some reprimand. And the reason for it still eluded him.

"What do you know about that plant Mura grows in the hydro— the one called 'catnip'?"

Tau did not appear surprised at that demand—the medic of a Free Trading spacer was never surprised at anything. He had his surfeit of shocks during his first years of service and after that accepted any occurrence, no matter how weird, as matter-of-fact. In addition Tau's hobby was "magic," the hidden knowledge possessed and used by witch doctors and medicine men on alien worlds. He had a library of recordings, of odd scraps of information, of certified results of certain very peculiar experiments. Now and then he wrote a report which was sent into Central Service, read with raised eyebrows by perhaps half a dozen incredulous desk warmers, and filed away to be safely forgotten. But even that had ceased to frustrate him.

"It's an herb of the mint family from Terra," he replied. "Mura grows it for Sinbad—has quite a marked influence on cats. Frank's been trying to keep him anchored to the ship by allowing him to roll in fresh leaves. He does it—then continues to sneak out whenever he can—"

That explained something for Dane—why the Salariki cub wished to enter the *Queen* tonight. Some of the scent of the plant had clung to Sinbad's fur, had been detected, and the Salarik had wanted to trace it to its source.

"Is it a drug?" Van Rycke prodded.

"In the way that all herbs are drugs. Human beings have dosed themselves in the past with a tea made of the dried leaves. It has no great medicinal properties. To felines it is a stimulant—and they get the same satisfaction from rolling in and eating the leaves as we do from drinking—"

"The Salariki are, in a manner of speaking, felines—" Van Rycke mused.

Tau straightened. "The Salariki have discovered catnip, I take it?"

Van Rycke nodded at Dane and for the second time the cargo-master apprentice made his report. When he was done Van Rycke asked a direct question of the medical officer:

"What affect would catnip have on a Salarik?"

It was only then that Dane grasped the enormity of what he had done. They had no way of gauging the influence of an off-world plant on alien metabolism. What if he had introduced to the natives of Sargol a dangerous drug—started that cub on some path of addiction. He was cold inside. Why, he might even have poisoned the child!

Tau picked up his cap, and after a second's hesitation, his emergency medical kit. He had only one question for Dane.

"Any idea of who the cub is—what clan he belongs to?"

And Dane, chill with real fear, was forced to answer in the negative. What *had* he done!

"Can you find him?" Van Rycke, ignoring Dane, spoke to Tau.

The medic shrugged. "I can try. I was out scouting this morning—met one of the storm priests who handles their medical work. But I wasn't welcomed. However, under the circumstances, we have to try something—"

In the corridor Van Rycke had an order for Dane. "I suggest that you keep to quarters, Thorson, until we know how matters stand."

Dane saluted. That note in his superior's voice was like a whip lash—much worse to take than the abuse of a lesser man. He swallowed as he shut himself into his own cramped cubby. This might be the end of their venture. And they would be lucky if their charter was not withdrawn. Let I-S get an inkling of his rash action and the Company would have them up before the Board to be stripped of all their rights in the Service. Just because of his own stupidity—his pride in being able to break through where Van Rycke and the Captain had faced a stone wall. And, worse than the future which could face the *Queen,* was the thought that he might have introduced some dangerous drug into Sargol with his gift of those few leaves. When would he learn? He threw himself facedown on his bunk and despondently pictured the string of calamities which could and maybe would stem from his thoughtless and hasty action.

Within the *Queen* night and day were mechanical—the lighting in the cabins did not vary much. Dane did not know how long he lay there forcing his mind to consider his stupid action, making himself face that in the Service there were no shortcuts which endangered others—not unless those taking the risks were Terrans.

"Dane—!" Rip Shannon's voice cut through his self-imposed nightmare. But he refused to answer. "Dane—Van wants you on the double!"

Why? To bring him up before Jellico probably. Dane schooled his expression, got up, pulling his tunic straight, still unable to meet Rip's eyes. Shannon was just one of those he had let down so badly. But the other did not notice his mood. "Wait 'til you see them—! Half Sargol must be here yelling for trade!"

That comment was so far from what he had been expecting that Dane was startled out of his own gloomy thoughts. Rip's brown face was one wide smile, his black eyes danced—it was plain he was honestly elated.

"Get a move on, fire rockets," he urged, "or Van will blast you for fair!"

Dane did move, up the ladder to the next level and out on the port ramp. What he saw below brought him up short. Evening had come to Sargol but the scene immediately below was not in darkness. Blazing torches advanced in lines from the grass forest and the portable flood light of the spacer added to the general glare, turning night into noonday.

Van Rycke and Jellico sat on stools facing at least five of the seven major chieftains with whom they had conferred to no purpose earlier. And behind these leaders milled a throng of lesser Salariki. Yes, there was at least one carrying chair—and also an orgel from the back of which a veiled noble-woman was being assisted to dismount by two retainers. The women of the clans were coming—which could mean only that trade was at last in progress. But trade for what?

Dane strode down the ramp. He saw Paft, his hand carefully covered by his trade cloth, advance to Van Rycke, whose own fingers were decently veiled by a handkerchief. Under the folds of fabric their hands touched. The bargaining was in the first stages. And it was important enough for the clan leaders to conduct themselves. Where, according to Cam's records, it had been usual to delegate that power to a favored liege man.

Catching the light from the ship's beam and from the softer flares of the Salariki torches was a small pile of stones resting on a stool to one side. Dane drew a deep breath. He had heard the Koros stones described, had seen the tri-dee print of one found among Cam's recordings but the reality was beyond his expectations. He knew the technical analysis of the gems—that they were, as the amber of Terra, the fossilized resin exuded by ancient plants (maybe the ancestors of the grass trees) long buried in the saline deposits of the shallow seas where chemical changes had taken place to produce the wonder jewels. In color they shaded from a rosy apricot to a rich mauve, but in their depths other colors, silver, fiery gold, spun sparks which seemed to move as the gem was turned. And—which was what first endeared them to the Salariki—when worn against the skin and warmed by body heat they gave off a perfume which enchanted not only the Sargolian natives but all in the Galaxy wealthy enough to own one.

On another stool placed at Van Rycke's right hand, as that bearing the Koros stones was at Paft's, was a transparent plastic box containing some wrinkled brownish leaves. Dane moved as unobtrusively as he could to his proper place at such a trading session, behind Van Rycke. More Salariki were tramping out of the forest, torch bearing retainers and cloaked warriors. A little to one side was a third party Dane had not seen before.

They were clustered about a staff which had been driven into the ground, a staff topped with a white streamer marking a temporary trading ground. These were Salariki right enough but they did not wear the colorful garb of those about them, instead they were all clad alike in muffling, sleeved robes of a drab green—the storm priests—their robes denoting the color of the Sargolian sky just before the onslaught of their worst tempests. Cam had not left many clues concerning the religion of the Salariki, but the storm priests had, in narrowly defined limits, power, and their recognition of the Terran Traders would add to good feeling.

In the knot of storm priests a Terran stood—Medic Tau—and he was talking earnestly with the leader of the religious party. Dane would have given much to have been free to cross and ask Tau a question or two. Was all this assembly the result of the discovery in the hydro? But even as he asked himself that, the trade cloths were shaken from the hands of the bargainers and Van Rycke gave an order over his shoulder.

"Measure out two spoonsful of the dried leaves into a box—" He pointed to a tiny plastic container.

With painstaking care Dane followed directions. At the same time a servant of the Salarik chief swept the handful of gems from the other stool and dropped them in a heap before Van Rycke, who transferred them to a strong box resting between his feet. Paft arose—but he had hardly quitted the trading seat before one of the lesser clan leaders had taken his place, the bargaining cloth ready looped loosely about his wrist.

It was at that point that the proceedings were interrupted. A new party came into the open, their utilitarian Trade tunics making a drab blot as they threaded their way in a compact group through the throng of Salariki. I-S men! So they had not lifted from Sargol.

They showed no signs of uneasiness—it was as if *their* rights were being infringed by the Free Traders. And Kallee, their cargo-master, swaggered straight to the bargaining point. The chatter of Salariki voices was stilled, the Sargolians withdrew a little, letting one party of Terrans face the other, sensing drama to come. Neither Van Rycke nor Jellico spoke, it was left to Kallee to state his case.

"You've crooked your orbit this time, bright boys," his jeer was a pean of triumph. "Code Three—Article Six—or can't you absorb rules tapes with your thick heads?"

Code Three—Article Six, Dane searched his memory for that law of the Service. The words flashed into his mind as the auto-learner had planted them during his first year of training back in the Pool.

"To no alien race shall any Trader introduce any drug, food, or drink from off world, until such a substance has been certified as nonharmful to the aliens."

There it was! I-S had them and it was all his fault. But if he had been so wrong, why in the world did Van Rycke sit there trading, condoning the error and making it into a crime for which they could be summoned before the Board and struck off the rolls of the Service?

Van Rycke smiled gently. "Code Four—Article Two," he quoted with the genial air of one playing gift-giver at a Forkidan feasting.

Code Four, Article Two: Any organic substance offered for trade must be examined by a committee of trained medical experts, an equal representation of Terrans and aliens.

Kallee's sneering smile did not vanish. "Well," he challenged, "where's your board of experts?"

"Tau!" Van Rycke called to the medic with the storm priests. "Will you ask your colleague to be so kind as to allow the cargo-master Kallee to be presented?"

The tall, dark young Terran medic spoke to the priest beside him and together they came across the clearing. Van Rycke and Jellico both arose and inclined their heads in honor to the priests, as did the chief with whom they had been about to deal.

"Reader of clouds and master of many winds," Tau's voice flowed with the many-voweled titles of the Sargolian, "may I bring before your face Cargo-Master Kallee, a servant of Inter-Solar in the realm of Trade?"

The storm priest's shaven skull and body gleamed steel gray in the light. His eyes, of that startling blue-green, regarded the I-S party with cynical detachment.

"You wish of me?" Plainly he was one who believed in getting down to essentials at once.

Kallee could not be overawed. "These Free Traders have introduced among your people a powerful drug which will bring much evil," he spoke slowly in simple words as if he were addressing a cub.

"You have evidence of such evil?" countered the storm priest. "In what manner is this new plant evil?"

For a moment Kallee was disconcerted. But he rallied quickly. "It has not been tested—you do not know how it will affect your people—"

The storm priest shook his head impatiently. "We are not lacking in intelligence, Trader. This plant *has* been tested, both by your master of life secrets and ours. There is no harm in it—rather it is a good thing, to be highly prized—so highly that we shall give thanks that it was brought unto us. This speech-together is finished." He pulled the loose folds of his robe closer about him and walked away.

"Now," Van Rycke addressed the I-S party, "I must ask you to withdraw. Under the rules of Trade your presence here can be actively resented—"

But Kallee had lost little of his assurance. "You haven't heard the last of this. A tape of the whole proceedings goes to the Board—"

"As you wish. But in the meantime—" Van Rycke gestured to the waiting Salariki who were beginning to mutter impatiently. Kallee glanced around, heard those mutters, and made the only move possible, away from the *Queen*. He was not quite so cocky, but neither had he surrendered.

Dane caught at Tau's sleeve and asked the question which had been burning in him since he had come upon the scene.

"What happened—about the catnip?"

There was lightening of the serious expression on Tau's face.

"Fortunately for you that child took the leaves to the storm priest. They tested and approved it. And I can't see that it has any ill effects. But you were just lucky, Thorson—it might have gone another way."

Dane sighed. "I know that, sir," he confessed. "I'm not trying to rocket out—"

Tau gave a half-smile. "We all off-fire our tubes at times," he conceded. "Only next time—"

He did not need to complete that warning as Dane caught him up:

"There isn't going to be a next time like this, sir—ever!"

GORP HUNT

4

But the interruption had disturbed the tenor of trading. The small chief who had so eagerly taken Paft's place had only two Koros stones to offer and even to Dane's inexperienced eyes they were inferior in size and color to those the other clan leader had tendered. The Terrans were aware that Koros mining was a dangerous business but they had not known that the stock of available stones was so very small. Within ten minutes the last of the serious bargaining was concluded and the clansmen were drifting away from the burned over space about the *Queen*'s standing fins.

Dane folded up the bargaining cloth, glad for a task. He sensed that he was far from being back in Van Rycke's good graces. The fact that his superior did not discuss any of the aspects of the deals with him was a bad sign.

Captain Jellico stretched. Although his was not, or never, what might be termed a good-humored face, he was at peace with his world. "That would seem to be all. What's the haul, Van?"

"Ten first-class stones, about fifty second grade, and twenty or so of third. The chiefs will go to the fisheries tomorrow. *Then* we'll be in to see the really good stuff."

"And how's the herbs holding out?" That interested Dane too. Surely the few plants in the hydro and the dried leaves could not be stretched too far.

"As well as we could expect." Van Rycke frowned. "But Craig thinks he's on the trail of something to help—"

The storm priests had uprooted the staff marking the trading station and were wrapping the white streamer about it. Their leader had already gone and now Tau came up to the group by the ramp.

"Van says you have an idea," the Captain hailed him.

"We haven't tried it yet. And we can't unless the priests give it a clear lane—"

"That goes without saying—" Jellico agreed.

The Captain had not addressed that remark to him personally, but Dane was sure it had been directed at him. Well, they needn't worry—never again was he going to make that mistake, they could be very sure of that.

He was part of the conference which followed in the mess cabin only because he was a member of the crew. How far the reason for his disgrace had spread he had no way of telling, but he made no overtures, even to Rip.

Tau had the floor with Mura as an efficient lieutenant. He discussed the properties of catnip and gave information on the limited supply the *Queen* carried. Then he launched into a new suggestion.

"Felines of Terra, in fact a great many other of our native mammals, have a similar affinity for this."

Mura produced a small flask and Tau opened it, passing it to Captain Jellico and so from hand to hand about the room. Each crewman sniffed at the strong aroma. It was a heavier scent than that given off by the crushed catnip—Dane was not sure he liked it. But a moment later Sinbad streaked in from the corridor and committed the unpardonable sin of leaping to the table top just before Mura who had taken the flask from Dane. He miaowed plaintively and clawed at the steward's cuff. Mura stoppered the flask and put the cat down on the floor.

"What is it?" Jellico wanted to know.

"Anisette, a liquor made from the oil of anise—from seeds of the anise plant. It is a stimulant, but we use it mainly as a condiment. If it is harmless for the Salariki it ought to be a bigger bargaining point than any perfumes or spices I-S can import. And remember, with their unlimited capital, they can flood the market with products we can't touch, selling at a loss if need be to cut us out. Because their ship is not going to lift from Sargol just because she has no legal right here."

"There's this point," Van Rycke added to the lecture. "The Eysies are trading or want to trade perfumes. But they stock only manufactured products, exotic stuff, but synthetic." He took from his belt pouch two tiny boxes.

Before he caught the rich scent of the paste inside them Dane had already identified each as luxury items from Casper—chemical products which sold well and at high prices in the civilized ports of the Galaxy. The cargo-master turned the boxes over, exposing the symbol on their undersides—the mark of I-S.

"These were offered to me in trade by a Salarik. I took them, just to have proof that the Eysies are operating here. But—note—they were offered to me in trade, along with two top Koros, for what? One spoonful of dried catnip leaves. Does that suggest anything?"

Mura answered first. "The Salariki prefer natural products to synthetic."

"I think so."

"D'you suppose that was Cam's secret?" speculated Astrogator Steen Wilcox.

"If it was," Jellico cut in, "he certainly kept it! If we had only known this earlier—"

They were all thinking of that, of their storage space carefully packed with useless trade goods. Where, if they had known, the same space could have carried herbs with five or twenty-five times as much buying power.

"Maybe now that their sales resistance is broken, we *can* switch to some of the other stuff," Tang Ya, torn away from his beloved communicators for the conference, said wistfully. "They like color—how about breaking out some rolls of Harlinian moth silk?"

Van Rycke sighed wearily. "Oh, we'll try. We'll bring out everything and anything. But we could have done so much better—" he brooded over the tricks of fate which had landed them on a planet wild for trade with no proper trade goods in either of their holds.

There was a nervous little sound of a throat being apologetically cleared. Jasper Weeks, the small wiper from the engine room detail, the third-generation Venusian colonist whom the more vocal members of the *Queen*'s compliment were apt to forget upon occasion, seeing all eyes upon him, spoke though his voice was hardly above a hoarse whisper.

"Cedar—lacquel bark—forsh weed—"

"Cinnamon," Mura added to the list. "Imported in small quantities—"

"Naturally! Only the problem now is—how much cedar, lacquel bark, forsh weed, cinnamon do we have on board?" demanded Van Rycke.

His sarcasm did not register with Weeks for the little man pushed by Dane and left the cabin to their surprise. In the quiet which followed they could hear the clatter of his boots on ladder rungs as he descended to the quarters of the engine room staff. Tang turned to his neighbor, Johan Stotz, the *Queen*'s engineer.

"What's he going for?"

Stotz shrugged. Weeks was a self-effacing man—so much so that even in the cramped quarters of the spacer very little about him as an individual impressed his mates—a fact which was slowly dawning on them all now. Then they heard the scramble of feet hurrying back and Weeks burst in with energy which carried him across to the table behind which the Captain and Van Rycke now sat.

In the wiper's hands was a plasta-steel box—the treasure chest of a spaceman. Its tough exterior was guaranteed to protect the contents against everything but outright disintegration. Weeks put it down on the table and snapped up the lid.

A new aroma, or aromas, was added to the scents now at war in the cabin. Weeks pulled out a handful of fluffy white stuff which frothed up about his fingers like soap lather. Then with more care he lifted up a tray divided into many small compartments, each with a separate sealing lid of its own. The men of the *Queen* moved in, their curiosity aroused, until they were jostling one another.

Being tall Dane had an advantage, though Van Rycke's bulk and the wide shoulders of the Captain were between him and the object they were so intent upon. In each division of the tray, easily seen through the transparent lids, was a carved figure. The weird denizens of the Venusian polar swamps were there, along with life-like effigies of Terran animals, a Martian sand-mouse in all its monstrous ferocity, and the native animal and reptile life of half a hundred different worlds. Weeks put down a second tray beside the first, again displaying a menagerie of strange life forms. But when he clicked open one of the compartments and handed the figurine it contained to the Captain, Dane understood the reason for now bringing forward the carvings.

The majority of them were fashioned from a dull blue-gray wood and Dane knew that if he picked one up he would discover that it weighed close to nothing in his hand. That was lacquel bark—the aromatic product of a Venusian vine. And each little animal or reptile lay encased in a soft dab of frothy white—frosh weed—the perfumed seed casing of the Martian canal plants. One or two figures on the second tray were of a red-brown wood and these Van Rycke sniffed at appreciatively.

"Cedar—Terran cedar," he murmured.

Weeks nodded eagerly, his eyes alight. "I am waiting now for sandlewood—it is also good for carving—"

Jellico stared at the array in puzzled wonder. "You have made these?"

Being an amateur xenobiologist of no small standing himself, the shapes of the carvings more than the material from which they fashioned held his attention.

All those on board the *Queen* had their own hobbies. The monotony of voyaging through hyper-space had long ago impressed upon men the need for occupying both hands and mind during the sterile days while they were forced into close companionship with few duties to keep them alert. Jellico's cabin was papered with tri-dee pictures of the rare animals and alien creatures he had studied in their native haunts or of which he kept careful and painstaking records. Tau had his magic, Mura not only his plants but the delicate miniature landscapes he fashioned, to be imprisoned forever in the hearts of protecting plasta balls. But Weeks had never shown his work before and now he had an artist's supreme pleasure of completely confounding his shipmates. The cargo-master returned to the business on hand first. "You're willing to transfer these to 'cargo'?" he asked briskly. "How many do you have?"

Weeks, now lifting a third and then a fourth tray from the box, replied without looking up.

"Two hundred. Yes, I'll transfer, sir."

The Captain was turning about in his fingers the beautifully shaped figure of an Astran duocorn. "Pity to trade these here," he mused aloud. "Will Paft or Halfner appreciate more than just their scent?"

Weeks smiled shyly. "I've filled this case, sir. I was going to offer them to Mr. Van Rycke on a venture. I can always make another set. And right now—well, maybe they'll be worth more to the *Queen,* seeing as how they're made out of aromatic woods, than they'd be elsewhere. Leastwise the Eysies aren't going to have anything like them to show!" he ended in a burst of honest pride.

"Indeed they aren't!" Van Rycke gave honor where it was due.

So they made plans and then separated to sleep out the rest of the night. Dane knew that his lapse was not forgotten nor forgiven, but now he was honestly too tired to care and slept as well as if his conscience were clear.

But morning brought only a trickle of lower-class clansmen for trading and none of them had much but news to offer. The storm priests, as neutral arbitrators, had divided up the Koros grounds. And the clansmen, under the personal supervision of their chieftains were busy hunting the stones. The Terrans gathered from scraps of information that gem seeking on such a large scale had never been attempted before.

Before night there came other news, and much more chilling. Paft, one of the two major chieftains of this section of Sargol—while supervising the efforts of his liege men on a newly discovered and richly strewn length of shoal water—had been attacked and killed by gorp. The unusual activity of the Salariki in the shallows had in turn drawn to the spot battalions of the intelligent, malignant reptiles who had struck in strength, slaying and escaping before the Salariki could form an adequate defense, having killed the land dwellers' sentries silently and effectively before advancing on the laboring main bodies of gem hunters.

A loss of a certain number of miners or fishers had been foreseen as the price one paid for Koros in quantity. But the death of a chieftain was another thing altogether, having repercussions which carried far beyond the fact of his death. When the news reached the Salariki about the *Queen* they melted away into the grass forest and for the first time the Terrans felt free of spying eyes.

"What happens now?" Ali inquired. "Do they declare all deals off?"

"That might just be the unfortunate answer," agreed Van Rycke.

"Could be," Rip commented to Dane, "that they'd think we were in some way responsible—"

But Dane's conscience, sensitive over the whole matter of Salariki trade, had already reached that conclusion.

The Terran party, unsure of what were the best tactics, wisely decided to do nothing at all for the time being. But, when the Salariki seemed to have completely vanished on the morning of the second day, the men were restless. Had Paft's death resulted in some inter-clan quarrel over the heirship and the other clans withdrawn to let the various contendents for that honor fight it out? Or—what was more probable and dangerous—had the aliens come to the point of view that the *Queen* was in the main responsible for the catastrophe and were engaged in preparing too warm a welcome for any Traders who dared to visit them?

With the latter idea in mind they did not stray far from the ship. And the limit of their traveling was the edge of the forest from which they could be covered and so they did not learn much.

It was well into the morning before they were dramatically appraised that, far from being considered in any way an enemy, they were about to be accepted in a tie as close as clan to clan during one of the temporary but binding truces.

The messenger came in state, a young Salarik warrior, his splendid cloak rent and hanging in tattered pieces from his shoulders as a sign of his official grief. He carried in one hand a burned out torch, and in the other an unsheathed claw knife, its blade reflecting the sunlight with a wicked glitter. Behind him trotted three couples of retainers, their cloaks also ragged fringes, their knives drawn.

Standing up on the ramp to receive what could only be a formal deputation were Captain, Astrogator, Cargo-Master and Engineer, the senior officers of the spacer.

In the rolling periods of the Trade Lingo the torch bearer identified himself as Groft, son and heir of the late lamented Paft. Until his chieftain father was avenged in blood he could not assume the high seat of his clan nor the leadership of the family. And now, following custom, he was inviting the friends and sometime allies of the dead Paft to a gorp hunt. Such a gorp hunt, Dane gathered from amidst the flowers of ceremonial Salariki speech, as had never been planned before on the face of Sargol. Salariki without number in the past had died beneath the ripping talons of the water reptiles, but it was seldom that a chieftain had so fallen and his clan were firm in their determination to take a full blood price from the killers.

"—and so, sky lords," Groft brought his oration to a close, "we come to ask that you send your young men to this hunting so that they may know the joy of plunging knives into the scaled death and see the horned ones die bathed in their own vile blood!"

Dane needed no hint from the *Queen*'s officers that this invitation was a sharp departure from custom. By joining with the natives in such a foray the Terrans were being admitted to kinship of a sort, cementing relations by a tie which the I-S, or any other interloper from off-world, would find hard to break. It was a piece of such excellent good fortune as they would not have dreamed of three days earlier.

Van Rycke replied, his voice properly sonorous, sounding out the rounded periods of the rolling tongue which they had all been taught during the voyage, using Cam's recordings. Yes, the Terrans would join with pleasure in so good and great a cause. They would lend the force of their arms to the defeat of all gorp they had the good fortune to meet. Groft need only name the hour for them to join him—

It was not needful, the young Salariki chieftain-to-be hastened to tell the cargo-master, that the senior sky lords concern themselves in this matter. In fact it would be against custom, for it was meet that such a hunt be left to warriors of few years, that they might earn glory and be able to stand before the fires at the Naming as men. Therefore—the thumb claw of Groft was extended to its greatest length as he used it to single out the Terrans he had been eyeing—let this one, and that, and that, and the fourth be ready to join with the Salariki party an hour after nooning on this very day and they would indeed teach the slimy, treacherous lurkers in the depths a well needed lesson.

The Salarik's choice with one exception had unerringly fallen upon the youngest members of the crew, Ali, Rip, and Dane in that order. But his fourth addition had been Jasper Weeks. Perhaps because of his native pallor of skin and slightness of body the oiler had seemed, to the alien, to be younger than his years. At any rate Groft had made it very plain that he chose these men and Dane knew that the *Queen*'s officers would raise no objection which might upset the delicate balance of favorable relations.

Van Rycke did ask for one concession which was reluctantly granted. He received permission for the spacer's men to carry their sleep rods. Though the Salariki, apparently for some reason of binding and hoary custom, were totally opposed to hunting their age-old enemy with anything other than their duelists' weapons of net and claw knife.

"Go along with them," Captain Jellico gave his final orders to the four, "as long as it doesn't mean your own necks—understand? On the other hand dead heroes have never helped to lift a ship. And these gorp are tough from all accounts. You'll just have to use your own judgment about springing your rods on them—" He looked distinctly unhappy at that thought.

Ali was grinning and little Weeks tightened his weapon belt with a touch of swagger he had never shown before. Rip was his usual soft voiced self, dependable as a rock and a good base for the rest of them—taking command without question as they marched off to join Groft's company.

THE PERILOUS SEAS

5 The gorp hunters straggled through the grass forest in family groups, and the Terrans saw that the enterprise had forced another uneasy truce upon the district, for there were representatives from more than just Paft's own clan. All the Salariki were young and the parties babbled together in excitement. It was plain that this hunt, staged upon a large scale, was not only a means of revenge upon a hated enemy but, also, a sporting event of outstanding prestige.

Now the grass trees began to show ragged gaps, open spaces between their clumps, until the forest was only scattered groups and the party the Terrans had joined walked along a trail cloaked in knee-high, yellow-red fern growth. Most of the Salariki carried unlit torches, some having four or five bundled together, as if gorp hunting must be done after nightfall. And it *was* fairly late in the afternoon before they topped a rise of ground and looked out upon one of Sargol's seas.

The water was a dull, metallic gray, broken by great swaths of purple as if an artist had slapped a brush of color across it in a hit or miss fashion. Sand of the red grit, lightened by the golden flecks which glittered in the sun, stretched to the edge of the wavelets breaking with oily languor on the curve of earth. The bulk of islands arose in serried ranks farther out—crowned with grass trees all rippling under the sea wind.

They came out upon the beach where one of the purple patches touched the shore and Dane noted that it left a scummy deposit there. The Terrans went on to the water's edge. Where it was clear of the purple stuff they could get a murky glimpse of the bottom, but the scum hid long stretches of shoreline and outer wave, and Dane wondered if the gorp used it as a protective covering.

For the moment the Salariki made no move toward the sea which was to be their hunting ground. Instead the youngest members of the party, some of whom were adolescents not yet entitled to wear the claw knife of manhood, spread out along the shore and set industriously to gathering driftwood, which they brought back to heap on the sand. Dane, watching that harvest, caught sight of a smoothly polished length. He called Weeks' attention to the water-rounded cylinder.

The oiler's eyes lighted and he stooped to pick it up. Where the other sticks were from grass trees this was something else. And among the bleached pile it had the vividness of flame. For it was a strident scarlet. Weeks turned it over in his hands, running his fingers lovingly across its perfect grain. Even in this crude state it had beauty. He stopped the Salarik who had just brought in another armload of wood.

"This is what?" he spoke the Trade Lingo haltingly.

The native gazed somewhat indifferently at the branch. "Tansil," he answered. "It grows on the islands—" He made a vague gesture to include a good section of the western sea before he hurried away.

Weeks now went along the tide line on his own quest, Dane trailing him. At the end of a quarter hour when a hail summoned them back to the site of the now lighted fire, they had some ten pieces of the tansil wood between them. The finds ranged from a three-foot section some four inches in diameter, to some slender twigs no larger than a writing steelo—but all with high polish, the warm flame coloring. Weeks lashed them together before he joined the group where Groft was outlining the technique of gorp hunting for the benefit of the Terrans.

Some two hundred feet away a reef, often awash and stained with the purple scum, angled out into the sea in a long curve which formed a natural breakwater. This was the point of attack. But first the purple film must be removed so that land and sea dwellers could meet on common terms.

The fire blazed up, eating hungrily into the driftwood. And from it ran the young Salariki with lighted brands, which at the water's edge they whirled about their heads and then hurled out onto the purple patches. Fire arose from the water and ran with frantic speed across the crests of the low waves, while the Salariki coughed and buried their noses in their perfume boxes, for the wind drove shoreward an overpowering stench.

Where the cleansing fire had run on the water there was now only the natural metallic gray of the liquid, the cover was gone. Older Salariki warriors were choosing torches from those they had brought, doing it with care. Groft approached the Terrans carrying four.

"These you use now—"

What for? Dane wondered. The sky was still sunlit. He held the torch watching to see how the Salariki made use of them.

Groft led the advance—running lightly out along the reef with agile and graceful leaps to cross the breaks where the sea hurled in over the rock. And after him followed the other natives, each with a lighted torch in hand—the torch they hunkered down to plant firmly in some crevice of the rock before taking a stand beside that beacon.

The Terrans, less surefooted in the space boots, picked their way along the same path, wet with spray, wrinkling their noses against the lingering puffs of the stench from the water.

Following the example of the Salariki they faced seaward—but Dane did not know what to watch for. Cam had left only the vaguest general descriptions of gorp and beyond the fact that they were reptilian, intelligent and dangerous, the Terrans had not been briefed.

Once the warriors had taken up their stand along the reef, the younger Salariki went into action once more. Lighting more torches at the fire, they ran out along the line of their elders and flung their torches as far as they could hurl them into the sea outside the reef.

The gray steel of the water was now yellow with the reflection of the sinking sun. But that ocher and gold became more brilliant yet as the torches of the Salariki set blazing up far floating patches of scum. Dane shielded his eyes against the glare and tried to watch the water, with some idea that this move must be provocation and what they hunted would so be driven into view.

He held his sleep rod ready, just as the Salarik on his right had claw knife in one hand and in the other, open and waiting, the net intended to entangle and hold fast a victim, binding him for the kill.

But it was at the far tip of the barrier—the post of greatest honor which Groft had jealously claimed as his, that the gorp struck first. At a wild shout of defiance Dane half turned to see the Salarik noble cast his net at sea level and then stab viciously with a well practiced blow. When he raised his arm for a second thrust, greenish ichor ran from the blade down his wrist.

"Dane!"

Thorson's head jerked around. He saw the vee of ripples headed straight for the rocks where he balanced. But he'd have to wait for a better target than a moving wedge of water. Instinctively he half crouched in the stance of an embattled spaceman, wishing now that he did have a blaster.

Neither of the Salariki stationed on either side of him made any move and he guessed that that was hunt etiquette. Each man was supposed to face and kill the monster that challenged him—without assistance. And upon his skill during the next few minutes might rest the reputation of all Terrans as far as the natives were concerned.

There was a shadow outline beneath the surface of the metallic water now, but he could not see well because of the distortion of the murky waves. He must wait until he was sure.

Then the thing gave a spurt and, only inches beyond the toes of his boots, a nightmare creature sprang halfway out of the water, pincher claws as long as his own arms snapping at him. Without being conscious of his act, he pressed the stud of the sleep rod, aiming in the general direction of that horror from the sea.

But to his utter amazement the creature did not fall supinely back into watery world from which it had emerged. Instead those claws snapped again, this time scraping across the top of Dane's foot, leaving a furrow in material the keenest of knives could not have scored.

"Give it to him!" That was Rip shouting encouragement from his own place farther along the reef.

Dane pressed the firing stud again and again. The claws waved as the monstrosity slavered from a gaping frog's mouth, a mouth which was fanged with a shark's vicious teeth. It was almost wholly out of the water, creeping on a crab's many legs, with the clawed upper limbs reaching for him, when suddenly it stopped, its huge head turning from side to side in the sheltering carapace of scaled natural armor. It settled back as if crouching for a final spring—a spring which would push Dane into the ocean.

But that attack never came. Instead the gorp drew in upon itself until it resembled an unwieldy ball of indestructible armor and there it remained.

The Salariki on either side of Dane let out cries of triumph and edged closer. One of them twirled his net suggestively, seeing that the Terran lacked what was to him an essential piece of hunting equipment. Dane nodded vigorously in agreement and the tough strands swung out in a skillful cast which engulfed the motionless creature on the reef. But it was so protected by its scales that there was no opening for the claw knife. They had made a capture but they could not make a kill.

However, the Salariki were highly delighted. And several abandoned their posts to help the boys drag the monster ashore where it was pinned down to the beach by stakes driven through the edges of the net.

But the hunting party was given little time to gloat over this stroke of fortune. The gorp killed by Groft and the one stunned by Dane were only the van of an army and within moments the hunters on the reef were confronted by trouble armed with slashing claws and diabolic fighting ability.

The battle was anything but one-sided. Dane whirled, as the air was rent by a shriek of agony, just in time to see one of the Salariki, already torn by the claws of a gorp, being drawn under the water. It was too late to save the hunter, though Dane, balanced on the very edge of the reef, aimed a beam into the bloody waves. If the gorp was affected by this attack he could not tell, for both attacker and victim could no longer be seen.

But Ali had better luck in rescuing the Salarik who shared his particular section of reef, and the native, gashed and spurting blood from a wound in his thigh, was hauled to safety. While the gorp, coiling too slowly under the Terran ray, was literally hewn to pieces by the revengeful knives of the hunter's kin.

The fight broke into a series of individual duels carried on now by the light of the torches as the evening closed in. The last of the purple patches had burned away to nothing. Dane crouched by his standard torch, his eyes fastened on the sea, watching for an ominous vee of ripples betraying another gorp on its way to launch against the rock barrier.

There was such wild confusion along that line of water-sprayed rocks that he had no idea of how the engagement was going. But so far the gorp showed no signs of having had enough.

Dane was shaken out of his absorption by another scream. One, he was sure, which had not come from any Salariki throat. He got to his feet. Rip was stationed four men beyond him. Yes, the tall astrogator-apprentice was there, outlined against torch flare. Ali? No—there was the assistant engineer. Weeks? But Weeks was picking his way back along the reef toward the shore, haste expressed in every line of his figure. The scream sounded for a second time, freezing the Terrans.

"Come back—!" That was Weeks gesturing violently at the shore and something floundering in the protecting circle of the reef. The younger Salariki who had been feeding the fire were now clustered at the water's edge.

Ali ran and with a leap covered the last few feet, landing recklessly knee deep in the waves. Dane saw light strike on his rod as he swung it in a wide arc to center on the struggle churning the water into foam. A third scream died to a moan and then the Salariki dashed into the sea, their nets spread, drawing back with them through the surf a dark and now quiet mass.

The fact that at least one gorp had managed to get on the inner side of the reef made an impression on the rest of the native hunters. After an uncertain minute or two Groft gave the signal to withdraw—which they did with grisly trophies. Dane counted seven gorp bodies—which did not include the prisoner ashore. And more might have slid into the sea to die. On the other hand two Salariki were dead—one had been drawn into the sea before Dane's eyes—and at least one was badly wounded. But who had been pulled down in the shallows—someone sent out from the *Queen* with a message?

Dane raced back along the reef, not waiting to pull up his torch, and before he reached the shore Rip was overtaking him. But the man who lay groaning on the sand was not from the *Queen*. The torn and bloodstained tunic covering his lacerated shoulders had the I-S badge. Ali was already at work on his wounds, giving temporary first aid from his belt kit. To all their questions he was stubbornly silent—either he couldn't or wouldn't answer.

In the end they helped the Salariki rig three stretchers. On one, the largest, the captive gorp, still curled in a round carapace protected ball, was bound with the net. The second supported the wounded Salarik clansman and onto the third the Terrans lifted the I-S man.

"We'll deliver him to his own ship," Rip decided. "He must have tailed us here as a spy—" He asked a passing Salarik as to where they could find the Company spacer.

"They might just think we are responsible," Ali pointed out. "But I see your point. If we do pack him back to the *Queen* and he doesn't make it, they might say that we fired his rockets for him. All right, boys, let's up-ship—he doesn't look too good to me."

With a torch-bearing Salarik boy as a guide, they hurried along a path taking in turns the burden of the stretcher. Luckily the I-S ship was even closer to the sea than the *Queen* and as they crossed the slagged ground, congealed by the break fire, they were trotting.

Though the Company ship was probably one of the smallest Inter-Solar carried on her rosters, it was a third again as large as the *Queen*—with part of that third undoubtedly dedicated to extra cargo space. Beside her their own spacer would seem not only smaller, but battered and worn. But no Free Trader would have willingly assumed the badges of a Company man, not even for the command of such a ship fresh from the cradles of a builder.

When a man went up from the training Pool for his first assign-ment, he was sent to the ship where his temperament, training and abilities best fitted. And those who were designated as Free Traders could never fit into the pattern of Company men. Of late years the breach between those who lived under the strict parental control of one of the five great galaxy-wide organizations and those still too much of an individual to live any life but that of the half-explorer-half-pioneer which was the Free Trader's, had widened alarmingly. Antagonism flared, rivalry was strong. But as yet the great Compa-nies themselves were at polite cold war with one another for the big plums of the scattered systems. The Free Traders took the crumbs and there was not much disputing—save in cases such as had arisen on Sargol, when suddenly crumbs assumed the guise of very rich cake, rich and large enough to attract a giant.

The party from the *Queen* was given a peremptory challenge as they reached the other ship's ramp. Rip demanded to see the officer of the watch and then told the story of the wounded man as far as they knew it. The Eysie was hurried aboard—nor did his shipmates give a word of thanks.

"That's that." Rip shrugged. "Let's go before they slam the hatch so hard they'll rock their ship off her fins!"

"Polite, aren't they?" asked Weeks mildly.

"What do you expect of Eysies?" Ali wanted to know. "To them Free Traders are just rim planet trash. Let's report back where we are appreciated."

They took a short cut which brought them back to the *Queen* and they filed up her ramp to make their report to the Captain.

But they were not yet satisfied with Groft and his gorp slayers. No Salarik appeared for trade in the morning—surprising the Terrans. Instead a second delegation, this time of older men and a storm priest, visited the spacer with an invitation to attend Paft's funeral feast, a rite which would be followed by the formal elevation of Groft to his father's position, now that he had revenged that parent. And from remarks dropped by members of the delegation it was plain that the bearing of the Terrans who had joined the hunting party was esteemed to have been in highest accord with Salariki tradition.

They drew lots to decide which two must remain with the ship and the rest perfumed themselves so as to give no offense which might upset their now cordial relations. Again it was mid-afternoon when the Salariki escort sent to do them honor waited at the edge of the wood and Mura and Tang saw them off. With a herald booming before them, they traveled the beaten earth road in the opposite direction from the trading center, off through the forest until they came to a wide section of several miles which had been rigorously cleared of any vegetation which might give cover to a lurking enemy. In the center of this was a twelve-foot-high stockade of the bright red, burnished wood which had attracted Weeks on the shore. Each paling was the trunk of a tree and it had been sharpened at the top to a wicked point. On the field side was a wide ditch, crossed at the gate by a bridge, the planking of which might be removed at will. And as

Dane passed over he looked down into a moat that was dry. The Salariki did not depend upon water for a defense—but on something else which his experience of the previous night had taught him to respect. There was no mistaking that shade of purple. The highly inflammable scum the hunters had burnt from the top of the waves had been brought inland and lay a greasy blanket some eight feet below. It would only be necessary to toss a torch on that and the defenders of the stockade would create a wall of fire to baffle any attacker. The Salariki knew how to make the most of their world's natural resources.

DUELIST'S CHALLENGE

6 Inside the red stockade there was a crowded community. The Salariki demanded privacy of a kind, and even the unmarried warriors did not share barracks, but each had a small cubicle of his own. So that the mud brick and timber erections of one of their clan cities resembled nothing so much as the comb cells of a busy beehive. Although Paft's was considered a large clan, it numbered only about two hundred fighting men and their numerous wives, children and captive servants. Not all of them normally lived at this center, but for the funeral feasting they had assembled—which meant a lot of doubling up and tenting out under makeshift cover between the regular buildings of the town. So that the Terrans were glad to be guided through this crowded maze to the Great Hall which was its heart.

As the trading center had been, the hall was a circular enclosure open to the sky above but divided in wheel-spoke fashion with posts of the red wood, each supporting a metal basket filled with inflammable material. Here were no lowly stools or trading tables. One vast circular board, broken only by a gap at the foot, ran completely around the wall. At the end opposite the entrance was the high chair of the chieftain, set on a two-step dais. Though the feast had not yet officially begun, the Terrans saw that the majority of the places were already occupied.

They were led around the perimeter of the enclosure to places not far from the high seat. Van Rycke settled down with a grunt of satisfaction. It was plain that the Free Traders were numbered among the nobility. They could be sure of good trade in the days to come.

Delegations from neighboring clans arrived in close companies of ten or twelve and were granted seats, as had been the Terrans, in groups. Dane noted that there was no intermingling of clan with clan. And, as they were to understand later that night, there was a very good reason for that precaution.

"Hope all our adaption shots work," Ali murmured, eyeing with no pleasure at all the succession of platters now being borne through the inner opening of the table.

While the Traders had learned long ago that the wisest part of valor was not to sample alien strong drinks, ceremony often required that they break bread (or its other world equivalent) on strange planets. And so science served expediency and now a Trader bound for any Galactic banquet was immunized, as far as was medically possible, against the evil consequences of consuming food not originally intended for Terran stomachs. One of the results being that Traders acquired a far flung reputation of possessing bird-like appetites— since it was always better to nibble and live, than to gorge and die.

Groft had not yet taken his place in the vacant chieftain's chair. For the present he stood in the center of the table circle, directing the captive slaves who circulated with the food. Until the magic moment when the clan themselves would proclaim him their overlord, he remained merely the eldest son of the house, relatively without power.

As the endless rows of platters made their way about the table the basket lights on the tops of the pillars were ignited, dispelling the dusk of evening. And there was an attendant stationed by each to throw on handsful of aromatic bark which burned with puffs of lavender smoke, adding to the many warring scents. The Terrans had recourse at intervals to their own pungent smelling bottles, merely to clear their heads of the drugging fumes.

Luckily, Dane thought as the feast proceeded, that smoke from the braziers went straight up. Had they been in a roofed space they might have been overcome. As it was—were they entirely conscious of all that was going on around them?

His reason for that speculation was the dance now being performed in the center of the hall—their fight with the gorp being enacted in a series of bounds and stabbings. He was sure that he could no longer trust his eyes when the claw knife of the victorious dancer-hunter apparently passed completely through the chest of another wearing a grotesque monster mask.

As a fitting climax to their horrific display, three of the men who had been with them on the reef entered, dragging behind them— still enmeshed in the hunting net—the gorp which Dane had stunned. It was uncurled now and very much alive, but the pincer claws which might have cut its way to safety were encased in balls of hard substance.

Freed from the net, suspended by its sealed claws, the gorp swung back and forth from a standard set up before the high seat. Its murderous jaws snapped futilely, and from it came an enraged snake's vicious hissing. Though totally in the power of its enemies it gave an impression of terrifying strength and menace.

The sight of their ancient foe aroused the Salariki, inflaming warriors who leaned across the table to hurl tongue-twisting invective at the captive monster. Dane gathered that seldom had a living gorp been delivered helpless into their hands and they proposed to make the most of this wonderful opportunity. And the Terran suddenly wished that the monstrosity had fallen back into the sea. He had no soft thoughts for the gorp after what he had seen at the reef and the tales he had heard, but neither did he like what he saw now expressed in gestures, heard in the tones of voices about them.

A storm priest put an end to the outcries. His dun cloak making a spot of darkness amid all the flashing color, he came straight to the place where the gorp swung. As he took his stand before the wriggling creature the din gradually faded, the warriors settled back into their seats, a pool of quiet spread through the enclosure.

Groft came up to take his position beside the priest. With both hands he carried a two-handled cup. It was not the ornamented goblet which stood before each diner, but a manifestly older artifact, fashioned of some dull black substance and having the appearance of being even older than the hall or town.

One of the warriors who had helped to bring in the gorp now made a quick and accurate cast with a looped rope, snaring the monster's head and pulling back almost at a right angle. With deliberation the storm priest produced a knife—the first straight bladed weapon Dane had seen on Sargol. He made a single thrust in the soft underpart of the gorp's throat, catching in the cup he took from Groft some of the ichor which spurted from the wound.

The gorp thrashed madly, spattering table and surrounding Salariki with its life fluid, but the attention of the crowd was riveted elsewhere. Into the old cup the priest poured another substance from a flask brought by an underling. He shook the cup back and forth, as if to mix its contents thoroughly and then handed it to Groft.

Holding it before him the young chieftain leaped to the table top and so to a stand before the high seat. There was a hush throughout the enclosure. Now even the gorp had ceased its wild struggles and hung limp in its bonds.

Groft raised the cup above his head and gave a loud shout in the archaic language of his clan. He was answered by a chant from the warriors who would in battle follow his banner, a chant punctuated with the clinking slap of knife blades brought down forcibly on the board.

Three times he recited some formula and was answered by the others. Then, in another period of sudden quiet, he raised the cup to his lips and drank off its contents in a single draught, turning the goblet upside down when he had done to prove that not a drop remained within. A shout tore through the great hall. The Salariki were all on their feet, waving their knives over their heads in honor to their new ruler. And Groft for the first time seated himself in the high seat. The clan was no longer without a chieftain, Groft held his father's place.

"Show over?" Dane heard Stotz murmur and Van Rycke's disappointing reply:

"Not yet. They'll probably make a night of it. Here comes another round of drinks—"

"And trouble with them." That was Captain Jellico being prophetic.

"By the Coalsack's Ripcord!" That exclamation had been jolted out of Rip and Dane turned to see what had so jarred the usually serene astrogator-apprentice. He was just in time to witness an important piece of Sargolian social practice.

A young warrior, surely only within a year or so of receiving his knife, was facing an older Salarik, both on their feet. The head and shoulder fur of the older fighter was dripping wet and an empty goblet rolled across the table to bump to the floor. A hush had fallen on the immediate neighbors of the pair, and there was an air of expectancy about the company.

"Threw his drink all over the other fellow," Rip's soft whisper explained. "That means a duel—"

"Here and now?" Dane had heard of the personal combat proclivities of the Salariki.

"Should be to the death for an insult such as that," Ali remarked, as usual surveying the scene from his chosen role as bystander. As a child he had survived the unspeakable massacres of the Crater War, nothing had been able to crack his surface armor since.

"The young fool!" That was Steen Wilcox sizing up the situation from the angle of a naturally cautious nature and some fifteen years of experience on a great many different worlds. "He'll be mustered out for good before he knows what happened to him!"

The younger Salarik had barked a question at his elder and had

been promptly answered by that dripping warrior. Now their neighbors came to life with an efficiency which suggested that they had
been waiting for such a move, it had happened so many times that
every man knew just the right procedure from that point on.

In order for a Sargolian feast to be a success, the Terrans gathered
from overhead remarks, at least one duel must be staged sometime
during the festivities. And those not actively engaged did a lot of
brisk betting in the background.

"Look there—at that fellow in the violet cloak," Rip directed
Dane. "See what he just laid down?"

The nobleman in the violet cloak was not one of Groft's liege
men, but a member of the delegation from another clan. And what he
had laid down on the table—indicating as he did so his choice as winner in the coming combat, the elder warrior—was a small piece of
white material on which reposed a slightly withered but familiar leaf.
The neighbor he wagered with, eyed the stake narrowly, bending
over to sniff at it, before he piled up two gem set armlets, a personal
scent box and a thumb ring to balance.

At this practical indication of just how much the Terran herb was
esteemed Dane regretted anew their earlier ignorance. He glanced
along the board and saw that Van Rycke had noted that stake and was
calling their Captain's attention to it.

But such side issues were forgotten as the duelists vaulted into the
circle rimmed by the table, a space now vacated for their action. They
were stripped to their loin cloths, their cloaks thrown aside. Each carried his net in his right hand, his claw knife ready in his left. As yet
the Traders had not seen Salarik against Salarik in action and in spite
of themselves they edged forward in their seats, as intent as the
natives upon what was to come. The finer points of the combat were
lost on them, and they did not understand the drilled casts of the net,
which had become as formalized through the centuries as the ancient
and now almost forgotten sword play of their own world. The young
Salarik had greater agility and speed, but the veteran who faced him
had the experience.

To Terran eyes the duel had some of the weaving, sweeping movements of the earlier ritual dance. The swift evasions of the nets were graceful and so timed that many times the meshes grazed the skin of the fighter who fled entrapment.

Dane believed that the elder man was tiring, and the youngster must have shared that opinion. There was a leap to the right, a sudden flurry of dart and retreat, and then a net curled high and fell, enfolding flailing arms and kicking legs. When the clutch rope was jerked tight, the captured youth was thrown off balance. He rolled frenziedly, but there was no escaping the imprisoning strands.

A shout applauded the victor. He stood now above his captive who lay supine, his throat or breast ready for either stroke of the knife his captor wished to deliver. But it appeared that the winner was not minded to end the encounter with blood. Instead he reached out a long, be-furred arm, took up a filled goblet from the table and with serious deliberation, poured its contents onto the upturned face of the loser.

For a moment there was a dead silence around the feast board and then a second roar, to which the honestly relieved Terrans added spurts of laughter. The sputtering youth was shaken free of the net and went down on his knees, tendering his opponent his knife, which the other thrust along with his own into his sash belt. Dane gathered from overheard remarks that the younger man was, for a period of time, to be determined by clan council, now the servant-slave of his overthrower and that since they were closely united by blood ties, this solution was considered eminently suitable—though had the elder killed his opponent, no one would have thought the worse of him for that deed.

It was the *Queen*'s men who were to provide the next center of attraction. Groft climbed down from his high seat and came to face across the board those who had accompanied him on the hunt. This time there was no escaping the sipping of the potent drink which the new chieftain slopped from his own goblet into each of theirs.

The fiery mouthful almost gagged Dane, but he swallowed manfully and hoped for the best as it burned like acid down his throat into his middle, there to mix uncomfortably with the viands he had eaten. Weeks' thin face looked very white, and Dane noticed, with malicious enjoyment, that Ali had an unobtrusive grip on the table which made his knuckles stand out in polished knobs—proving that there *were* things which could upset the imperturbable Kamil.

Fortunately they were *not* required to empty that flowing bowl in one gulp as Groft had done. The ceremonial mouthful was deemed enough and Dane sat down thankfully—but with uneasy fears for the future.

Groft had started back to his high seat when there was an interruption which had not been foreseen. A messenger threaded his way among the serving men and spoke to the chieftain, who glanced at the Terrans and then nodded.

Dane, his queasiness growing every second, was not attending until he heard a bitten off word from Rip's direction and looked up to see a party of I-S men coming into the open space before the high seat. The men from the *Queen* stiffened—there was something in the attitude of the newcomers which hinted at trouble.

"What do you wish, sky lords?" That was Groft using the Trade Lingo, his eyes half closed as he lolled in his chair of state, almost as if he were about to witness some entertainment provided for his pleasure.

"We wish to offer you the good fortune desires of our hearts—" That was Kallee, the flowery words rolling with the proper accent from his tongue. "And that you shall not forget us—we also offer gifts—"

At a gesture from their cargo-master, the I-S men set down a small chest. Groft, his chin resting on a clenched fist, lost none of his lazy air.

"They are received," he retorted with the formal acceptance. "And no one can have too much good fortune. The Howlers of the Black Winds know that." But he tendered no invitation to join the feast.

Kallee did not appear to be disconcerted. His next move was one which took his rivals by surprise, in spite of their suspicions.

"Under the laws of the Fellowship, O, Groft," he clung to the formal speech, "I claim redress—"

Ali's hand moved. Through his growing distress Dane saw Van Rycke's jaw tighten, the fighting mask snap back on Captain Jellico's face. Whatever came now was real trouble.

Groft's eyes flickered over the party from the *Queen*. Though he had just pledged cup friendship with four of them, he had the malicious humor of his race. He would make no move to head off what might be coming.

"By the right of the knife and the net," he intoned, "you have the power to claim personal satisfaction. Where is your enemy?"

Kallee turned to face the Free Traders. "I hereby challenge a champion to be set out from these off-worlders to meet by the blood and by the water my champion—"

The Salariki were getting excited. This was superb entertainment, an engagement such as they had never hoped to see—alien against alien. The rising murmur of their voices was like the growl of a hunting beast.

Groft smiled and the pleasure that expression displayed was neither Terran—nor human. But then the clan leader was not either, Dane reminded himself.

"Four of these warriors are clan-bound," he said. "But the others may produce a champion—"

Dane looked along the line of his comrades—Ali, Rip, Weeks and himself had just been ruled out. That left Jellico, Van Rycke, Karl Kosti, the giant jetman whose strength they had to rely upon before, Stotz the engineer, Medic Tau and Steen Wilcox. If it were strength alone he would have chosen Kosti, but the big man was not too quick a thinker—

Jellico got to his feet, the embodiment of a star lane fighting man. In the flickering light the scar on his cheek seemed to ripple. "Who's your champion?" he asked Kallee.

The Eysie cargo-master was grinning. He was confident he had pushed them into a position from which they could not extricate themselves.

"You accept challenge?" he countered.

Jellico merely repeated his question and Kallee beckoned forward one of his men.

The Eysie who stepped up was no match for Kosti. He was a slender, almost wand-slim young man, whose pleased smirk said that he, too, was about to put something over on the notorious Free Traders. Jellico studied him for a couple of long seconds during which the hum of Salariki voices was the threatening buzz of a disturbed wasps' nest. There was no way out of this—to refuse conflict was to lose all they had won with the clansmen. And they did not doubt that Kallee had, in some way, triggered the scales against them.

Jellico made the best of it. "We accept challenge," his voice was level. "We, being guesting in Groft's holding, will fight after the manner of the Salariki who are proven warriors—" He paused as roars of pleased acknowledgment arose around the board.

"Therefore let us follow the custom of warriors and take up the net and the knife—"

Was there a shade of dismay on Kallee's face?

"And the time?" Groft leaned forward to ask—but his satisfaction at such a fine ending for his feast was apparent. This would be talked over by every Sargolian for many storm seasons to come!

Jellico glanced up at the sky. "Say an hour after dawn, Chieftain. With your leave, we shall confer concerning a champion."

"My council room is yours," Groft signed for a liege man to guide them.

BARRING ACCIDENT

7 The morning winds rustled through the grass forest and, closer to hand, it pulled at the cloaks of the Salariki. Clan nobles sat on stools, lesser folk squatted on the trampled stubble of the cleared ground outside the stockade. In their many colored splendor the drab tunics of the Terrans were a blot of darkness at either end of the makeshift arena which had been marked out for them.

At the conclusion of their conference the *Queen*'s men had been forced into a course Jellico had urged from the first. He, and he alone, would represent the Free Traders in the coming duel. And now he stood there in the early morning, stripped down to shorts and boots, wearing nothing on which a net could catch and so trap him. The Free Traders were certain that the I-S men having any advantage would press it to the ultimate limit and the death of Captain Jellico would make a great impression on the Salariki.

Jellico was taller than the Eysie who faced him, but almost as lean. Hard muscles moved under his skin, pale where space tan had not burned in the years of his star voyaging. And his every movement was with the liquid grace of a man who, in his time, had been a master of

the force blade. Now he gripped in his left hand the claw knife given
him by Groft himself and in the other he looped the throwing rope
of the net.

At the other end of the field, the Eysie man was industriously moving his bootsoles back and forth across the ground, intent upon coating them with as much of the gritty sand as would adhere. And he
displayed the supreme confidence in himself which he had shown at
the moment of challenge in the Great Hall.

None of the Free Trading party made the mistake of trying to
give Jellico advice. The Captain had not risen to his command without learning his duties. And the duties of a Free Trader covered a
wide range of knowledge and practice. One had to be equally expert
with a blaster and a slingshot when the occasion demanded. Though
Jellico had not fought a Salariki duel with net and knife before, he
had a deep memory of other weapons, other tactics which could be
drawn upon and adapted to his present need.

There was none of the casual atmosphere which had surrounded
the affair between the Salariki clansmen in the hall. Here was ceremony. The storm priests invoked their own particular grim Provi-
dence, and there was an oath taken over the weapons of battle. When
the actual engagement began the betting among the spectators had
reached, Dane decided, epic proportions. Large sections of Sargolian
personal property were due to change hands as a result of this
encounter.

As the chief priest gave the order to engage both Terrans advanced
from their respective ends of the fighting space with the half crouching, light footed tread of spacemen. Jellico had pulled his net into as
close a resemblance to rope as its bulk would allow. The very type of
weapon, so far removed from any the Traders knew, made it a disad-
vantage rather than an asset.

But it was when the Eysie moved out to meet the Captain that Rip's
fingers closed about Dane's upper arm in an almost paralyzing grip.

"He knows—"

Dane had not needed that bad news to be made vocal. Having seen the exploits of the Salariki duelists earlier, he had already caught the significance of that glide, of the way the I-S champion carried his net. The Eysie had not had any last minute instruction in the use of Sargolian weapons—he had practiced and, by his stance, knew enough to make him a formidable menace. The clamor about the *Queen*'s party rose as the battle-wise eyes of the clansmen noted that and the odds against Jellico reached fantastic heights while the hearts of his crew sank.

Only Van Rycke was not disturbed. Now and then he raised his smelling bottle to his nose with an elegant gesture which matched those of the befurred nobility around him, as if not a thought of care ruffled his mind.

The Eysie feinted in an opening which was a rather ragged copy of the young Salarik's more fluid moves some hours before. But, when the net settled, Jellico was simply not there, his quick drop to one knee had sent the mesh flailing in an arc over his bowed shoulders with a good six inches to spare. And a cry of approval came not only from his comrades, but from those natives who had been gamblers enough to venture their wagers on his performance.

Dane watched the field and the fighters through a watery film. The discomfort he had experienced since downing that mouthful of the cup of friendship had tightened into a fist of pain clutching his middle in a torturing grip. But he knew he must stick it out until Jellico's ordeal was over. Someone stumbled against him and he glanced up to see Ali's face, a horrible gray-green under the tan, close to his own. For a moment the engineer-apprentice caught at his arm for support and then with a visible effort straightened up. So he wasn't the only one— He looked for Rip and Weeks and saw that they, too, were ill.

But for the moment all that mattered was the stretch of trampled earth and the two men facing each other. The Eysie made another cast and this time, although Jellico was not caught, the slap of the mesh raised a red welt on his forearm. So far the Captain had been content to play the defensive role of retreat, studying his enemy, planning ahead.

The Eysie plainly thought the game his, that he had only to wait for a favorable moment and cinch the victory. Dane began to think it had gone on for weary hours. And he was dimly aware that the Salariki were also restless. One or two shouted angrily at Jellico in their own tongue.

The end came suddenly. Jellico lost his footing, stumbled, and went down. But before his men could move, the Eysie champion bounded forward, his net whirling out. Only he never reached the Captain. In the very act of falling Jellico had pulled his legs under him so that he was not supine but crouched, and his net swept out at ground level, clipping the I-S man about the shins, entangling his feet so that he crashed heavily to the sod and lay still.

"The whip—that Lalox whip trick!" Wilcox's voice rose triumphantly above the babble of the crowd. Using his net as if it had been a thong, Jellico had brought down the Eysie with a move the other had not foreseen.

Breathing hard, sweat running down his shoulders and making tracks through the powdery red dust which streaked him, Jellico got to his feet and walked over to the I-S champion who had not moved or made a sound since his fall. The Captain went down on one knee to examine him.

"Kill! Kill!" That was the Salariki, all their instinctive savagery aroused.

But Jellico spoke to Groft. "By our customs we do not kill the conquered. Let his friends bear him hence." He took the claw knife the Eysie still clutched in his hand and thrust it into his own belt. Then he faced the I-S party and Kallee.

"Take your man and get out!" The rein he had kept on his temper these past days was growing very thin. "You've made your last play here."

Kallee's thick lips drew back in something close to a Salarik snarl.

But neither he nor his men made any reply. They bundled up their unconscious fighter and disappeared.

Of their own return to the sanctuary of the *Queen* Dane had only the dimmest of memories afterwards. He had made the privacy of the forest road before he yielded to the demands of his outraged interior. And after that he had stumbled along with Van Rycke's hand under his arm, knowing from other miserable sounds that he was not alone in his torment.

It was some time later, months he thought when he first roused, that he found himself lying in his bunk, feeling very weak and empty as if a large section of his middle had been removed, but also at peace with his world. As he levered himself up the cabin had a nasty tendency to move slowly to the right as if he were a pivot on which it swung, and he had all the sensations of being in free fall though the *Queen* was still firmly planeted. But that was only a minor discomfort compared to the disturbance he remembered.

Fed the semi-liquid diet prescribed by Tau and served up by Mura to him and his fellow sufferers, he speedily got back his strength. But it had been a close call, he did not need Tau's explanation to underline that. Weeks had suffered the least of the four, he the most—though none of them had had an easy time. And they had been out of circulation three days.

"The Eysie blasted last night," Rip informed him as they lounged in the sun on the ramp, sharing the blessed lazy hours of invalidism.

But somehow that news gave Dane no lift of spirit. "I didn't think they'd give up—"

Rip shrugged. "They may be off to make a dust-off before the Board. Only, thanks to Van and the Old Man, we're covered all along the line. There's nothing they can use against us to break our contract. And now we're in so solid they can't cut us out with the Salariki. Groft asked the Captain to teach him that trick with the net. I didn't know the Old Man knew Lalox whip fighting—it's about one of the nastiest ways to get cut to pieces in this universe—"

"How's trade going?"

Rip's sunniness clouded. "Supplies have given out. Weeks had an idea—but it won't bring in Koros. That red wood he's so mad about, he's persuaded Van to stow some in the cargo holds since we have enough Koros stones to cover the voyage. Luckily the clansmen will take ordinary trade goods in exchange for that and Weeks thinks it will sell on Terra. It's tough enough to turn a steel knife blade and yet it is light and easy to handle when it's cured. Queer stuff and the color's interesting. That stockade of it planted around Groft's town has been up close to a hundred years and not a sign of rot in a log of it!"

"Where is Van?"

"The storm priests sent for him. Some kind of a gabble-fest on the star-star level, I gather. Otherwise we're almost ready to blast. And we know what kind of cargo to bring next time."

They certainly did, Dane agreed. But he was not to idle away his morning. An hour later a caravan came out of the forest, a line of complaining, burdened orgels, their tiny heads hanging low as they moaned their woes, the hard life which sent them on their sluggish way with piles of red logs lashed to their broad toads' backs. Weeks was in charge of the procession and Dane went to work with the cargo plan Van had left, seeing that the brilliant scarlet lengths were hoisted into the lower cargo hatch and stacked according to the science of stowage. He discovered that Rip had been right, the wood for all its incredible hardness was light of weight. Weak as he still was he could lift and stow a full sized log with no great difficulty. And he thought Weeks was correct in thinking that it would sell on their home world. The color was novel, the durability an asset. It would not make fortunes as the Koros stones might, but every bit of profit helped and this cargo might cover their fielding fees on Terra.

Sinbad was in the cargo space when the first of the logs came in. With his usual curiosity the striped tom cat prowled along the wood, sniffing industriously. Suddenly he stopped short, spat and backed away, his spine fur a roughened crest. Having backed as far as the inner door he turned and slunk out. Puzzled, Dane gave the wood a

swift inspection. There were no cracks or crevices in the smooth surfaces, but as he stopped over the logs he became conscious of a sharp
odor. So this was one scent of the perfumed planet Sinbad did not
like. Dane laughed. Maybe they had better have Weeks make a gate
of the stuff and slip it across the ramp, keeping Sinbad on ship board.
Odd—it wasn't an unpleasant odor—at least to him it wasn't—just
sharp and pungent. He sniffed again and was vaguely surprised to
discover that it was less noticeable now. Perhaps the wood when
taken out of the sunlight lost its scent.

They packed the lower hold solid in accordance with the rules of
stowage and locked the hatch before Van Rycke returned from his
meeting with the storm priests. When the cargo-master came back he
was followed by two servants bearing between them a chest.

But there was something in Van Rycke's attitude, apparent to those
who knew him best, that proclaimed he was not too well pleased with
his morning's work. Sparing the feelings of the accompanying storm
priests about the offensiveness of the spacer Captain Jellico and Steen
Wilcox went out to receive them in the open. Dane watched from the
hatch, aware that in his present pariah-hood it would not be wise to
venture closer.

The Terran Traders were protesting some course of action that
the Salariki were firmly insistent upon. In the end the natives won
and Kosti was summoned to carry on board the chest which the servants had brought. Having seen it carried safely inside the spacer,
the aliens departed, but Van Rycke was frowning and Jellico's fingers were beating a tattoo on his belt as they came up the ramp.

"I don't like it," Jellico stated as he entered.

"It was none of my doing," Van Rycke snapped. "I'll take risks if I
have to—but there's something about this one—" He broke off, two
deep lines showing between his thick brows. "Well, you can't teach a
sasseral to spit," he ended philosophically. "We'll have to do the best
we can."

But Jellico did not look at all happy as he climbed to the control section. And before the hour was out the reason for the Captain's uneasiness was common property throughout the ship.

Having sampled the delights of off-world herbs, the Salariki were determined to not be cut off from their source of supply. Six Terran months from the present Sargolian date would come the great yearly feast of the Fifty Storms, and the priests were agreed that this year their influence and power would be doubled if they could offer the devout certain privileges in the form of Terran plants. Consequently they had produced and forced upon the reluctant Van Rycke the Koros collection of their order, with instructions that it be sold on Terra and the price returned to them in the precious seeds and plants. In vain the cargo-master and Captain had pointed out that Galactic trade was a chancy thing at the best, that accident might prevent return of the *Queen* to Sargol. But the priests had remained adamant and saw in all such arguments only a devious attempt to raise prices. They quoted in their turn the information they had levered out of the Company men—that Traders had their code and that once pay had been given in advance the contract *must* be fulfilled. They, and they alone, wanted the full cargo of the *Queen* on her next voyage, and they were taking the one way they were sure of achieving that result.

So a fortune in Koros stones which as yet did not rightfully belong to the Traders was now in the *Queen*'s strong-room and her crew were pledged by the strongest possible tie known in their Service to set down on Sargol once more before the allotted time had passed. The Free Traders did not like it, there was even a vaguely superstitious feeling that such a bargain would inevitably draw ill luck to them. But they were left with no choice if they wanted to retain their influence with the Salariki.

"Cutting orbit pretty fine, aren't we?" Ali asked Rip across the mess table. "I saw your two star man sweating it out before he came down to shoot the breeze with us rocket monkeys—"

Rip nodded. "Steen's double checked every computation and some he's done four times." He ran his hands over his close cropped head with a weary gesture. As a semi-invalid he had been herded down with his fellows to swallow the builder Mura had concocted and Tau insisted that they take, but he had been doing half a night's work on the plotter under his chief's exacting eye before he came. "The latest news is that, barring accident, we can make it with about three weeks' grace, give or take a day or two—"

"Barring accident—" The words rang in the air. Here on the frontiers of the star lanes there were so many accidents, so many delays which could put a ship behind schedule. Only on the main star trails did the huge liners or Company ships attempt to keep on regularly timed trips. A Free Trader did not really dare to have an inelastic contract.

"What does Stotz say?" Dane asked Ali.

"He says he can deliver. We don't have the headache about setting a course—you point the nose and we only give her the boost to send her along."

Rip sighed. "Yes—point her nose." He inspected his nails. "Goodbye," he added gravely. "These won't be here by the time we planet here again. I'll have my fingers gnawed off to the first knuckle. Well, we lift at six hours. Pleasant strap down." He drank the last of the stuff in his mug, made a face at the flavor, and got to his feet, due back at his post in control.

Dane, free of duty until the ship earthed, drifted back to his own cabin, sure of part of a night's undisturbed rest before they blasted off. Sinbad was curled on his bunk. For some reason the cat had not been prowling the ship before takeoff as he usually did. First he had sat on Van's desk and now he was here, almost as if he wanted human company. Dane picked him up and Sinbad rumbled a purr, arching his head so that it rubbed against the young man's chin in an extremely uncharacteristic show of affection. Smoothing the fur along the cat's jawline Dane carried him back to the cargo-master's cabin.

With some hesitation he knocked at the panel and did not step in until he had Van Rycke's muffled invitation. The cargo-master was stretched on the bunk, two of the takeoff straps already fastened across his bulk as if he intended to sleep through the blast-off.

"Sinbad, sir. Shall I stow him?"

Van Rycke grunted an assent and Dane dropped the cat in the small hammock which was his particular station, fastening the safety cords. For once Sinbad made no protest but rolled into a ball and was promptly fast asleep. For a moment or two Dane thought about this unnatural behavior and wondered if he should call it to the cargomaster's attention. Perhaps on Sargol Sinbad had had *his* equivalent of a friendship cup and needed a checkup by Tau.

"Stowage correct?" The question, coming from Van Rycke, was also unusual. The seal would not have been put across the hold lock had its contents not been checked and rechecked.

"Yes, sir," Dane replied woodenly, knowing he was still in the outer darkness. "There was just the wood—we stowed it according to chart."

Van Rycke grunted once more. "Feeling top layer again?"

"Yes, sir. Any orders, sir?"

"No. Blastoff's at six."

"Yes, sir." Dane left the cabin, closing the panel carefully behind him. Would he—or could he—he thought drearily, get back in Van Rycke's profit column again? Sargol had been unlucky as far as he was concerned. First he had made that stupid mistake and then he got sick and now—And now—what *was* the matter? Was it just the general attack of nerves over their voyage and the commitments which forced their haste, or was it something else? He could not rid himself of a vague sense that the *Queen* was about to take off into real trouble. And he did not like the sensation at all!

HEADACHES

8 They lifted from Sargol as scheduled and went into Hyper also on schedule. From that point on there was nothing to do but wait out the usual dull time of flight between systems and hope that Steen Wilcox had plotted a course which would cut that flight time to a minimum. But this voyage there was little relaxation once they were in Hyper. No matter when Dane dropped into the mess cabin, which was the common meeting place of the spacer, he was apt to find others there before him, usually with a mug of one of Mura's special brews close at hand, speculating about their landing date.

Dane, himself, once he had thrown off the lingering effects of his Sargolian illness, applied time to his studies. When he had first joined the *Queen* as a recruit straight out of the training Pool, he had speedily learned that all the ten years of intensive study then behind him had only been an introduction to the amount he still had to absorb before he could take his place as an equal with such a trader as Van Rycke—if he had the stuff which would raise him in time to that exalted level. While he had still had his superior's favor he had dared to treat him as an instructor, going to him with perplexing problems of stowage or barter. But now he had no desire to intrude upon the cargo-master, and doggedly wrestled with the microtapes of old records on his own, painfully working out the why and wherefore for any departure from the regular procedure. He had no inkling of his own future status—whether the return to Terra would find him permanently earthed. And he would ask no questions.

They had been four days of ship's time in Hyper when Dane walked into the mess cabin, tired after his work with old records, to discover no Mura busy in the galley beyond, no brew steaming on the heat coil. Rip sat at the table, his long legs stuck out, his usually happy face very sober.

"What's wrong?" Dane reached for a mug, then seeing no pot of drink, put it back in place.

"Frank's sick—"

"What!" Dane turned. Illness such as they had run into on Sargol had a logical base. But illness on board ship was something else.

"Tau has him isolated. He has a bad headache and he blacked out when he tried to sit up. Tau's running tests."

Dane sat down. "Could be something he ate—"

Rip shook his head. "He wasn't at the feast—remember? And he didn't eat anything from outside, he swore that to Tau. In fact he didn't go dirt much while we were down—"

That was only too true as Dane could now recall. And the fact that the steward had not been at the feast, had not sampled native food products, wiped out the simplest and most comforting reasons for his present collapse.

"What's this about Frank?" Ali stood in the doorway. "He said yesterday that he had a headache. But now Tau has him shut off—"

"He blacked out. Tau's running tests," Rip repeated.

"But he wasn't at that feast." Ali stopped short as the implications of that struck him. "How's Tang feeling?"

"Fine—why?" The com-tech had come up behind Kamil and was answering for himself. "Why this interest in the state of my health?"

"Frank's down with something—in isolation," Rip replied bluntly. "Did he do anything out of the ordinary when we were off ship?"

For a long moment the other stared at Shannon and then he shook his head. "No. And he wasn't dirt-side to any extent either. So Tau's running tests—" He lapsed into silence. None of them wished to put their thoughts into words.

Dane picked up the microtape he had brought with him and went on down the corridor to return it. The panel of the cargo office was ajar and to his relief he found Van Rycke out. He shoved the tape back in its case and pulled out the next one. Sinbad was there, not in his own private hammock, but sprawled out on the cargo-master's bunk. He watched Dane lazily, mouthing a silent mew of welcome. For some reason since they had blasted from Sargol the cat had been lazy—as if his adventures afield there had sapped much of his vitality.

"Why aren't you out working?" Dane asked as he leaned over to scratch under a furry chin raised for the benefit of such a caress. "You inspected the hold lately, boy?"

Sinbad merely blinked and after the manner of his species looked infinitely bored. As Dane turned to go the cargo-master came in. He showed no surprise at Dane's presence. Instead he reached out and fingered the label of the tape Dane had just chosen. After a glance at the identifying symbol he took it out of his assistant's hand, plopped it back in its case, and stood for a moment eyeing the selection of past voyage records. With a tongue-click of satisfaction he pulled out another and tossed it across the desk to Dane.

"See what you can make out of this tangle," he ordered. But Dane's shoulders went back as if some weight had been lifted from them. The old easiness was still lacking, but he was no longer exiled to the outer darkness of Van Rycke's displeasure.

Holding the microtape as if it were a first grade Koros stone Dane went back to his own cabin, snapped the tape into his reader, adjusted the ear buttons and lay back on his bunk to listen.

He was deep in the intricacy of a deal so complicated that he was lost after the first two moves, when he opened his eyes to see Ali at the door panel. The Engineer-apprentice made an emphatic beckoning wave and Dane slipped off the ear buttons.

"What is it?" His question lacked a cordial note.

"I've got to have help." Ali was terse. "Kosti's blacked out!"

"What!" Dane sat up and dropped his feet to the deck in almost one movement.

"I can't shift him alone," Ali stated the obvious. The giant jetman was almost double his size. "We must get him to his quarters. And I won't ask Stotz—"

For a perfectly good reason Dane knew. An assistant—two of the apprentices—could go sick, but their officers continued good health meant the most to the *Queen*. If some infection were aboard it would be better for Ali and himself to be exposed, than to have Johan Stotz with all his encyclopedic knowledge of the ship's engines contract any disease.

They found the jetman half sitting, half lying in the short foot or so of corridor which led to his own cubby. He had been making for his quarters when the seizure had taken him. And by the time the two reached his side, he was beginning to come around, moaning, his hands going to his head.

Together they got him on his feet and guided him to his bunk where he collapsed again, a dead weight they had to push into place. Dane looked at Ali—

"Tau?"

"Haven't had time to call him yet." Ali was jerking at the thigh straps which fastened Kosti's space boots.

"I'll go." Glad for the task Dane sped up the ladder to the next section and threaded the narrow side hall to the medic's cabin where he knocked on the panel.

There was a pause before Craig Tau looked out, deep lines of weariness bracketing his mouth, etched between his eyes.

"Kosti, sir," Dane gave his bad news quickly. "He's collapsed. We got him to his cabin—"

Tau showed no sign of surprise. His hand shot out for his kit.

"You touched him?" At the other's nod he added an order. "Stay in your quarters until I have a chance to look you over—understand?"

Dane had no chance to answer, the medic was already on his way. He went to his own cabin, understanding the reason for his imprisonment, but inwardly rebelling against it. Rather than sit idle he snapped on the reader—but, although facts and figures were dunned into his ears—he really heard very little. He couldn't apply himself— not with a new specter leering at him from the bulkhead.

The dangers of the space lanes were not to be numbered, death walked among the stars a familiar companion of all spacemen. And to the Free Trader it was the extra and invisible crewman on every ship that raised. But there were deaths and deaths— And Dane could not forget the gruesome legends Van Rycke collected avidly as his hobby—had recorded in his private library of the folklore of space.

Stories such as that of the ghostly *New Hope* carrying refugees from the first Martian Rebellion—the ship which had lifted for the stars but had never arrived, which wandered for a timeless eternity, a derelict in free fall, its port closed but the warning "dead" lights on at its nose—a ship which through five centuries had been sighted only by a spacer in similar distress. Such stories were numerous. There were other tales of "plague" ships wandering free with their dead crews, or discovered and shot into some sun by a Patrol cruiser so that they might not carry their infection farther. Plague—the nebulous "worst" the Traders had to face. Dane screwed his eyes shut, tried to concentrate upon the droning voice in his ears, but he could not control his thoughts nor—his fears.

At a touch on his arm he started so wildly that he jerked the cord loose from the reader and sat up, somewhat shamefaced, to greet Tau. At the medic's orders he stripped for one of the most complete examinations he had ever undergone outside a quarantine port. It included an almost microscopic inspection of the skin on his neck and shoulders, but when Tau had done he gave a sigh of relief.

"Well, you haven't got it—at least you don't show any signs yet," he amended his first statement almost before the words were out of his mouth.

"What were you looking for?"

Tau took time out to explain. "Here," his fingers touched the small hollow at the base of Dane's throat and then swung him around and indicated two places on the back of his neck and under his shoulder blades. "Kosti and Mura both have red eruptions here. It's as if they have been given an injection of some narcotic." Tau sat down on the jump seat while Dane dressed. "Kosti was dirt-side—he might have picked up something—"

"But Mura—"

"That's it!" Tau brought his fist down on the edge of the bunk. "Frank hardly left the ship—yet he showed the first signs. On the other hand you are all right so far and you were off ship. And Ali's clean and he was with you on the hunt. We'll just have to wait and see." He got up wearily. "If your head begins to ache," he told Dane, "you get back here in a hurry and stay put—understand?"

As Dane learned all the other members of the crew were given the same type of inspection. But none of them showed the characteristic marks which meant trouble. They were on course for Terra—but— and that but must have loomed large in all their minds—once there would they be allowed to land? Could they even hope for a hearing? Plague ship—Tau must find the answer before they came into normal space about their own solar system or they were in for such trouble as made a broken contract seem the simplest of mishaps.

Kosti and Mura were in isolation. There were volunteers for nursing and Tau, unable to be in two places at once, finally picked Weeks to look after his crewmate in the engineering section.

There was doubling up of duties. Tau could no longer share with Mura the care of the hydro garden so Van Rycke took over. While Dane found himself in charge of the galley and, while he did not have Mura's deft hand at disguising the monotonous concentrates to the point they resembled fresh food, after a day or two he began to experiment cautiously and produced a stew which brought some short words of appreciation from Captain Jellico.

They all breathed a sigh of relief when, after three days, no more signs of the mysterious illness showed on new members of the crew. It became routine to parade before Tau stripped to the waist each morning for the inspection of the danger points, and the medic's vigilance did not relax.

In the meantime neither Mura nor Kosti appeared to suffer. Once the initial stages of headaches and blackouts were passed, the patients lapsed into a semi-conscious state as if they were under sedation of some type. They would eat, if the food was placed in their mouths, but they did not seem to know what was going on about them, nor did they answer when spoken to.

Tau, between visits to them, worked feverishly in his tiny lab, analyzing blood samples, reading the records of obscure diseases, trying to find the reason for their attacks. But as yet his discoveries were exactly nothing. He had come out of his quarters and sat in limp exhaustion at the mess table while Dane placed before him a mug of stimulating caf-hag.

"I don't get it!" The medic addressed the table top rather than the amateur cook. "It's a poison of some kind. Kosti went dirt-side—Mura didn't. Yet Mura came down with it first. And we didn't ship any food from Sargol. Neither did he eat any while we were there. Unless he did and we didn't know about it. If I could just bring him to long enough to answer a couple of questions!" Sighing he dropped his weary head on his folded arms and within seconds was asleep.

Dane put the mug back on the heating unit and sat down at the other end of the table. He did not have the heart to shake Tau into wakefulness—let the poor devil get a slice of bunk time, he certainly needed it after the fatigues of the past four days.

Van Rycke passed along the corridor on his way to the hydro, Sinbad at his heels. But in a moment the cat was back, leaping up on Dane's knee. He did not curl up, but rubbed against the young man's arm, finally reaching up with a paw to touch Dane's chin, uttering one of the soundless mews which were his bid for attention.

"What's the matter, boy?" Dane fondled the cat's ears. "You haven't got a headache—have you?" In that second a wild surmise came into his mind. Sinbad had been planet-side on Sargol as much as he could, and on ship board he was equally at home in all their cabins—could he be the carrier of the disease?

A good idea—only if it were true, then logically the second victim should have been Van, or Dane—where as Sinbad lingered most of the time in their cabins—not Kosti. The cat, as far as he knew, had never shown any particular fondness for the jetman and certainly did not sleep in Karl's quarters. No—that point did not fit. But he would mention it to Tau—no use overlooking anything—no matter how wild.

It was the sequence of victims which puzzled them all. As far as Tau had been able to discover Mura and Kosti had nothing much in common except that they were crewmates on the same spacer. They did not bunk in the same section, their fields of labor were totally different, they had no special food or drink tastes in common, they were not even of the same race. Frank Mura was one of the few descendants of a mysterious (or now mysterious) people who had had their home on a series of islands in one of Terra's seas, islands which almost a hundred years before had been swallowed up in a series of world-rending quakes—Japan was the ancient name of that nation. While Karl Kosti had come from the once thickly populated land masses half the planet away which had borne the geographical name of "Europe." No, all the way along the two victims had only very general meeting points—they both shipped on the *Solar Queen* and they were both of Terran birth.

Tau stirred and sat up, blinking bemusedly at Dane, then pushed back his wiry black hair and assumed a measure of alertness. Dane dropped the now purring cat in the medic's lap and in a few sentences outlined his suspicion. Tau's hands closed about Sinbad.

"There's a chance in that—" He looked a little less beat and he drank thirstily from the mug Dane gave him for the second time. Then he hurried out with Sinbad under one arm—bound for his lab.

Dane slicked up the galley, trying to put things away as neatly as Mura kept them. He didn't have much faith in the Sinbad lead, but in this case everything must be checked out.

When the medic did not appear during the rest of the ship's day Dane was not greatly concerned. But he was alerted to trouble when Ali came in with an inquiry and a complaint.

"Seen anything of Craig?"

"He's in the lab," Dane answered.

"He didn't answer my knock," Ali protested. "And Weeks says he hasn't been in to see Karl all day—"

That did catch Dane's attention. Had his half hunch been right? Was Tau on the trail of a discovery which had kept him chained to the lab? But it wasn't like the medic not to look in on his patients.

"You're sure he isn't in the lab?"

"I told you that he didn't answer my knock. I didn't open the panel—" But now Ali was already in the corridor heading back the way he had come, with Dane on his heels, an unwelcome explanation for that silence in both their minds. And their fears were reinforced by what they heard as they approached the panel—a low moan wrung out of unbearable pain. Dane thrust the sliding door open.

Tau had slipped from his stool to the floor. His hands were at his head which rolled from side to side as if he were trying to quiet some agony. Dane stripped down the medic's under tunic. There was no need to make a careful examination, in the hollow of Craig Tau's throat was the tell-tale red blotch.

"Sinbad!" Dane glanced about the cabin. "Did Sinbad get out past you?" he demanded of the puzzled Ali.

"No—I haven't seen him all day—"

Yet the cat was nowhere in the tiny cabin and it had no concealed hiding place. To make doubly sure Dane secured the panel before they carried Tau to his bunk. The medic had blacked out again, passed into the lethargic second stage of the malady. At least he was out of the pain which appeared to be the worst symptom of the disease.

"It must be Sinbad!" Dane said as he made his report directly to Captain Jellico. "And yet—"

"Yes, he's been staying in Van's cabin," the Captain mused. "And you've handled him, he slept on your bunk. Yet you and Van are all right. I don't understand that. Anyway—to be on the safe side—we'd better find and isolate him before—"

He didn't have to underline any words for the grim-faced men who listened. With Tau—their one hope of fighting the disease—gone, they had a black future facing them.

They did not have to search for Sinbad. Dane coming down to his own section found the cat crouched before the panel of Van Rycke's cabin, his eyes glued to the thin crack of the door. Dane scooped him up and took him to the small cargo space intended for the safeguarding of choice items of commerce. To his vast surprise Sinbad began fighting wildly as he opened the hatch, kicking and then slashing with ready claws. The cat seemed to go mad and Dane had all he could do to shut him in. When he snapped the panel he heard Sinbad launch himself against the barrier as if to batter his way out. Dane, blood welling in several deep scratches, went in search of first aid. But some suspicion led him to pause as he passed Van Rycke's door. And when his knock brought no answer he pushed the panel open.

Van Rycke lay on his bunk, his eyes half closed in a way which had become only too familiar to the crew of the *Solar Queen*. And Dane knew that when he looked for it he would find the mark of the strange plague on the cargo-master's body.

PLAGUE!

9 Jellico and Steen Wilcox pored over the few notes Tau had made before he was stricken. But apparently the medic had found nothing to indicate that Sinbad was the carrier of any disease. Meanwhile the Captain gave orders for the cat to be confined. A difficult task—since Sinbad crouched close to the door of the storage cabin and was ready to dart out when food was taken in for him. Once he got a good way down the corridor before Dane was able to corner and return him to keeping.

Dane, Ali and Weeks took on the full care of the four sick men, leaving the few regular duties of the ship to the senior officers, while Rip was installed in charge of the hydro garden.

Mura, the first to be taken ill, showed no change. He was semi-conscious, he swallowed food if it were put in his mouth, he responded to nothing around him. And Kosti, Tau, and Van Rycke followed the same pattern. They still held morning inspection of those on their feet for signs of a new outbreak, but when no one else went down during the next two days, they regained a faint spark of hope.

Hope which was snapped out when Ali brought the news that

Stotz could not be roused and must have taken ill during a sleep period. One more inert patient was added to the list—and nothing learned about how he was infected. Except that they could eliminate Sinbad, since the cat had been in custody during the time Stotz had apparently contracted the disease.

Weeks, Ali and Dane, though they were in constant contact with the sick men, and though Dane had repeatedly handled Sinbad, continued to be immune. A fact, Dane thought more than once, which must have significance—if someone with Tau's medical knowledge had been able to study it. By all rights they should be the most susceptible—but the opposite seemed true. And Wilcox duly noted that fact among the data they had recorded.

It became a matter of watching each other, waiting for another collapse. And they were not surprised when Tang Ya reeled into the mess, his face livid and drawn with pain. Rip and Dane got him to his cabin before he blacked out. But all they could learn from him during the interval before he lost consciousness was that his head was bursting and he couldn't stand it. Over his limp body they stared at one another bleakly.

"Six down," Ali observed, "and six to go. How do you feel?"

"Tired, that's all. What I don't understand is that once they go into this stupor they just stay. They don't get any worse, they have no rise in temperature—it's as if they are in a modified form of cold sleep!"

"How is Tang?" Rip asked from the corridor.

"Usual pattern," Ali answered. "He's sleeping. Got a pain, fella?"

Rip shook his head. "Right as a com-unit. I don't get it. Why does it strike Tang who didn't even hit dirt much—and yet you keep on—?"

Dane grimaced. "If we had an answer to that, maybe we'd know what caused the whole thing—"

Ali's eyes narrowed. He was staring straight at the unconscious com-tech as if he did not see that supine body at all. "I wonder if we've been salted—" he said slowly.

"We've been *what*?" Dane demanded.

"Look here, we three—with Weeks—drank that brew of the Salariki, didn't we? And we—"

"Were as sick as Venusian gobblers afterwards," agreed Rip.

Light dawned. "Do you mean—" began Dane.

"So that's it!" flashed Rip.

"It might just be," Ali said. "Do you remember how the settlers on Camblyne brought their Terran cattle through the first year? They fed them salt mixed with fansel grass. The result was that the herds didn't take the fansel grass fever when they turned them out to pasture in the dry season. All right, maybe we had our 'salt' in that drink. The fansel-salt makes the cattle filthy sick when it's forced down their throats, but after they recover they're immune to the fever. And nobody on Camblyne buys unsalted cattle now."

"It sounds logical," admitted Rip. "But how are we going to prove it?"

Ali's face was black once more. "Probably by elimination," he said morosely. "If we keep our feet and all the rest go down—that's our proof."

"But we ought to be able to do something—" protested Shannon.

"Just how?" Ali's slender brows arched. "Do you have a gallon of that Salariki brew on board you can serve out? We don't know what was in it. Nor are we sure that this whole idea has any value."

All of them had had first aid and basic preventive medicine as part of their training, but the more advanced laboratory experimentation was beyond their knowledge and skill. Had Tau still been on his feet perhaps he could have traced that lead and brought order out of the chaos which was closing in upon the *Solar Queen*. But, though they reported their suggestion to the Captain, Jellico was powerless to do anything about it. If the four who had shared that upsetting friendship cup were immune to the doom which now overhung the ship, there was no possible way for them to discover why or how.

Ship's time came to have little meaning. And they were not surprised when Steen Wilcox slipped from his seat before the computer—to be stowed away with what had become a familiar procedure. Only Jellico withstood the contagion apart from the younger four, taking his turn at caring for the helpless men. There was no change in their condition. They neither roused nor grew worse as the hours and then the days sped by. But each of those units of time in passing brought them nearer to greater danger. Sooner or later they must make the transition out of Hyper into system space, and the jump out of warp was something not even a veteran took lightly. Rip's round face thinned while they watched. Jellico was still functioning. But if the Captain collapsed the whole responsibility for the snapout would fall directly on Shannon. An infinitesimal error would condemn them to almost hopeless wandering—perhaps forever.

Dane and Ali relieved Rip of all duty but that which kept him chained in Wilcox's chair before the computers. He went over and over the data of the course the Astrogator had set. And Captain Jellico, his eyes sunk in dark pits, checked and rechecked.

When the fatal moment came Ali manned the engine room with Weeks at his elbow to tend the controls the acting-engineer could not reach. And Dane, having seen the sick all safely stowed in crash webbing, came up to the control cabin, riding out the transfer in Tang Ya's place.

Rip's voice hoarsened into a croak, calling out the data. Dane, though he had had basic theory, was completely lost before Shannon had finished the first set of coordinates. But Jellico replied, hands playing across the pilot's board.

"Stand-by for snap-out—" The croak went down to the engines where Ali now held Stotz's post.

"Engines ready!" The voice came back, thinned by its journey from the *Queen*'s interior.

"Ought-five-nine—" That was Jellico.

Dane found himself suddenly unable to watch. He shut his eyes and braced himself against the vertigo of snap-out. It came and he whirled sickeningly through unstable space. Then he was sitting in the laced com-tech's seat looking at Rip.

Runnels of sweat streaked Shannon's brown face. There was a damp patch darkening his tunic between his shoulder blades, a patch which it would take both of Dane's hands to cover.

For a moment he did not raise his head to look at the vision plate which would tell him whether or not they had made it. But when he did familiar constellations made the patterns they knew. They were out—and they couldn't be too far off the course Wilcox had plotted. There was still the system run to make—but snap-out was behind them. Rip gave a deep sigh and buried his head in his hands.

With a throb of fear Dane unhooked his safety belt and hurried over to him. When he clutched at Shannon's shoulder the astrogator-apprentice's head rolled limply. Was Rip down with the illness too? But the other muttered and opened his eyes.

"Does your head ache?" Dane shook him.

"Head? No—" Rip's words came drowsily. "Jus' sleepy—so sleepy—"

He did not seem to be in pain. But Dane's hands were shaking as he hoisted the other out of his seat and half carried, half led him to his cabin, praying as he went that it was only fatigue and not the disease. The ship was on auto now until Jellico as pilot set a course—

Dane got Rip down on the bunk and stripped off his tunic. The fine-drawn face of the sleeper looked wan against the foam rest, and he snuggled into the softness like a child as he turned over and curled up. But his skin was clear—it was real sleep and not the plague which had claimed him.

Impulse sent Dane back to the control cabin. He was not an experienced pilot officer, but there might be some assistance he could offer the Captain now that Rip was washed out, perhaps for hours.

Jellico hunched before the smaller computer, feeding pilot tape into its slot. His face was a skull under a thin coating of skin, the bones marking it sharply at jaw, nose and eye socket.

"Shannon down?" His voice was a mere whisper of its powerful self, he did not turn his head.

"He's just worn out, sir," Dane hastened to give reassurance. "The marks aren't on him."

"When he comes around tell him the co-ords are in," Jellico murmured. "See he checks course in ten hours—"

"But, sir—" Dane's protest failed as he watched the Captain struggle to his feet, pulling himself up with shaking hands. As Thorson reached forward to steady the other, one of those hands tore at tunic collar, ripping loose the sealing—

There was no need for explanation—the red splotch signaled from Jellico's sweating throat. He kept his feet, holding out against the waves of pain by sheer will power. Then Dane had a grip on him, got him away from the computer, hoping he could keep him going until they reached Jellico's cabin.

Somehow they made that journey, being greeted with raucous screams from the Hoobat. Furiously Dane slapped the cage, setting it to swinging and so silencing the creature which stared at him with round, malignant eyes as he got the Captain to bed.

Only four of them on their feet now, Dane thought bleakly as he left the cabin. If Rip came out of it in time they could land—Dane's breath caught as he made himself face up to the fact that Shannon might be ill, that it might be up to *him* to bring the *Queen* in for a landing. And in where? The Terra quarantine was Luna City on the Moon. But let them signal for a set-down there—let them describe what had happened and they might face death as a plague ship.

Wearily he climbed down to the mess cabin to discover Weeks and Ali there before him. They did not look up as he entered.

"Old Man's got it," he reported.

"Rip?" was Ali's crossing question.

"Asleep. He passed out—"

"What!" Weeks swung around.

"Worn out," Dane amended. "Captain fed in a pilot tape before he gave up."

"So—now we are three," was Ali's comment. "Where do we set down—Luna City?"

"If they let us," Dane hinted at the worst.

"But they've got to let us!" Weeks exclaimed. "We can't just wander around out here—"

"It's been done," Ali reminded them brutally and that silenced Weeks.

"Did the Old Man set Luna?" After a long pause Ali inquired.

"I didn't check," Dane confessed. "He was giving out and I had to get him to his bunk."

"It might be well to know." The engineer-apprentice got up, his movements lacking much of the elastic spring which was normally his. When he climbed to control both the others followed him.

Ali's slender fingers played across a set of keys and in the small screen mounting on the computer a set of figures appeared. Dane took up the master course book, read the connotation and blinked.

"Not Luna?" Ali asked.

"No. But I don't understand. This must be for somewhere in the asteroid belt."

Ali's lips stretched into a pale caricature of a smile. "Good for the Old Man, he still had his wits about him, even after the bug bit him!"

"But why are we going to the asteroids?" Weeks asked reasonably enough. "There's medics at Luna City—they can help us—"

"They can handle known diseases," Ali pointed out. "But what of the Code?"

Weeks dropped into the com-tech's place as if some of the stiffening had vanished from his thin but sturdy legs. "They wouldn't do that—" he protested, but his eyes said that he knew that they might— they well might.

"Oh, no? Face the facts, man." Ali sounded almost savage. "We come from a frontier planet, we're a plague ship—"

He did not have to underline that. They all knew too well the danger in which they now stood.

"Nobody's died yet," Weeks tried to find an opening in the net being drawn about them.

"And nobody's recovered," Ali crushed that thread of hope. "We don't know what it is, how it is contracted—anything about it. Let us make a report saying that and you know what will happen—don't you?"

They weren't sure of the details, but they could guess.

"So I say," Ali continued, "the Old Man was right when he set us on an evasion course. If we can stay out until we really know what is the matter we'll have some chance of talking over the high brass at Luna when we do planet—"

In the end they decided not to interfere with the course the Captain had set. It would take them into the fringes of solar civilization, but give them a fighting chance at solving their problem before they had to report to the authorities. In the meantime they tended their charges, let Rip sleep, and watched each other with desperate but hidden intentness, ready for another to be stricken. However, they remained, although almost stupid with fatigue at times, reasonably healthy. Time was proving that their guess had been correct—they had been somehow inoculated against the germ or virus which had struck the ship.

Rip slept for twenty-four hours, ship time, and then came into the mess cabin ravenously hungry, to catch up on both food and news. And he refused to join with the prevailing pessimistic view of the future. Instead he was sure that their own immunity having been proven, they had a talking point to use with the medical officials at Luna and he was eager to alter course directly for the quarantine station. Only the combined arguments of the other three made him, unwillingly, agree to a short delay.

And how grateful they should be for Captain Jellico's foresight they learned within the next day. Ali was at the com-unit, trying to pick up Solarian news reports. When the red alert flashed on throughout the ship it brought the others hurrying to the control cabin. The code squeaks were magnified as Ali switched on the receiver full strength, to be translated as he pressed a second button.

"Repeat, repeat, repeat. Free Trader, *Solar Queen,* Terra Registry 65-724910-Jk, suspected plague ship—took off from infected planet.

Warn off—warn off—report such ship to Luna Station. *Solar Queen* from infected planet—to be warned off and reported." The same message was repeated three times before going off ether.

The four in the control cabin looked at each other blankly.

"But," Dane broke the silence, "how did they know? We haven't reported in—"

"The Eysies!" Ali had the answer ready. "That I-S ship must be having the same sort of trouble and reported to her Company. They would include us in their report and believe that we were infected too—or it would be easy to convince the authorities that we were."

"I wonder," Rip's eyes were narrowed slits as he leaned back against the wall. "Look at the facts. The Survey ship which charted Sargol—they were dirt-side there about three—four months. Yet they gave it a clean bill of health and put it up for trading rights auction. Then Cam bought those rights—he made at least two trips in and out before he was blasted on Limbo. No infection bothered him or Survey—"

"But you've got to admit it hit us," Weeks protested.

"Yes, and the Eysie ship was able to foresee it—report us before we snapped out of Hyper. Sounds almost as if they expected us to carry plague, doesn't it?" Shannon wanted to know.

"Planted?" Ali frowned at the banks of controls. "But how—no Eysie came on board—no Salarik either, except for the cub who showed us what they thought of catnip."

Rip shrugged. "How would I know how they did—" he was beginning when Dane cut in:

"If they didn't know about our immunity the *Queen* might stay in Hyper and never come out—there wouldn't be anyone to set the snap-out."

"Right enough. But on the chance that somebody did keep on his feet and bring her home, they were ready with a cover. If no one raises a howl Sargol will be written off the charts as infected. I-S sits on her tail fins a year or so and then she promotes an investigation before the Board. The Survey records are trotted out—no infection recorded.

So they send in a Patrol Probe. Everything is all right—so it wasn't the planet after all—it was that dirty old Free Trader. And she's out of the way. I-S gets the Koros trade all square and legal and we're no longer around to worry about! Neat as a Salariki net cast—and right around our collective throats, my friends!"

"So what do we do now?" Weeks wanted to know.

"We keep on the Old Man's course, get lost in the asteroids until we can do some heavy thinking and see a way out. But if I-S gave us this prize package, some trace of its origin is still aboard. And if we can find that—why, then we have something to start from."

"Mura went down first—and then Karl. Nothing in common," the old problem faced Dane for the hundredth time.

"No. But," Ali arose from his place at the com-unit. "I'd suggest a real search of first Frank's and then Karl's quarters. A regular turn out down to the bare walls of their cabins. Are you with me?"

"Fly boy, we're ahead of you!" Rip contributed, already at the door panel. "Down to the bare walls it is."

E-STAT LANDING

10

Since Mura was in the isolation of ship sick bay the stripping of his cabin was a relatively simple job. But, though Rip and Dane went over it literally by inches, they found nothing unusual—in fact nothing from Sargol except a small twig of the red wood which lay on the steward's worktable where he had been fashioning something to incorporate in one of his miniature fairy landscapes, to be imprisoned for all time in a plasta-bubble. Dane turned this around in his fingers. Because it was the only link with the perfumed planet he couldn't help but feel that it had some importance.

But Kosti had not shown any interest in the wood. And he, himself, and Weeks had handled it freely *before* they had tasted Groft's friendship cup and had no ill effects—so it couldn't be the wood. Dane put the twig back on the worktable and snapped the protecting cover over the delicate tools—never realizing until days later how very close he had been in that moment to the solution of their problem.

After two hours of shifting every one of the steward's belongings, of crawling on hands and knees about the deck and climbing to inspect perfectly bare walls, they had found exactly nothing. Rip sat down on the end of the denuded bunk.

"There's the hydro—Frank spent a lot of time in there—and the storeroom," he told the places off on his fingers. "The galley and the mess cabin."

Those had been the extent of Mura's world. They could search the storeroom, the galley and the mess cabin—but to interfere with the hydro would endanger their air supply. It was for that very reason that they now looked at each other in startled surprise.

"The perfect place to plant something!" Dane spoke first.

Rip's teeth caught his underlip. The hydro—something planted there could not be routed out unless they made a landing on a port field and had the whole section stripped.

"Devilish—" Rip's mobile lips drew tight. "But how could they do it?"

Dane didn't see how it could have been done either. No one but the *Queen's* own crew had been on board the ship during their entire stay on Sargol, except for the young Salarik. Could that cub have brought something? But he and Mura had been with the youngster every minute that he had been in the hydro. To the best of Dane's memory the cub had touched nothing and had been there only for a few moments. That had been before the feast also—

Rip got to his feet. "We can't strip the hydro in space," he pointed out the obvious quietly.

Dane had the answer. "Then we've got to earth!"

"You heard that warn-off. If we try it—"

"What about an Emergency station?"

Rip stood very still, his big hands locked about the buckle of his arms belt. Then, without another word, he went out of the cabin and at a pounding pace up the ladder, bound for the Captain's cabin and the records Jellico kept there. It was such a slim chance—but it was better than none at all.

Dane shouldered into the small space in his wake, to find Rip making a selection from the astrogation tapes. There were E-Stats among the asteroids—points prospectors or small traders in sudden difficulties might contact for supplies or repairs. The big Companies maintained their own—the Patrol had several for independents.

"No Patrol one—"

Rip managed a smile. "I haven't gone space whirly yet," was his comment. He was feeding a tape into the reader on the Captain's desk. In the cage over his head the blue Hoobat squatted watching him intently—for the first time since Dane could remember showing no sign of resentment by weird screams or wild spitting.

"Patrol E-Stat A-54—" The reader squeaked. Rip hit a key and the wire clicked to the next entry. "Combine E-Stat—" Another punch and click. "Patrol E-Stat A-55—" punch-click. "Inter-Solar—" This time Rip's hand did not hit the key and the squeak continued— "Coordinates—" Rip reached for a steelo and jotted down the list of figures.

"Got to compare this with our present course—"

"But that's an I-S Stat," began Dane and then he laughed as the justice of such a move struck him. They did not dare set the *Queen* down at any Patrol Station. But a Company one which would be manned by only two or three men and not expecting any but their own people—and I-S owed them help now!

"There may be trouble," he said, not that he would have any regrets if there was. If the Eysies were responsible for the present plight of the *Queen* he would welcome trouble, the kind which would plant his fists on some sneering Eysie face.

"We'll see about that when we come to it," Rip went on to the control cabin with his figures. Carefully he punched the combination on the plotter and watched it be compared with the course Jellico had set before his collapse.

"Good enough," he commented as the result flashed on. "We can make it without using too much fuel—"

"Make what?" That was Ali up from the search of Kosti's quarters. "Nothing," he gave his report of what he had found there and then returned to the earlier question. "Make what?"

Swiftly Dane outlined their suspicions—that the seat of the trouble lay in the hydro and that they should clean out that section, drawing upon emergency materials at the I-S E-Stat.

"Sounds all right. But you know what they do to pirates?" inquired the engineer-apprentice.

Space law came into Dane's field, he needed no prompting. " 'Any ship in emergency,' " he recited automatically, " 'may claim supplies from the nearest E-Stat—paying for them when the voyage is completed.' "

"That means any Patrol E-Stat. The Companies' are private property."

"But," Dane pointed out triumphantly, "the law doesn't say so—there is nothing about any difference between Company and Patrol E-Stat in the law—"

"He's right," Rip agreed. "That law was framed when only the Patrol had such stations. Companies put them in later to save tax—remember? Legally we're all right."

"Unless the agents on duty raise a howl," Ali amended. "Oh, don't give me that look, Rip. I'm not sounding any warn-off on this, but I just want you to be prepared to find a cruiser riding our fins and giving us the hot flash as bandits. If you want to spoil the Eysies, I'm all for it. Got a stat of theirs pinpointed?"

Rip pointed to the figures on the computer. "There she is. We can set down in about five hours' ship time. How long will it take to strip the hydro and re-install?"

"How can I tell?" Ali sounded irritable. "I can give you oxyg for quarters for about two hours. Depends upon how fast we can move. No telling until we make a start."

He started for the corridor and then added over his shoulder: "You'll have to answer a com challenge—thought about that?"

"Why?" Rip asked. "It might be com repairs bringing us in. They won't be expecting trouble and we will—we'll have the advantage."

But Ali was not to be shaken out of his usual dim view of the future. "All right—so we land, blaster in hand, and take the place. And they get off one little squeak to the Patrol. Well, a short life but an interesting one. And we'll make all the Video channels for sure when we go out with rockets blasting. Nothing like having a little excitement to break the dull routine of a voyage."

"We aren't going to, are we—" Dane protested, "land armed, I mean?"

Ali stared at him and Rip, to Dane's surprise, did not immediately repudiate that thought.

"Sleep rods, certainly," the Astrogator-apprentice said after a pause. "We'll have to be prepared for the moment when they find out who we are. And you can't reset a hydro in a few minutes, not when we have to keep oxgy on for the others. If we were able to turn that off and work in suits it'd be a quicker job—we could dump before we set down and then pile it in at once. But this way it's going to be piece work. And it all depends on the agents at the Stat whether we have trouble or not."

"We had better break out the suits now," Ali added to Rip's estimate of the situation. "If we set down and pile out wearing suits at once it will build up our tale of being poor wrecked spacemen—"

Sleep rods or not, Dane thought to himself, the whole plan was one born of desperation. It would depend upon who manned the E-Stat and how fast the Free Traders could move once the *Queen* touched her fins to earth.

"Knock out their coms," that was Ali continuing to plan. "Do that first and then we don't have to worry about someone calling in the Patrol."

Rip stretched. For the first time in hours he seemed to have returned to his usual placid self. "Good thing somebody in this spacer watches Video serials—Ali, you can brief us on all the latest tricks of space pirates. Nothing is so wildly improbable that you can't make use of it sometime during a checkered career."

He glanced over the board before he brought his hand down on a single key set a distance apart from the other controls. "Put some local color into it," was his comment.

Dane understood. Rip had turned on the distress signal at the *Queen*'s nose. When she set down on the Stat field she would be flaming a banner of trouble. Next to the wan dead lights, set only when a ship had no hope of ever reaching port at all, that signal was one every spacer dreaded having to flash. But it was *not* the dead lights—not yet for the *Queen*.

Working together they brought out the space suits and readied them at the hatch. Then Weeks and Dane took up the task of tending their unconscious charges while Rip and Ali prepared for landing.

There was no change in the sleepers. And in Jellico's cabin even Queex appeared to be influenced by the plight of its master, for instead of greeting Dane with its normal aspect of rage, the Hoobat stayed quiescent on the floor of its cage, its top claws hooked about two of the wires, its protruding eyes staring out into the room with what seemed close to a malignant intelligence. It did not even spit as Dane passed under its abode to pour thin soup into his patient.

As for Sinbad, the cat had retreated to Dane's cabin and steadily refused to leave the quarters he had chosen, resisting with tooth and claw the one time Dane had tried to take him back to Van Rycke's office and his own hammock there. Afterwards the cargo-apprentice did not try to evict him—there was comfort in seeing that plump gray body curled on the bunk he had little chance to use.

His nursing duties performed for the moment, Dane ventured into the hydro. He was practiced in tending this vital heart of the ship's air supply. But outfitting a hydro was something else again. In his cadet years he had aided in such a program at least twice as a matter of learning the basic training of the Service. But then they had had unlimited supplies to draw on and the action had taken place under no more pressure than that exerted by the instructors. Now it was going to be a far more tricky job—

He went slowly down the aisle between the banks of green things. Plants from all over the Galaxy, grown for their contribution to the air renewal—as well as side products such as fresh fruit and vegetables, were banked there. The sweet odor of their verdant life was strong. But how could any of the four now on duty tell what was rightfully there and what might have been brought in? And could they be sure anything *had* been introduced?

Dane stood there, his eyes searching those lines of greens—such a mixture of greens from the familiar shade of Terra's fields to greens tinged with shades first bestowed by other suns on other worlds—looking for one which was alien enough to be noticeable. Only Mura, who knew this garden as he knew his own cabin, could have differentiated between them. They would just dump everything and trust to luck—

He was suddenly aware of a slight movement in the banks—a shivering of stem, quiver of leaf. The mere act of his passing had set some sensitive plant to register his presence. A lacy, fern-like thing was contracting its fronds into balls. He should not stay—disturbing the peace of the hydro. But it made little difference now—within a matter of hours all this luxuriance would be thrust out to die and they would have to depend upon canned oxyg and algae tanks. Too bad—the hydro represented much time and labor on Mura's part and Tau had medical plants growing there he had been observing for a long time.

As Dane closed the door behind him, seeing the line of balled fern which had marked his passage, he heard a faint rustling, a sound as if a wind had swept across the green room within. That imagination which was a Trader's asset (when it was kept within bounds) suggested that the plants inside guessed— With a frown for his own sentimentality, Dane strode down the corridor and climbed to check with Rip in control.

The Astrogator-apprentice had his own problems. To bring the *Queen* down on the circumscribed field of an E-Stat—without a guide beam to ride in—since if they contacted the Stat they must reveal their *own* com was working and they would have to answer questions—was the sort of test even a seasoned pilot would tense over. Yet Rip was sitting now in the Captain's place, his broad hands spread out on the edge of the control board waiting. And below in the engine room Ali was in Stotz's place ready to fire and cut rockets at order. Of course they were both several years ahead of him in Service, Dane knew. But he wondered at their quick assumption of responsibility and whether he himself could ever reach that point of self-confidence—his memory turning to the bad mistake he had made on Sargol.

There was the sharp note of a warning gong, the flash of red light on the control board. They were off automatic, from here on in it was all Rip's work. Dane strapped down at the silent com-unit and was startled a moment later when it spat words at him, translated from space code.

"Identify—identify—I-S E-Stat calling spacer—identify—"

So compelling was that demand that Dane's fingers went to the answer key before he remembered and snatched them back, to fold his hands in his lap.

"Identify—" the expressionless voice of the translator droned over their heads.

Rip's hands were on the control board, playing the buttons there with the precision of a musician creating some symphonic master-piece. And the *Queen* was alive, now quivering through her stout plates, coming into a landing.

Dane watched the visa-plate. The E-Stat asteroid was of a reasonable size, but in their eyes it was a bleak, torn mote of stuff swimming through vast emptiness.

"Identify—" the drone heightened in pitch.

Rip's lips were compressed, he made quick calculations. And Dane saw that, though Jellico was the master, Rip was fully fit to follow in the Captain's boot prints.

There was a sudden silence in the cabin—the demand had stopped. The agents below must now have realized that the ship with the distress signals blazing on her nose was not going to reply. Dane found he could not watch the visa-plate now, Rip's hands about their task filled his whole range of sight.

He knew that Shannon was using every bit of his skill and knowledge to jockey them into the position where they could ride their tail rockets down to the scorched rock of the E-Stat field. Perhaps it wasn't as smooth a landing as Jellico could have made. But they did it. Rip's hands were quiet, again that patch of darkness showed on the back of his tunic. He made no move from his seat.

"Secure—" Ali's voice floated up to them.

Dane unbuckled his safety webbing and got up, looking to Shannon for orders. This was Rip's plan they were to carry through. Then something moved him to give honor where it was due. He touched that bowed shoulder before him.

"Fin landing, brother! Four points and down!"

Rip glanced up, a grin made him look his old self. "Ought to have a recording of that for the Board when I go up for my pass-through."

Dane matched his smile. "Too bad we didn't have someone out there with a tri-dee machine."

"More likely it'd be evidence at our trial for piracy—" their words must have reached Ali on the ship's inter-com, for his deflating reply came back, to remind them of why they had made that particular landing. "Do we move now?"

"Check first," Rip said into the mike.

Dane looked at the visa-plate. Against a background of jagged rock teeth was the bubble of the E-Stat housing—more than three-quarters of it being in the hollowed out sections below the surface of the miniature world which supported it, as Dane knew. But a beam of light shone from the dome to center on the grounded *Queen*. They had not caught the Stat agents napping.

They made the rounds of the spacer, checking on each of the semi-conscious men. Ali had ready the artificial oxyg tanks—they must move fast once they began the actual task of clearing and restocking the hydro.

"Hope you have a good story ready," he commented as the other three joined him by the hatch to don the suits which would enable them to cross the airless, heatless surface of the asteroid.

"We have a poisoned hydro," Dane said.

"One look at the plants we dump will give you the lie. They won't accept our story without investigation."

Dane was aroused. Did Ali think he was as stupid as all that? "If you'd take a look in there now you'd believe me," he snapped.

"What did you do?" Ali sounded genuinely interested.

"Chuckled a heated can of lacoil over a good section. It's wilting down fast in big patches."

Rip snorted. "Good old lacoil. You drink it, you wash in it, and now you kill off the hydro with it. Maybe we can give the company an extra testimonial for the official jabber and collect when we hit Terra. All right—Weeks," he spoke to the little man, "you listen in on the com—it's tuned to our helmet units. We'll climb into these pipe suits and see how many tears we can wring out of the Eysies with our sad, sad tale."

They got into the awkward, bulky suits and squeezed into the hatch while Weeks slammed the lock door at their backs and operated the outer opening. Then they were looking out across the ground, still showing signs of the heat of their landing, and lighted by the dome beam.

"Nobody hurrying out with an aid and comfort kit," Rip's voice sounded in Dane's earphones. "A little slack, aren't they?"

Slack—or was it that the Eysies had recognized the *Queen* and was preparing the sort of welcome the remnant of her crew could not withstand? Dane, wanting very much in his heart to be elsewhere, climbed down the ladder in Rip's wake, both of them spotlighted by the immovable beam from the Stat dome.

DESPERATE MEASURES

11 Measured in distance and time that rough walk in the ponderous suits across the broken terrain of the asteroid was a short one; measured by the beating of his own heart, Dane thought it much too long. There was no sign of life by the air lock of the bubble—no move on the part of the men stationed there to come to their assistance.

"D'you suppose we're invisible?" Ali's disembodied voice clicked in the helmet earphones.

"Maybe we'll wish we were," Dane could not forego that return.

Rip was almost to the air lock door now. His massively suited arm was outstretched toward the control bar when the com-unit in all three helmets caught the same demand:

"Identify!" The crisp order had enough snap to warn them that an answer was the best policy.

"Shannon—A-A of the *Polestar*," Rip gave the required information. "We claim E rights—"

But would they get them? Dane wondered. There was a click loud in his ears. The metal door was yielding to Rip's hand. At least those on the inside had taken off the lock. Dane quickened pace to join his leader.

Together the three from the *Queen* crowded through the lock door, saw that swing shut and seal behind them, as they stood waiting for the moment they could discard the suits and enter the dome. The odds against them could not be too high, this was a small Stat. It would not house more than four agents at the most. And they were familiar enough with the basic architecture of such stations to know just what move to make. Ali was to go to the com room where he could take over if they did meet with trouble. Dane and Rip would have to handle any dissenters in the main section. But they still hoped that luck might ride their fins and they could put over a story which would keep them out of active conflict with the Eysies.

The gauge on the wall registered safety and they unfastened the protective clasps of the suits. Standing the cumbersome things against the wall as the inner door to the lock rolled back, they walked into Eysie territory.

As Free Traders they had the advantage of being uniformly tunicked—with no Company badge to betray their ship or status. So that could well *be* the *Polestar* standing needle slim behind them—and not the notorious *Solar Queen*. But each, as he passed through the inner lock, gave a hitch to his belt which brought the butt of his sleep rod closer to hand. Innocuous as that weapon was, in close quarters its effect, if only temporary, was to some purpose. And since they were prepared for trouble, they might have a slight edge over the Eysies in attack.

A Company man, his tunic shabby and open in a negligent fashion at his thick throat, stood waiting for them. His unhelmeted head was grizzled, his coarse, tanned face with heavy jowls bristly enough to suggest he had not bothered to use smooth-cream for some days. An under officer of some spacer, retired to finish out the few years before pension in this nominal duty—fast letting down the standards of personal regime he had had to maintain on ship board. But he wasn't all fat and soft living, the glance with which he measured them was shrewdly appraising.

"What's your trouble?" he demanded without greeting. "You didn't I-dent coming in."

"Coms are out," Rip replied as shortly. "We need E-Hydro—"

"First time I ever heard it that the coms were wired in with the grass," the Eysie's hands were on his hips—in close proximity to something which made Dane's eyes narrow. The fellow was wearing a flare-blaster! That might be regulation equipment for an E-Stat agent on a lonely asteroid—but he didn't quite believe it. And probably the other was quick on the draw too.

"The coms are something else," Rip answered readily. "Our tech is working on them. But the hydro's bad all through. We'll have to dump and restock. Give you a voucher on Terra for the stuff."

The Eysie agent continued to block the doorway into the station. "This is private—I-S property. You should hit the Patrol post—they cater to you F-Ts."

"We hit the nearest E-Stat when we discovered that we were contaminated," Rip spoke with an assumption of patience. "That's the law, and you know it. You have to supply us and take a voucher—"

"How do I know that your voucher is worth the film it's recorded on?" asked the agent reasonably.

"All right," Rip shrugged. "If we have to do it the hard way, we'll cargo dump to cover your bill."

"Not on this field." The other shook his head. "I'll flash in your voucher first."

He had them, Dane thought bitterly. Their luck had run out. Because what he was going to do was a move they dared not protest. It was one any canny agent would make in the present situation. And if they were what they said they were, they must readily agree to let him flash their voucher of payment to I-S headquarters, to be checked and okayed before they took the hydro stock.

But Rip merely registered a mild resignation. "You the com-tech? Where's your unit? I'll indit at once if you want it that way."

Whether their readiness to cooperate allayed some of the agent's suspicion or not, he relaxed some, giving them one more stare all around before he turned on his heel. "This way."

They followed him down the narrow hall, Rip on his heels, the others behind.

"Lonely post," Rip commented. "I'd think you boys'd get space-whirly out here."

The other snorted. "We're not star lovers. And the pay's worth a three-month stretch. They take us down for Terra leave before we start talking to the Whisperers."

"How many of you here at a time?" Rip edged the question in casually.

But the other might have been expecting it by the way he avoided giving a direct answer. "Enough to run the place—and not enough to help you clean out your wagon," he was short about it. "Any dumping you do is strictly on your own. You've enough hands on a spacer that size to manage—"

Rip laughed. "Far be it from me to ask an Eysie to do any real work," was his counter. "We know all about you Company men—"

But the agent did not take fire at that jib. Instead he pushed back a panel and they were looking into a com-unit room where another man in the tunic of the I-S lounged on what was by law twenty-four-hour duty, divided into three watches.

"These F-Ts want to flash a voucher request through," their guide informed the tech. The other, interested, gave them a searching once-over before he pushed a small scriber toward Rip.

"It's all yours—clear ether," he reported.

Ali stood with his back to the wall and Dane still lingered in the portal. Both of them fixed their attention on Rip's left hand. If he gave the agreed upon signal! Their fingers were linked loosely in their belts only an inch or so from their sleep rods.

With his right hand Rip scooped up the scribbler while the com-tech half turned to make adjustments to the controls, picking up a speaker to call the I-S headquarters.

Rip's left index finger snapped across his thumb to form a circle. Ali's rod did not even leave his belt, it tilted up and the invisible deadening stream from it centered upon the seated tech. At the same instant Dane shot at the agent who had guided them there. The latter had time for a surprised grunt and his hand was at his blaster as he sagged to his knees and then relaxed on the floor. The tech slumped across the call board as if sleep had overtaken him at his post.

Rip crossed the room and snapped off the switch which opened the wire for broadcasting. While Ali, with Dane's help, quietly and effectively immobilized the Eysies with their own belts.

"There should be at least three men here," Rip waited by the door. "We have to get them all under control before we start work."

However, the interior of the bubble, extending as it did on levels beneath the outer crust of the asteroid, was not an easy place to search. An enemy, warned of the invasion, could easily keep ahead of the party from the *Queen,* spying on them at his leisure or preparing traps for them. In the end, afraid of wasting time, they contented themselves with locking the doors of the corridor leading to the lower levels, making ready to raid the storeroom they had discovered during their search.

Emergency hydro supplies consisted mainly of algae which could be stored in tanks and hastily put to use—as the plants now in the *Queen* took much longer to grow even under forcing methods. Dane volunteered to remain inside the E-Stat and assemble the necessary containers at the air lock while the other two, having had more experience, went back to the spacer to strip the hydro and prepare to switch contents.

But, when Rip and Ali left, the younger cargo-apprentice began to find the bubble a haunted place. He took the sealed containers out of their storage racks, stood them on a small hand truck, and pushed them to the foot of the stairs, up which he then climbed carrying two of the cylinders at a time.

The swish of the air current through the narrow corridors made a constant murmur of sound, but he found himself listening for something else, for a footfall other than his own, for the betraying rasp of clothing against a wall—for even a whisper of voice. And time and time again he paused suddenly to listen—sure that the faintest hint of such a sound had reached his ears. He had a dozen containers lined up when the welcome signal reached him by the com-unit of his field helmet. To transfer the cylinders to the lock, get out, and then open the outer door, did not take long. But as he waited he still listened for a sound which did not come—the notice that someone besides himself was free to move about the Stat.

Not knowing just how many of the supply tins were needed, he worked on transferring all there were in the storage racks to the upper corridor and the lock. But he still had half a dozen left to pass through when Rip sent a message that he was coming in.

Out of his pressure suit, the astrogator-apprentice stepped lightly into the corridor, looked at the array of containers and shook his head.

"We don't need all those. No, leave them—" he added as Dane, with a sigh, started to pick up two for a return trip. "There's something more important just now—" He turned into the side hall which led to the com room.

Both the I-S men had awakened. The com-tech appeared to accept his bonds philosophically. He was quiet and flat on his back, staring pensively at the ceiling. But the other agent had made a worm's progress half across the room and Rip had to halt in haste to prevent stepping on him.

Shannon stooped and, hooking his fingers in the other's tunic, heaved him back while the helpless man favored them with some of the ripest speech—and NOT Trade Lingo—Dane had ever heard. Rip waited until the man began to run down and then he broke in with his pleasant soft drawl.

"Oh, sure, we're all that. But time runs on, Eysie, and I'd like a couple of answers which may mean something to you. First—when do you expect your relief?"

That set the agent off again. And his remarks—edited—were that no something, something F-T was going to get any something, something information out of him!

But it was his companion in misfortune—the com-tech—who guessed the reason behind Rip's question.

"Cut jets!" he advised the other. "They're just being softhearted. I take it," he spoke over the other agent's sputtering to Rip, "that you're worried about leaving us fin down— That's it, isn't it?"

Rip nodded. "In spite of what you think about us," he replied, "We're not Patrol Posted outlaws—"

"No, you're just from a plague ship," the Com-tech remarked calmly. And his words struck his comrade dumb. "*Solar Queen?*"

"You got the warn-off then?"

"Who didn't? You really have plague on board?" The thought did not appear to alarm the com-tech unduly. But his fellow suddenly heaved his bound body some distance away from the Free Traders and his face displayed mixed emotions—most of them fearful.

"We have something—probably supplied," Rip straightened. "Might pass along to your bosses that we know that. Now suppose you tell me about your relief. When is it due?"

"Not until after we take off on the Long Orbit if you leave us like this. On the other hand," the other added coolly, "I don't see how you can do otherwise. We've still got those—" with his chin he pointed to the com-unit.

"After a few alterations," Rip amended. The bulk of the com was in a tightly sealed case which they would need a flamer to open. But he could and did wreak havoc with the exposed portions. The tech watching this destruction spouted at least two expressions his companion had not used. But when Rip finished he was his unruffled self again.

"Now," Rip drew his sleep rod. "A little rest and when you wake it will all be a bad dream." He carefully beamed each man into slumber and helped Dane strip off their bonds. But before he left the room he placed on the recorder the voucher for the supplies they had taken.

The *Queen* was not stealing—under the law she still had some shadow of rights.

Suited they crossed the rough rock to the ship. And there about the fins, already frozen into brittle spikes was a tangle of plants—the rich result of years of collecting.

"Did you find anything?" Dane asked as they rounded that mess on their way to the ladder.

Rip's voice came back through the helmet com. "Nothing we know how to interpret. I wish Frank or Craig had had a chance to check. We took tri-dees of everything before we dumped. Maybe they can learn something from these when—"

His voice trailed off leaving that "when" to ring in both their minds. It was such an important "when." When *would* either the steward or the medic recover enough to view those tri-dee shots? Or was that "when" really an ominous "if"?

Back in the *Queen,* sealed once more for blast-off, they took their stations. Dane speculated as to the course Rip had set—were they just going to wander about the system hoping to escape notice until they had somehow solved their problem? Or did Shannon have some definite port in mind? He did not have time to ask before they lifted. But once they were space borne again he voiced his question.

Rip's face was serious. "Frankly—" he began and then hesitated for a long moment before he added, "I don't know. If we can only get the Captain or Craig on their feet again—"

"One thing," Ali materialized to join them, "Sinbad's back in the hydro. And this morning you couldn't get him inside the door. It's not a very good piece of evidence—"

No, it wasn't but they clung to it as backing for their actions of the past few hours. The cat that had shown such a marked distaste for the company of the stricken, and then for the hydro, was now content to visit the latter as if some evil he has sensed there had been cleansed with the dumping of the garden. They had not yet solved their mystery but another clue had come into their hands.

But now the care of the sick occupied hours and Rip insisted that a watch be maintained by the com—listening in for news which might concern the *Queen*. They had done a good job at silencing the E-Stat, for they had been almost six hours in space before the news of their raid was beamed to the nearest Patrol post.

Ali laughed. "Told you we'd be pirates," he said when he listened to that account of their descent upon the I-S station. "Though I didn't see all that blaster work they're now raving about. You'd think we fought a major battle there!"

Weeks growled. "The Eysies are trying to make it look good. Make us into outlaws—"

But Rip did not share in the general amusement at the wild extravagance of the report from the ether. "I notice they didn't say anything about the voucher we left."

Ali's cynical smile curled. "Did you expect them to? The Eysies think they have us by the tail fins now—why should they give us any benefit of the doubt? We junked all our boosters behind us on this takeoff, and don't forget that, my friends."

Weeks looked confused. "But I thought you said we could do this legal," he appealed to Rip. "If we're Patrol Posted as outlaws—"

"They can't do any more to us than they can for running in a plague ship," Ali pointed out. "Either will get us blasted if we happen into the wrong vector now. So—what do we do?"

"We find out what the plague really is," Dane said and meant every word of it.

"How?" Ali inquired. "Through some of Craig's magic?"

Dane was forced to answer with the truth. "I don't know yet—but it's our only chance."

Rip rubbed his eyes wearily. "Don't think I'm disagreeing—but just where do we start? We've already combed Frank's quarters and Kosti's—we cleaned out the hydro—"

"Those tri-dee shots of the hydro—have you checked them yet?" Dane countered.

Without a word Ali arose and left the cabin. He came back with a microfilm roll. Fitting it into the large projector he focused it on the wall and snapped the button.

They were looking at the hydro—down the length of space so accurately recorded that it seemed they might walk straight into it. The greenery of the plants was so vivid and alive Dane felt that he could reach out and pluck a leaf. Inch by inch he examined those ranks, looking for something which was not in order, had no right to be there.

The long shot of the hydro as it had been merged into a series of sectional groupings. In silence they studied it intently, using all their field lore in an attempt to spot what each one was certain must be there somewhere. But they were all handicapped by their lack of intimate knowledge of the garden.

"Wait!" Weeks' voice scaled up. "Left hand corner—there!" His pointing hand broke and shadowed the portion he was calling to their attention. Ali jumped to the projector and made a quick adjustment.

Plants four and five times life size glowed green on the wall. What Weeks had caught they all saw now—ragged leaves, stripped stems.

"Chewed!" Dane supplied the answer.

It was only one species of plant which had been so mangled. Other varieties in the same bank showed no signs of disturbance. But all of that one type had at least one stripped branch and two were virtual skeletons.

"A pest!" said Rip.

"But Sinbad," Dane began a protest before the memory of the cat's peculiar actions of the past weeks stopped him. Sinbad had slipped up, the hunter who had kept the *Queen* free of the outré alien life which came aboard from time to time with cargo, had not attacked that which had ravaged the hydro plants. Or if he had done so, he had not, after his usual custom, presented the bodies of the slain to any crew member.

"It looks as if we have something at last," Ali observed and someone echoed that with a sigh of heartdeep relief.

STRANGE BEHAVIOR
OF A HOOBAT

12

"All right, so we think we know a little more," Ali added a moment later. "Just what are we going to do? We can't stay in space forever—there're the small items of fuel and supplies and—"

Rip had come to a decision. "We're not going to remain space borne," he stated with the confidence of one who now saw an open road before him.

"Luna—" Weeks was plainly doubtful.

"No. Not after that warn-off. Terra!"

For a second or two the other three stared at Rip agape. The audacity and danger of what he suggested was a little stunning. Since men had taken regularly to space no ship had made a direct landing on their home planet—all had passed through the quarantine on Luna. It was not only risky—it was so unheard of that for some minutes they did not understand him.

"We try to set down at Terraport," Dane found his tongue first; "and they flame us out—"

Rip was smiling. "The trouble with you," he addressed them all, "is that you think of earth only in terms of Terraport—"

"Well, there *is* the Patrol field at Stella," Weeks agreed doubtfully. "But we'd be right in the middle of trouble there—"

"Did we have a regular port on Sargol—on Limbo—on fifty others I can name out of our log?" Rip wanted to know.

Ali voiced a new objection. "So—we have the luck of Jones and we set down somewhere out of sight. Then what do we do?"

"We seal ship until we find the pest—then we bring in a medic and get to the bottom of the whole thing," Rip's confidence was contagious. Dane almost believed that it *could* be done that way.

"Did you ever think," Ali cut in, "what would happen if we were wrong—if the *Queen* really is a plague carrier?"

"I said—we seal the ship-tight," countered Shannon. "And when we earth it'll be where we won't have visitors to infect—"

"And that is where?" Ali, who knew the deserts of Mars better than he did the greener planet from which his stock had sprung, pursued the question.

"Right in the middle of the Big Burn!"

Dane, Terra-born and -bred, realized first what Rip was planning and what it meant. Sealed off was right—the *Queen* would be amply protected from investigation. Whether her crew would survive was another matter—whether she could even make a landing there was also to be considered.

The Big Burn was the horrible scar left by the last of the Atomic Wars—a section of radiation-poisoned land comprising hundreds of square miles—land which generations had never dared to penetrate. Originally the survivors of that war had shunned the whole continent which it disfigured. It had been close to two centuries before men had gone into the still wholesome land laying to the far west and the south. And, through the years, the avoidance of the Big Burn had become part of their racial instinct so they shrank from it. It was a symbol of something no Terran wanted to remember.

But Ali now had only one question to ask. "Can we do it?"

"We'll never know until we try," was Rip's reply.

"The Patrol'll be watching—" That was Weeks. With his Venusian background he had less respect for the dangers of the Big Burn than he did for the forces of Law and order which ranged the star lanes.

"They'll be watching the routine lanes," Rip pointed out. "They won't expect a ship to come in on that vector, steering away from the ports. Why should they? As far as I know it's never been tried since Terraport was laid out. It'll be tricky—" And he himself would have to bear most of the responsibility for it. "But I believe that it can be done. And we can't just roam around out here. With I-S out for our blood and a Patrol warn-off it won't do us any good to head for Luna—"

None of his listeners could argue with that. And, Dane's spirits began to rise, after all they knew so little about the Big Burn—it might afford them just the temporary sanctuary they needed. In the end they agreed to try it, mainly because none of them could see any alternative, except the too dangerous one of trying to contact the authorities and being summarily treated as a plague ship before they could defend themselves.

And their decision was ably endorsed not long afterwards by a sardonic warning on the com—a warning which Ali who had been tending the machine passed along to them.

"Greetings, pirates—"

"What do you mean?" Dane was heating broth to feed to Captain Jellico.

"The word has gone out—our raid on the E-Stat is now a matter of history and Patrol record—we've been Posted!"

Dane felt a cold finger drawn along his backbone. Now they were fair game for the whole system. Any Patrol ship that wanted could shoot them down with no questions asked. Of course that had always been a possibility from the first after their raid on the E-Stat. But to realize that it was now true was a different matter altogether. This was one occasion when realization was worse than anticipation. He tried to keep his voice level as he answered:

"Let us hope we can pull off Rip's plan—"

"We'd better. What about the Big Burn anyway, Thorson? Is it as tough as the stories say?"

"We don't know what it's like. It's never been explored—or at least those who tried to explore its interior never reported in afterwards. As far as I know it's left strictly alone."

"Is it still all 'hot'?"

"Parts of it must be. But all—we don't know."

With the bottle of soup in his hand Dane climbed to Jellico's cabin. And he was so occupied with the problem at hand that at first he did not see what was happening in the small room. He had braced the Captain up into a half-sitting position and was patiently ladling the liquid into his mouth a spoonful at a time when a thin squeak drew his attention to the top of Jellico's desk.

From the half open lid of a microtape compartment something long and dark projected, beating the air feebly. Dane, easing the Captain back on the bunk, was going to investigate when the Hoobat broke its unnatural quiet of the past few days with an ear-splitting screech of fury. Dane struck at the bottom of its cage—the move its master always used to silence it—but this time the results were spectacular.

The cage bounced up and down on the spring which secured it to the ceiling of the cabin and the blue feathered horror slammed against the wires. Either its clawing had weakened them, or some fault had developed, for they parted and the Hoobat came through them to land with a sullen plop on the desk. Its screams stopped as suddenly as they had begun and it scuttled on its spider-toad legs to the microtape compartment, acting with purposeful dispatch and paying no attention to Dane.

Its claws shot out and with ease it extracted from the compartment a creature as weird as itself—one which came fighting and of which Dane could not get a very clear idea. Struggling they battled across the surface of the desk and flopped to the floor. There the hunted broke loose from the hunter and fled with fantastic speed into the corridor. And before Dane could move the Hoobat was after it.

He gained the passage just in time to see Queex disappear down the ladder, climbing with the aid of its pincher claws, apparently grimly determined to catch up with the thing it pursued. And Dane went after them.

There was no sign of the creature who fled on the next level. But Dane made no move to recapture the blue hunter who squatted at the foot of the ladder staring unblinkingly into space. Dane waited, afraid to disturb the Hoobat. He had not had a good look at the thing which had run from Queex—but he knew that it was something which had no business aboard the *Queen*. And it might be the disturbing factor they were searching for. If the Hoobat would only lead him to it—

The Hoobat moved, rearing up on the tips of its six legs, its neckless head slowly revolving on its puffy shoulders. Along the ridge of its backbone its blue feathers were rising into a crest much as Sinbad's fur rose when the cat was afraid or angry. Then, without any sign of haste, it crawled over and began descending the ladder once more, heading toward the lower section which housed the Hydro.

Dane remained where he was until it had almost reached the deck of the next level and then he followed, one step at a time. He was sure that the Hoobat's peculiar construction of body prevented it from looking up—unless it turned upon its back—but he did not want to do anything which would alarm it or deter Queex from what he was sure was a methodical chase.

Queex stopped again at the foot of the second descent and sat in its toad stance, apparently brooding, a round blue blot. Dane clung to the ladder and prayed that no one would happen along to frighten it. Then, just as he was beginning to wonder if it had lost contact with its prey, once more it arose and with the same speed it had displayed in the Captain's cabin it shot along the corridor to the hydro.

To Dane's knowledge the door of the garden was not only shut but sealed. And how either the stranger or Queex could get through it he did not see.

"What the—?" Ali clattered down the ladder to halt abruptly as Dane waved at him.

"Queex," the cargo-apprentice kept his voice to a half whisper, "it got loose and chased something out of the Old Man's cabin down here."

"Queex—!" Ali began and then shut his mouth, moving noiselessly up to join Dane.

The short corridor ended at the hydro entrance. And Dane had been right, there they found the Hoobat, crouched at the closed panel, its claws clicking against the metal as it picked away uselessly at the portal which would not admit it.

"Whatever it's after must be in there," Dane said softly.

And the hydro, stripped of its luxuriance of plant life, occupied now by the tanks of green scum, would not afford too many hiding places. They had only to let Queex in and keep watch.

As they came up the Hoobat flattened to the floor and shrilled its war cry, spitting at their boots and then flashing claws against the stout metal-enforced hide. However, though it was prepared to fight them, it showed no signs of wishing to retreat, and for that Dane was thankful. He quickly pressed the release and tugged open the panel.

At the first crack of its opening Queex turned with one of those bursts of astounding speed and clawed for admittance, its protest against the men forgotten. And it squeezed through a space Dane would have thought too narrow to accommodate its bloated body. Both men slipped around the door behind it and closed the panel tight.

The air was not as fresh as it had been when the plants were there. And the vats which had taken the places of the banked greenery were certainly nothing to look at. Queex humped itself into a clod of blue, immovable, halfway down the aisle.

Dane tried to subdue his breathing, to listen. The Hoobat's actions certainly argued that the alien thing had taken refuge here, though how it had gotten through——? But if it were in the hydro it was well hidden.

He had just begun to wonder how long they must wait when Queex again went into action. Its clawed front legs upraised, it brought the pinchers deliberately together and sawed one across the other, producing a rasping sound which was almost a vibration in the air. Back and forth, back and forth, moved the claws. Watching them produced almost a hypnotic affect, and the reason for such a maneuver was totally beyond the human watchers.

But Queex knew what it was doing all right. Ali's fingers closed on Dane's arm in a pincher grip as painful as if he had been equipped with the horny armament of the Hoobat.

Something, a flitting shadow, had rounded one vat and was that much closer to the industrious fiddler on the floor. By some weird magic of its own the Hoobat was calling its prey to it.

Scrape, scrape——the unmusical performance continued with monotonous regularity. Again the shadow flashed——one vat closer. The Hoobat now presented the appearance of one charmed by its own art—— sunk in a lethargy of weird music making.

At last the enchanted came into full view, though lingering at the round side of a container, very apparently longing to flee again, but under some compulsion to approach its enchanter. Dane blinked, not quite sure that his eyes were not playing tricks on him. He had seen the almost transparent globe "bogies" of Limbo, had been fascinated by the weird and ugly pictures in Captain Jellico's collection of tridee prints. But this creature was as impossible in its way as the horrific blue thing dragging it out of concealment.

It walked erect on two threads of legs, with four knobby joints easily detected. A bulging abdomen sheathed in the horny substance of a beetle's shell ended in a sharp point. Two pairs of small legs, folded close to the much smaller upper portion of its body, were equipped with thorn sharp terminations. The head, which constantly turned back and forth on the armor-plated shoulders, was long and narrow and split for half its length by a mouth above which were deep pits which must harbor eyes, though actual organs were not visible to the watching men. It was a palish gray in color—which surprised Dane a little. His memory of the few seconds he had seen it on the Captain's desk had suggested that it was much darker. And erect as it was, it stood about eighteen inches high.

With head turning rapidly, it still hesitated by the side of the vat, so nearly the color of the metal that unless it moved it was difficult to distinguish. As far as Dane could see the Hoobat was paying it no attention. Queex might be lost in a happy dream, the result of its own fiddling. Nor did the rhythm of that scraping vary.

The nightmare thing made the last foot in a rush of speed which reduced it to a blur, coming to a halt before the Hoobat. Its front legs whipped out to strike at its enemy. But Queex was no longer dreaming. This was the moment the Hoobat had been awaiting. One of the sawing claws opened and closed, separating the head of the lurker from its body. And before either of the men could interfere Queex had dismembered the prey with dispatch.

"Look there!" Dane pointed.

The Hoobat held close the body of the stranger and where the ashy corpse came into contact with Queex's blue feathered skin it was slowly changing hue—as if some of the color of its hunter had rubbed off on it.

"Chameleon!" Ali went down on one knee the better to view the grisly feast now in progress. "Watch out!" he added sharply as Dane came to join him.

One of the thin upper limbs lay where Queex had discarded it. And from the needle tip was oozing some colorless drops of fluid. Poison?

Dane looked around for something which he could use to pick up the still jerking appendage. But before he could find anything Queex had appropriated it. And in the end they had to allow the Hoobat its victim in its entirety. But once Queex had consumed its prey it lapsed into its usual hunched immobility. Dane went for the cage and working gingerly he and Ali got the creature back in captivity. But all the evidence now left were some smears on the floor of the hydro, smears which Ali blotted up for future research in the lab.

An hour later the four who now comprised the crew of the *Queen* gathered in the mess for a conference. Queex was in its cage on the table before them, asleep after all its untoward activity.

"There must be more than just one," Weeks said. "But how are we going to hunt them down? With Sinbad?"

Dane shook his head. Once the Hoobat had been caged and the more prominent evidence of the battle scrapped from the floor, he had brought the cat into the hydro and forced him to sniff at the site of the engagement. The result was that Sinbad had gone raving mad and Dane's hands were now covered with claw tears which ran viciously deep. It was plain that the ship's cat was having none of the intruders, alive or dead. He had fled to Dane's cabin where he had taken refuge on the bunk and snarled wild eyed when anyone looked in from the corridor.

"Queex has to do it," Rip said. "But will it hunt unless it is hungry?"

He surveyed the now comatose creature skeptically. They had never seen the Captain's pet eat anything except some pellets which Jellico kept in his desk, and they were aware that the intervals between such feedings were quite lengthy. If they had to wait the usual time for Queex to feel hunger pangs once more, they might have to wait a long time.

"We should catch one alive," Ali remarked thoughtfully. "If we could get Queex to fiddle it out to where we could net it—"

Weeks nodded eagerly. "A small net like those the Salariki use. Drop it over the thing—"

While Queex still drowsed in its cage, Weeks went to work with fine cord. Holding the color-changing abilities of the enemy in mind they could not tell how many of the creatures might be roaming the ship. It could only be proved where they *weren't* by where Sinbad would consent to stay. So they made plans which included both the cat and the Hoobat.

Sinbad, much against his will, was buckled into an improvised harness by which he could be controlled without the handler losing too much valuable skin.

And then the hunt started at the top of the ship, proceeding downward section by section. Sinbad raised no protest in the control cabin, nor in the private cabins of the officers' thereabouts. If they could interpret his reactions the center section was free of the invaders. So with Dane in control of the cat and Ali carrying the caged Hoobat, they descended once more to the level which housed the hydro galley, steward's quarters and ship's sick bay.

Sinbad proceeded on his own four feet into the galley and the mess. He was not uneasy in the sick bay, nor in Mura's cabin, and this time he even paced the hydro without being dragged—much to their surprise as they had thought that the headquarters of the stowaways.

"Could there only have been one?" Weeks wanted to know as he stood by ready with the net in his hands.

"Either that—or else we're wrong about the hydro being their main hideout. If they're afraid of Queex now they may have withdrawn to the place they feel the safest," Rip said.

It was when they were on the ladder leading to the cargo level that Sinbad balked. He planted himself firmly and yowled against further progress until Dane, with the harness, pulled him along.

"Look at Queex!"

They followed Weeks' order. The Hoobat was no longer lethargic. It was raising itself, leaning forward to clasp the bars of its cage, and now it uttered one of its screams of rage. And as Ali went on down the ladder it rattled the bars in a determined effort for freedom. Sinbad, spitting and yowling refused to walk. Rip nodded to Ali.

"Let it out."

Tipped out of its cage the Hoobat scuttled forward, straight for the panel which opened on the large cargo space and there waited, as if for them to open the portal and admit the hunter to its hunting territory.

OFF THE MAP

13 Across the lock of the panel was the seal set in place by Van Rycke before the spacer had lifted from Sargol. Under Dane's inspection it showed no crack. To all evidences the hatch had not been opened since they left the perfumed planet. And yet the hunting Hoobat was sure that the invading pests were within.

It took only a second for Dane to commit an act which, if he could not defend it later, would blacklist him out of space. He twisted off the official seal which should remain there while the freighter was space borne.

With Ali's help he shouldered aside the heavy sliding panel and they looked into the cargo space, now filled with the red wood from Sarbol. The red wood! When he saw it Dane was struck with their stupidity. Aside from the Koros stones in the stone box, only the wood had come from the Salariki world. What if the pests had not been planted by I-S agents, but were natives of Sargol being brought in with the wood?

The men remained at the hatch to allow the Hoobat freedom in its hunt. And Sinbad crouched behind them, snarling and giving voice to a rumbling growl which was his negative opinion of the proceedings.

They were conscious of an odor—the sharp, unidentifiable scent Dane had noticed during the loading of the wood. It was not unpleasant—merely different. And it—or something—had an electrifying effect upon Queex. The blue hunter climbed with the aid of its claws to the top of the nearest pile of wood and there settled down. For a space it was apparently contemplating the area about it.

Then it raised its claws and began the scraping fiddle which once before had drawn its prey out of hiding. Oddly enough that dry rasp of sound had a quieting effect upon Sinbad and Dane felt the drag of the harness lessen as the cat moved, not toward escape, but to the scene of action, humping himself at last in the open panel, his round eyes fixed upon the Hoobat with a fascinated stare.

Scrape-scrape—the monotonous noise bit into the ears of the men, gnawed at their nerves.

"Ahhh—" Ali kept his voice to a whisper, but his hand jerked to draw their attention to the right at deck level. Dane saw that flicker along a log. The stowaway pest was now the same brilliant color as the wood, indistinguishable until it moved, which probably explained how it had come on board.

But that was only the first arrival. A second flash of movement and a third followed. Then the hunted remained stationary, able to resist for a period the insidious summoning of Queex. The Hoobat maintained an attitude of indifference, of being so wrapped in its music that nothing else existed. Rip whispered to Weeks:

"There's one to the left—on the very end of that log. Can you net it?"

The small oiler slipped the coiled mesh through his calloused hands. He edged around Ali, keeping his eyes on the protruding bump of red upon red which was his quarry.

"—two—three—four—five—" Ali was counting under his breath but Dane could not see that many. He was sure of only four, and those because he had seen them move.

The things were ringing in the pile of wood where the Hoobat fiddled, and two had ascended the first logs toward their doom.

Weeks went down on one knee, ready to cast his net, when Dane had his first inspiration. He drew his sleep rod, easing it out of its holster, set the lever on "spray" and beamed it at three of those humps.

Rip, seeing what he was doing, dropped a hand on Weeks' shoulder, holding the oiler in check. A hump moved, slid down the rounded side of the log into the narrow aisle of deck between two piles of wood. It lay quiet, a bright scarlet blot against the gray.

Then Weeks did move, throwing his net over it and jerking the draw string tight, at the same time pulling the captive toward him over the deck. But, even as it came, the scarlet of the thing's body was fast fading to an ashy pink and at last taking on a gray as dull as the metal on which it lay—the complete camouflage. Had they not had it enmeshed they might have lost it altogether, so well did it now blend with the surface.

The other two in the path of the ray had not lost their grip upon the logs, and the men could not advance to scoop them up. Not while there were others not affected, free to flee back into hiding. Weeks bound the net about the captive and looked to Rip for orders.

"Deep freeze," the acting-commander of the *Queen* said succinctly. "Let me see it get out of that!"

Surely the cold of the deep freeze, united to the sleep ray, would keep the creature under control until they had a chance to study it. But, as Weeks passed Sinbad on his errand, the cat was so frantic to avoid him, that he reared up on his hind legs, almost turning a somersault, snarling and spitting until Weeks was up the ladder to the next level. It was very evident that the ship's cat was having none of this pest.

They might have been invisible and their actions nonexistent as far as Queex was concerned. For the Hoobat continued its siren concert. The lured became more reckless, mounting the logs to Queex's post in sudden darts. Dane wondered how the Hoobat proposed handling four of the creatures at once. For, although the other two which had been in the path of the ray had not moved, he now counted four climbing.

"Stand by to ray—" That was Rip.

But it would have been interesting to see how Queex *was* prepared to handle the four. And, though Rip had given the order to stand by, he had not ordered the ray to be used. Was he, too, interested in that?

The first red projection was within a foot of the Hoobat now and its fellows had frozen as if to allow it the honor of battle with the feathered enemy. To all appearances Queex did not see it, but when it sprang with a whir of speed which would baffle a human, the Hoobat was ready and its claws, halting their rasp, met around the wasp-thin waist of the pest, speedily cutting it in two. Only this time the Hoobat made no move to unjoint and consume the victim. Instead it squatted in utter silence, as motionless as a tri-dee print.

The heavy lower half of the creature rolled down the pile of logs to the deck and there paled to the gray of its background. None of its kind appeared to be interested in its fate. The two which had been in the path of the ray continued to be humps on the wood, the others faced the Hoobat.

But Rip was ready to waste no more time. "Ray them!" he snapped.

All three of their sleep rods sprayed the pile, catching in passing the Hoobat. Queex's pop eyes closed, but it showed no other sign of falling under the spell of the beam.

Certain that all the creatures in sight were now relatively harmless, the three approached the logs. But it was necessary to get into touching distance before they could even make out the outlines of the nightmare things, so well did their protective coloring conceal them. Wearing gloves Ali detached the little monsters from their holds on the wood and put them for temporary safekeeping—during a transfer to the deep freeze—into the Hoobat's cage. Queex, they decided to leave where it was for a space, to awaken and trap any survivor which had been too wary to emerge at the first siren song. As far as they could tell the Hoobat was their only possible protection against the pest and to leave it in the center of infection was the wisest course.

Having dumped the now metal-colored catch into the freeze, they held a conference.

"No plague—" Weeks breathed a sigh of relief.

"No proof of that yet," Ali caught him up short. "We have to prove it past any reasonable doubt."

"And how are we going to do—?" Dane began when he saw what the other had brought in from Tau's stores. A lancet and the upper half of the creature Queex had killed in the cargo hold.

The needle-pointed front feet of the thing were curled up in its death throes and it was now a dirty white shade as if the ability to change color had been lost before it matched the cotton on which it lay. With the lancet Ali forced a claw away from the body. It was oozing the watery liquid which they had seen on the one in the hydro.

"I have an idea," he said slowly, his eyes on the mangled creature rather than on his shipmates, "that we might have escaped being attacked because they sheered off from us. But if we were clawed we might take it too. Remember those marks on the throats and backs of the rest? That might be the entry point of this poison—if poison it is—"

Dane could see the end of that line of reasoning. Rip and Ali— they couldn't be spared. The knowledge they had would bring the *Queen* to earth. But a cargo-master was excess baggage when there was no reason for trade. It was his place to try out the truth of Ali's surmise.

But while he thought another acted. Weeks leaned over and twitched the lancet out of Ali's fingers. Then, before any of them could move, he thrust its contaminated point into the back of his hand.

"Don't!"

Both Dane's cry and Rip's hand came too late. It had been done. And Weeks sat there, looking alone and frightened, studying the droop of blood which marked the dig of the surgeon's keen knife. But when he spoke his voice sounded perfectly natural.

"Headache first, isn't it?"

Only Ali was outwardly unaffected by what the little man had just done. "Just be sure you have a real one," he warned with what Dane privately considered real callousness.

Weeks nodded. "Don't let my imagination work," he answered shrewdly. "I know. It has to be real. How long do you suppose?"

"We don't know," Rip sounded tired, beaten. "Meanwhile," he got to his feet, "we'd better set a course home—"

"Home," Weeks repeated. To him Terra was not his own home— he had been born in the polar swamps of Venus. But to all Solarians—no matter which planet had nurtured them—Terra was home.

"You," Rip's big hand fell gently on the little oiler's shoulder, "stay here with Thorson—"

"No," Weeks shook his head. "Unless I black out, I'm riding station in the engine room. Maybe the bug won't work on me anyway."

And because he had done what he had done they could not deny him the right to ride his station as long as he could during the grueling hours to come.

Dane visited the cargo hold once more. To be greeted by an irate scream which assured him that Queex was again awake and on guard. Although the Hoobat was ready enough to give tongue, it still squatted in its chosen position on top of the log stack and he did not try to dislodge it. Perhaps with Queex planted in the enemies' territory they would have nothing to fear from any pests not now confined in the deep freeze.

Rip set his course for Terra—for that plague spot on their native world where they might hide out the *Queen* until they could prove their point—that the spacer was not a disease-ridden ship to be feared. He kept to the control cabin, shifting only between the astrogator's and the pilot's station. Upon him alone rested the responsibility of bringing in the ship along a vector which crossed no well traveled space lane where the Patrol might challenge them. Dane rode out the orbiting in the com-tech's seat, listening in for the first warning of danger—that they had been detected.

The mechanical repetition of their list of crimes was now stale news and largely off-ether. And from all traces he could pick up, they were lost as far as the authorities were concerned. On the other hand, the Patrol might indeed be as far knowing as its propaganda stated and the *Queen* was running headlong into a trap. Only they had no choice in the matter.

It was the ship's inter-com bringing Ali's voice from the engine room which broke the concentration in the control cabin.

"Weeks is down!"

Rip barked into the mike. "How bad?"

"He hasn't blacked out yet. The pains in his head are pretty bad and his hand is swelling—"

"He's given us our proof. Tell him to report off—"

But the disembodied voice which answered that was Weeks'.

"I haven't got it as bad as the others. I'll ride this out."

Rip shook his head. But short-handed as they were he could not argue Weeks away from his post if the man insisted upon staying. He had other, and for the time being, more important matters before him.

How long they sweated out that descent upon their native world Dane could never afterwards have testified. He only knew that hours must have passed, until he thought groggily that he could not remember a time he was not glued in the seat which had been Tang's, the earphones pressing against his sweating skull, his fatigue-drugged mind being held with difficulty to the duty at hand.

Sometime during that haze they made their landing. He had a dim memory of Rip sprawled across the pilot's control board and then utter exhaustion claimed him also and the darkness closed in. When he roused it was to look about a cabin tilted to one side. Rip was still slumped in a muscle cramping posture, breathing heavily. Dane bit out a forceful word born of twinges of his own, and then snapped on the visa-plate.

For a long moment he was sure that he was not yet awake. And then, as his dazed mind supplied names for what he saw, he knew that Rip had failed. Far from being in the center—or at least well within the perimeter of the dread Big Burn—they must have landed in some civic park or national forest. For the massed green outside, the bright flowers; the bird he sighted as a brilliant flash of wind coasting color—those were not to be found in the twisted horror left by man's last attempt to impress his will upon his resisting kind.

Well, it had been a good try, but there was no use expecting luck to ride their fins all the way, and they had had more than their share in the E-Stat affair. How long would it be before the Law arrived to collect them? Would they have time to state their case?

The faint hope that they might aroused him. He reached for the com key and a second later tore the headphones from his appalled ears. The crackle of static he knew—and the numerous strange noises which broke in upon the lanes of communication in space— but this solid, paralyzing roar was something totally new—new, and frightening.

And because it was new and he could not account for it, he turned back to regard the scene on the viewer with a more critical eye. The foliage which grew in riotous profusion was green right enough, and Terra green into the bargain—there was no mistaking that. But— Dane caught at the edge of the com-unit for support. But—What was that liver-red blossom which had just reached out to engulf a small flying thing?

Feverishly he tried to remember the little natural history he knew. Sure that what he had just witnessed was unnatural—un-Terran— and to be suspect!

He started the spy lens on its slow revolution in the *Queen*'s nose, to get a full picture of their immediate surroundings. It was tilted at an angle—apparently they had *not* made a fin-point landing this time—and sometimes it merely reflected slices of sky. But when it swept earthward he saw enough to make him believe that wherever the spacer had set down it was not on the Terra he knew.

Subconsciously he had expected the Big Burn to be barren land— curdled rock with rivers of frozen quartz, substances boiled up through the crust of the planet by the action of the atomic explosives. That was the way it had been on Limbo—on the other "burnt-off" worlds they had discovered where those who had preceded mankind into the Galaxy—the mysterious, long vanished "Forerunners"—had fought their grim and totally annihilating wars.

But it would seem that the Big Burn was altogether different—at least here it was. There was no rock sterile of life outside—in fact there would appear to be too much life. What Dane could sight on his limited field of vision was a teeming jungle. And the thrill of that discovery almost made him forget their present circumstances. He was still staring bemused at the screen when Rip muttered, turned his head on his folded arms and opened his sunken eyes:

"Did we make it?" he asked dully.

Dane, not taking his eyes from that fascinating scene without, answered: "You brought us down. But I don't know where—"

"Unless our instruments were way off, we're near to the heart of the Burn."

"Some heart!"

"What does it look like?" Rip sounded too tired to cross the cabin and see for himself. "Barren as Limbo?"

"Hardly! Rip, did you ever see a tomato as big as a melon— At least it looks like a tomato," Dane halted the spy lens as it focused upon this new phenomena.

"A what?" There was a note of concern in Shannon's voice. "What's the matter with you, Dane?"

"Come and see," Dane willingly yielded his place to Rip but he did not step out of range of the screen. Surely that did have the likeness to a good, old-fashioned earthside tomato—but it was melon size and it hung from a bush which was close to a ten foot tree!

Rip stumbled across to drop into the Com-tech's place. But his expression of worry changed to one of simple astonishment as he saw that picture.

"Where are we?"

"You name it," Dane had had longer to adjust, the excitement of an explorer sighting virgin territory worked in his veins, banishing fatigue. "It must be the Big Burn!"

"But," Rip shook his head slowly as if with that gesture to deny the evidence before his eyes, "that country's all bare rock. I've seen pictures—"

"Of the outer rim," Dane corrected, having already solved that problem for himself. "This must be farther in than any survey ship ever came. Great Spirit of Outer Space, what has happened here?"

Rip had enough technical training to know how to get part of the answer. He leaned halfway across the com, and was able to flick down a lever with the very tip of his longest finger. Instantly the cabin was filled with a clicking so loud as to make an almost continuous drone of sound.

Dane knew that danger signal, he didn't need Rip's words to underline it for him.

"That's what's happened. This country is pile 'hot' out there!"

SPECIAL MISSION

14 That click, the dial beneath the counter, warned them that they were as cut off from the luxuriance outside as if they were viewing a scene on Mars or Sargol from their present position. To go beyond the shielding walls of the spacer into that riotous green world would sentence them to death as surely as if the Patrol was without, with a flamer trained on their hatch. There was no escape from that radiation—it would be in the air one breathed, strike through one's skin. And yet the wilderness flourished and beckoned.

"Mutations—" Rip mused. "Space, Tau'd go wild if he could see it!"

And that mention of the medic brought them back to the problem which had earthed them. Dane leaned back against the slanting wall of the cabin.

"We have to have a medic—"

Rip nodded without looking away from the screen.

"Can one of the flitters be shielded?" The cargo-apprentice persisted.

"That's a thought! Ali should know—" Rip reached for the inter-com mike. "Engines!"

"So you *are live?*" Ali's voice had a bite in it. "About time you're contacting. Where are we? Besides being lopsided from a recruit's scrambled set-down, I mean."

"In the Big Burn. Come top-side. Wait—how's Weeks?"

"He has a devil's own headache, but he hasn't blacked out yet. Looks like his immunity holds in part. I've sent him bunkside for a while with a couple of pain pills. So we've made it—"

He must have left to join them for when Rip answered: "After a fashion," into the mike there was no reply.

And the clang of his boot plates on the ladder heralded his arrival at their post. There was an interval for him to view the outer world and accept the verdict of the counter and then Rip voiced Dane's question:

"Can we shield one of the flitters well enough to cross that? I can't take the *Queen* up and earth her again—"

"I know you can't!" the acting-engineer cut in. "Maybe you could get her off world, but you'll come close to blasting out when you try for another landing. Fuel doesn't go on forever—though some of you space jockeys seem to think it does. The flitter? Well, we've some spare rocket linings. But it's going to be a job and a half to get those beaten out and reassembled. And, frankly, the space whirly one who flies her had better be suited and praying loudly when he takes off. We can always try—" He was frowning, already busied with the problem which was one for his department.

So with intervals of snatched sleep, hurried meals, and the time which must be given to tending their unconscious charges, Rip and Dane became only hands to be directed by Ali's brain and garnered knowledge. Weeks slept off the worst of his pain and, though he complained of weakness, he tottered back on duty to help.

The flitter—an air sled intended to hold three men and supplies for exploring trips on strange worlds—was first stripped of all nonessentials until what remained was not much more than the pilot's seat and the motor. Then they labored to build up a shielding of the tough radiation dulling alloy which was used to line rocket tubes. And they could only praise the foresight of Stotz who carried such a full supply of spare parts and tools. It was a task over which they often despaired, and Ali improvised frantically, performing weird adjustments of engineering structure. He was still unsatisfied when they had done.

"She'll fly," he admitted. "And she's the best we can do. But it'll depend a lot on how far she has to go over 'hot' country. Which way do we head her?"

Rip had been busy with a map of Terra—a small thing he had discovered in one of the travel recordings carried for crew entertainment.

"The Big Burn covers three quarters of this continent. There's no use going north—the devastated area extends into the arctic regions. I'd say west—there's some fringe settlements on the sea coast and we need to contact a frontier territory. Now do we have it straight—? I take the flitter, get a medic and bring him back—"

Dane cut in at that point. "Correct course! You stay here. If the *Queen* has to lift, you're the only one who can take her off world. And the same's true for Ali. I can't ride out a blastoff in either the pilot's or the engineer's seat. And Weeks is on the sick list. So I'm elected to do the medic hunting—"

They were forced to agree to that. He was no hero, Dane thought, as he gave a last glance about his cabin early the next morning. The small cubby, utilitarian and bare as it was, never looked more inviting or secure. No, no hero, it was merely a matter of common sense. And although his imagination—that deeply hidden imagination with which few of his fellows credited him—shrank from the ordeal ahead, he had not the slightest intention of allowing that to deter him.

The space suit, which had been bulky and clumsy enough on the E-Stat asteroid under limited gravity, was almost twice as poorly adapted to progression on earth. But he climbed into it with Rip's aid, while Ali lashed a second suit under the seat—ready to encase the man Dane must bring back with him. Before he closed he helmet, Rip had one last order to give, along with an unexpected piece of equipment. And, when Dane saw that, he knew just how desperate Shannon considered their situation to be. For only on life or death terms would the astrogator-apprentice have used Jellico's private key, opened the forbidden arms cabinet, and withdrawn that blaster.

"If you need it—use this—" Rip's face was very sober.

Ali arose from fastening the extra suit in place. "It's ready—"

He came back into the corridor and Dane clanked out in his place, settling himself behind the controls. When they saw him there, the inner hatch closed and he was alone in the bay.

With tantalizing slowness the outer wall of the spacer slid back. His hands, blundering within the metallic claws of the gloves, Dane buckled two safety belts about him. Then the skeleton flitter moved to the left—out into the glare of the early day, a light too bright, even through the shielded viewplates of his helmet.

For some dangerous moment the machine creaked out and down on the landing cranes, the warning counter on its control panel going into a mad whirl of color as it tried to record the radiation. There came a jar as it touched the scorched earth at the foot of the *Queen*'s fins.

Dane pressed the release and watched the lines whip up and the hatch above snap shut. Then he opened the controls. He used too much energy and shot into the air, tearing a wide gap through what was luckily a thin screen of the matted foliage, before he gained complete mastery.

Then he was able to level out and bore westward, the rising sun at his back, the sea of deadly green beneath him, and somewhere far ahead the faint promise of clean, radiation-free land holding the help they needed.

Mile after mile of the green jungle swept under the flitter, and the flash of the counter's light continued to record a land unfit for mankind. Even with the equipment used on distant worlds to protect what spacemen had come to recognize was a reasonably tough human frame, no ground force could hope to explore that wilderness in person. And flying above it, as well insulated as he was, Dane knew that he could be dangerously exposed. If the contaminated territory extended more than a thousand miles, his danger was no longer problematical—it was an established fact.

He had only the vague directions from the scrap of map Rip had uncovered. To the west—he had no idea how far away—there stretched a length of coastline, far enough from the radiation blasted area to allow small settlements. For generations the population of Terra, decimated by the atomic wars, and then drained by first system and then Galactic exploration and colonization, had been decreasing. But within the past hundred years it was again on the upswing. Men retiring from space were returning to their native planet to live out their remaining years. The descendants of far-flung colonists, coming home on visits, found the sparsely populated mother world appealed to some basic instinct so that they remained. And now the settlements of mankind were on the march, spreading out from the well established sections which had not been blighted by ancient wars.

It was mid-afternoon when Dane noted that the green carpet beneath the flitter was displaying holes—that small breaks in the vegetation became sizable stretches of rocky waste. He kept one eye on the counter and what, when he left the spacer, had been an almost steady beam of warning light was now a well defined succession of blinks. The land below was cooling off—perhaps he had passed the worst of the journey. But in that passing how much had he and the flitter become contaminated? Ali had devised a method of protection for the empty suit the medic would wear—had that held? There were an alarming number of dark ifs in the immediate future.

The mutant growths were now only thin patches of stunted and yellowish green. Had man penetrated only this far into the Burn, the knowledge of what lay beyond would be totally false. This effect of dreary waste might well discourage exploration.

Now the blink of the counter was deliberate, with whole seconds of pause between the flashes. Cooling off—? It was getting cold fast! He wished that he had a com-unit. Because of the interference in the Burn he had left it behind—but with one he might be able now to locate some settlement. All that remained was to find the seashore and, with it as a guide, flit south towards the center of modern civilization.

He laid no plans of action—this whole exploit must depend upon improvisation. And, as a Free Trader, spur-of-the-moment action was a necessary way of life. On the frontier Rim of the Galaxy, where the independent spacers traced the star trails, fast thinking and the ability to change plans on an instant were as important as skill in aiming a blaster. And it was very often proven that the tongue—and the brain behind it—were more deadly than a flamer.

The sun was in Dane's face now and he caught sight of patches of uncontaminated earth with honest vegetation—in place of the "hot" jungle now miles behind. That night he camped out on the edge of rough pasturage where the counter no longer flashed its warning and he was able to shed the suit and sleep under the stars with the fresh air of early summer against his cheek and the smell of honest growing things replacing the dry scent of the spacer and the languorous perfumes of Sargol.

He lay on his back, flat against the earth of which he was truly a part, staring up into the dark, inverted bowl of the heavens. It was so hard to connect those distant points of icy light making the well remembered patterns overhead with the suns whose rays had added to the brown stain on his skin. Sargol's sun—the one which gave such limited light to dead Limbo—the sun under which Naxos, his first Galactic port, grew its food. He could not pick them out—was not even sure that any could be sighted from Terra. Strange suns, red, orange, blue, green, white—yet here all looked alike—points of glitter.

Tomorrow at dawn he must go on. He turned his head away from the sky and grass, green Terran grass, was soft beneath his cheek. Yet unless he was successful tomorrow—or the next day—he might never have the right to feel that grass again. Resolutely Dane willed that thought out of his mind, tried to fix upon something more lulling which would bring with it the sleep he must have before he went on. And in the end he did sleep, deeply, dreamlessly, as if the touch of Terra's soil was in itself the sedative his tautly strung nerves needed.

It was before sunrise that he awoke, stiff, and chilled. The grayness of pre-dawn gave partial light and somewhere a bird was twittering. There had been birds—or things whose far off ancestors had been birds—in the "hot" forest. Did they also sing to greet the dawn?

Dane went over the flitter with his small counter and was relieved to find that they had done a good job of shielding under Ali's supervision. Once the suit he had worn was stored, he could sit at the controls without danger and in comfort. And it was good to be free of that metal prison.

This time he took to the air with ease, the salt taste of food concentrate on his tongue as he sucked a cube. And his confidence arose with the flitter. This was *the* day, somehow he knew it. He was going to find what he sought.

It was less than two hours after sunrise that he did so. A village which was a cluster of perhaps fifty or so house units strung along into the land. He skimmed across it and brought the flitter down in a rock-cliff-walled sand pocket with surf booming some yards away, where he would be reasonably sure of safe hiding.

All right, he had found a village. Now what? A medic—A stranger appearing on the lane which served the town, a stranger in a distinctive uniform of Trade, would only incite conjecture and betrayal. He had to plan now—

Dane unsealed his tunic. He should, by rights, shed his space boots too. But perhaps he could use those to color his story. He thrust the blaster into hiding at his waist. A rip or two in his undertunic, a shallow cut from his bush knife allowed to bleed messily. He could not see himself to judge the general effect, but had to hope it was the right one.

His chance to test his acting powers came sooner than he had anticipated. Luckily he had climbed out of the hidden cove before he was spotted by the boy who came whistling along the path, a fishing pole over his shoulder, a basket swinging from his hand. Dane assumed an expression which he thought would suggest fatigue, pain, and bewilderment and lurched forward as if, in sighting the oncoming boy, he had also sighed hope.

"Help—!" Perhaps it was excitement which gave his utterance that convincing croak.

Rod and basket fell to the ground as the boy, after one astounded stare, ran forward.

"What's the matter!" His eyes were on those space boots and he added a "sir" which had the ring of hero worship.

"Escape boat—" Dane waved toward the sea's general direction. "Medic—must get to medic—"

"Yes, sir," the boy's basic Terran sounded good. "Can you walk if I help you?"

Dane managed a weak nod, but contrived that he did not lean too heavily on his avidly helpful guide.

"The medic's my father, sir. We're right down this slope—third house. And Father hasn't left—he's supposed to go on a northern inspection tour today—"

Dane felt a stab of distaste for the role being forced upon him. When he had visualized the medic he must abduct to serve the *Queen* in her need, he had not expected to have to kidnap a family man. Only the knowledge that he did have the extra suit, and that he had made the outward trip without dangerous exposure, bolstered up his determination to see the plan through.

When they came out at the end of the single long lane which tied the houses of the village together, Dane was puzzled to see the place so deserted. But, since it was not within his role of dazed sufferer to ask questions, he did not do so. It was his young guide who volunteered the information he wanted.

"Most everyone is out with the fleet. There's a run of red-backs—"

Dane understood. Within recent times the "red-backs" of the

north had become a desirable luxury item for Terran tables. If a school of them were to be found in the vicinity no wonder this village was now deserted as its fleet went out to garner in the elusive but highly succulent fish.

"In here, sir—" Dane found himself being led to a house on the right. "Are you in Trade—?"

He suppressed a start, shedding his uniform tunic had not done much in the way of disguise. It would be nice, he thought a little bitterly, if he could flash an I-S badge now to completely confuse the issue. But he answered with the partial truth and did not enlarge.

"Yes—"

The boy was flushed with excitement. "I'm trying for Trade Service medic," he confided. "Passed the Directive exam last month. But I still have to go up for Prelim psycho—"

Dane had a flash of memory. Not too many months before not the Prelim psycho, but the big machine at the Assignment Center had decided his own future arbitrarily, fitting him into the crew of the *Solar Queen* as the ship where his abilities, knowledge and potentialities could best work to the good of the Service. At the time he had resented, had even been slightly ashamed of being relegated to a Free Trading spacer while Artur Sands and other classmates from the Pool had walked off with Company assignments. Now he knew that he would not trade the smallest and most rusty bolt from the *Solar Queen* for the newest scout ship in I-S or Combine registry. And this boy from the frontier village might be himself as he was five years earlier. Though he had never known a real home or family, scrapping into the Pool from one of the children's Depots.

"Good luck!" He meant that and the boy's flush deepened.

"Thank you, sir. Around here—Father's treatment room has this other door—"

Dane allowed himself to be helped into the treatment room and sat down in a chair while the boy hurried off to locate the medic. The Trader's hand went to the butt of his concealed blaster. It was a job he had to do—one he had volunteered for—and there was no backing out. But his mouth had a wry twist as he drew out the blaster and made ready to point it at the inner door. Or—his mind leaped to another idea—could he get the medic safely out of the village? A story about another man badly injured—perhaps pinned in the wreckage of an escape boat—He could try it. He thrust the blaster back inside his torn undertunic, hoping the bulge would pass unnoticed.

"My son says—"

Dane looked up. The man who came through the inner door was in early middle age, thin, wiry, with a hard, fined-down look about him. He could almost be Tau's elder brother. He crossed the room with a brisk stride and came to stand over Dane, his hand reaching to pull aside the bloody cloth covering the Trader's breast. But Dane fended off that examination.

"My partner," he said. "Back there—pinned in—" He jerked his hand southward. "Needs help—"

The medic frowned. "Most of the men are out with the fleet. Jorge," he spoke to the boy who had followed him, "go and get Lex and Hartog. Here," he tried to push Dane back into the chair as the Trader got up, "let me look at that cut—"

Dane shook his head. "No time now, sir. My partner's hurt bad. Can you come?"

"Certainly." The medic reached for the emergency kit on the shelf behind him. "You able to make it?"

"Yes," Dane was exultant. It was going to work! He could toll the medic away from the village. Once out among the rocks on the shoreline he could pull the blaster and herd the man to the flitter. His luck was going to hold after all!

MEDIC HOVAN REPORTS

15 Fortunately the path out of the straggling town was a twisted one and in a very short space they were hidden from view. Dane paused as if the pace was too much for an injured man. The medic put out a steadying hand, only to drop it quickly when he saw the weapon which had appeared in Dane's grip.

"What—?" His mouth snapped shut, his jaw tightened.

"You will march ahead of me," Dane's low voice was steady. "Beyond that rock spur to the left you'll find a place where it is possible to climb down to sea level. Do it!"

"I suppose I shouldn't ask why?"

"Not now. We haven't much time. Get moving!"

The medic mastered his surprise and without further protest obeyed orders. It was only when they were standing by the flitter and he saw the suits that his eyes widened and he said:

"The Big Burn!"

"Yes, and I'm desperate—"

"You must be—or mad—" The medic stared at Dane for a long moment and then shook his head. "What is it? A plague ship?"

Dane bit his lip. The other was too astute. But he did not ask why or how he had been able to guess so shrewdly. Instead he gestured to the suit Ali had lashed beneath the seat in the flitter. "Get into that and be quick about it!"

The medic rubbed his hand across his jaw. "I think that you might just be desperate enough to use that thing you're brandishing about so melodramatically if I don't," he remarked in a calmly conversational tone.

"I won't kill. But a blaster burn—"

"Can be pretty painful. Yes, I know that, young man. And," suddenly he shrugged, put down his kit and started donning the suit, "I wouldn't put it past you to knock me out and load me aboard if I did say no. All right—"

Suited, he took his place on the seat as Dane directed, and then the Trader followed the additional precaution of lashing the medic's metal encased arms to his body before he climbed into his own protective covering. Now they could only communicate by sight through the vision plates of their helmets.

Dane triggered the controls and they arose out of the sand and rock hollow just as a party of two men and a boy came hurrying along the top of the cliff—Jorge and the rescuers arriving too late. The flitter spiraled up into the sunlight and Dane wondered how long it would be before this outrage was reported to the nearest Planet Police base. But would any Police cruiser have the hardihood to follow him into the Big Burn? He hoped that the radiation would hold them back.

There was no navigation to be done. The flitter's "memory" should deposit them at the *Queen*. Dane wondered at what his silent companion was now thinking. The medic had accepted his kidnaping with such docility that the very ease of their departure began to bother Dane. Was the other expecting a trailer? Had exploration into the Big Burn from the seaside villages been more extensive than reported officially?

He stepped up the power of the flitter to the top notch and saw with some relief that the ground beneath them was now the rocky waste bordering the devastated area. The metal encased figure that shared his seat had not moved, but now the bubble head turned as if the medic were intent upon the ground flowing beneath them.

The flicker of the counter began and Dane realized that nightfall would find them still airborne. But so far he had not been aware of any pursuit. Again he wished he had the use of a com—only here the radiation would blanket sound with that continuous roar.

Patches of the radiation vegetation showed now and something in the lines of the medic's tense figure suggested that these were new to him. Afternoon waned as the patches united, spread into the beginning of the jungle as the counter was once more an almost steady light. When evening closed in they were not caught in darkness—for below trees, looping vines, brush, had a pale, evil glow of their own, proclaiming their toxicity with bluish halos. Sometimes pockets of these made a core of light which pulsed, sending warning fingers at the flitter which sped across it.

The hour was close on midnight before Dane sighted the other light, the pink-red of which winked through the ghastly blue-white with a natural and comforting promise, even though it had been meant for an entirely different purpose. The *Queen* had earthed with her distress lights on and no one had remembered to snap them off. Now they acted as a beacon to draw the flitter to its berth.

Dane brought the stripped flyer down on the fused ground as close to the spot from which he had taken off as he could remember. Now—if those on the spacer would only move fast enough—!

But he need not have worried, his arrival had been anticipated. Above, the rounded side of the spacer bulged as the hatch opened. Lines swung down to fasten their magnetic clamps on the flitter. Then once more they were airborne, swinging up to be warped into the side of the ship. As the outer port of the flitter berth closed Dane reached over and pulled loose the lashing which immobilized his companion. The medic stood up, a little awkwardly as might any man who wore space armor the first time.

The inner hatch now opened and Dane waved his captive into the small section which must serve them as a decontamination space. Free at last of the suits, they went through one more improvised hatch to the main corridor of the *Queen* where Rip and Ali stood waiting, their weary faces lighting as they saw the Medic.

It was the latter who spoke first. "This *is* a plague ship—"

Rip shook his head. "It is *not,* sir. And you're the one who is going to help us prove that."

The man leaned back against the wall, his face expressionless. "You take a rather tough way of trying to get help."

"It was the only way left us. I'll be frank," Rip continued, "we're Patrol Posted."

The medic's shrewd eyes went from one drawn young face to the next. "You don't look like very desperate criminals," was his comment. "This your full crew?"

"All the rest are your concern. That is—if you will take the job—" Rip's shoulders slumped a little.

"You haven't left me much choice, have you? If there is illness on board, I'm under the Oath—whether you are Patrol Posted or not. What's the trouble?"

They got him down to Tau's laboratory and told him their story. From a slight incredulity his expression changed to an alert interest and he demanded to see, first the patients and then the pests now immured in the deep freeze. Sometime in the middle of this, Dane, overcome by fatigue which was partly relief from tension, sought his cabin and the bunk from which he wearily disposed Sinbad, only to have the purring cat crawl back once more when he had lain down.

And when he awoke, renewed in body and spirit, it was in a new *Queen,* a ship in which hope and confidence now ruled.

"Hovan's already got it!" Rip told him exultantly. "It's that poison from the little devils' claws right enough! A narcotic—produces some of the affects of deep sleep. In fact—it may have a medical use. He's excited about it—"

"All right," Dane waved aside information which under other circumstances, promising as it did a chance for future trade, would have engrossed him, to ask a question which at the moment seemed far more to the point. "Can he get our men back on their feet?"

A little of Rip's exuberance faded. "Not right away. He's given them all shots. But he thinks they'll have to sleep it off."

"And we have no idea how long that is going to take," Ali contributed.

Time—for the first time in days Dane was struck by that—time! Because of his training a fact he had forgotten in the past weeks of worry now came to mind—their contract with the storm priests. Even if they were able to clear themselves of the plague charge, even if the rest of the crew were speedily restored to health, he was sure that they could not hope to return to Sargol with the promised cargo, the pay for which was already on board the *Queen*. They would have broken their pledge and there could be no hope of holding to their trading rights on that world—if they were not blacklisted for breaking contract into the bargain. I-S would be able to move in and clean up and probably they could never prove that the Company was behind their misfortunes—though the men of the *Queen* would always be convinced that that fact was the truth.

"We're going to break contract—" he said aloud and that shook the other two, knocked some of their assurance out of them.

"How about that?" Rip asked Ali.

The acting-engineer nodded. "We have fuel enough to lift from here and maybe set down at Terraport—if we take it careful and cut vectors. We can't lift from there without refueling—and of course the Patrol are going to sit on their hands while we do that—with us Posted! No, put out of your heads any plan for getting back to Sargol within the time limit. Thorson's right—that way we're flamed out!"

Rip slumped in his seat. "So the Eysies can take over after all?"

"As I see it," Dane cut in, "let's just take one thing at a time. We may have to argue a broken contract out before the Board. But first we have to get off the Posted hook with the Patrol. Have you any idea about how we are going to handle that?"

"Hovan's on our side. In fact if we let him have the bugs to play with he'll back us all the way. He can swear us a clean bill of health before the Medic Control Center."

"How much will that count after we've broken all their regs?" Ali wanted to know. "If we surrender now we're not going to have much chance, no matter what Hovan does or does not swear to. Hovan's a frontier medic—I won't say that he's not a member in good standing of their association—but he doesn't have top star rating. And with the Eysies and the Patrol on our necks, we'll need more than one medic's word—"

But Rip looked from the pessimistic Kamil to Dane. Now he asked a question which was more than half statement.

"You've thought of something?"

"I've remembered something," the cargo-apprentice corrected. "Recall the trick Van pulled on Limbo when the Patrol was trying to ease us out of our rights there after they took over the outlaw hold?"

Ali was impatient. "He threatened to talk to the Video people and broadcast—tell everyone about the ships wrecked by the Forerunner installation and left lying about full of treasure. But what has that to do with us now—? We bargained away our rights on Limbo for the rest of Cam's monopoly on Sargol—not that it's done us much good—"

"The Video," Dane fastened on the important point, "Van threatened publicity which would embarrass the Patrol and he was legally within his rights. We're outside the law now—but publicity might help again. How many earth-side people know of the unwritten law about open war on plague ships? How many who aren't spacemen know that we could be legally pushed into the sun and fried without any chance to prove we're innocent of carrying a new disease? If we could talk loud and clear to the people at large maybe we'd have a chance for a real hearing—"

"Right from the Terraport broadcast station, I suppose?" Ali taunted.

"Why not?"

There was silence in the cabin as the other two chewed upon that and he broke it again:

"We set down here when it had never been done before."

With one brown forefinger Rip traced some pattern known only to himself on the top of the table. Ali stared at the opposite wall as if it were a bank of machinery he must master.

"It just might be whirly enough to work—" Kamil commented softly. "Or maybe we've been spaced too long and the Whisperers have been chattering into our ears. What about it, Rip, could you set us down close enough to Center Block there?"

"We can try anything once. But we might crash the old girl bringing her in. There's that apron between the Companies' Launching cradles and the Center— It's clear there and we could give an E signal coming down which would make them stay rid of it. But I won't try it except as a last resort."

Dane noticed that after that discouraging statement Rip made straight for Jellico's record tapes and routed out the one which dealt with Terraport and the landing instructions for that metropolis of the star ships. To land unbidden would certainly bring them publicity—and to get to the Video broadcast and tell their story would grant them not only worldwide, but systemwide hearing. News from Terraport was broadcast on every channel every hour of the day and night and not a single viewer could miss their appeal.

But first there was Hovan to be consulted. Would he be willing to back them with his professional knowledge and assurance? Or would their high-handed method of recruiting his services operate against them now? They decided to let Rip ask such questions of the medic.

"So you're going to set us down in the center of the big jump-off?" was his first comment, as the acting-Captain of the *Queen* stated their case. "Then you want me to fire my rockets to certify you are harmless. You don't ask for very much, do you, son?"

Rip spread his hands. "I can understand how its looks to you, sir.

We grabbed you and brought you here by force. We can't make you testify for us if you decide not to—"

"Can't you?" The medic cocked an eyebrow at him. "What about this bully boy of yours with his little blaster? He could herd me right up to the telecast, couldn't he? There's a lot of persuasion in one of those nasty little arms. On the other hand, I've a son who's set on taking out on one of these tin pots to go star hunting. If I handed you over to the Patrol he might make some remarks to me in private. You may be Posted, but you don't look like very hardened criminals to me. It seems that you've been handed a bad situation and handled it as best you know. And I'm willing to ride along the rest of the way on your tail blast. Let me see how many pieces you land us in at Terraport and I'll give you my final answer. If luck holds we may have a couple more of your crew present by that time, also—"

They had had no indication that the *Queen* had been located, that any posse hunting the kidnaped medic had followed them into the Big Burn. And they could only hope that they would continue to remain unsighted as they upped-ship once more and cruised into a regular traffic lane for earthing at the port. It would be a chancy thing and Ali and Rip spent hours checking the mechanics of that flight, while Dane and the recovering Weeks worked with Hovan in an effort to restore the sleeping crew.

After three visits to the hold and the discovery that the Hoobat had uncovered no more of the pests, Dane caged the angry blue horror and returned it to its usual stand in Jellico's cabin, certain that the ship was clean for Sinbad now confidently prowled the corridors and went into every cabin or storage space Dane opened for him.

And on the morning of the day they had planned for takeoff, Hovan at last had a definite response to his treatment. Craig Tau roused, stared dazedly around, and asked a vague question. The fact that he immediately relapsed once more into semi-coma did not discourage the other medic. Progress had been made and he was now sure that he knew the proper treatment.

They strapped down at zero hour and blasted out of the weird green wilderness they had not dared to explore, lifting into the arch of the sky, depending upon Rip's knowledge to put them safely down again.

Dane once more rode out the takeoff at the com-unit, waiting for the blast of radiation-borne static to fade so that he could catch any broadcast.

"—turned back last night. The high level of radiation makes it almost certain that the outlaws could not have headed into the dangerous central portion. Search is now spreading north. Authorities are inclined to believe that this last outrage may be a clew to the vanished *Solar Queen,* a plague ship, warned off and Patrol Posted after her crew plundered an E-Stat belonging to the Inter-Solar Corporation. Anyone having any information concerning this ship—or any strange spacer—report at once to the nearest Terrapolice or Patrol station. Do not take chances—report any contact at once to the nearest Terrapolice or Patrol station!"

"That's putting it strongly," Dane commented as he relayed the message. "Good as giving orders for us to be flamed down at sight—"

"Well, if we set down in the right spot," Rip replied, "they can't flame us out without blasting the larger part of Terraport field with us. And I don't think they are going to do that in a hurry."

Dane hoped Shannon was correct in that belief. It would be more chancy than landing at the E-Stat or in the Big Burn—to gauge it just right and put them down on the Terraport apron where they could not be flamed out without destroying too much, where their very position would give them a bargaining point, was going to be a top star job. If Rip could only pull it off!

He could not evaluate the niceties of that flight, he did not understand all Rip was doing. But he did know enough to remain quietly in his place, ask no questions, and await results with a dry mouth and a wildly beating heart. There came a moment when Rip glanced up at him, one hand poised over the control board. The pilot's voice came tersely, thin and queer:

"Pray it out, Dane—here we go!"

Dane heard the shrill of a riding beam, so tearing he had to move his earphones. They must be almost on top of the control tower to get it like that! Rip was planning on a set down where the *Queen* would block things neatly. He brought his own fingers down on the E-E-Red button to give the last and most powerful warning. That, to be used only when a ship landing was out of control, should clear the ground below. They could only pray it would vacate the port they were still far from seeing.

"Make it a fin-point, Rip," he couldn't repress that one bit of advice. And was glad he had given it when he saw a ghost grin tug for a moment at Rip's full lips.

"Good enough for a check-ride?"

They were riding her flaming jets down as they would on a strange world. Below the port must be wild. Dane counted off the seconds. Two—three—four—five—just a few more and they would be too low to intercept—without endangering innocent coasters and groundhuggers. When the last minute during which they were still vulnerable passed, he gave a sigh of relief. That was one more point on their side. In the earphones was a crackle of frantic questions, a gabble of orders screaming at him. Let them rave, they'd know soon enough what it was all about.

THE BATTLE OF THE VIDEO

16

Oddly enough, in spite of the tension which must have boiled within him, Rip brought them in with a perfect four fin-point landing—one which, under the circumstances, must win him the respect of master star-star pilots from the Rim. Though Dane doubted whether if they lost, that skill would bring Shannon anything but a long term in the moon mines. The actual jar of their landing contact was mostly absorbed by the webbing of their shock seats and they were on their feet, ready to move almost at once.

The next operation had been planned. Dane gave a glance at the screen. Ringed now about the *Queen* were the buildings of Terraport. Yes, any attempt to attack the ship would endanger too much of the permanent structure of the field itself. Rip had brought them down—not on the rocket-scarred outer landing space—but on the concrete apron between the Assignment Center and the control tower—a smooth strip usually sacred to the parking of officials' ground scooters. He speculated as to whether any of the latter had been converted to molten metal by the exhausts of the *Queen*'s descent.

Like the team they had come to be the four active members of the crew went into action. Ali and Weeks were waiting by an inner hatch, Medic Hovan with them. The engineer-apprentice was bulky in a space suit, and two more of the unwieldy body coverings waited beside him for Rip and Dane. With fingers which were inclined to act like thumbs they were sealed into what would provide some protection against any blaster or sleep ray. Then with Hovan, conspicuously wearing no such armor, they climbed into one of the ship's crawlers.

Weeks activated the outer hatch and the crane lines plucked the small vehicle out of the *Queen,* swinging it dizzily down to the blast scored apron.

"Make for the tower—" Rip's voice was thin in the helmet coms.

Dane at the controls of the crawler pulled on as Ali cast off the lines which anchored them to the spacer.

Through the bubble helmet he could see the frenzied activity in the aroused port. An ant hill into which some idle investigator had thrust a stick and given it a turn or two was nothing compared with Terraport after the unorthodox arrival of the *Solar Queen.*

"Patrol mobile coming in on southeast vector," Ali announced calmly. "Looks like she mounts a portable flamer on her nose—"

"So." Dane changed direction, putting behind him a customs check point, aware as he ground by that stand of a line of faces at its vision ports. Evasive action—and he'd have to get the top speed from the clumsy crawler.

"Police 'copter over us—" That was Rip reporting.

Well, they couldn't very well avoid *that*. But at the same time Dane was reasonably sure that its attack would not be an overt one—not with the unarmed, unprotected Hovan prominently displayed in their midst.

But there he was too sanguine. A muffled exclamation from Rip made him glance at the medic beside him. Just in time to see Hovan slump limply forward, about to tumble from the crawler when Shannon caught him from behind. Dane was too familiar with the results of sleep rays to have any doubts as to what had happened.

The P-copter had sprayed them with its most harmless weapon. Only the suits, insulated to the best of their makers' ability against most of the dangers of space, real and anticipated, had kept the three Traders from being overcome as well. Dane suspected that his own responses were a trifle sluggish, that while he had not succumbed to that attack, he had been slowed. But with Rip holding the unconscious medic in his seat, Thorson continued to head the crawler for the tower and its promise of a systemwide hearing for their appeal.

"There's a P-mobile coming in ahead—"

Dane was irritated by that warning from Rip. He had already sighted that black and silver ground car himself. And he was only too keenly conscious of the nasty threat of the snub nosed weapon mounted on its hood, now pointed straight at the oncoming, too deliberate Traders' crawler. Then he saw what he believed would be their only chance—to play once more the same type of trick as Rip had used to earth them safely.

"Get Hovan under cover," he ordered. "I'm going to crash the tower door!"

Hasty movements answered that as the medic's limp body was thrust under the cover offered by the upper framework of the crawler. Luckily the machine had been built for heavy duty on rugged worlds where roadways were unknown. Dane was sure he could build up the power and speed necessary to take them into the lower floor of the tower—no matter if its door was now barred against them.

Whether his audacity daunted the P-mobile, or whether they held off from an all out attack because of Hovan, Dane could not guess. But he was glad for a few minutes of grace as he raced the protesting engine of the heavy machine to its last and greatest effort. The treads of the crawler bit on the steps leading up to the impressive entrance of the tower. There was a second or two before traction caught and then the driver's heart snapped back into place as the machine tilted its nose up and headed straight for the portal.

They struck the closed doors with a shock which almost hurled them from their seats. But that engraved bronze expanse had not been cast to withstand a head-on blow from a heavy duty off-world vehicle and the leaves tore apart letting them into the wide hall beyond.

"Take Hovan and make for the riser!" For the second time it was Dane who gave the orders. "I have a blocking job to do here." He expected every second to feel the bit of a police blaster somewhere along his shrinking body—could even a space suit protect him now?

At the far end of the corridor were the attendants and visitors, trapped in the building, who had fled in an attempt to find safety at the crashing entrance of the crawler. These flung themselves flat at the steady advance of the two space-suited Traders who supported the unconscious medic between them, using the low-powered anti-grav units on their belts to take most of his weight so each had one hand free to hold a sleep rod. And they did not hesitate to use those weapons—spraying the rightful inhabitants of the tower until all lay unmoving.

Having seen that Ali and Rip appeared to have the situation in hand, Dane turned to his own self-appointed job. He jammed the machine on reverse, maneuvering it with an ease learned by practice on the rough terrain of Limbo, until the gate doors were pushed shut again. Then he swung the machine around so that its bulk would afford an effective bar to keep the door locked for some very precious moments to come. Short of using a flamer full power to cut their way in, no one was going to force an entrance now.

He climbed out of the machine, to discover, when he turned, that the trio from the *Queen* had disappeared—leaving all possible opposition asleep on the floor. They must have taken a riser to the broadcasting floor. Dane clanked on to join them, carrying in plated fingers their most important weapon to awake public opinion—an improvised cage in which was housed one of the pests from the cargo hold—the proof of their plague-free state which they intended Hovan to present, via the telecast, to the whole system.

Dane reached the shaft of the riser—to find the platform gone. Would either Rip or Ali have presence of mind enough to send it down to him on automatic?

"Rip—return the riser," he spoke urgently into the throat mike of his helmet com.

"Keep your rockets straight," Ali's cool voice was in his earphones, "it's on its way down. Did *you* remember to bring Exhibit A?"

Dane did not answer. For he was very much occupied with another problem. On the bronze doors he had been at such pains to seal shut there had come into being a round circle of dull red which was speedily changing into a coruscating incandescence. They *had* brought a flamer to bear! It would be a very short time now before the Police could come through. That riser—

Afraid of overbalancing in the bulky suit, Dane did not lean forward to stare up into the shaft. But, as his uncertainty reached a fever pitch, the platform descended and he took two steps forward into temporary safety, still clutching the cage. At the first try the thick fingers of his gloved hand slipped from the lever and he hit it again, harder than he intended, so that he found himself being wafted upward with a speed which did not agree with a stomach, even one long accustomed to space flight. And he almost lost his balance when it came to a stop many floors above.

But he had not lost his wits. Before he stepped from the platform he set the dial on a point which would lift the riser to the top of the shaft and hold it there. That might trap the Traders on the broadcasting floor, but it would also insure them time before the forces of the Law could reach them.

Dane located the rest of his party in the circular core chamber of the broadcasting section. He recognized a backdrop he had seen thousands of times behind the announcer who introduced the newscasts. In one corner Rip, his suit off, was working over the still relaxed form of the medic. While Ali, a grim set to his mouth, was standing with a man who wore the insignia of a com-tech.

"All set?" Rip looked up from his futile ministrations.

Dane put down the cage and began the business of unhooking his own protective covering. "They were burning through the outer doors of the entrance hall when I took off."

"You're not going to get away with this—" That was the com-tech.

Ali smiled wearily, a stretch of lips in which there was little or no mirth. "Listen, my friend. Since I started to ride rockets I've been told I wasn't going to get away with this or that. Why not be more original? Use what is between those outsize ears of yours. We fought our way in here—we landed at Terraport against orders—we're Patrol Posted. Do you think that one man, one lone man, is going to keep us now from doing what we came to do? And don't look around for any reinforcements. We sprayed both those rooms. You can run the emergency hook-up singlehanded and you're going to. We're Free Traders— Ha," the man had lost some of his assurance as he stared from one drawn young face to another, "I see you begin to realize what that means. Out on the Rim we play rough, and we play for keeps. I know half a hundred ways to set you screaming in three minutes and at least ten of them will not even leave a mark on your skin! Now do we get Service—or don't we?"

"You'll go to the Chamber for this—!" snarled the tech.

"All right. But first we broadcast. Then maybe someday a ship that's run into bad luck'll have a straighter deal than we've had. You get on your post. And we'll have the playback on—remember that. If you don't give us a clear channel we'll know it. How about it, Rip— how's Hovan?"

Rip's face was a mask of worry. "He must have had a full dose. I can't bring him around."

Was this the end of their bold bid? Let each or all of them go before the screen to plead their case, let them show the caged pest. But without the professional testimony of the medic, the weight of an expert opinion on their side, they were licked. Well, sometimes luck did not ride a man's fins all the way in.

But some stubborn core within Dane refused to let him believe that they had lost. He went over to the medic huddled in a chair. To all appearances Hovan was deeply asleep, sunk in the semi-coma the sleep ray produced. And the frustrating thing was that the man himself could have supplied the counter to his condition, given them the instructions how to bring him around. How many hours away was a natural awaking? Long before that their hold on the station would be broken—they would be in the custody of either Police or Patrol.

"He's sunk—" Dane voiced the belief which put an end to their hopes. But Ali did not seem concerned.

Kamil was standing with their captive, an odd expression on his handsome face as if he were striving to recall some dim memory. When he spoke it was to the com-tech. "You have an HD OS here?"

The other registered surprise. "I think so—"

Ali made an abrupt gesture. "Make sure," he ordered, following the man into another room. Dane looked to Rip for enlightenment.

"What in the Great Nebula is an HD OS?"

"I'm no engineer. It may be some gadget to get us out of here—"

"Such as a pair of wings?" Dane was inclined to be sarcastic. The memory of that incandescent circle on the door some twenty floors below stayed with him. Tempers of Police and Patrol were not going to be improved by fighting their way around or over the obstacles the Traders had arranged to delay them. If they caught up to the outlaws before the latter had their chance for an impartial hearing, the result was not going to be a happy one as far as the *Queen*'s men were concerned.

Ali appeared in the doorway. "Bring Hovan in here."

Together Rip and Dane carried the medic into a smaller chamber where they found Ali and the tech busy lashing a small, lightweight tube chair to a machine which, to their untutored eyes, had the semblance of a collection of bars. Obeying instructions they seated Hovan in that chair, fastening him in, while the medic continued to slumber peacefully. Uncomprehendingly Rip and Dane stepped back while, under Ali's watchful eye, the com-tech made adjustments and finally snapped some hidden switch.

Dane discovered that he dared not watch too closely what followed. Inured as he thought he was to the tricks of Hyperspace, to acceleration and anti-gravity, the oscillation of that swinging seat, the weird swaying of the half-recumbent figure, did things to his sight and to his sense of balance which seemed perilous in the extreme. But when a groan broke through the hum of Ali's mysterious machine, all of them knew that the engineer-apprentice had found the answer to their problem, that Hovan was waking.

The medic was bleary-eyed and inclined to stagger when they freed him. And for several minutes he seemed unable to grasp either his surroundings or the train of events which had brought him there.

Long since the Police must have broken into the entrance corridor below. Perhaps they had by now secured a riser which would bring them up. Ali had forced the com-tech to throw the emergency control which was designed to seal off from the outer world the entire unit in which they now were. But whether that protective device would continue to hold now, none of the three were certain. Time was running out fast.

Supporting the wobbling Hovan, they went back into the panel room and under Ali's supervision the com-tech took his place at the control board. Dane put the cage with the pest well to the fore on the table of the announcer and waited for Rip to take his place there with the trembling medic. When Shannon did not move Dane glanced up in surprise—this was no time to hesitate. But he discovered that the attention of both his shipmates was now centered on him. Rip pointed to the seat.

"You're the talk merchant, aren't you?" the acting commander of the *Queen* asked crisply. "Now's the time to shout the Lingo—"

They couldn't mean—! But it was very evident that they did. Of course, a cargo-master was supposed to be the spokesman of a ship. But that was in matters of trade. And how could *he* stand there and argue the case for the *Queen*? He was the newest joined, the greenest member of her crew. Already his mouth was dry and his nerves tense. But Dane didn't know that none of that was revealed by his face or manner. The usual impassiveness which had masked his inner conflicts since his first days at the Pool served him now. And the others never noted the hesitation with which he approached the announcer's place.

Dane had scarcely seated himself, one hand resting on the cage of the pest, before Ali brought down two fingers in the sharp sweep which signaled the com-tech to duty. Far above them there was a whisper of sound which signified the opening of the playback. They would be able to check on whether the broadcast was going out or not. Although Dane could see nothing of the systemwide audience which he currently faced, he realized that the room and those in it were now visible on every tuned-in Video set. Instead of the factual cast, the listeners were about to be treated to a melodrama which was as wild as their favorite romances. It only needed the break-in of the Patrol to complete the illusion of action-fiction—crime variety.

A second finger moved in his direction and Dane leaned forward. He faced only the folds of a wall wide curtain, but he must keep in mind that in truth there was a sea of faces before him, the faces of those whom he and Hovan, working together, must convince if he were to save the *Queen* and her crew.

He found his voice and it was steady and even, he might have been outlining some stowage problem for Van Rycke's approval.

"People of Terra—"

Martian, Venusian, Asteroid colonist—inwardly they were still all Terran and on that point he would rest. He was a Terran appealing to his own kind.

"People of Terra, we come before you to ask justice—" From somewhere the words came easily, flowing from his lips to center on a patch of light ahead. And that "justice" rang with a kind of reassurance.

IN CUSTODY

17

"To those of you who do not travel the star trails our case may seem puzzling—" The words were coming easily. Dane gathered confidence as he spoke, intent on making those others out there know what it meant to be outlawed.

"We are Patrol Posted, outlawed as a plague ship," he confessed frankly. "But this is our true story—"

Swiftly, with a flow of language he had not known he could command, Dane swung into the story of Sargol, of the pest they had carried away from that world. And at the proper moment he thrust a gloved hand into the cage and brought out the wriggling thing which struck vainly with its poisoned talons, holding it above the dark table so that those unseen watchers could witness that dramatic change of color which made it such a menace. Dane continued the story of the *Queen*'s ill-fated voyage—of their forced descent upon the E-Stat.

"Ask the truth of Inter-Solar," he demanded of the audience beyond those walls. "We were no pirates. They will discover in their records the vouchers we left." Then Dane described the weird hunt when, led by the Hoobat, they had finally found and isolated the menace, and their landing in the heart of the Big Burn. He followed that with his own quest for medical aid and the kidnaping of Hovan. At that point he turned to the medic.

"This is Medic Hovan. He has consented to appear in our behalf and to testify to the truth—that the *Solar Queen* has not been stricken by some unknown plague, but infested with a living organism we now have under control—" For a suspenseful second or two he wondered if Hovan was going to make it. The man looked shaken and sick, as if the drastic awaking they had subjected him to had left him too dazed to pull himself together.

But out of some hidden reservoir of strength the medic summoned the energy he needed. And his testimony was all they had hoped it would be. Though now and then he strayed into technical terms. But, Dane thought, their use only enhanced the authority of his description of what he had discovered on board the spacer and what he had done to counteract the power of the poison. When he had done Dane added a few last words.

"We have broken the law," he admitted forthrightly, "but we were fighting in self-defense. All we ask now is the privilege of an impartial investigation, a chance to defend ourselves—such as any of you take for granted on Terra—before the courts of this planet—" But he was not to finish without interruption.

From the playback over their heads another voice blared, breaking across his last words:

"Surrender! This is the Patrol. Surrender or take the consequences!" And that faint sighing which signaled their open contact with the outer world was cut off. The com-tech turned away from the control board, a sneering half smile on his face.

"They've reached the circuit and cut you off. You're done!"

Dane stared into the cage where the now almost invisible thing sat humped together. He had done his best—they had all done their best. He felt nothing but a vast fatigue, an overwhelming weariness, not so much of body, but of nerve and spirit too.

Rip broke the silence with a question aimed at the tech. "Can you signal below?"

"Going to give up?" The fellow brightened. "Yes, there's an inter-com I can cut in."

Rip stood up. He unbuckled the belt about his waist and laid it on the table—disarming himself. Without words Ali and Dane followed his example. They had played their hand—to prolong the struggle would mean nothing. The acting Captain of the *Queen* gave a last order:

"Tell them we are coming down—unarmed—to surrender." He paused in front of Hovan. "You'd better stay here. If there's any trou-ble—no reason for you to be caught in the middle."

Hovan nodded as the three left the room. Dane, remembering the trick he had pulled with the riser, made a comment:

"We may be marooned here—"

Ali shrugged. "Then we can just wait and let them collect us." He yawned, his dark eyes set in smudges. "I don't care if they'll just let us sleep the clock around afterwards. D'you really think," he addressed Rip, "that we've done ourselves any good?"

Rip neither denied nor confirmed. "We took our only chance. Now it's up to them—" He pointed to the wall and the teeming world which lay beyond it.

Ali grinned wryly. "I note you left the what-you-call-it with Hovan."

"He wanted one to experiment with," Dane replied. "I thought he'd earned it."

"And now here comes what we've earned—" Rip cut in as the hum of the riser came to their ears.

"Should we take to cover?" Ali's mobile eyebrows underlined his demand. "The forces of law and order may erupt with blasters blazing."

But Rip did not move. He faced the riser door squarely and, drawn by something in that stance of his, the other two stepped in on either side so that they fronted the dubious future as a united group. Whatever came now, the *Queen*'s men would meet it together.

In a way Ali was right. The four men who emerged all had their blasters or riot stun-rifles at ready, and the sights of those weapons were trained at the middles of the Free Traders. As Dane's empty hands, palm out, went up on a line with his shoulders, he estimated the opposition. Two were in the silver and black of the Patrol, two wore the forest green of the Terrapolice. But they all looked like men with whom it was better not to play games.

And it was clear they were prepared to take no chances with the outlaws. In spite of the passiveness of the *Queen*'s men, their hands were locked behind them with force bars about their wrists. When a quick search revealed that the three were unarmed, they were herded onto the riser by two of their captors, while the other pair remained behind, presumably to uncover any damage they had done to the Tower installations.

The police did not speak except for a few terse words among themselves and a barked order to march, delivered to the prisoners. Very shortly they were in the entrance hall facing the wreckage of the crawler and doors through which a ragged gap had been burned. Ali viewed the scene with his usual detachment.

"Nice job," he commended Dane's enterprise. "They'll have a moving—"

"Get going!" A heavy hand between his shoulder blades urged him on.

The engineer-apprentice whirled, his eyes blazing. "Keep your hands to yourself! We aren't mine fodder yet. I think that the little matter of a trial comes first—"

"You're Posted," the Patrolman was openly contemptuous.

Dane was chilled. For the first time that aspect of their predicament really registered. Posted outlaws might, within reason, be shot on sight without further recourse to the law. If that label stuck on the crew of the *Queen,* they had practically no chance at all. And when he saw that Ali was no longer inclined to retort, he knew that fact had dawned upon Kamil also. It would all depend upon how big an impression their broadcast had made. If public opinion veered to their side—then they could defend themselves legally. Otherwise the moon mines might be the best sentence they dare hope for.

They were pushed out into the brilliant sunlight. There stood the *Queen,* her meteor-scarred sides reflecting the light of her native sun. And ringed around her at a safe distance was what seemed to be a small mechanized army corps. The authorities were making very sure that no more rebels would burst from her interior.

Dane thought that they would be loaded into a mobile or 'copter and taken away. But instead they were marched down, through the ranks of portable flamers, scramblers, and other equipment, to an open space where anyone on duty at the visa-screen within the control cabin of the spacer could see them. An officer of the Patrol, the sun making an eye-blinding flash of his lightning sword breast badge, stood behind a loud speaker. When he perceived that the three prisoners were present, he picked up a hand mike and spoke into it— his voice so being relayed over the field as clearly as it must be reaching Weeks inside the sealed freighter.

"You have five minutes to open hatch. Your men have been taken. Five minutes to open hatch and surrender."

Ali chuckled. "And how does he think he's going to enforce that?" he inquired of the air and incidentally of the guards now forming a square about the three. "He'll need more than a flamer to unlatch the old girl if she doesn't care for his offer."

Privately Dane agreed with that. He hoped that Weeks would decide to hold out—at least until they had a better idea of what the future would be. No tool or weapon he saw in the assembly about them was forceful enough to penetrate the shell of the *Queen*. And there were sufficient supplies on board to keep Weeks and his charges going for at least a week. Since Tau had shown signs of coming out of his coma, it might even be that the crew of the ship would arouse to their own defense in that time. It all depended upon Weeks' present decision.

No hatch yawned in the ship's sleek sides. She might have been an inert derelict for all response to that demand. Dane's confidence began to rise. Weeks had picked up the challenge, he would continue to baffle police and Patrol.

Just how long that stalemate would have lasted they were not to know for another player came on the board. Through the lines of besiegers Hovan, escorted by the Patrolmen, made his way up to the officer at the mike station. There was something in his air which suggested that he was about to give battle. And the conversation at the mike was relayed across the field, a fact of which they were not at once aware.

"There are sick men in there—" Hovan's voice boomed out. "I demand the right to return to duty—"

"If and when they surrender they shall all be accorded necessary aid," that was the officer. But he made no impression on the medic from the frontier. Dane, by chance, had chosen better support than he had guessed.

"Pro Bono Publico—" Hovan invoked the battle cry of his own Service. "For the Public Good—"

"A plague ship—" the officer was beginning. Hovan waved that aside impatiently.

"Nonsense!" His voice scaled up across the field. "There is no plague aboard. I am willing to certify that before the Council. And if you refuse these men medical attention—which they need—I shall cite the case all the way to my Board!"

Dane drew a deep breath. That *was* taking off on their orbit! Not being one of the *Queen*'s crew, in fact having good reason to be angry over his treatment at their hands, Hovan's present attitude would or should carry weight.

The Patrol officer who was not yet ready to concede all points had an answer: "If you are able to get on board—go."

Hovan snatched the mike from the astonished officer. "Weeks!" His voice was imperative. "I'm coming aboard—alone!"

All eyes were on the ship and for a short period it would seem that Weeks did not trust the medic. Then, high in her needle nose, one of the escape ports, not intended for use except in dire emergency, opened and allowed a plastic link ladder to fall link by link.

Out of the corner of his eye Dane caught a flash of movement to his left. Manacled as he was he threw himself on the policeman who was aiming a stun rifle into the port. His shoulder struck the fellow waist high and his weight carried them both with a bruising crash to the concrete pavement as Rip shouted and hands clutched roughly at the now helpless cargo-apprentice.

He was pulled to his feet, tasting the flat sweetness of blood where a flailing blow from the surprised and frightened policeman had cut his lip against his teeth. He spat red and glowered at the ring of angry men.

"Why don't you kick him?" Ali inquired, a vast and blistering contempt sawtoothing his voice. "He's got his hands cuffed so he's fair game—"

"What's going on here?" An officer broke through the ring. The policeman, on his feet once more, snatched up the rifle Dane's attack had knocked out of his hold.

"Your boy here," Ali was ready with an answer, "tried to find a target inside the hatch. Is this the usual way you conduct a truce, sir?"

He was answered by a glare and the rifleman was abruptly ordered to the rear. Dane, his head clearing, looked at the *Queen*. Hovan was climbing the ladder—he was within arm's length of that half open hatch. The very fact that the medic had managed to make his point stick was, in a faint way, encouraging. But the three were not allowed to enjoy that small victory for long. They were marched from the field, loaded into a mobile and taken to the city several miles away. It was the Patrol who held them in custody—not the Terrapolice. Dane was not sure whether that was to be reckoned favorable or not. As a Free Trader he had a grudging respect for the organization he had seen in action on Limbo.

Sometime later they found themselves, freed of the force bars, alone in a room which, bare walled as it was, did have a bench on which all three sank thankfully. Dane caught the warning gesture from Ali—they were under unseen observation and they must have a listening audience too—located somewhere in the maze of offices.

"They can't make up their minds," the engineer-apprentice settled his shoulders against the wall. "Either we're desperate criminals, or we're heroes. They're going to let time decide."

"If we're heroes," Dane asked a little querulously, "what are we doing locked up here? I'd like a few earth-side comforts—beginning with a full meal—"

"No thumb printing, no psycho testing," Rip mused. "Yes, they haven't put us through the system yet."

"And we decidedly aren't the forgotten men. Wipe your face, child," Ali said to Dane, "you're still dribbling."

The cargo-apprentice smeared his hand across his chin and brought it away red and sticky. Luckily his teeth remained intact.

"We need Hovan to read them more law," observed Kamil. "You should have medical attention."

Dane dabbed at his mouth. He didn't need all that solicitude, but he guessed that Ali was talking for the benefit of those who now kept them under surveillance.

"Speaking of Hovan—I wonder what became of that pest he was supposed to have under control. He didn't bring the cage with him when he came out of the Tower, did he?" asked Rip.

"If it gets loose in that building," Dane decided to give the powers who held them in custody something to think about, "they'll have trouble. Practically invisible and poisonous. And maybe it can reproduce its kind, too. We don't know anything about it—"

Ali laughed. "Such fun and games! Imagine a hundred of the dear creatures flitting in and out of the broadcasting section. And Captain Jellico has the only Hoobat on Terra! He can name his own terms for rounding up the plague. The whole place will be filled with sleepers before they're through—"

Would that scrap of information send some Patrolmen hurtling off to the Tower in search of the caged creature? The thought of such an expedition was, in a small way, comforting to the captives.

An hour or so later they were fed, noiselessly and without visible attendants, when three trays slid through a slit in the wall at floor level. Rip's nose wrinkled.

"Now I get the vector! We're plague-ridden—keep aloof and watch to see if we break out in purple spots!"

Ali was lifting thermo lids from the containers and now he suddenly arose and bowed in the direction of the blank wall. "Many, many thanks," he intoned. "Nothing but the best—a sub-commander's rations at least! We shall deliver top star rating to this thoughtfulness when we are questioned by the powers that shine."

It *was* good food. Dane ate cautiously because of his torn lip, but the whole adventure took on a more rose-colored hue. The lapse of time before they were put through the usual procedure followed with criminals, this excellent dinner—it was all promising. The Patrol could not yet be sure how they were to be handled.

"They've fed us," Ali observed as he clanged the last dish back on a tray. "Now you'd think they'd bed us. I could do with several days—and nights—of bunk time right about now."

But that hint was not taken up and they continued to sit on the bench as time limped by. According to Dane's watch it must be night now, though the steady light in the windowless room did not vary. What had Hovan discovered in the *Queen*? Had he been able to rouse any of the crew? And was the spacer still inviolate, or had the Terrapolice and the Patrol managed to take her over?

He was so very tired, his eyes felt as if hot sand had been poured beneath the lids, his body ached. And at last he nodded into naps from which he awoke with jerks of the neck. Rip was frankly asleep, his shoulders and head resting against the wall, while Ali lounged with closed eyes. Though the cargo-apprentice was sure that Kamil was more alert than his comrades, as if he waited for something he thought was soon to occur.

Dane dreamed. Once more he trod the reef rising out of Sargol's shallow sea. But he held no weapon and beneath the surface of the water a gorp lurked. When he reached the break in the water-washed rock just ahead, the spidery horror would strike and against its attack he was defenseless. Yet he must march on for he had no control over his own actions!

"Wake up!" Ali's hand was on his shoulder, shaking him back and forth with something close to gentleness. "Must you give an imitation of a space-whirly moonbat?"

"The gorp—" Dane came back to the present and flushed. He dreaded admitting to a nightmare—especially to Ali whose poise he had always found disconcerting.

"No gorps here. Nothing but—"

Kamil's words were lost in the escape of metal against metal as a panel slid back in the wall. But no guard wearing the black and silver of the Patrol stepped through to summon them to trial. Van Rycke stood in the opening, half smiling at them with his customary sleepy benevolence.

"Well, well, and here's our missing ones." His purring voice was the most beautiful sound Dane thought he had ever heard.

BARGAIN CONCLUDED

18

"—And so we landed here, sir." Rip concluded his report in the matter-of-fact tone he might have used in describing a perfectly ordinary voyage, say between Terraport and Luna City, a run of no incident and dull cargo carrying.

The crew of the *Solar Queen,* save for Tau, were assembled in a room somewhere in the vastness of Patrol Headquarters. Since the room seemed a comfortable conference chamber, Dane thought that their status must now be on a higher level than that of Patrol Posted outlaws. But he was also sure that if they attempted to walk out of the building that effort would not be successful.

Van Rycke sat stolidly in his chosen seat, fingers of both hands laced across his substantial middle. He had sat as impassively as the Captain while Rip had outlined their adventures since they had all been stricken. Though the other listeners had betrayed interest in the story, the senior officers made no comments. Now Jellico turned to his cargo-master.

"How about it, Van?"

"What's done is done—"

Dane's elation vanished as if ripped away by a Sargolian storm wind. The cargo-master didn't approve. So there must have been another way to achieve their ends—one the younger members of the crew had been too inexperienced or too dense to see—

"If we blasted off today we might just make cargo contract."

Dane started. That was it! The point they had lost sight of during their struggles to get aid. There was no possible chance of upping the ship today—probably not for days to come—or ever, if the case went against them. So they had broken contract—and the Board would be down on them for that. Dane shivered inside. He could try to fight back against the Patrol—there had always been a slight feeling of rivalry between the Free Traders and the space police. But you couldn't buck the Board—and keep your license and so have a means of staying in space. A broken contract could cut one off from the stars forever. Captain Jellico looked very bleak at that reminder.

"The Eysies will be all ready to step in. I'd like to know why they were so sure we had the plague on board—"

Van Rycke snorted. "I can supply you five answers to that—for one they may have known the affinity of those creatures for the wood, and it would be easy to predict as a result of our taking a load on board—or again they may have deliberately planted the things on us through the Salariki— But we can't ever prove it. It remains that they are going to get for themselves the Sargolian contract unless—" He stopped short, staring straight ahead of him at the wall between Rip and Dane. And his assistant knew that Van was exploring a fresh idea. Van's ideas were never to be despised and Jellico did not now disturb the cargo-master with questions.

It was Rip who spoke next and directly to the Captain. "Do you know what they plan to do about us, sir?"

Captain Jellico grunted and there was a sardonic twist to his mouth as he replied, "It's my opinion that they're now busy adding up the list of crimes you four have committed—maybe they had to turn the big HG computer loose on the problem. The tally isn't in yet.

We gave them our automat flight record and that ought to give them more food for thought."

Dane speculated as to what the experts *would* make of the mechanical record of the *Queen*'s past few weeks—the section dealing with their landing in the Big Burn ought to be a little surprising. Van Rycke got to his feet and marched to the door of the conference room. It was opened from without so quickly Dane was sure that they had been under constant surveillance.

"Trade business," snapped the cargo-master, "contract deal. Take me to a sealed com booth!"

Contracts might not be as sacred to the protective Service as they were to Trade, but Trade had its powers and since Van Rycke, an innocent bystander of the *Queen*'s troubles, could not legally be charged with any crime, he was escorted out of the room. But the door panel was sealed behind him, shutting in the rest with the unspoken warning that they were not free agents. Jellico leaned back in his chair and stretched. Long years of close friendship had taught him that his cargo-master was to be trusted with not only the actual trading and cargo tending, but could also think them out of some of the tangles which could not be solved by his own direct action methods. Direct action had been applied to their present problem—now the rest was up to Van, and he was willing to delegate all responsibility.

But they were not left long to themselves. The door opened once more to admit star rank Patrolmen. None of the Free Traders arose. As members of another Service they considered themselves equals. And it was their private boast that the interests of Galactic civilization, as represented by the black and silver, often followed, not preceded, the brown tunics into new quarters of the universe.

However, Rip, Ali, Dane, and Weeks answered as fully as they could the flood of questions which engulfed them. They explained in detail their visit to the E-Stat, the landing in the Big Burn, the kidnaping of Hovan. Dane's stubborn feeling of being in the right grew in opposition to the questioning. Under the same set of circumstances how

would that Commander—that Wing Officer—that Senior Scout—
now all seated there—have acted? And every time they inferred that
his part in the affair had been illegal he stiffened.

Sure, there had to be law and order out on the Rim—and doubly
sure it had to cover and protect life on the softer planets of the inner systems. He wasn't denying that on Limbo, he, for one, had been very glad
to see the Patrol blast their way into the headquarters of the pirates
holed up on that half-dead world. And he was never contemptuous of
the men in the field. But like all Free Traders he was influenced by a
belief that too often the laws as enforced by the Patrol favored the
wealth and might of the Companies, that law could be twisted and the
Patrol sent to push through actions which, though legal, were inher-
ently unfair to those who had not the funds to fight it out in the far-off
Council courts. Just as now he was certain that the Eysies were bringing all the influence they had to bear here against the *Queen*'s men.
And Inter-Solar had a lot of influence.

At the end of their ordeal their statements were read back to them
from the recording tape and they thumb signed them. Were these
statements or confessions, Dane mused. Perhaps in their honest reports
they had just signed their way into the moon mines. Only there was
no move to lead them out and book them. And when Weeks pressed
his thumb at the bottom of the tape, Captain Jellico took a hand. He
looked at his watch.

"It is now ten hours," he observed. "My men need rest, and we all
want food. Are you through with us?"

The Commander was spokesman for the other group. "You are to
remain in quarantine, Captain. Your ship has not yet been passed as
port-free. But you will be assigned quarters—"

Once again they were marched through blank halls to the other
section of the sprawling Patrol Headquarters. No windows looked
upon the outer world, but there were bunks and a small mess alcove.
Ali, Dane, and Rip turned in, more interested in sleep than food. And
the last thing the cargo-apprentice remembered was seeing Jellico

talking earnestly with Steen Wilcox as they both sipped steaming mugs of real Terran coffee.

But with twelve hours of sleep behind them the three were less contented in confinement. No one had come near them and Van Rycke had not returned. Which fact the crew clung to as a ray of hope. Somewhere the cargo-master must be fighting their battle. And all Van's vast store of Trade knowledge, all his knack of cutting corners and driving a shrewd bargain, enlisted on their behalf, must win them some concessions.

Medic Tau came in, bringing Hovan with him. Both looked tired but triumphant. And their report was a shot in the arm for the now uneasy Traders.

"We've rammed it down their throats," Tau announced. "They're willing to admit that it was those poison bugs and not a plague. Incidentally," he grinned at Jellico and then looked around expectantly, "where's Van? This comes in his department. We're going to cash in on those the kids dumped in the deep freeze. Terra-Lab is bidding on them. I said to see Van—he can arrange the best deal for us. Where is he?"

"Gone to see about our contract," Jellico reported. "What's the news about our status now?"

"Well, they've got to wipe out the plague ship listing. Also—we're big news. There're about twenty Video men rocketing around out in the offices trying to get in and have us do some spot broadcasts. Seems that the children here," he jerked his thumb at the three apprentices, "started something. An inter solar invasion couldn't be bigger news! Human interest by the tankful. I've been on Video twice and they're trying to sign up Hovan almost steady—"

The medic from the frontier nodded. "Wanted me to appear on a three-week schedule," he chuckled. "I was asked to come in on *Our Heroes of the Starlines* and two quiz programs. As for you, you young criminal," he swung to Dane, "you're going to be fair game for about three networks. It seems you transmit well." He uttered the last as if it were an accusation and Dane squirmed. "Anyway you did something with your crazy stunt. And, Captain, three men want to buy your Hoobat. I gather they are planning a showing of how it captures those pests. So be prepared—"

Dane tried to visualize a scene in which he shared top billing with Queex and shuddered. All he wanted now was to get free of Terra for a nice, quiet, uncomplicated world where problems could be settled with a sleep rod or a blaster and the Video screen was unknown.

Having heard of what awaited them without the men of the *Queen* were more content to be incarcerated in the quarantine section. But as time wore on and the cargo-master did not return, their anxieties awoke. They were fairly sure by now that any penalty the Patrol or the Terrapolice would impose would not be too drastic. But a broken contract was another and more serious affair—a matter which might ground them more effectively than any rule of the law enforcement bodies. And Jellico took to pacing the room, while Tang and Wilcox who had started a game of four-dimensional chess made countless errors of move, and Stotz glared moodily at the wall, apparently too sunk in his own gloomy thoughts to rise from the mess table in the alcove.

Though time had ceased to have much meaning for them except as an irritating reminder of the now sure failure of their Sargolian venture, they marked the hours into a second full day of detention before Van Rycke finally put in appearance. The cargo-master was plainly tired, but he showed no signs of discomposure. In fact as he came in he was humming what he fondly imagined was a popular tune.

Jellico asked no questions, he merely regarded his trusted officer with a quizzically raised eyebrow. But the others drew around. It was so apparent that Van Rycke was pleased with himself. Which could only mean that in some fantastic way he had managed to bring their venture down in a full fin landing, that somehow he had argued the *Queen* out of danger into a position where he could control the situation.

He halted just within the doorway and eyed Dane, Ali, and Rip with mock severity. "You're baaaad boys," he told them with a shake of the head and a drawl of the adjective. "You've been demoted ten files each on the list."

Which must put him on the bottom rung once more, Dane calculated swiftly. Or even below—though he didn't see how he could fall beneath the rank he held at assignment. However, he found the news heartening instead of discouraging. Compared to a bleak sentence at the moon mines such demotion was absolutely nothing and he knew that Van Rycke was breaking the worst news first.

"You also forfeit all pay for this voyage," the cargo-master was continuing. But Jellico broke in.

"Board fine?"

At the cargo-master's nod, Jellico added, "Ship pays that."

"So I told them," Van Rycke agreed. "The *Queen*'s warned off Terra for ten solar years—"

They could take that, too. Other Free Traders got back to their home ports perhaps once in a quarter century. It was so much less than they had expected that the sentence was greeted with a concentrated sigh of relief.

"No earth-side leave—"

All right—no leave. They were not, after their late experiences so entranced with Terraport that they wanted to linger in its environs any longer than they had to.

"We lose the Sargol contract—"

That did hurt. But they had resigned themselves to it since the hour when they had realized that they could not make it back to the perfumed planet.

"To Inter-Solar?" Wilcox asked the important question.

Van Rycke was smiling broadly, as if the loss he had just announced was in some way a gain. "No—to Combine!"

"Combine?" the Captain echoed and his puzzlement was duplicated around the circle. How did Inter-Solar's principal rival come into it?

"We've made a deal with Combine," Van Rycke informed them. "I wasn't going to let I-S cash in on our loss. So I went to Vickers at Combine and told him the situation. He understands that we were in solid with the Salariki and that the Eysies are not. And a chance to point a blaster at I-S's tail is just what he has been waiting for. The shipment will go out to the storm priests tomorrow on a light cruiser—it'll make it on time."

Yes, a light cruiser, one of the fast ships maintained by the big Companies, could make the transition to Sargol with a slight margin to spare. Stotz nodded his approval at this practical solution.

"I'm going with it—" That did jerk them all up short. For Van Rycke to leave the *Queen—that* was as unthinkable as if Captain Jellico had suddenly announced that he was about to retire and become a kelp farmer. "Just for the one trip," the cargo-master hastened to assure them. "I smooth their vector with the storm priests and hand over so the Eysies will be frozen out—"

Captain Jellico interrupted at that point. "D'you mean that Combine is *buying* us out—not just taking over? What kind of a deal—"

But Van Rycke, his smile a brilliant stretch across his plump face, was nodding in agreement. "They're taking over our contract and our place with the Salariki."

"In return for what?" Steen Wilcox asked for them all.

"For twenty-five thousand credits and a mail run between Xecho and Trewsworld—frontier planets. They're far enough from Terra to get around the exile ruling. The Patrol will escort us out and see that we get down to work like good little space men. We'll have two years of a nice, quiet run on regular pay. Then, when all the powers that shine have forgotten about us, we can cut in on the trade routes again."

"And the pay?" "First or second class mail?" "When do we start?"

"Standard pay on the completion of each run—Board rates," he made replies in order. "First, second and third class mail—anything that bears the government seal and out in those quarters it is apt to be *anything*! And you start as soon as you can get to Xecho and relieve the Combine scout which has been holding down the run."

"While you go to Sargol—" commented Jellico.

"While I make one voyage to Sargol. You can spare me," he dropped one of his big hands on Dane's shoulder and gave the flesh beneath it a quick squeeze. "Seeing as how our juniors helped pull us out of this last mix-up we can trust them about an inch farther than we did before. Anyway—cargo-master on a mail run is more or less a thumb-twiddling job at the best. And you can trust Thorson on stowage—that's one thing he *does* know." Which dubious ending left Dane wondering as to whether he had been complimented or warned. "I'll be on board again before you know it—the Combine will ship me out to Trewsworld on your second trip across and I'll join ship there. For once we won't have to worry for awhile. Nothing can happen on a mail run." He shook his head at the three youngest members of the crew. "You're in for a very dull time—and it will serve you right. Give you a chance to learn your jobs so that when you come up for reassignment you can pick up some of those files you were just demoted. Now," he started briskly for the door. "I'll tranship to the Combine cruiser. I take it that you *don't* want to meet the Video people?"

At their hasty agreement to that, he laughed. "Well, the Patrol doesn't want the Video spouting about 'high-handed official news suppression' so about an hour or so from now you'll be let out the back way. They put the *Queen* in a cradle and a field scooter will take you to her. You'll find her serviced for a take-off to Luna City. You can refit there for deep space. Frankly the sooner you get off-world the happier all ranks are going to be—both here and on the Board. It will be better for us to walk softly for a while and let them forget that the *Solar Queen* and her crazy crew exists. Separately and together you've managed to break—or at least bend—half the laws in the books and they'd like to have us out of their minds."

Captain Jellico stood up. "They aren't any more anxious to see us go than we are to get out of here. You've pulled it off for us again, Van, and we're lucky to get out of it this easy—"

Van Rycke rolled his eyes ceilingward. "You'll never know how lucky! Be glad Combine hates the space I-S blasts through. We were able to use that to our advantage. Get the big fellows at each other's throats and they'll stop annoying us—simple proposition but it works. Anyway we're set in blessed and peaceful obscurity now. Thank the Spirit of Free Space there's practically no trouble one can get into on a safe and sane mail route!"

But Cargo-master Van Rycke, in spite of knowing the *Solar Queen* and the temper of her crew, was exceedingly over-optimistic when he made that emphatic statement.

ABOUT THE AUTHOR

For more than fifty years, Andre Norton, "one of the most distin-
guished living SF and fantasy writers" (*Booklist*), has been penning
bestselling novels that have earned her a unique place in the hearts
and minds of millions of readers worldwide. She has been honored
with a Life Achievement Award by the World Fantasy Convention,
and with the Grand Master Nebula Award by her peers in the Science
Fiction Writers of America. Works set in her fabled Witch World, as
well as others, such as The Time Traders, Solar Queen, and Beast
Master series, to name but a few in her great oeuvre, have made her
"one of the most popular authors of our time" (*Publishers Weekly*). She
lives in Murfreesboro, Tennessee, where she presides over High Hallack, a writers' resource and retreat. More can be learned about Miss
Norton's work, and about High Hallack, at www.andre-norton.org.